THE PY

Graeme McCaig is thirteen a ʼs uncle.

Lord Raversham, head of the Ra and ensconced in his castle on Raversham Isle, is dying say) and seemingly powerless to stop his grown–up children from vanishing.

Could these disappearances have anything to do with the strangers with large sacks who are gathering at night, down on the beach? Who is their cloaked, silver–masked leader and what is his plan?

Graeme starts to investigate and finds himself caught up in an adventure that will see him collide with the Raversham family in more ways than one.

He will make new friends.
He will hate Calamara Jones.
He will fly.
He will fall.
He will meet royalty.
He will meet cannibalistic child assassins.
He will learn of the legend of the Pyn King.
He will find a new world.
But can he save ours?

THE PYN KING

Published by lulu.com

First published 2008
This edition published 2009

tpk@thepynking.com

ISBN 978-1-4092-2513-3

Edition 1950i

The Pyn King

By

Alistair Sowerbutts

Contents

The Raversham Family

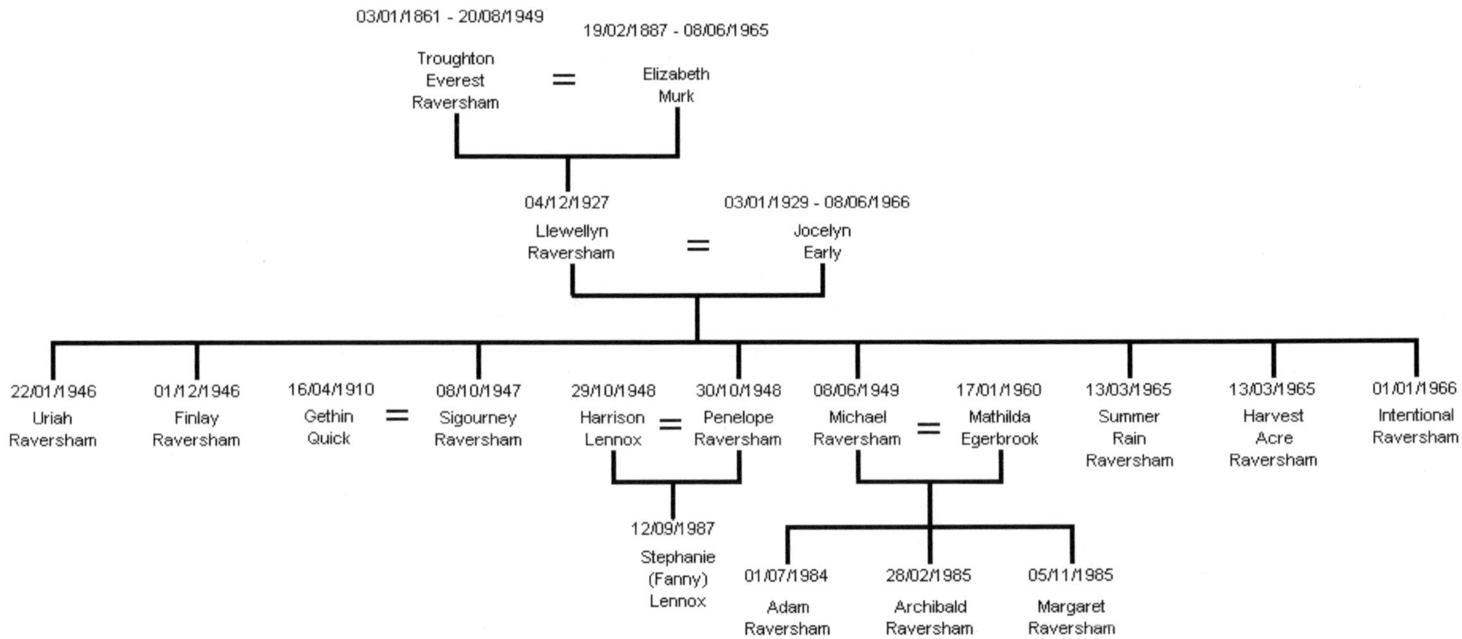

CHAPTER ONE

Arrival: Monday, 21st December 1998

Graeme McCaig, thirteen and travelling alone, stepped off the coach, his ticket still clutched in his hand, right into a puddle of water. It had obviously rained recently. The sky was clearing now but it was still cold.

The coach station (if a glorified lay–by could qualify as such) contained one small office building plastered in layer upon layer of old, ripped timetables, and two elongated bus shelters that between them formed an effective wind tunnel. The wind whipped past Graeme, catching at his clothes as he stood in the queue alongside the coach waiting his turn to collect his belongings from the driver.

This was the end of the line; everybody had disembarked. Graeme stared at the side of the coach, watching the reflections of his fellow queuing passengers as everyone shuffled forward. There was the old man who had shouted out, "Gorilla! Gotcha!" in his sleep; there were the teenagers, a boy and a girl, not much older than Graeme – they had sat in the back, snogging and giggling all the way; there was the woman in the green coat who had tried to force–feed him an apple every ten minutes (which he'd refused – he had read the odd book and knew the kind of trouble you could get into, accepting offers like that – never put a gift apple in your mouth); and then there, in the middle of the queue, was Graeme himself: a short, skinny kid, skin pale, hollow–eyed, shoulders hunched, wrapped up in a jacket that was hardy but really more suited to late summer, autumn at a push, rather than the dead of winter. He didn't look like your typical moody teenager; he didn't look as if he was resentful, annoyed at having been forced to go anywhere against his will; he just looked like he hadn't slept properly in fair few months; and he was lost in thought.

"Oy!"

Graeme had reached the front of the queue and the driver, a dour man dressed in a crumpled suit and hastily–tied tie, was waiting.

"Don't mind me. Got all day, I have," said the driver. "You going to rejoin the real world anytime soon?"

Graeme pointed wordlessly to his suitcase – massive, old, no wheels. The driver picked it out, dumped it on the ground and gave Graeme an odd look. "Think you'll manage to lift that?"

Graeme didn't reply. He reached out to pick it up. The ticket, which he'd stared at, crumpled in the palm of his hand for the entire journey, was caught in a gust of air and went skittering away.

The driver gave him a look of disgust. "You mind? Littering is an offence."

Graeme hadn't meant to let it go. It had just happened; it was one of those things. Perhaps he should have said something, but different rules apply when you're young. Answering back isn't the smart thing to do. Besides, the words would have gone if he tried to say them out loud. They always did.

So instead, he just said, "Sorry," picked up his case (it was heavy but he was stronger than people gave him credit for) and walked out to the main road to wait for his lift. The road, with its narrow, uneven pavements, stretched in a straight line to his left, with festively decorated shops on either side of the street. Not far on his right it curved away, leading, if he remembered right, to the car park.

The street was surprisingly deserted, considering how close Christmas was, which made him feel all the more stupid when he bumped into a man in a brown suit. He dropped his suitcase on the man's foot.

"Whoa, there!" the man laughed, "mind where you're going, sonny!"

"Sorry," said Graeme.

"That's perfectly fine, no bones broken, no bones broken," the man replied, smiling. Standing behind him were a woman and three children: two boys and a girl. They were all looking at Graeme as if he were something they'd just scraped off the bottom of their shoe. Graeme didn't look directly at them.

“Michael!” the woman barked. “Never mind him. We’ll be late for dinner.”

“Is everything okay?” It was Graeme’s uncle, Adrian, who had come running from around the corner, looking slightly out of breath.

“Not a problem,” the man grinned, looking down at Graeme. “Not a problem! I think the boy’s just in a bit of a hurry to get to the beach and start skimming stones! That’ll put a bit of colour in his cheeks! Here for the hols, is he?”

“Yes, I am” said Graeme, sounding irritated. He hated it when people talked as if he wasn’t there.

The man didn’t seem to mind Graeme’s tone of voice. In fact, he laughed. “How splendid! He’ll be bound to get up to all sorts of japes, no doubt!”

“Michael!” the woman said again.

The man looked directly at Graeme and rolled his eyes in a conspiratorial way. “Well, got to go!” He ruffled Graeme’s hair, turned and walked off.

“You don’t know what you could have caught. You don’t know where he’s been,” the woman was saying as she and the children followed the man towards a large silver Rolls Royce. A short chauffeur was holding the doors open. The doors had a red and gold crest painted on them.

Graeme’s uncle wasn’t looking happy. He had obviously also heard the woman’s comment. The whole street had probably heard. “People!” he said. “Sorry I’m late. They’ve put temporary traffic lights up at Pointer’s Cross. I was stuck for ages.”

“That’s okay,” Graeme told him.

“Good, good,” said Adrian. He picked up Graeme’s case and the two of them began walking back towards the car park. There was a kind of pause. It seemed to go on forever. Graeme had to remind himself that Doctor Willis had said not to panic, that it would be awkward for everyone at first.

“Was the journey okay?” Adrian asked after an age.

“Fine,” Graeme said abruptly. He looked at the case. “I can carry that,” he offered.

“Oh, right,” Adrian said, sounding unsure. “Sorry, Graeme. I still see you as a six year old sometimes.”

Graeme took his suitcase and walked with his uncle. Adrian was Graeme’s mum’s younger brother. He was thirty–nine; so although from Graeme’s point of view he was old, he definitely wasn’t doddery with a long grey beard and a walking stick, if you were picturing something like that.

"So, how was it? The trip, I mean?" Adrian asked again.

Graeme wondered if he should point out that this was the second time his uncle had asked, but in the end he just said, "Fine."

They walked the rest of the way in silence. When they got back to the car, a nineteen–sixty something cream coloured Saab, Graeme put his case in the back and then they set off to Port Stilton.

Port Stilton: I know what you're thinking. I know it's a funny name. *Everyone* knows it's a funny name but the last thing you want to do is laugh about it in front of the locals. It's okay for them to crack a joke or two because they live there. It's their name to make fun of. But outsiders can't, unless they want to end up with a black eye. One wag of a visitor once said something clever in front of the Port Stilton Rotary. He was black balled for life.

"It really has been a while since you've been down, hasn't it?" Adrian asked as they drove along the increasingly narrow lanes.

"Yeah," Graeme said. His family (him, his mum and dad) had always come here for holidays, mostly in the summer but occasionally for Christmas. Adrian had joined them a couple of times and loved the area. He'd bought one of the local cottages almost five years ago now and had been steadily doing it up. At first he had stayed in London and just come down from time to time, but now he lived in the port permanently. He was an architect, so he'd built a studio at the back of the cottage and worked from home most of the time.

"Jim knows you're coming," Adrian said. "I, um, I told him about everything. Hope that's okay."

There was that silence again. Graeme licked his lips. They were cracked. He could almost hear the rasp of his tongue running over them, they were so dry. "Okay."

Jim was a boy who Graeme had met during one of their holidays. There weren't that many kids around in Port Stilton and it was far from the well–beaten tourist track, so the two of them had fallen in together within five minutes of meeting. Jim was deaf and had spent the first week they'd hung out teaching Graeme (at Graeme's request) rude words in sign language. It had got Graeme into a lot of hot water back home, but his parents were over the moon that he'd got "an interest" at last. They signed him up for signing evening classes straight away. His mum and dad always had the knack of taking the fun out of everything.

Jim and Graeme hadn't spoken in ages. The hospital had let Graeme use one of their computers to email him – Jim was really brainy and into computers in a big way – but he hadn't replied. Doctor Willis said that it was probably just the computer playing up but Graeme hadn't been so sure.

"Jim's really excited that you're going to be around," Adrian continued. "I don't think he's been very happy lately. His mum and dad sent him away to boarding school after all the trouble and he doesn't like it much."

"What trouble?" Graeme asked.

"Maybe trouble's the wrong word," Adrian corrected himself. "To be honest, nobody's said that much about it but there was some sort of kafuffle not so long ago. Anyway, whatever happened, Jim got sent away to school but he's back for the holidays. He's been hanging around with some girl in a wheelchair. Her family moved into the old lighthouse last summer. You'll be able to form a little gang!" he teased.

Graeme looked out the window. Bramble hedges, about eight feet high, were on either side of the road and the road was the width of a single car. It was almost suffocating and felt to Graeme as if they were driving through a maze. Only occasionally did they come across passing points, where the road had been widened to allow one vehicle to pull aside so another coming from the opposite direction could get by. Every now and then there would be a gap in the hedge, for a gate or just where the brambles had been trampled. Looking through, Graeme could see the ocean, all grey and still.

"Sorry we haven't got better weather for you," Adrian said. "At least the sun's poking through a bit now. It tipped down not long ago."

Graeme shrugged. "Doesn't bother me."

"Here, you should take a look as we come to the top of this hill," said Adrian. "You can see home and out to sea as well."

He was right. The road got no wider but the maze was left behind them as they crested the hill. Now they could see everything: the huddled homes of Port Stilton; the sloping road that led down to the harbour; the beached fishing boats leaning drunkenly to one side; and out beyond the headland there was Raversham Isle, a hulking pile of rock covered in trees, home of the Raversham family. They were one of the oldest families in the world; it was said they could trace their ancestors back to "before the beginning of time", which sounded good but was, of course, codswallop. The current Lord Raversham had eight children, all grown up and some with children of their own, so the family legacy was set to continue for another few generations at least.

"Do you want to stop?" Adrian asked. "There's a great view from up here."

"Okay," said Graeme.

Adrian pulled the car over into a handy passing point. They got out and leaned on a low wall that looked like it pre–dated Stonehenge. At the bottom of the hill was Pointer's Cross, where the so–called main road ended and the even more twisty lanes of Port Stilton began. It looked in a right state. Workmen were up to their waists in a trench, digging for England.

"They're repairing a broken cable and replacing a telegraph pole," Adrian told Graeme, following his eye–line. "They said they'd have finished last week but they just keep on digging. I think they're heading for Australia."

The peaceful moment was shattered by the thunderous sound of a helicopter zooming overhead. It tilted forwards and roared out over the water, towards Raversham Isle.

The sun was setting just behind the island, breaking through the low–lying cloud and sending the castle standing at the centre into relief. The castle itself was a rag–tag collection of stonework, with walls that meandered in and out of the trees, up and down across the rocks. The sun streamed between two tall towers of unequal height that were at the western corner, their turrets spearing the clouds. A steep staircase connected them.

"Now that's what I call a building," Adrian said, staring at the island all misty–eyed.

"*That's* what you call a building?" Graeme asked him. For the first time since he'd arrived, Graeme's voice sounded bright, and alive. "It's falling apart!"

Adrian looked at his nephew. "It's a Parkes," he said, as if that explained everything. Graeme had almost forgotten how his uncle tended to get a bit over enthusiastic about buildings, sometimes.

The helicopter had now reached the isle. It hovered over the castle like a bird of prey and then dropped out of sight behind the walls.

"Must be visitors," said Adrian. "They're a bit early!"

Graeme didn't know what he'd meant by that.

"You'll be here for the party this year," Adrian said. "I can bring you along as my guest! You'll come, won't you?"

It dawned on Graeme, then, what his uncle was talking about. "They're still doing that?" he asked. The Ravershams threw a party on the island for the locals every Christmas. It was a pretty big deal, with music, dancing, a funfair, films and huge amounts of food and fireworks. There was so much food, in fact, the story went that they weighed you before letting you get on the boat back to the mainland.

"Oh yeah," Adrian said. "Every year. We're pretty traditional in these parts!"

Somewhere behind them, distorted by the wind but getting closer, was the sound of a bell. Looking around, Graeme saw a tiny woman approach on an old, rusty bicycle. There was very little paint left on it, but it had probably once been red. A yellow flag stuck up from the pannier bags over the rear wheel. The woman attempted to smile as she got closer, but was obviously out of breath. She wore a small blue cagoule. Her hair was lank, black and dripping with sweat.

"That," she puffed, "hill – is – a – killer!"

Getting off the bike, she bent over with her hands on her knees and breathed heavily. "Hello, Adrian!" she said, looking up for a moment. Her cagoule fell open and Graeme could see that underneath it she was wearing a policeman's uniform.

"Hi Rob," Adrian said. "This is my nephew, Graeme. Graeme, this is Roberta Plastic. She's our local bobby."

Roberta, who was still doubled over trying to catch her breath, lifted one hand in a sort of half–wave.

"What are you doing cycling this way?" asked Adrian.

"Ah, well, don't know if I can say," Roberta puffed, sucking a breath in from between her teeth. "Business out on Raversham Isle. Of course, Lord Muck won't leave the island, so muggins here had to go all the way out there. Not only that, but I get back and find that those bloody workmen have only gone and cut their way through the phone line, the idiots! So now I'm cycling to Peashingle to further my investigation."

"Can't you use a mobile phone?" Graeme asked her.

Roberta looked at him and gave a hollow laugh, her emerald eyes fierce. "Oh, don't get me started on that one!"

"Can't get any kind of signal down here," Adrian explained. "There's talk of putting an aerial up, but that's all it is at the moment."

Roberta took a deep breath. Her face was now a mild pink, rather than red. "Right," she said. "I shouldn't dawdle. I'll bet the old codger's got his telescope trained on me."

“Well the cycling will keep you fit,” Adrian grinned.

Roberta pursed her lips. “Keep on making remarks like that and you’ll find me commandeering your car,” she snapped.

“Sorry,” Adrian apologised, his grin turning into a grimace.

“Never mind,” she replied, mounting the bike and kicking the pedals round, ready to push off. “See you later!” she called out and began to pedal away.

“What’s that all about?” Adrian wondered aloud as Roberta disappeared round a bend in the road. “Must be quite important if she’s cycling off to Peashingle right now.”

Graeme shivered. The afternoon was wearing on and the air was getting chillier.

“Oh, sorry Graeme. You’re turning blue there! You still feeling the cold?”

Graeme nodded. For some reason since he’d been in hospital he’d become really sensitive to changes in temperature and couldn’t stand the cold at all. During one of their many chats, Doctor Willis had jokingly mentioned that the heating bill had tripled after Graeme arrived.

“Come on,” Adrian said, putting an arm round Graeme’s shoulders. “Let’s get you into the warm. You hungry?” he asked. Graeme nodded.

Adrian grimaced again. “Actually, I’m not sure what I’ve got to feed you. I think I’ve got some pasta lurking somewhere …”

CHAPTER TWO

The Boats at Midnight

Adrian was a world–class liar. When he said he had pasta lurking "somewhere", Graeme had thought that his uncle had no food at all. Instead, as they stepped through the front door it looked as if he planned to never go shopping again. There were crisps and chocolate in the lounge and in the kitchen Graeme couldn't open a cupboard without something falling out. A few bulging shopping bags were still waiting to be unpacked on the worktop.

"There's more in the freezer," Adrian told him, rummaging through one of the shopping bags. "Are you hungry?"

Graeme was speechless. He didn't think he'd ever seen so much food in one place at one time.

"Well, I'll take your silence as a yes, then," said Adrian. "I know it's here somewhere," he muttered, frowning as he continued to delve into the bags. "I might have gone a bit overboard," he admitted, glancing up for a moment to indicate all the shopping, "but your grandma put the fear of God into me. She said that when she'd been up to see you that you'd looked like a walking skeleton, so I'd better feed you up or she'd be having my guts for garters. So you've got to eat, okay? Or it'll be my head on the block!"

"Okay," Graeme said. Actually, he'd always been thin and it had never bothered anybody before, but for some reason everyone had now decided that fattening him up was the answer to all his problems.

"Got it!" Adrian shouted, lifting a pack of spaghetti above his head like he was carrying the Olympic torch. "We shall eat! If I can find the pasta sauce."

Graeme could see the sauce from where he was standing. He thought about letting Adrian fly from pillar to post like a mad thing hunting for it, which would have been quite a laugh, but was kind of aware that his uncle was trying to make an effort so instead he walked over, picked it up and handed it to him.

They cooked dinner together. For someone who lived alone Adrian was useless in the kitchen. Graeme had to show him how to do virtually everything. Pasta is, however, quite quick to prepare, even allowing for breaks to put out minor fires, so it wasn't long before they were sitting at the kitchen table with two huge bowls of steaming spaghetti and meatballs smothered with sauce. They'd probably made enough for five people. Six, if you included the burnt bits coating the bottom of the saucepan.

"Sticky Toffee Pudding for afters," Adrian burbled through a mouthful of food.

Graeme stared at him.

"Don't worry," said Adrian, "We can do that in the microwave. I'm king of the microwave."

*

After Graeme and the king of the microwave had wiped the remains of the exploded pudding from inside the oven they moved to the living room and sat in front of the fire.

"It's never done that before," Adrian was saying, shifting the glowing logs with a poker. Sparks whirled from the embers and danced in the air before vanishing up the chimney.

"Never mind," Graeme yawned. It was good to feel warm again. He stretched out his legs and half closed his eyes. Out in the cold night, the wind was whistling down the street and around the house; but inside the fire was warming the soles of his feet and the tips of his fingers, his face was bright red and his ears were glowing. The firelight flickered on the bare stone walls, over tables and chairs, into the shadowy corners at the edge of the room.

Before Graeme knew it, Adrian was shaking his arm to wake him up.

"You've been asleep for hours," he said.

"Have I?" Graeme asked, shielding his eyes as he opened them.

"Do you want to watch some TV?" Adrian asked.

Graeme shook his head. "No, thanks. I should really go to bed."

"Okay," Adrian said. "You know where your room is."

"Mmm–hmm." Graeme felt so exhausted he thought it was likely that he'd fall asleep again as soon as his head hit the pillow. He got up and mumbled goodnight, trying not to lose that warm, sleepy feeling you have when you're not quite awake, and made his way up the spiral staircase that stood at the back of the lounge.

Graeme's room was right at the very top of the house. On the landing there was a rope hanging down. You pulled the rope and a hatch popped open and a spiral staircase unfolded, winding round and round until it hit the floor. Adrian had a thing for spiral staircases, which was just as well: there wasn't a straight set of steps in the house. Climbing up took you into the loft, into the room in the roof.

It had a sloping ceiling with thick, dark brown wooden beams. The floor was bare wood with a massive straw–coloured rug in the middle. There was a hammock set up in one corner and a bunk bed was over against the far wall with Graeme's suitcase lying open on the bottom bunk. On the other side of the room there was an alcove with a window that looked across the harbour and out to sea. It had a wide windowsill, covered in cushions, that was almost large enough to stretch right out on. Graeme pulled the duvet off his bed and wrapped himself up in it, then shuffled across to the window. He clambered onto the cushions and fell asleep with his head against the window frame, listening to the sound of the wind and the waves lapping the shore.

*

Graeme didn't know what made him wake up. He'd had the duvet pulled almost completely over his head, so even though the light from the moon was shining right through the window he wasn't aware of it. The sea was little more than a murmur in the background. Nevertheless, he woke up. He sat up on one elbow and rubbed his eyes. Pressing his face to the window, he squinted at the world outside. There were still clouds in the sky, but he could see stars shining through. The moon was partially obscured by a thin layer of cloud and looked hazy. It was still very bright.

Graeme's eyes darted downwards as he noticed a movement in next door's front garden. Someone – he couldn't make out who – was inching across the lawn, heading away from the house. Whoever it was opened the gate. The latch made a clack–clack sound as it was operated and the figure froze on the spot. It stayed motionless for a minute then crept out into the lane and across the street where it paused and turned to look up at something. For a minute Graeme thought it was staring right at him, but then it ran off between two houses, towards the beach.

Graeme looked out to sea. Ripples of light covered the surface of the water. There appeared to be dark shapes at the shoreline. At first he thought they were the shadows of clouds, but as his eyes grew accustomed to the level of light he realised they were boats. He opened his window a bit, which let in a rush of cold air. His teeth chattered. A bat flapped by in front of his eyes, startled in the midst of its mad flight. With the window open, the rush of the surf on the beach was clear. Now he could make out people milling about at the water's edge.

He was wide–awake. Sometimes being up while it's dark makes everything seem unreal, as if the normal rules don't apply. When he had the time to look back, Graeme could only think that's why he threw the duvet to the floor and fumbled for his trainers. He hopped across the room, pulling them on one at a time, and jumped down the staircase. The house was in darkness. Adrian must have gone to bed.

Graeme trod carefully along the landing, not wanting to wake his uncle, and down the steps into the lounge. He picked his jacket off the hook by the front door and sneaked out into the night.

The garden gate was shut and Graeme knew it squeaked loud enough to wake the dead, so he clambered over the hedge instead. The prickles dug into his jumper, which stuck out the bottom of his jacket. He tugged at it to get it free and then slipped into the narrow alley that the stranger had darted down only moments before, bursting out on the other side by the Radley Guest House. Graeme crept past its darkened porch, where a rocking chair was creaking to and fro, and then pelted down the slope that led to the beach. He was going so fast that before he knew it he found his feet crunching on the gravel that separated the sand from roadway.

"What was that?" snapped someone in a deep, hollow voice.

Graeme managed to stop dead in his tracks, right by a line of boulders at the edge of the sand. The people on the beach all looked around. It was lucky his clothes were so dark or they'd have easily spotted him.

"Shine the torch over there," commanded the man standing at the front of the group. He spoke in that same hollow voice that Graeme had heard moments before.

There was a click as one of the others switched on a torch.

Something pulled at Graeme's jumper.

"Get down!"

He was dragged behind one of the boulders. A boy wearing night vision goggles was crouched there.

"Jim?" Graeme whispered. "Is that you?"

A grin flashed on and off. It was Jim, all right, all boundless enthusiasm, even this late at night. He raised a finger to his lips, and then grinned again.

Light splashed over the boys' heads as the man with the torch scanned the area. "There's nothing there, Lord."

The hollow voiced man let out a blast of air through his nostrils. "Your word is not the most reliable."

Graeme could hear the man's footsteps as he started to move around the beach. Gravel crunched as he neared their hiding place. They tried to flatten themselves against the rock as the footsteps got closer and closer. The man smelled the air, as if he could sniff them out. He started to talk as he searched.

"Have you found it yet?"

"Found what, my Lord?"

"You know what."

"Oh. No, my Lord, not as yet." The other speaker hesitated. "I think you had it last."

"What?"

"Nothing, my Lord. In any case, sir, *bob amser arall ffordd*, sir."

There was a moment's silence; and then the man, the leader, said, "Are you trying to be funny?"

"No, my Lord. It's just, I mean, there's always another way, sir. We have the boats, after all."

"Indeed we do," said the leader. Graeme heard the sound of him hitting his companion.

"Ow!"

"I don't forget failure," the leader said; and then he sighed. "And I hate travelling by row boat," he added in a much quieter voice.

They must have been really close if Graeme could hear such a whisper.

The leader harrumphed. “Shine the light here,” he called over his shoulder.

The light from the torch flooded around the boulder that the boys were crouched behind. Jim tapped Graeme on the shoulder and pointed. Graeme’s foot was casting a long shadow off into the road. It looked like a bit of the boulder, but if he moved by so much as a centimetre, the men would realise that someone was watching them.

The leader snorted once in frustration and his fingers drummed on something metallic. “Move the torch around this way,” he said.

Graeme and Jim held their breath.

“My Lord, I beg your pardon, sir, but surely if we don’t want any witnesses, we shouldn’t really be wangin’ a torch about in the dead of night.”

The leader brought his hand down, right above Graeme’s head, so it smacked the top of the boulder. “For once,” he fumed, “for once, you are right.”

There was more crunching on the gravel as he returned to the others.

“Get the boats in the water,” he instructed, “and you – take your own advice and put that light out!”

The light went out.

The boys stayed where they were, listening to the splashing of feet as the others launched the boats. When Graeme finally risked peeking over the top of the boulder, he was in time to see the last few stragglers lurching into the sea. They struggled to load a large, lumpy sack with a red circle printed on it, then half leapt, half fell into their boat. They scrambled to get their oars in place and then rowed like mad to try and catch up to the others.

A lone figure in the lead boat was standing, with a foot placed forward on the prow. Graeme watched as they rowed further out. It didn’t look like they were heading for sea at all. They were aiming for the island. Whoever was in the lead boat held out an arm and flashed a light on and off. An answering light came from somewhere along the rocky coast, diffused by the mist that had settled around the isle. The mist made it appear that the isle was floating on a cloud.

The person with the light called out, “Row on!” and turned to sit back down. It was the hollow voiced leader. The boat rocked to and fro and then began to pitch and toss in a more violent manner as he gingerly twisted around. He seemed to be having trouble keeping his balance.

"Watch out!" he cried, that echoing voice carrying quite clearly back to shore. His arms pinwheeled as he tried to steady himself; and then he fell overboard.

The people in the other boats all dropped their oars and tried to lean over and help their struggling companion. He was splashing around, cursing between taking great gulps of seawater.

"You utter dolt!" he half shouted at the oarsman of his boat. "You imbecile!"

The oarsman said something that Graeme couldn't make out.

"Oh, shut up you fool," the leader said through mouthfuls of water. He hooked his arm over the edge of the boat. "Well, don't just sit there, cretin! Help me!"

The oarsman tried to help his master back on board. After struggling for several minutes, the leader hit his fist on the surface of the water.

"Oh, just let go! Let go!" he snapped. "I'll do it myself. Like everything else around here! You're all useless! Incompetent!"

The oarsman muttered again.

"One more clever remark and it'll be the end of you," said the leader, treading water. "Why on earth do I always allow myself to be surrounded by idiots?"

The oarsman, who clearly felt he had something to say on every issue, said something.

"I'll give you cheap," the leader snarled, lifting himself out of the water. There was a yelp as he hit the oarsman. "Now get rowing!"

The boat rowed off. There was a general shuffling as the others got back into position and also went on their way. As they neared the island and began navigating amongst the rocks, they slowly vanished into the mist.

Jim bounced upright, ripped off his goggles and bounded onto the beach, splashing a way into the water before stopping and looking back at Graeme. *"It's incredible!"* he signed. His eyes were shining.

Graeme followed him out from their hiding place. *"Who are they?"* he signed back; not very well, it seemed, judging by the look Jim gave him, tutting once.

"I thought you'd taken lessons," he accused Graeme out loud. Jim had a very good speaking voice, better than many with perfect hearing. About the only giveaway that he was deaf was that his voice was a bit flat and he tended to lisp occasionally on certain words.

"Sorry," Graeme apologised. "Who are they?" he said and signed again at the same time.

"That's better," Jim signed. He shrugged. *"Dunno. We've been watching them for a few weeks now."*

"Who's 'we'?"

"Calamara and I. Of course, you haven't met her yet." He noticed Graeme's worried expression and added, *"She kind of takes a bit of getting used to, but she's okay."* He glanced back out to sea. *"We first spied them mooching around, here on the beach. I dashed down to see what was going on but by the time I got here they'd always be gone. Then about a week ago they started using the boats. The sacks are new!"*

He stood there for a moment, his breath steaming in the chill air. Then he ran to the rock face on the right. "They came from here," he said, running his hand over the stone. He turned to look at Graeme. *"The boats, I mean,"* he explained. *"There was an opening right here. I got down here just in time to see them closing it. Now, if I'm lucky,"* he signed, starting to examine the cracks that riddled the rock.

Graeme pulled him round so they were face to face. "If you're lucky what?"

Jim shrugged Graeme off and turned back to the rocks. As his hands were busy probing he had no choice but to speak out loud. "If I'm lucky, the stone I threw into the path of the closing door will have been strong enough to…" his face lit up. "Got it!"

Graeme followed his finger as it pointed to a crack that looked no different to any of the others. There was a small rock lodged there at ground level.

Jim smiled. "This is it!" he said, putting on his goggles and trying to peer inside. He shifted from one position to another, trying to see in. Eventually he gave up with an exasperated sigh. *"The gap's too narrow. There's definitely something in there, though. Help me to pull it open."*

They got their fingers jammed in the opening and started to heave at it. No matter how hard they pulled, it refused to budge. A plank of driftwood lay nearby, so Graeme picked it up, startling a tiny crab which scuttled away into the night. Pushing the plank into the gap, they tried using it to lever the door open but it was no good. The wood was far too rotten and just broke up in their hands as soon as they applied pressure. They looked down at the sodden splinters in the sand at their feet.

"There's got to be something else we can use," Jim mused, wiping his hands on his jeans. He let out a strangled yell. "Oh, no!" he wailed.

The small crab Graeme had disturbed earlier was crawling over the stone that was holding the door open. It turned itself on its side to squeeze through, then grabbed hold of the stone in one pincer and pulled it inside.

The door shut with a quiet click.

Jim collapsed on the sand with his back to the rock. "No!" he cried again.

"Did you see how they got it open in the first place?" Graeme asked.

"No, I only just made it down here in time to see the thing close. Calamara's going to kill me!"

"If she's so bothered why isn't she here?"

"It's difficult to get the wheelchair down from the lighthouse in the dark," Jim said. *"Don't mention that in front of her, though."* He started to run sand through his fingers. *"Well, I suppose that's it for tonight, then."*

"Did any of the people have a key?" Graeme asked him. "You saw the door shutting, but did anybody have to lock it afterwards?"

"I didn't see anybody lock it."

"Well, if nobody locked it, then it probably doesn't need a key, which means it must open and close another way."

"What are you thinking?" Jim asked.

"Well, maybe it has a password."

"Voice recognition," Jim nodded. *"You mean like* 'Open Sesame'!" He said "Open Sesame" aloud.

"Yeah. All we have to do is work out what word someone would use to unlock rock."

Jim fell forward and was pushed across the sand as the door swung open.

The boys looked at each other.

"That," Jim congratulated Graeme, "was a piece of luck."

Graeme frowned. "It does seem a bit simple, doesn't it?"

"It was probably set by an adult. They can't cope with complicated passwords. My mum has the same password for everything: credit cards, e–mail, you name it."

"Lock rock," Graeme tried.

Nothing happened.

"What are you doing?" Jim asked, open–mouthed.

"I thought that maybe it might be..."

The door swept in a wide arc and shut again.

"No!" Jim held his head in his hands. *"What have you done?"*

"I don't think it was me," Graeme told him.

"Do you see anybody else around here?" Jim asked.

"Maybe it shuts by itself after a certain amount of time."

Jim didn't look convinced.

"Let me give it another go," Graeme said. "Unlock rock."

The door did not re–appear.

Jim gave Graeme an accusing look. *"They're probably using a rotating password."*

"How many people do you know who rotate their passwords?" Graeme asked him.

Jim's fingers moved but he didn't form the words properly. Graeme had to get him to repeat it before he could make out what Jim was trying to say. *"Well, I do."*

Graeme tried to keep his face blank. *"Okay,"* he said, nodding. "Well, maybe it was just a co–incidence that what I said opened it up," he suggested.

"Yeah." Jim folded his arms.

"It's the only explanation..."

The door opened.

Graeme pinched his bottom lip. "This doesn't make sense."

Jim got up, smiling as he dusted himself off. *"I'm glad you're here,"* he said and patted Graeme on the shoulder. *"Let's go in."*

This all seemed more than weird to Graeme, but he followed Jim.

They walked through the opening into a cave. Graeme couldn't see the crab. It was probably huddled in a corner wondering what it had done to deserve being bothered all night by a couple of boys. To either side of them, hung on the walls, were six row–boats, three on each wall. Cables ran across the ceiling above them and down the walls to four security lights, which had flickered on as they entered.

Jim scratched his head. *"That's odd."*

"What's odd?"

"There aren't any empty spaces. They had six boats tonight, but there are still six here and no room for any others."

Graeme's eyes were beginning to sting a bit. He rubbed them. "Well, maybe," he started, but stopped as he heard a movement behind them. He turned around. In the doorway was a tall, cloaked figure. Mist flowed around its robes. It hissed at them.

Graeme took a step back into the cave and collided with Jim, who looked over his shoulder and howled as he saw the stranger. Both boys stumbled back and fell to the ground.

The cloaked figure advanced on them. The hissing grew louder, echoing off the walls. Clouds of smoke curled around Graeme's head and the last things he remembered were the dark stranger towering over him; the hissing that seemed to be coming from everywhere; and the crab, which had come out of hiding and was crawling across his chest.

*

"Thanks for coming along, Rob."

It was Adrian.

Graeme opened his eyes and the world span around. He closed them. It felt like he was going to be sick.

"Not a problem, Adrian." It was the voice of Roberta, the policewoman they'd met the day before.

"I can't believe this," Adrian was saying. "He's been here less than a day and he's already missing!"

"It might help if you remember what you were like when you were young," Roberta said. "It's quite normal, especially in an area like this. If I had a pound for every child who went AWOL in the past year I'd be a rich woman. They go off convinced they'll find pirate treasure or whatever. All they ever come back with is a stinking cold. It's quite ordinary for boys to do stupid things."

"I haven't forgotten what it was like to be that age, Rob. Ordinarily I'd agree with you, but he's not any ordinary boy. Not right now. If anything's happened to him…"

"You did look all the way round the house, didn't you?"

"Yes."

"I mean, he's not hiding in a cupboard or something, as a prank?"

"He's not really a prankster. And he's thirteen, as he pointed out to me, not eight."

A new voice said, “Some eight year olds I know might consider that an insult.”

Curiosity overrode Graeme’s fear of throwing up and he opened his eyes again. It wasn’t so bad as long as he moved slowly. He could see the sky, so he was outside. It wasn’t quite light yet. His clothes felt a bit damp. Turning his head, he could see that Jim was beside him, fast asleep. They were behind another rock.

“Morning, Josephine,” Roberta was saying. There was a slight edge to her voice.

“Lost something, have we?” Josephine asked. She sounded as if she were enjoying herself immensely.

Graeme propped himself up, just enough to peer over the top of the rock. He and Jim were a little way up the cliff, on a natural shelf formed in the rock face. He couldn’t see Adrian or Roberta, so they must’ve been directly below. He could see the newcomer, Josephine. It would have been hard to miss her.

She stood at the edge of the beach, by the boulder he and Jim had hidden behind the previous night. She looked sort of like Graeme’s grandma, only Graeme’s grandma had never dressed in a fur coat, high–heeled shoes and very little else (to his knowledge). Her greying hair was piled atop her head and even from where he was, Graeme could see her bright red lips, drawn into a tight smile. He got the feeling that she was biting the inside of her cheeks to stop herself from laughing out loud at the joke, whatever the joke was.

“We’re looking for my nephew, Graeme,” Adrian told her. “He’s about so high, brown hair, blue–ish eyes.”

“What was he wearing?”

Adrian’s voice sounded strained. “I don’t really remember. Jeans, I think, a jacket, and a jumper, maybe. God, I hope he’s got a jumper on. What if he’s freezing to death somewhere?”

“Jeans, jumper and jacket, eh? I think you’ve just about described every teenage boy I’ve ever known.”

“Now, Josephine,” said Roberta, her tone reproachful.

“Now, Roberta,” Josephine sang, “why don’t you let me help? I’ll bet he’s not far. Boys love the beach,” she said. Lifting her legs one at a time, she removed her shoes. Holding them in one hand by the straps, she tiptoed onto the beach. “Don’t you just love the feeling of sand in your toes?”

“Josephine,” Roberta said again, but Josephine wasn’t listening. She was drawing pictures in the sand with her feet.

"How old did you say your nephew was again?" she asked.

"Thirteen," Adrian said.

Josephine wrinkled her nose. "Oh." Her shoulders gave an involuntary shudder. "Sorry," she apologised. "I had to oversee the Peashingle Baby Races the other day and what a hullabaloo that was. I haven't quite recovered yet. You mentioning… that age… thirteen is too near the wrong side of puberty… talk of children brings the whole day rushing back."

Roberta laughed. "I'll bet the poo was flying everywhere!"

"Oh, I don't mind that," said Josephine, waving a hand in the air. "That is, after all, one of the great levellers of life. We all do it, don't we?"

Graeme didn't hear Roberta or Adrian say anything in reply to that.

"If it were just the poo I wouldn't have a problem," said Josephine. "It's the child that comes with it, that's what I have the problem with! I made up a rhyme. Do you want to hear it?"

"Not really," said Roberta.

Josephine paddled in the surf and then started to sing:

"Hello my son did you do a number two?
Was it large, was it lumpy, as it plopped into the…"

"Lovely," said Roberta.

"I'd hardly started!" complained Josephine. "There are two verses."

"Do you think we could get back to the matter at hand?" Adrian asked them.

"Of course, of course," said Josephine. "The teenagers? They're up there!" She pointed straight at Graeme, no hesitation. "Hello," she called, waggling her fingers in a silly wave. "Were you planning on announcing your presence at any point in the near future or were you holding out until your uncle had a heart attack?"

Adrian and Roberta both stepped back and looked up.

"Graeme!" Adrian shouted.

Graeme struggled to stand as Adrian and Roberta climbed up to him.

"What are you doing here?" Adrian asked, grabbing hold of Graeme. "Have you been out all night?"

Roberta looked past the two of them. "Is that Jim?" She stepped carefully over Graeme, sank to Jim's side and patted him on the cheek. "He's just asleep," she said. "Come on, boy," she urged, shaking him, "wake up."

Jim sat up almost immediately. He didn't seem to be feeling as ill as Graeme; he was fully alert and didn't seem surprised or in any way concerned as he quickly assessed where he was and what was going on. Roberta started to sign something to him.

"Why don't you just speak?" he asked. *"I can lip read you know."*

"Listen here, my lad," Roberta lectured him, "good taxpayers' money was spent so I could converse in sign language, so converse in sign language I bloody well will. Now, what were you two up to, out here all night?"

"We were just having a sleep out," Jim said before Graeme had the chance to say anything. *"You could see the stars and everything. We wore warm clothes,"* he added.

"Well, they're soggy clothes now," Adrian told the boys, fixing a stern stare on his nephew. Graeme felt his cheeks flush.

Roberta pulled Jim to his feet. "Let's get you down, then."

They picked their way over the rocks and back onto the beach, where Josephine was still standing in the surf, wriggling her toes in the wet sand.

"Hope they didn't try and fob you off with some story about being out to watch the stars." She washed her feet off and then came over to them. "How lovely," she sang, gripping Graeme on the shoulder. "Everyone re–united." She looked deep into his eyes; hers were extraordinary, brilliant green. "Someone's going to be very interested to see you're here," she whispered in his ear. "He'll want a word, no doubt."

Jim had something in his hand and Josephine's eyes darted to him. She let go of Graeme, virtually pushing him out of the way, causing him to trip backwards, and clutched Jim instead, pulling him up, holding him fast and squeezing his arms. "And you, little James," she licked her lips. "How you've grown. What is that you have there?"

"Nothing," said Jim, stuffing his hands in his pockets. Josephine eyed him with a suspicious stare.

"Idle boys are rarely up to any good," she said. "You should come and see me. I can always find something useful for a strapping lad like you to do."

Roberta put an arm around a confused looking Jim and pulled him away. "Yes, thank you, Josephine, for all your help."

Josephine curtsied. "Not at all," she said in that singsong voice. "Glad to be of assistance."

With her stilettos still clasped in one hand, she sauntered off up the road, humming a little tune to herself.

"Right," Roberta clapped her hands together. "Let's get you all home. Jim, I'll come with you and try and stop your dad from grounding you for the next year."

"Okay," Jim agreed. Just as they were walking away, he turned to Graeme and signed something. He signed it so quickly that it was a miracle Graeme caught any of it. This is what he signed: *"I'll come round later. Got a plan. We're going to that island."*

CHAPTER THREE
A Passage to the Isle

"I called your parents last night."

The spoonful of porridge froze half way to Graeme's mouth. Adrian had gone out to the local shop first thing to get a paper; he'd come back, made Graeme's breakfast, sat down, shaken the paper, got up, and then, from the safety of the kitchen, made the announcement. He obviously knew that he was bringing up a dangerous subject. "The phones came on for all of ten minutes or so. I got cut off right in the middle of talking to your mum," he continued in a jolly voice that sounded more than a little forced.

Graeme smiled ever so briefly; he didn't stop eating; he didn't look up.

Adrian was quiet for a while longer as he fixed himself a bowl of cornflakes and came to sit at the table again. "They were glad to know you'd got here safely," he said.

Graeme just wasn't in the mood for this. "Okay," he replied, hoping that the monosyllabic answer would be a broad hint to Adrian that this was not a subject he wanted to discuss at that moment; *or ever*, he thought to himself.

Adrian hadn't taken the hint though; he was nervously licking his lips as he continued, "They said they'd call on Christmas Day."

"Okay."

"Okay," Adrian nodded and bit his lip, finally getting the message. He paused again and then said, "Let's have the radio on."

He leaned over and switched on the small, old fashioned wireless that was sitting on the sideboard. Then he started eating his cornflakes, while peering at the paper.

Graeme continued to eat as the awful presenters of some morning magazine programme rambled on in the background. He wasn't particularly interested in stuff about the price of cranberries, but he did raise his head out of his breakfast bowl when the next item started.

"We have exclusively learnt of a strange set of events concerning the millionaire recluse Lord Llewellyn Raversham. It's over to Georgette for more on this story."

"Thanks, Roger. The news broke late last night that Lord Raversham, who followed family tradition in making this tiny corner of the world his home, has 'lost contact' with several of his children. By all accounts, they have simply vanished off the face of the planet. His eldest son, Uriah, has not been heard from in over two weeks. He was not on his return flight from the Amazon basin; despite repeated attempts, nobody at his base camp can be reached. Uriah's younger brother, Finlay, has been missing for a similar amount of time; and now it appears that yet another member of the family has gone missing. Only yesterday, the private jet that Penelope Raversham–Lennox and her husband, Harrison, were travelling in vanished as it flew over the Western Ghats.

"And now, what might have been viewed as an unfortunate string of co–incidences is turning, well, I can only describe it as sinister. For the latest developments in this extraordinary story we've linked up with LVFM9 in Las Vegas to hear about an incident involving Intentional Raversham, the youngest of Lord Raversham's children. LVFM9's top reporter, Anna Kay, should be on the other end of the line. Hello, Anna. Are you there?"

There was a burst of static from the radio.

"Yes Georgette this really is a weird one," a slightly distorted but very perky American voice announced, talking at nine to the dozen, "weird and mysterious! I'm standing here on the very spot where last night Intentional Raversham says he was accosted by a monstrous attacker! And by monstrous I mean monstrous, Georgette! Intentional was interviewed by local police last night after reporting that a white monster, with purple eyes, no less, materialised out of nowhere and tried to grab him, right here on the strip! With me now are Kevin and

Valerie Quintent of Budding, Earwax, who witnessed the whole thing. Mr and Mrs Quintent, can you tell me what you saw?"

"Yeah," said Mrs Quintent, "well, we were on our way back to our hotel. It was late – "

"We'd just seen a show at Ptolemy's Palace Pizzeria," her husband interrupted her.

"It was so good, I can't tell you!" raved Mrs Quintent.

"Yeah, anyway," said Mr Quintent, "we were driving back to our hotel and all of a sudden this guy appears, dressed in red pants and a damn ugly yellow shirt. He's standing in the middle of the road right in front of us!"

"He was dressed all in black," Mrs Quintent argued, "and he was running about all over the place!"

"He was standing in the middle of the road," insisted Mr Quintent.

"No, babe," laughed Mrs Quintent, "he wasn't! You downed your thirtieth pinacolada before we left the dinner show!"

"You're exaggerating! I know when I've had enough and I was nowhere near – "

"You were blotto! *I* had to drive, remember?"

"Excuse me," Anna interrupted them. "What happened next?"

There was a slight pause before Mr Quintent continued. "Well, it was lucky for that guy I'd just had my brakes serviced before we came on vacation, otherwise, well, I think he'd be a pancake right now, you know what I mean? So, my wife is screaming, I mean, it's just not what you expect to see, is it? A guy in the middle of the street!"

"He wasn't in the middle of the street and I didn't make a sound. *You* were the one screaming… like a little girl!"

"So I get out of my car and start yelling at him, I mean, he gave me a scare, right? But he's not listening! He's curled up on the ground, swatting at the air and he's yowling louder than my wife, and she's got a pair of lungs on her like you wouldn't believe."

"He didn't shriek until you got out and started on him," said Mrs Quintent. "You can be real intimidating, 'specially when you've had a few! My husband's a big guy, y'know? Not many people'd have him, the great lug, but I like a cuddly man!"

"Hmm," said Mr Quintent. "So I'm, like, talking to the guy but I can't get any sense outta him, so I call the police…"

"I called the police," said Mrs Quintent. "You were talking at a trash can on the sidewalk by then! He can't work a cell, anyway,

Anna. Big fingers, you know! So the police came – they were quick, I tell ya, real fast, I wish they were that fast at home – and they took that poor man away. They thought he was as high as a kite, but he seemed okay to me, just really, really scared."

"Don't pay no attention to her! All she has to hear is a hint of a British accent and she's away!" said Mr Quintent. "He was out of it, I tell ya! Crazy drunk Brit – "

"Thanks," the reporter cut him off. "But you didn't see any monsters trying to grab Intentional – Mr Raversham?"

"Nah. I mean, please! Monsters! Damn Brit – "

"Well, there you have it, Georgette," said Anna. "On the face of it, it's just another night in Las Vegas, but given the other stories you're reporting, maybe there's more to this that meets the eye! This is Anna Kay, reporting for LVFM9, in Las Vegas."

"Thank you, Anna," said Georgette. "Well, whatever conclusions we may draw, it does seem that this chain of events has scared the Raversham family. Rumour has it that they are converging on Raversham Isle for the holidays. A statement has been released by the police on behalf of Lord Raversham to the effect that that the family are returning for the annual Christmas Eve party on Raversham Isle, which all locals are traditionally invited to. One thing is certain: none of this can have improved Lord Raversham's failing health; another reason, as if one were needed, that he will be grateful to have his family about him during the Christmas festivities."

"Poor souls," Adrian said, as the presenters moved on to interview an enthusiastic scientist who was predicting that humanity would be extinct by 2083 and the turkey would then evolve to be the dominant form of life on Earth.

"The world can be an awful place, can't it?" Adrian continued. (Graeme assumed his uncle was talking about the Ravershams rather than the turkeys.) "At this time of year, too..."

Seeing as they appeared to be past the awkward moment, Graeme felt it would be safe to put his spoon in the empty bowl and sit up.

"That was great," he said.

Adrian made a face. "It wasn't proper porridge," he admitted. "I got the easy instant stuff. The last time I made proper porridge I had to throw out the saucepan I made it in."

"Well it was very tasty anyway," Graeme told him.

Adrian's eyes narrowed. "Complementing my cooking? What are you after, I wonder?"

"Well, Jim said he'd come round. We were going to hang out."

"Thick as thieves again, are you?" Adrian smiled.

"Eh?"

"You seemed a bit worried yesterday when I mentioned him."

"Oh." Graeme didn't think he'd been that obvious about it. "No, he's … I mean, we're fine."

Even as he spoke, Graeme realised that he hadn't asked Jim about why he had never received a reply to his email. He made a mental note to ask later on.

"He's a good lad," Adrian was saying. He levelled his gaze and pointed at Graeme with his spoon. "Promise me if you two go out and about you won't get in anybody's way."

"I promise."

"I want your word," Adrian persisted. "No shenanigans."

Graeme laughed. "No shenanigans? You sound like Grandpa."

"Do I?" Adrian's face creased with worry. "Oh, God. I'm turning into my father!" he cried out in a tragic voice.

They both laughed.

"I was thinking of us going out today," Adrian said, "but seeing as things are going well with you and Jim I'll work instead. I have got some stuff – for a theme park, actually – that ought to be finished before Christmas. What do you think about us picking a Christmas tree tomorrow? The paper says they've got carolling and stuff on at the garden centre in Peashingle. Did you ever go there while you were down here with your Mum and Dad?"

"No. We never went there," Graeme assured him. Then, as Adrian seemed to be expecting more, he added, "You know what they're like. Remember when you came along those times? When we only ever seemed to go to the beach or to castles? Well, when you weren't there it was just castles. Castles, castles and more castles, until I was castle sick."

"Well there are a few around," Adrian grinned. "So you think you'd be up for it? The garden centre, I mean? I thought we could pop along and get in the Christmas spirit."

Graeme didn't know what to say. A garden centre…

"It's not just a place for plant pots and fertiliser and, um, crazy paving and so on," said Adrian, starting to babble, aware he wasn't necessarily presenting an attractive proposition. "There's, y'know, acres of actual gardens, tearooms… not that you'd be interested in those… I'm not selling this very well, am I? It's got a maze, though, and an art centre, that sort of thing. Oh, and they have homemade doughnuts! Fabulous doughnuts!"

Graeme looked at his uncle, who seemed desperate to please, who was trying so hard. "Sounds great," he lied. Well, he liked doughnuts. It might not be as bad as all that.

*

Jim came round about half an hour later and Adrian treated both boys to the "no shenanigans" lecture before letting them out the door. He also made Graeme dress as if they were preparing an expedition to the North Pole.

"Why was he so fussed about you putting on so many jumpers?" Jim asked as they walked along. He was walking backwards just ahead of Graeme, apparently because he could.

Graeme frowned. "He wants me to keep warm." His voice was becoming tight and he was sure how uncomfortable he felt showed in his expression.

Jim just looked puzzled. *"It is winter, but it's not that cold,"* he said.

"They think my lungs are still weak," said Graeme, not bothering to sign it. "Everyone's afraid I'll get pneumonia again or worse."

"Oh yeah," Jim nodded. *"Yeah, smoke damage. We had a film about it in school."* He looked off at nothing in particular, as if he were trying to remember something. *"Yeah, now, how did it go?"*

Graeme started concentrating hard on Jim's fingers, not looking him in the face.

"Smoke inhalation and asphyxiation is the main cause of house fire injuries and – " Jim stopped, mid–flow. He'd finally noticed how uncomfortable Graeme was. *"Or something,"* he finished. *"You seem fine, anyway,"* he added. Unlike Adrian, Jim was definitely not a good liar. He tried a grin but it didn't help.

Graeme changed the subject. "Where are we headed? Are we going to meet, um, Clarmara later?"

"We're off to the quay, and it's Cal–a–mar–a,*"* Jim corrected him, saying and spelling it. *"Yeah, she'll find us, don't you worry. I called and told her about last night before I came over to you. I had to*

try seven times. Dad's really in a stew about the phones. Still, took his mind off punishing me!"

"What was it that you found on the beach?" Graeme asked him.

"Oh," he said, his eyes widening. "*This was where we woke up, in the rocks. Look!*"

He reached into his jeans pocket.

"Watch out!"

They'd walked right down to the road along the front and Jim was on the verge of falling into a pit the workmen had dug. No one had bothered to mark the area where the work was being carried out with tape or anything. Two men in blue overalls were standing with their arms folded. They glowered at Graeme and Jim as if the boys were the enemy.

"Don't complain to us," one said.

"It's nothing to do with us," said the other. "It's not our fault. We've checked. Speak to them, down in the pit. Address all complaints to them."

Jim and Graeme looked at each other and back to the men. "We're not complaining," Jim said.

A head popped up from the hole. It belonged to a ruddy–faced workman.

"You kids ought to be more careful," he cautioned them.

"Sorry," Jim said out loud.

The workman scowled and said something under his breath. He didn't seem all that impressed with the apology.

Another head appeared from the depths. "Unwin, what are you up to?" This was a woman, wearing a yellow hardhat that was smeared with dirt. She looked at the men in overalls. "Are you still here?" she asked, putting her hands on her hips.

"We aren't going anywhere," said the man who had first spoken to Graeme and Jim, "until you admit it was you lot who fouled up the phones, *love*."

The woman wasn't amused. "I am not your love," she told him in a dangerously flat voice. "My name is Facility, if you feel the need to address me again; and let me assure you if it had been us who knocked out the phone lines then I think they'd have stayed down."

"Not gone up and down like a horse draws," Unwin added, nodding.

Facility looked at Unwin, closed her eyes and shook her head. She turned back to the men in overalls. "When we muck things up, we do it properly. Now why don't you two skedaddle and see if you can't actually fix something as opposed to standing around trying to shift the blame onto the innocent?"

The men in overalls looked at each other. "We'll be back," they said as one, then turned and trudged off.

Facility finally seemed to notice Graeme and Jim at that point. "Oh, hello."

"Hello," they chorused back.

"You two shouldn't be playing around here," she said. "Unwin's spadework is a bit haphazard at the best of times."

"It weren't me that took out the phones," Unwin whined. "I can't throw a spade that high." He pointed to the telegraph poles that were dotted at regular intervals along the road.

"Of course not, Unwin," Facility agreed in a condescending tone. "And that's the story we're sticking to as long as those two idiots from the telephone company are around, right? And put your hardhat on."

Unwin grumbled but reached down to grab his yellow hat. Facility turned back to the boys.

"Despite Unwin's assurances I wouldn't hang around where we're working. I'm okay," she rapped her knuckles on her hardhat twice to illustrate the point, "but I don't want your brains dashed out all over. There's enough of a mess here already and I don't need it being added to, thank you very much."

Jim and Graeme looked at each other.

Facility stood there watching them for a moment, then said very slowly, "Go – away – please. Now!"

The boys walked carefully around the hole and continued on their way, leaving the workers to resume digging.

*

The quay was little more than a rough wall of stone that ran alongside the beach. A seagull, a canary and some other bird that Graeme didn't recognise were strutting about as if they owned the place. There were quite a few boats moored there, mostly of the fishing variety, with their nets hung out to dry on the decks. There were two others right alongside the wall, both with gangplanks down. They were ordinary looking and quite small, but one was in much better shape than the other. The one furthest away had a split wooden nameplate nailed to its side. Graeme could just about read the name, though the paint was peeling. He didn't know much about boats, but the *Salty Gull* hardly qualified as such. It was a miracle it was afloat given the number of holes in the hull. There were so many barnacles that you couldn't make out any wood; the cabin probably hadn't seen a lick of paint since the day it left the shipyard where it was built; and the mast looked like it had been snapped in half at some point and was now held together with sticky tape and a few frayed ropes. A small, rusted bell hung just outside the cabin and was tolling softly in the breeze. From somewhere in the depths there was the mournful sound of a cello.

The other boat was called *Oregon Blaze* and compared to its neighbour looked like it would be able to withstand the end of the world. A few crates marked *"R.I."* were sitting on the freshly washed deck. More crates and boxes of all shapes and sizes, identically marked, were piled high on the quay.

"These are the two boats that are delivering stuff for the party," Jim said.

"That thing goes to sea?" Graeme asked, pointing at the *Salty Gull*.

Jim nodded. Then he called out loud, "Hey, Mortimer!"

A man about the same age as Adrian, with short, curly blond hair, climbed out of the hold on the *Oregon Blaze*. He was wearing faded jeans and a chunky, cream coloured sweater.

"Hey, Jim," he said, walking down the gangplank. He had an American accent.

"Canadian," Jim signed to Graeme.

"What?" Graeme asked.

"You were thinking he's American. He's Canadian," Jim explained.

"You explaining that I'm Canadian?" Mortimer asked. His tone suggested that he was used to people making the mistake.

"Yes," Jim told him, grinning.

Mortimer held out his hand to Graeme. "I'm Mort," he introduced himself.

They shook hands. "I'm Graeme," Graeme said.

"Jim said you might drop by. You warm enough, there?"

Graeme grimaced. "Yeah. My uncle made me put all this stuff on."

"Your uncle? That's Adrian, right?" Mortimer asked.

"Yeah."

Mort nodded. "I would've guessed, I think. You have his ears."

"Yeah, well, I also have a few of his jumpers on here," said Graeme, tugging at his collar.

Mortimer and Jim both laughed at that.

"I thought you'd be spending time with him," Mort commented, picking at a loose thread on his jumper, "rather than lurking down here."

"He had to work today. We're going to the garden centre tomorrow to pick a Christmas tree," Graeme told him.

"Really?" Mortimer asked, still concentrating on his jumper. "I'm sure that'll be... fun. Anyway," he looked up at the boys, rubbing his hands together and blowing on them to keep warm, "so you two are going to help me load up?"

Graeme looked at Jim. "We are?"

"Sure."

"Well, I've already made a start," said Mort. "Why don't you two grab some of the smaller stuff over there?" He indicated a cluster of boxes just to the left of the larger crates on the quay. "I'll get a trolley to handle the rest." He turned and looked towards the *Salty Gull*. "I wish Dad would stop playing for a while or just CHANGE THE TUNE!" he shouted. The music didn't change or stop, though.

"What am I missing?" Jim asked.

Mort stopped half way along the gangplank to his boat. "It's my Dad," he explained. "He's playing his cello again. I wish he'd learn some other tunes."

"Oh."

"Well, hop to it, grab those boxes!" Mort ordered with a grin spread across his face, "and don't worry about the birds. Just push them out of the way if they get under your feet."

They started loading the boxes. The seagull seemed very interested in what they were doing; they had to shoo it away several times. The canary and the other bird hopped about just out of reach. All three of them seemed pretty tame.

"This is your plan?" Graeme asked Jim as they put their first load down on the deck.

"*Yeah,*" he replied.

"Those people on the beach, do you think they're smugglers?" Graeme asked him as they walked off the boat.

"*Only holidayers would think that*," scoffed Jim.

Graeme felt his ears burning up.

Jim continued, "*I thought they might be transporting stuff for the party: a big surprise like the inflatable nativity last year; but then I don't think delivery men dress up in masks and robes, even if they are delivering in the dead of night. If we can get closer to the isle we can start looking for where those boats are docking. There's got to be a cave, I think. The problem is that Raversham Isle's strictly off limits to everyone apart from people on official business until the night of the party. Helping Mort and his dad gives us an excuse to be there, you see? I was going to help anyway. It's what my Mum calls a 'happy co–incidence'.*"

"You told your Mum about what's been going on?"

"Hardly!" Jim laughed. "*I mean, don't get me wrong, I don't think Mum and Dad are mixed up in this, any more than your uncle or Roberta are. They like nothing better than going to bed with cocoa by nine o'clock. Parents talk, though, you know? To all the wrong people, normally.*"

Graeme nodded. "Yes."

"Are you two old women going to stand around gassing all day or are you actually going to roll up your sleeves at some point?" Mort was standing just behind them with a trolley.

"Sorry," Graeme apologised, his cheeks flushing.

Mort, noticing how embarrassed Graeme was, shook his head, smiled and said, "I was joking. Give me a hand with this crate."

All three of them took an edge of one of the larger crates and heaved it onto the trolley. Then Jim grabbed a box and he and Mort went on board. Graeme went to pick up something himself but whenever he went near anything one or all of the birds would settle on it and fix him with what his grandma had always referred to as "the evil eye".

As he stared at them and tried to work out his next move, he noticed the Rolls Royce from outside the coach station pulling up at the side of the road. The driver door popped open and the short chauffeur scurried to open the back doors. The woman who had thought Graeme was contagious emerged from inside the car and surveyed her surroundings.

"Hey there!" she called out in a haughty voice, then turned back and leaned into the car. "You!" the woman shouted over her shoulder, "You! Boy!"

The air was filled with the sound of flapping wings as the birds retreated to the top of the highest stack of crates.

"You!" the woman shouted again.

Graeme realised she must be speaking to him. "Yes?" he said.

"Go and wake your captain or master or whatever!" she commanded. "We wish to take passage to the island."

With that, her head vanished inside the car again. There was a brief exchange of sharp words and then one by one her children emerged. Their faces were all scrunched up as they stood blinking in the sunlight. It wasn't that bright.

"Didn't you hear me, boy?" the woman snapped. "Get the captain of the boat, now!"

The children had started pointing at Graeme. They were whispering to each other. Graeme hadn't really taken much notice of them yesterday. They were all stick thin.

"Boy!" the woman shouted again.

"Have you got me confused with somebody else?" Graeme asked her.

"What?" she asked as she strode along the quay towards him. The children shuffled along behind her. "What?" Her voice was getting higher in pitch by the second. "Pray tell me, are you," she closed her eyes and shook her head as she spoke, slowing her words right down as if she were speaking to an idiot, "or are you not, the ca – bin boy?"

Graeme stared back at her. "I," he said, "am – not."

She momentarily looked lost for words. "Then what are you doing, loitering here?" she asked.

Everyone winced as a hideous screeching sound came from the bowels of the *Salty Gull*.

The woman put the back of one hand on her forehead. "What is that dreadful racket?"

On the *Oregon Blaze*, Mort and Jim came up on deck. Jim walked off the boat to stand alongside Graeme.

"Ah!" said the woman's husband, coming to join his family. "Look, it's the boy from yesterday, dear. You remember? He's probably planning a prank with his pal, there. Hello, again!" He grinned.

"Hello," said Graeme.

The woman sniffed. "They all look the same to me."

"And hello to you," the man said to Jim. "Fancy! I didn't know you lived in this neck of the woods!"

"Hello, sir," Jim replied, nudging Graeme. "*He teaches history at my school*," he signed. He looked meaningfully at the three children, who were still engrossed in their own hushed conversation of giggles. He scowled. "*And they go there, too*."

The woman had decided that Graeme and Jim weren't worth bothering with; she had now focused on Mort. Drawing herself fully upright, she greeted him. "Ah, Captain! I am Mrs Mathilda Raversham. These are my children. Say good day, my dears."

The three kids swivelled as one to look at Mort. Their mouths stretched into smiles. It looked like they each had far too many teeth, all glistening white; and their huge, watery blue eyes were wide open. Mort shivered and it was easy to see why: those kids looked like three corpses standing in a row.

"This," Mathilda continued, indicating her husband, "is my husband, Michael."

Mort was still staring at their children like a rabbit caught in headlights.

"Captain?" Mathilda prompted him.

Mort blinked and shook his head. "What? Oh, right. Hello, yes. Hi," he said. "And yes, I know who you are, Mathilda. We have met before."

"We have?" Mathilda looked nonplussed.

"Only about five times or so. I'm Mortimer Murgatroyd?"

"Oh." She obviously wasn't bothered in the slightest that she couldn't remember him. "Well, we wish to go to the isle," she continued. "Is Captain Yale about? He normally takes us across but I can't see his boat."

"Captain Yale retired to Newfoundland three months ago," said Mort.

"Really?" Mathilda was shocked. "Michael! Has it been that long since we last visited? I can't believe it!"

Michael shrugged. "Probably, but I recall speaking to my dear Papa on the telephone only the other week."

Mathilda looked aghast. "You never mentioned that you'd spoken to him," she said. She appeared ready to slap her husband, but then seemed to dismiss the matter and continued speaking to Mort. "Well, as Captain Yale has deserted us I suppose we'll have to look elsewhere." She didn't say another word but just from her expression you could tell she was expecting an offer to be ferried across.

"Um," Mort said, looking skyward for inspiration, "I'm afraid I can't help you, there." He indicated the boxes and crates that were still to be loaded. "I have to take all this stuff across for the party. What with that and my crew," and here he pointed at Graeme and Jim, "I'm afraid I don't have room for passengers. Sorry."

There was a screech as Mort's father continued to torture his cello. The vibrations went right through to the bone. Nearly everyone, including Jim, cringed. The Raversham children didn't, though; their heads wobbled slightly as they watched Graeme, as if he were an insect they were considering pulling the legs off.

Mort's brown eyes got a glint in them. Hearing the cello had given him an idea. "Why don't you try my father, Captain Johan Murgatroyd?" He pointed towards the *Salty Gull*.

Mathilda looked down her nose at it. "Really?" she asked.

"Oh yes, he'll have room," Mort assured her.

Mathilda looked as if she were about to say something but her husband took her arm.

"Old Captain Murgatroyd," he sighed. "Well, well. Is he back? He's been gone for yonks, absolute yonks! How marvellous! What a splendid idea, that he should take us!"

Mathilda gave Mort a sour look and turned to her children. "Come along then," she said.

The birds, all three of which had watched without so much as a sound so far, started to shuffle about. The one Graeme hadn't been able to identify opened its beak and let out a rasping cry: several short bursts that sounded like someone running a stone down a cheese grater. It was so loud it must have carried for miles. Mathilda stopped in her tracks and briefly closed her eyes, her teeth set on edge. She glared at the bird and then resolutely turned her back on it. Her face set with a determined frown, she marched her husband along the quay towards the decrepit boat, crossed the gangplank and rang the bell.

The Raversham children hadn't followed their parents. They had finished their assessment of Graeme and were now grinning at Jim.

"Hello," they said to him in reed–thin voices. "Hello, James."

"Hi," Jim said out loud. He didn't sound pleased to see them. Exactly who *would* be pleased to see them, beyond their parents, was a mystery.

The kids all giggled and waggled their fingers in Jim's face. He just stood there.

"What did you say? What did you say?" they all chanted, beginning to dance around. Their bones were clicking.

"Hi," Jim said again and the children all broke into gales of laughter.

"Listen to Mister Thicky," said one of the boys. "Say something else, go on, say something!"

"Yes," the other two cried out, their voices shrill. "Say something! Say something! Say something! Say something!"

The girl in the wheelchair barrelled out of the blue like an out–of–control express train. The Raversham kids never stood a chance. She simply ran them down, paused long enough to give them a contemptuous sneer and then proceeded to roll backwards and forwards over their hands and feet.

They wailed and screamed and tears rolled down their faces.

"This is Calamara," Jim told Graeme.

The girl beamed triumphantly. She was beautiful, with long dark hair and glasses. "Hello," she said. She glanced down at the wailing children at her feet, her eyes sparkling with a vicious satisfaction.

"Ow! Ow! Ow!" the youngest boy was crying. One of the wheels on Calamara's chair was crushing his fingers.

"Oh, sorry," Calamara said in a tone that made it clear that she wasn't sorry at all. She wheeled her chair off his fingers and back over them once or twice more for good measure, smiling every time he hollered in agony.

"Adam! Archibald! Margaret!" Mathilda's voice rang out, far louder and more piercing than that odd bird's call. She had noticed that her children weren't with her. "Stop playing with your cripple friends and get over here!"

She rang the bell again. The cello music had stopped now.

The three children, still blubbering, got up and limped away.

"Shoulders back! Stand up straight!" barked Mathilda. Those kids snapped to attention as soon as they heard their mother's voice. They frogmarched to her.

Mathilda rang the bell again, almost shaking it off its rope.

A trap door on the boat sprang open.

"You should watch this," said Mort, his eyes bright as he walked off the *Oregon Blaze*. "Hi, Calamara. Nice going, there."

Calamara smiled a crooked smile. "Thanks."

A puppet made from old baked bean tins had popped out of the hold on Captain Murgatroyd's boat. Its head, which was one tin, had eyes and a smiley mouth painted on it and lolled to one side.

Calamara wasn't impressed. "Puppets?" she asked. "Are we now six?"

"Can you tell me," came a thickly accented voice from the hold of the *Salty Gull*, "who has disturbed me, my faithful friend?"

The baked bean tin man moved, looking first one way and then the other, until it rested its gaze (sort of) on the Raversham family.

"Ah–ha," said the voice. "So, the vultures gather."

Mathilda rang the bell again. Then she rang it again. And once more for luck.

The puppet vanished below decks and an old man with a weathered face leaned over the top of the hatch. As he appeared, the birds flew down from their vantage point on top of the crates and hopped along the quay until they were standing right beside the *Salty Gull*.

"Hallo," the old man said. "Little Michael, how are you?"

"As well as can be expected, thank you, Captain," replied Michael. "I see your first mate is still in fine fettle."

"Ah, well," Captain Murgatroyd swung himself up on deck in one smooth movement, "McGinty Tin Ribs ages no better than a lot of us, I dare say. He's had his head replaced, what, eighteen times, it must be."

"I know a good few people who could use that sort of treatment," said Michael in a merry voice.

Captain Murgatroyd looked over at his son, Graeme, Jim and Calamara. He wasn't very impressed with having an audience. "Are you enjoying yourselves?"

"Yes, thanks, Dad!" Mort shouted.

"I'm so glad." The Captain then switched his attention back to the Ravershams. "So, what do you want? Can I help you?"

"Indeed," Mathilda confirmed, stepping back into the conversation. "I understand from your son that you can offer us passage to the island."

Captain Murgatroyd and Mort exchanged a steady look.

"Yes," Captain Murgatroyd said, his eyes never leaving his son, "yes, it would be an honour." It didn't sound like he meant that. "We will leave shortly. Wait here."

He walked off the boat. He had an odd, bow–legged gait. The birds fluttered around him; he kicked at them when they were on the ground and reached up to brush them aside when they took to the air but they couldn't be driven away.

"Thank you, Mortimer," he said to his son.

"You're welcome."

The Captain briefly took note of Graeme, Jim and Calamara. "And you are employing child labour today?"

"They offered."

"You know that Llewellyn does not like strangers on his island. He is going to be especially stringent at the moment."

"*Why especially at the moment?*" Jim asked.

"*Didn't you see the news this morning?*" Calamara asked him in return.

"*No.*"

"*His children are vanishing. They're falling off the face of the planet!*"

"*Do you think that has anything to do with the boats?*"

"*Don't start leaping to conclusions,*" Calamara warned him.

"I'm sure they'll behave, Pop," Mort was saying to his dad.

"Hmm, well, if he wants a head he can have yours."

With that said, Captain Murgatroyd turned his attention to Graeme. "A new arrival," he said.

"Adrian's nephew," said Mort. "I've told you about Adrian."

"You mentioned him… once or twice," said the Captain. "Anyone would think you were fifteen again." He hadn't moved his brown, prune–like face from Graeme. "Nice to meet you," he said, taking Graeme's hand and shaking it vigorously. "I should tell you that people think I am Russian." He paused for a moment and his brow creased even more. "Uneducated people think I am Russian, I should say. Americans think I am Scottish and I have never bothered to find out why. I am," he said with a burst of pride, "Hungarian."

"Okay," said Graeme. He didn't know quite what else to say.

"Our family's a mixed bunch," Mort joked.

The Captain nodded in agreement with his son. "Okay, so we are all off to the isle? Okay." He looked up at the birds circling above him. "Settle down! Crazy birds!" he shouted.

Back on the *Salty Gull*, Mathilda was watching the proceedings with an increasingly irritated look on her face. Captain Murgatroyd didn't notice, or didn't care. He waved at the birds for a bit longer before giving up with a disgusted sigh. "They are my birds," he said. "Ever thought about having a bird for a pet? Don't. Don't have birds. They claw at you, they squawk and their droppings set like concrete in the summer. Want to know the names of these three? This is Canary, this is Corncrake, whose beak I should tape up, and this," he pointed at the seagull, "is Joan."

"He's going to tell you why two of them don't have proper names now," said Mort, squinting up at the sky.

Captain Murgatroyd nodded at his son and hunkered down, leaning in close. "You never know, one Christmas I may be far from home with nothing to eat. I don't like giving names to creatures I would eat."

Corncrake let out another couple of ear splitting croaks.

"So why give the seagull a name, Pop?" Mort asked.

"You only eat seagull once."

"Oh, Pop," Mort shook his head.

"What?" Murgatroyd shrugged. "It's the truth."

"You'd really eat them?" Jim asked.

The Captain's crinkled face crinkled some more. "What did he say?"

"He asked if you would really eat them," Calamara translated. "He's such a soft touch. I don't see anything wrong with it."

"Thank you for that, intelligent girl," said the Captain, smiling at her and standing up. "I could never get Mortimer to understand. Perhaps I will adopt you." His eyes narrowed and he surveyed the area before continuing, as if what he was about to say were top secret. "Of course I would really eat them. They would eat me if our positions were reversed. They give it a good go from time to time as it is." He held up his hands, which were covered in gouge marks, as evidence. "And why should they not? In some corners of this vast globe," he said in a deadly earnest tone of voice, "we humans are simply known as 'long pig'."

He nodded sagely, as if that should mean something. It certainly didn't mean anything to Graeme.

"Captain!" Mathilda shouted.

Captain Murgatroyd cursed under his breath. "I shall prepare to go now," he announced and kind of waddled back to his boat. The birds all hopped after him, settling on the roof of the *Salty Gull*'s cabin.

“That’s my Dad,” Mort said. His voice was odd; it was difficult to tell if he was proud or not.

“Let’s get the rest of this loaded,” Mort told Jim and Graeme. “Then we’ll be off. You think you can help, miss?” he asked Calamara.

“Of course,” Calamara said, heaving a box onto her lap and wheeling herself up the ramp onto the boat.

Jim picked up a box and ran to catch up with her.

Graeme helped Mort load another crate onto the trolley, picked yet another one up himself and took it aboard the *Oregon Blaze*.

On the *Salty Gull*, Mathilda was clearly pensive. “Are we in danger of getting going any time soon?” her voice rang out.

Captain Murgatroyd was in the cabin. He turned his head as she spoke, so had obviously heard her, but he didn’t say anything.

“Michael!” Mathilda called out to her husband.

Michael was on the other side of the boat to his wife and was leaning on the rail, looking out to sea. “Mmm?”

“Do something!”

“I’m sure the Captain has it in hand, dear.”

Mathilda made a disgusted sound and tossed her head to one side. Their children followed suit, one after the other.

It didn’t take too much longer for Mort and his new crew to finish transferring everything from the quay to the *Oregon Blaze*. Calamara being there certainly speeded things up: she was like a whirling dervish and loaded more than Graeme and Jim managed between them. She didn’t talk much. It was true that they were too busy and Mort was always around, so they couldn’t exactly discuss anything about the previous night right then and there, but still, Graeme got the distinct impression that she was avoiding talking to him. He thought more than once that he had caught her casting a suspicious glance his way. His brain started ticking over, wondering what Jim might have told her. He began to feel really uneasy.

When the last of the boxes had been brought on board, Mort walked to the front of the boat and waved at his dad. “We’re all done,” he called out.

Captain Murgatroyd waved back. “Ready for the off, then?”

“Finally!” Mathilda exclaimed, tapping her foot on the deck. “I trust the crossing will not take long, Captain.”

“Are you giving me orders?” the Captain asked, turning to stare at her. His voice sounded dangerous, threatening.

"No." Mathilda strode right into the cabin. "But I do – "

"Passengers are not allowed in here," said Captain Murgatroyd. Mathilda raised one eyebrow, but she did take a step back. Joan the seagull, who was edging along the ridge of the cabin roof, lifted her tail and pooed on Mathilda's head. Judging by the fact she didn't react, Mathilda was oblivious to what had happened; but her children weren't. They grinned.

Captain Murgatroyd bowed slightly. "A speedy crossing it is, then."

He turned back to the controls. The engine of the *Salty Gull* coughed and spluttered as it tried, against the odds, to start. It didn't sound healthy.

Mathilda faced her children. "Have you all taken your sea sickness pills?" she asked. "And have you re–applied your sunscreen? Margaret, you're looking a tad pink. We don't want you burning."

The boys smirked as their sister raised a hand to the see–through skin on her cheek.

"Unfasten the ropes, boy," Captain Murgatroyd called out from his cabin.

"You okay, Pop?" Mort jumped across to the quay and untied the ropes that secured both boats.

"Fine, fine," Murgatroyd shouted back.

Mort pushed the gangplank of the *Salty Gull* onto the boat, then ran back on board the *Blaze*, lifted the plank and went into the cabin.

"Hold on, you three," he said.

The engine purred and they started to manoeuvre away from the quay, a trail of froth left in the water behind them.

Mathilda looked at Graeme, Jim and Calamara with an indignant frown on her face as the *Blaze* pulled up alongside the *Salty Gull*. She was outraged that her boat wasn't pulling out first.

Michael, who was still leaning on the rail, smiled and waved. He appeared not to have a care in the world. He winked at Graeme.

Mathilda huffed. "Is there a problem, Captain?"

"None at all," the Captain told her.

Something didn't sound quite right, though. The *Salty Gull's* engine was coughing and popping. Captain Murgatroyd began hammering on the controls.

Mort let the engine idle now that the *Oregon Blaze* was level with his dad's boat. "Are you sure you're okay, Pop?" He shouted to be heard over the strangled sounds of the *Salty Gull's* engine refusing to start.

Captain Murgatroyd swore profusely and slammed his fist on the wall of the cabin. "It will not start," he admitted. "I will have to switch to the backup power."

"Oh," said Mort, like he knew what was coming.

Captain Murgatroyd reached up and pulled a lever. There was a loud clanking sound and the water around the base of the boat started to churn. The *Salty Gull* shook, rocked from side to side and then, creaking and groaning, began to rise up. At first, with all the white water surging around its hull, it seemed for all the world as if the boat was levitating. As it got higher, though, Graeme could see that in fact it was being pushed upwards by two stilt–like legs that were extending and extending, one from each side of the hull. It was a good thirty metres in the air by the time the legs stopped growing.

The *Salty Gull* rocked gently in place. The fact it was being supported by such thin legs was an engineering miracle. Graeme, Jim and Calamara moved to the rail of the *Blaze* and looked up into the faces of the Raversham family.

"Help!" screamed Mathilda.

The *Salty Gull* started to rock back and forth, pivoting on the legs, the boat itself always staying level. Each time it rocked, it leaned further back and, in turn, further forward, slowly at first and then with increasing speed.

"You might want to think about coming in here," Mort called from the safety of the cabin. Calamara was already heading for cover while Graeme let Jim know what Mort had said.

"Good idea," Jim agreed and the boys hurried to squeeze into the cabin as well.

Back and forth the *Salty Gull* went, building momentum until, with an awful creaking moan that would have made anybody think the entire thing was going to break up, it leaned so far forward that it toppled over and crashed back down into the sea, thus moving forward, the legs stretched out behind it. Seawater flew everywhere and waves rushed at the *Oregon Blaze*, tossing it about like it was in the midst of the worst storm. Everything on deck got deluged in salt water but that was nothing compared to the passengers on the *Salty Gull*. Graeme could see the Raversham family, all of whom were soaked to the skin and, aside from Michael, looking thoroughly miserable and not a little panicked.

"Wagons roll!" Captain Murgatroyd laughed like a lunatic.

The spindly legs on the *Salty Gull* were now rotating, lifting up so they looked like aerials that could pick up signals from Mars and then smoothly lowering so they pointed forward for a brief moment before vanishing back into the sea. Once again, the *Salty Gull* started to rise into the air. The whole process happened faster the second time, and faster still the third. Momentum was the key.

"We should try and get underway," Mort said in a matter of fact voice, steering his boat out after the *Salty Gull*, which was now well in the lead and would remain so, not because it was faster than the *Blaze* (because it wasn't); more because every time it returned to earth the *Blaze* was thrown about as if it were no more than a toy ship in a bathtub. Graeme could hear the distorted screams of the Ravershams; and over their warbling boomed the mad cries of Captain Murgatroyd.

Mort did do his best to keep a safe distance from the *Salty Gull*, but there wasn't a lot he could do to escape the havoc that Captain Murgatroyd was causing. Eventually, he decided to just wait it out, so he dropped his speed, leaving the *Blaze* bobbing in the water while the *Gull* pulled further and further away. When they were safely out of the splash–zone, Calamara pulled Jim out on deck to enjoy the show. She said nothing whatsoever to Graeme and it seemed to Graeme that this was on purpose. Jim beckoned him out to join them, though.

During a quiet moment, as the *Salty Gull* was going up for the umpteenth time and Mathilda's hysterical wailing grew fainter, Graeme leaned on the rail and closed his eyes, trying to forget about whether Calamara was trying to avoid him, or freeze him out, or whatever. He breathed deeply. The wind whipped at his hair and the salty spray flecked his face. It had been an age since he'd been near the sea; he'd almost forgotten how alive the tang in the air could make him feel.

The *Salty Gull* splashed down again.

"Ha! Ha! Ha!" Captain Murgatroyd was really enjoying himself.

Mort leaned out of the cabin. "I think we'll let Dad get a mite more ahead," he said as this latest mini–tsunami hit and once more the *Blaze* pitched in the wake of the *Salty Gull*. One of the crates stacked nearby tipped over and its lid fell off. A few bundles of newspapers spilled out. As Jim righted the crate and put the papers back in, Graeme caught a glimpse of part of a headline. It read, "FALLOW". The full headline had been "FALLOWSTONE FIRE". Graeme knew because that was a copy of one of his local papers, from home. He'd been headline news for a day or so. What on earth was a copy of that paper doing in Port Stilton? He stared at the spot where it had been and started to worry. His eyes darted from Jim to Calamara and back. Maybe they'd seen it; but that was a stupid thought, really. Even if they had, they'd never have known that it was about him unless they stopped to read it, and why would they? And in any case, a small voice at the back of his mind reminded him, Jim knew what happened; but that didn't make him rest easy. He began to feel ill, and Calamara did notice that.

"You about to puke?" she asked, as if feeling seasick were the crime of the century. She didn't wait for an answer, though. Instead, she turned, very business–like, to Jim. "Let's see the thingumy, then," she said.

Graeme was still worrying about that newspaper.

"Oh, yeah," said Jim. He looked around to make sure that Mort was occupied elsewhere and then reached into his pocket, pulling out a weird wooden carving hanging from a chain. It was of a little old man, wearing a top hat with a wide brim. The man had pinprick eyes and a long, pig–like snout. His arms were outstretched; and in them he was holding a heart shaped emblem which had tiny, multicoloured flowers all the way round it. Running around the inside of the flowery border there were two wolves, nipping at each other's tails; and in the very centre there was a golden sword. Graeme thought the emblem (minus the flowers) looked kind of familiar.

"Ugh!" said Calamara, screwing up her nose. "Someone's got very bad taste."

Jim put the carving back in his pocket. *"It's a piskie,"* he said.

Calamara shook her head. "Well, I knew that, obviously."

"Did you recognise anything else?"

"Of course I did." Calamara sounded haughty. She reached behind her and brought out a small gold and silver disc. It was no larger than a two pound coin and very gaudy; etched onto it was exactly the same design that they'd just seen in the arms of the piskie. Around the rim were the words:

BOB AMSER ARALL FFORDD – ALWAYS ANOTHER WAY

"We found this on the beach as well, just over a week ago," she told Graeme, proudly. "See the design? That's the Raversham crest. You wouldn't know."

For a moment Graeme's mind snapped back into focus. She was just so rude. He *would* know, actually. He'd seen that crest before and now he remembered where. It'd been on the doors of the Raversham' Rolls Royce, which he supposed kind of made sense. And he'd heard the motto recently as well.

Jim was nodding and looking at Calamara in a curious way. "*We don't know what it's for, though. It must have a purpose.*"

"I have an idea," said Calamara. "Look."

She squeezed the coin and a thin metal rod sprang out. It had teeth cut into it. "It's a key," she said, as if Graeme and Jim couldn't see that for themselves.

"Wow!" said Jim, the odd look still on his face. "*How did you figure that out?*"

"It was simple, really," said Calamara with a smug shrug. "I was studying it while you were mucking around last night."

"*Yeah?*" said Jim.

"Yes."

Jim smiled. "*So when I called you and your little brother answered and said that he'd found a coin that turned into a key...*"

Calamara cursed. "He nicked it off me," she said. "I *had* figured it out and then he took it. I was forcing him to give it back and it clicked open as we fought. *I* had hold of it at the time. Me. Not him."

"Well done," Jim congratulated her. Graeme remembered how easy–going Jim was, but still, he couldn't believe that Jim just seemed amused at her having lied like that. Graeme thought how mad he would have been, if a friend had lied to him.

"*How are we going to work out what it opens?*" Jim said, then. "*We can hardly try every keyhole on the isle. There must be thousands of them!*"

Calamara looked at him as if he'd insulted her. She stuck her nose in the air. "Well at least I figured out what it was."

"*Do you think it might open the boat cave on the beach?*" Jim suggested.

"We're going in entirely the wrong direction to check that out," snapped Calamara. She was pretty full of herself.

Graeme took a deep breath and watched the sea, lost in thoughts of newspapers and wondering how Jim put up with that girl.

Once the *Gull* was a safe distance in front, Mort got the *Blaze* going again and before too long, Raversham Isle loomed large in front of them.

"*Keep an eye open for caves*," said Jim.

"Oh, please," said Calamara, as if looking for caves was so last year.

It was surprising how high the cliffs were when you got up close. There were loads of ledges and alcoves in the rock; seagulls were perched on most of them. Captain Murgatroyd's gull, Joan, had flown up and was pestering her fellow birds. Some didn't seem to notice the boats' passage at all; others watched, their heads clicking around like clockwork. A few even left their nests and circled high above, crying as they swooped overhead.

The *Salty Gull*, still a way in front, stopped dead at the rocky entrance to a channel that split the cliff walls from top to bottom. Its legs were holding it up out of the water. As Graeme watched, the legs started acting like stilts, picking a safe way through the reef and into the channel. He couldn't help but wonder why Captain Murgatroyd hadn't used the stilts for the whole crossing and saved everything (and especially the Ravershams) a drenching.

When the *Blaze* reached the entrance, Mort took the speed down again so they were moving at a virtual crawl.

Entering the narrow passage, almost all light was blocked out, so they were travelling in an eerie twilight; neither was there much noise, other than the sound of the engine and the water softly sloshing against the hull. A couple of times the passage narrowed so much that the boat literally squealed as it squeezed through the gap. Vines and creepers were crawling all over the walls to either side of the *Blaze*. Water dripped from outcroppings far above.

It seemed like an age before they emerged on the other side, light flooding all over them. They had come out in a lagoon. There was a quay, smaller even than the one back in Port Stilton, and a massive wall with a pair of black gates set into it. The wall snaked away in either direction, vanishing into the vegetation.

They sailed past the *Salty Gull* and prepared to dock.

"Quite remarkable," Michael was saying to Captain Murgatroyd. "And look, Mathilda, the birdie doo–dah has been completely washed out of your hair!" He was supporting his wet wife and waving a small bottle of something under her nose while he and the Captain watched the gangly legs retract.

"What? What?" Mathilda asked; her eyes were unfocused, her voice feeble.

"You have created a most ingenious contraption," Michael praised Murgatroyd.

"It can go higher," the Captain bragged. "But I cannot take credit. In truth, I am not the designer." He grabbed the plank and pushed it onto the cobblestone quay. "Everybody off!"

Mort brought the *Blaze* to a halt behind the *Salty Gull*. He shut down the engine, jumped ashore and secured the boat. Jim nudged Graeme; between them they manhandled the plank into place. Calamara hardly waited for them to get their fingers out of the way before she rolled onto dry land.

"*Are you all right*?" Jim asked Graeme. Graeme didn't answer. He couldn't shake the thought of that newspaper; and Calamara… well, his first impressions weren't good.

"Hey!" said Jim, tugging at Graeme's arm. "You okay?"

Graeme smiled and nodded.

"We'll unload once they've opened up," Mort said. Graeme glanced, only for an instant, at the crate that held the newspaper, then followed Jim and Calamara as they moved to one side of the gates, slightly apart from the others.

"I didn't spot any caves," said Jim.

"Nor did I," said Graeme.

Calamara gave Graeme a withering look. She had an uncanny ability to make him feel utterly stupid without saying anything. "What is it with boys and caves? Whoever said there was a cave? Maybe they aren't going into a *cave* at all," she pointed out. "Look what we've got: one piskie, holding the Raversham crest; one key… with the Raversham crest on it. Spot the connection? Do you think, just maybe, the Ravershams might be mixed up in all this? And if they are, then isn't it more likely that they'd be coming ashore here, rather than sailing into a grotty little cave?"

"*Well…*" said Jim.

"How useless are you?"

"You could be right."

"Could be?" Calamara arched her eyebrows. She was acting so superior.

Jim thought for a moment. *"Well, we can find out,"* he said. "*The piskie's the thing, wherein we'll catch the conscience of the king*!"

Calamara leaned forward in her chair. "Don't paraphrase Shakespeare at me," she said, "not during the holidays. What half–baked scheme have you got fermenting in that brain of yours? You'd better not muck anything up, not now we've got this far."

"Shut up," said Graeme. He was as surprised as anyone when he said it. Calamara was certainly shocked.

"What?" she said, her voice flat.

"Shut up," Graeme said again.

"What is it with you?" She fired the question at him, gripping the wheels of her chair, as if she were about to charge.

"What is it with you, you mean!" Graeme shouted. "You're so… so…"

"So, so… what?"

Graeme stared at her. He could feel himself shaking, his heart pounding. For some reason he was suddenly really angry. He had all these feelings bubbling around inside, twisting his guts; and she was there, being… being… the words just wouldn't come. Why couldn't he think straight?

Jim stared at the two of them, caught in the middle. "Are you sure you're feeling all right?" he asked Graeme. "You look really… icky."

Graeme couldn't answer him; his eyes felt like they were bulging out of their sockets.

Calamara started to smile as Graeme spluttered. That just made him madder. He opened and closed his mouth, trying to force the words out.

Calamara continued to smile sweetly at Graeme, but she spoke to Jim. "Why did you let him in on this? He's mental. Hardly says a word all the way over here, tells me to shut up, and now stands there like a simpleton. Do you think a cat has got his tongue?"

Graeme started to yell. He opened his mouth wide and yelled and yelled. No words. Just noise.

A heavy hand landed on his shoulder; his voice faded to nothing.

"That's enough," someone growled behind him. "This is why children should be gagged on sight. Someone fetch an iron mask or three."

CHAPTER FOUR
On and Off

Graeme didn't often get angry; it tended to shake him up too much. He could count on one thing, though: he always opened his big mouth at the wrong time.

He was pulled around and found himself staring into the unshaven face of a haggard, scraggly old man in a threadbare brown overcoat. The old man was standing so close that everything else was blocked from view.

"Children," the old man croaked, "should be locked up until they are at least thirty–two. What," he asked, "are you doing here? What makes you think you have the right to trespass on my island? I throw my doors open once a year and still people think they can traipse all over my property any time they like. Do I invite myself to your house? Do I cavort on your front lawn?"

"No," said Graeme.

Lord Raversham let go of him, raised his face to the heavens and spread his arms wide. "Then kindly do me the same courtesy!"

Graeme's ears turned a violent shade of red. They felt like they'd burn right off at any moment. At the same time, the small part of him that wasn't dying of embarrassment marvelled that this shabby tramp was actually Lord Raversham. He'd kind of expected him to be a regal old gentleman.

"My Lord," a calm male voice said, though from where Graeme still couldn't see.

"What?" snapped Lord Raversham. He brought his arms down and cocked his head to one side. His eyes, which had deep, dark circles under them, fixed on Graeme's equally shadowed face even as he listened to the voice behind him.

"Remember your health, sir," the voice continued.

Lord Raversham stepped to one side and turned to see the speaker. As he moved he revealed a perfectly presented man in a butler's uniform.

"My health," Lord Raversham echoed in a quiet voice, "my health, indeed. This sort of thing doesn't help my health."

"Quite, sir," the butler agreed.

"I am not a well man," Lord Raversham said and grabbed hold of Graeme again. He had a very strong grip for an unwell man. He looked at Mort, the Captain and his relatives. "Which of you brought this loudmouth and his cohorts onto my island?"

"Him!" Mathilda piped up, pointing at Mort.

"You're looking a bit soggy, Mathilda. Did you come through a storm, perchance?" Lord Raversham was very amused to see the state his family had arrived in. His tone of voice suggested that seeing his daughter–in–law soaked to the skin was something he'd pay good money for any day of the week.

*

Lord Raversham had never quite come to terms with Michael's choice of wife. Michael had always been a quiet child: not mopey, not moody; just quiet. He was unique amongst the Raversham children, since the others were outgoing to the point of precociousness (and some, way beyond that). Lord Raversham might have worried about this quietness; if he did, he never spoke of his concerns to anyone. It was far more likely that he wasn't troubled at all: men of his generation and class didn't get involved with the day–to–day raising of children; and lest we forget, Michael had four older siblings who had practically raised themselves and not turned out too badly.

Lord and Lady Raversham had always spent a fair amount of time away from home. Having an inherited fortune meant they were invited to the best parties, where good, rich people could knock back good, rich food and wine and then give a bit to charity to show they cared. But never let it be said that Lady Jocelyn Raversham was one of the idle rich; not only did she put her money where her mouth was, she invariably put her best foot, if not feet, forward, to help her favoured causes. Lord Raversham was fiercely proud of his wife; he always travelled with and supported her, although this support was usually offered from a comfortable armchair in a five star hotel. (If their visit entailed travel to a country that offered no more than four star accommodations, the family yacht was used.)

When they did occasionally return, Lord Raversham liked to walk the halls and gardens of Raversham Isle, a literal Lord of all he surveyed. He would often see, from the corner of his eye, a young Michael watching him from a distance. Once spotted, the boy vanished like a ghost. Discovering anything about him became a task that would have stumped a master sleuth; it was a sheer accident when the family found out that he had followed in his mother's footsteps and taken an interest in music, but discussing it with him was next to impossible: he shied away from the subject whenever it was brought up at the dinner table and despite a course of very expensive lessons he eventually, as far as anyone was aware, gave up on it completely.

As if proving the validity of Lord Raversham's detached attitude to parenting, Michael did come out of his shell once he was past his teenage years. He decided to study anthropology and history, worthy subjects that led him to a teaching career at the acclaimed Peashingle Academy, just up the road from Port Stilton.

Being so close, you'd think that Michael would have been a regular visitor to Raversham Isle; on the contrary, Lord Raversham probably saw less of him than he did of his other children, but then none of them visited that often. Lord Raversham put that down to the fact their mother was no longer around.

(Lady Raversham had gone to her well–earned, yet untimely, rest in 1966. She had been on a trip with the Forests First Organisation to fight the large–scale deforestation taking place in the tiny country of Preneuraid. There, tramping towards the picket line to hold back bulldozers preparing to tear into the ancient habitat, she saw a Gwasgu–Cragen snail a second too late. She tried to stop herself treading on it by contorting her body but nothing could stop the hobnail sole of her shoe coming down on the creature, crushing it, its noxious guts splattering everywhere. Jocelyn, caught in the face, died within the hour. The sad irony was that she was there in an effort to protect the migratory path of that very species.)

Lord Raversham was seen to go out less and less following his wife's death. It became apparent she had been the driving force behind the marriage and the couple's whirl of a social life. He spent his days in splendid isolation on his island. His children may have rarely visited him; he never visited them.

In 1987, Michael made one of his rare trips home. With him came his rather officious wife–to–be and three toddlers that looked nothing like either of them. Lord Raversham had hated Mathilda on sight and that was something that time and familiarly did not rectify. She treated everybody except for him as if they were filth personified. Him, she fawned over, persistently asked about his health (always a sore subject) and went on (and on) about the importance of family, like he couldn't see the woman for what she was. His one regret in life was that he wouldn't be alive to see her face during the reading of his will, when she would discover that he had ensured she would inherit not a single ha'penny. Instead, he made do with any opportunity presenting itself that enabled him to poke fun or insult the toadying, money–grubbing schemer. Those moments were most welcome, indeed.

*

"Not a storm, no," Mathilda replied to Lord Raversham's question. As ever, she ignored the fact he was making fun of her. "The journey was… unorthodox, though."

"I don't doubt it," chuckled Lord Raversham. He winked at Captain Murgatroyd, who winked back. They looked like a couple of errant schoolboys. Everyone (apart from Mathilda, who simpered in an effort to look good–natured and patted her sodden hairdo) started to relax.

Lord Raversham's mischievous expression vanished as he caught sight of Graeme again. "Let's not get too far off–topic," he said, seriously. "These three hooligans. Brought to my island by…?"

Mathilda again seized the opportunity to try and get in her father–in–law's good graces, pointing at Mort. "I said before! It was him! Him!"

"I can't deny it," said Mort.

Lord Raversham snorted. "I don't want strangers on my island."

"I'm sorry," Mort apologised. "They helped me to load up, that's all. I thought they'd enjoy the trip here and back. They're not troublemakers."

"You obviously don't have much experience with children," snapped Lord Raversham. "Children *are* trouble. Synonymous, I think you'll find the word is."

"But Father," Michael said, "every young chap wants to explore. It's an inbuilt instinct."

"Don't I know it! And you wonder why I want them off my island!" said Lord Raversham, twisting round and giving Jim and Calamara a dirty look. His eyes widened and then narrowed. "How come I get the feeling that I know you?" he asked, pushing Graeme over to join them. He started stalking up and down in front of the trio. "Where have I seen you – all three of you – before? Not together, no, not together, but…"

Graeme and Jim looked at each other.

Lord Raversham jumped, like he'd had an electric shock. "I know! I know! This," he said, extending a bony finger towards Jim, "this is the Gunpowder Boy!"

Jim's mouth had just fallen wide open. "Nobody's supposed to know that," he said out loud. "It was meant to be a secret!"

"A secret?" scoffed Lord Raversham. "A secret? In the Houses of Parliament? Don't make me laugh." He pointed at Calamara. "And you," he cried, "you're the girl who mugged the Queen!"

Calamara stared back at him with a haughty look on her face. "I have never done any such thing."

"You bloody bit her on the nose!" Lord Raversham started to cough.

Calamara glowered at him. "She was about to be condescending."

Lord Raversham had rested one hand on his butler's shoulder and was wheezing. "I'll bet."

"How does he know all this?" Jim asked. "*Why does he know all about us?*"

Lord Raversham frowned. "Eh?"

"He wants to know how you know what you know about us," Graeme told him. Even as he spoke, Graeme realised that Jim had probably not meant that as a comment for everyone's ears. He found himself cursing his big mouth again.

Lord Raversham was livid. His eyebrows collided and he shook his head from side to side. "You think I'm so secluded I don't know what's going on in the world? I get out!" he shouted, staggering towards Graeme.

Graeme hadn't meant anything of the sort, but given that his mouth had done nothing but get him in trouble lately he decided to keep it shut while the old man ranted on.

“What is it,” Lord Raversham was asking the world at large, “about me that makes people think I don’t get out? Just because I don’t travel everywhere with a huge retinue and trumpets blaring it doesn’t mean I don’t get out! I get out! And even if I didn’t, there are such things as telephones; and the radio; and television; and newspapers!”

His eyes fell on Graeme; but then he started to have another coughing fit.

The butler put a restraining hand on Lord Raversham’s left arm. “My Lord.”

“Oh, for goodness’ sake Kendall, let me be!” Lord Raversham didn’t sound angry now; instead, he seemed a bit distracted. He was still looking in Graeme’s direction.

The butler removed his hand.

Lord Raversham shrugged and adjusted his coat. “That’s better,” he said, wiping spittle from his mouth with one cuff. He lowered his arm and rubbed it on his coat. His tongue ran over his front teeth. “How do I know you?” he asked. His voice was quiet; he seemed to be talking to himself rather than asking Graeme anything. “I nearly had it then, a second ago,” he said. “Why are you so familiar to me?”

Nobody said anything. Nobody seemed about to help Graeme out. Jim was looking at him and Graeme knew what he was thinking. He was thinking that Lord Raversham could only have recognised them if he had been the cloaked figure who had attacked them in the cave. He could have recognised Graeme from there, of course, but there was another, just as likely explanation.

“I’m Graeme McCaig,” said Graeme.

Lord Raversham started to chew at a fingernail. “I don’t care about your name, boy.”

“He’s here for the holidays. He’s staying with his uncle, Adrian Oxford,” said Mort.

“Still doesn’t…” Lord Raversham began, but then he stopped and stepped back and back again. Kendall the butler looked concerned. He almost instinctively held out a hand, but didn’t interfere.

“I’m not ready,” Lord Raversham was whispering. “Not ready.” His eyes darted left and right, as if he’d seen a ghost. Graeme couldn’t tell if he was talking to him, or him and Jim and Calamara, or everyone.

Lord Raversham had closed his eyes. He looked less disturbed when he opened them but he didn’t look at Graeme again; he concentrated on Jim and Calamara instead. “You were not invited here," he said, his voice firm. "I should put you in my dungeons and let you rot in there with the rats."

Kendall leaned and murmured in Lord Raversham's ear, "Not the best idea, my Lord, if your aim is to get them off the property."

Lord Raversham gnashed his teeth. "We could load them into catapults and hurl them across the bay."

"I don't think we have any working trebuchets, sir; and I think it might be illegal in any case."

Lord Raversham's face was wild as he searched for ideas. He certainly seemed to be over his bout of the willies. A mad glint appeared in his eyes. "I could make them swim back to the mainland. Murgatroyd! You had a shark in your hold, once upon a time, didn't you? Still got it? We could set that on them!"

Captain Murgatroyd did have a live, great white shark tucked away in the bowels of his boat. It wasn't a big boat, but it was big enough.

Kendall said, "Again, I think the legality of such a course of action is questionable, my Lord."

"Stop shooting all my best ideas down in flames, Kendall!"

"Surely, sir, there must be another way to deal with this situation; one that doesn't involve murdering minors."

Lord Raversham was shocked. "I wasn't planning on murdering them! Well, not directly. I was quite happy to give them a sporting chance."

"Even so, sir." Kendall's voice had remained totally calm throughout the conversation. He had served the Raversham family for long enough that he was unfazed by their wildest proclamations. "Let us not forget that the estate makes annual donations to a number of children's charities…"

Lord Raversham grunted. "All right, all right," he grumbled. "Bloody NSPCC."

Kendall nodded. "Indeed, my Lord."

"You'll have to wait here," Lord Raversham instructed Graeme, Jim and Calamara. He sounded really put out about it. "Don't even try and get inside the grounds. When everything has been unloaded and taken inside – which you will not help with – you can go back with the boats." He shook his coat sleeve back to look at his watch. "I'm expecting the plod out here today, as if I didn't have enough on my plate. She can have the honour of taking you back if she arrives first.

It's about time she made herself useful in some way. I won't press charges," he promised, "this time."

With that, he turned ninety degrees to face his family. Kendall scurried around so he was still behind his master. They started to walk away, with Lord Raversham's long coat dragging behind, uncovering the cobblestones… and something else. Kendall stooped to pick it up.

It was the piskie. Jim winked at Graeme. Graeme hadn't noticed him taking it off the chain and dropping it.

"Look, sir," said Kendall. "Did you drop...isn't, wasn't this Lady Raversham's?"

Lord Raversham stopped in his tracks and, without turning around, held out his hand. "Yes," he said as Kendall gave the piskie to him. "It's hers." He was spinning it with his fingers, poring over every ugly detail. He appeared to be mystified. "I thought I'd lost it last…"

"You thought you'd what, sir?" Kendall asked him, almost bouncing up and down behind Lord Raversham in an effort to get a look.

"Nothing," said Lord Raversham.

"You didn't… go out last night, did you?"

"With you on guard? What makes you think that?"

Kendall sighed. Lord Raversham scowled and clutched the piskie to his chest, cradling it like a baby.

"I do wish you'd pay attention to your doctors, my Lord," said Kendall. "Need I remind you that they have recommended bed rest – "

Lord Raversham held up one hand to silence Kendall; and then he bent over and poked his bottom in the air. "What's this?" he asked his butler.

"It's your… posterior, sir."

"Good, good," said Lord Raversham. There were several loud cracking sounds as he straightened up. Crooking one arm, he asked, "And this?"

Kendall's face took on a weary expression, as if he knew what was coming. "It's your elbow, my Lord."

Lord Raversham smiled. "Congratulations. You officially know more than all of my quacks combined."

"Thank you, sir," said Kendall, dropping the subject.

"Is that Mother's piskie, Father?" asked Michael, stepping forward. "I haven't seen that in absolute ages."

"Get away from me. You're all wet," said Lord Raversham.

"I thought it had been… how should I put this? I thought it had been 'lost'," said Kendall.

Mathilda moved every which way to get a peek; when she finally did see, she recoiled as if she'd been stung. "Burnt, one would have hoped," she said. "It really is the most frightful thing imaginable. She never wore it."

"*She* never threw it out, either," Lord Raversham snarled. Then his voice became softer; when he next spoke he was having another one of those private conversations where he was the sole participant. "It's always on my person," he said, "on its …" He was distracted by another thought, patting his coat, searching for something. "On its chain," he said. "Sometimes, in the night, it stops me, I don't feel so…"

His face became even more haggard than it already was. His eyes locked with Graeme's once more and then he shook his head and pushed past his butler and family to reach Captain Murgatroyd.

"You're back then, Murgatroyd."

"I am," said Captain Murgatroyd.

"Would you have leant me your shark?"

"Of course," said the Captain, without hesitation. Graeme didn't doubt it.

Lord Raversham glanced back at the trio with a wistful look on his face. "Another time, maybe."

"You seem to be in fine spirits," Captain Murgatroyd said then, "which I find hard to believe, given the circumstances. How are you really?"

"Hmm?" said Lord Raversham, who was still looking Graeme's way. "Oh, dying, as ever," he replied, returning his attention to the Captain. "It seems to be catching, if you believe those misery–mongers who write the news. They'd love nothing better than to have a Raversham corpse or two turn up in time for Christmas."

"You do not seem overly worried."

"I know my own children," said Lord Raversham. Again, he cast a suspicious eye towards Graeme, Jim and Calamara. "I don't want to talk out here. Kendall will organise some people to help unload this lot. I hope you've brought the spices that Tatum was after or she'll have you strung up and roasted on a spit."

"I've had worse done to me," Murgatroyd replied.

"I'm sure," Lord Raversham chuckled. He walked to the large gates and opened a small door set into the one on the left. He stepped through into the hallowed grounds of the castle with Murgatroyd and Mort, hardly registering his family, who filed, or dripped, more like, in behind them.

Kendall remained outside for a moment. "You mind his Lordship's instructions," he told the trio; and then he too went inside. The door shut behind him, leaving the three of them alone with only Captain Murgatroyd's birds for company. The birds seemed quite happy to hop about and peck at each other.

"*Did you see him? Did you see him with that piskie? It's him!*" said Jim. "*It's Lord Raversham. 'I get out,' says he! He gets out all right, out in the night!*"

"Fat lot of good that does us," said Calamara, levelling her gaze at Graeme. Graeme just glared at her. She waved an arm in his direction. "*Now* he's quiet. *Now* he keeps his mouth shut," she complained. "It doesn't matter now! You can scream and yell all you want."

"*You're not really doing any good,*" Jim told her. "*We've found out that Lord Raversham must be involved, so that's something.*"

"And a fat lot of good that does us!" said Calamara. "If it weren't for Sir Screamalot here we'd be inside that gate! We'd be able to see what Lord Raversham is up to!"

"*Calamara, don't.*"

"You're just sticking up for him." She poked Graeme. "Why don't you think?"

Jim looked hopelessly on at the standoff between Graeme and Calamara. "*We could still get inside the grounds,*" he said, trying to make peace. "*I mean, Calamara, you said they must be coming ashore here. The key has the crest on it; it looks kind of impressive. Maybe it's for the gate? Try it.*"

Calamara grunted, made her way to the gate, pulled out the key and tried it in the lock. "It's not turning," she said.

"Let me have a go," said Jim.

"I can do it. It fits in there, but it just won't turn."

She took the key out and made her way back to Jim. "Any more bright…" she started to say, but her voice trailed off. She was staring at the key in the palm of her hand. She chewed on her tongue. "Always Another Way…"

"Eh?" asked Jim, also peering at the key.

Graeme leaned in as well. Calamara was staring at the rim of the key's head.

"Always Another Way," she repeated.

"That's what they were saying last night," Graeme said, "when we were hiding behind the boulder."

"Wow!" said Jim.

Graeme nodded.

"And you were thinking of revealing this nugget of information when?" Calamara asked him.

Graeme didn't reply.

Jim grinned at them both. "It's like a password hint! There must be another way in!" he announced. "The key must open it! That's what it's telling us! There's always another way!"

"I was about to say that," Calamara raged, incensed that someone had beaten her to the punch. "But," she added after a moment's reflection, "it's just the stupid Raversham family's meaningless motto, like… 'Once a fool, always a fool'; and I don't see another gate, or anything like one, do you?"

Graeme wondered if she would have added that last sentence if she had been the one to voice their idea first.

"*Once a fool: that's more of a phrase,*" said Jim. "*I can't think anyone would want that as their motto.*"

"No?"

Jim ignored Calamara's Gaze Of Death and continued, "*If there is another gate, it must be somewhere round the walls. Come on! We might as well have a look as stand around here! All those in favour, raise your hand!*"

Jim raised his arm. Graeme automatically raised his.

Calamara took one look at the dense undergrowth to either side of the gates and folded her arms.

"*Two to one,*" Jim told her.

"Who gave him the vote?" she complained, nodding at Graeme.

"*Come on,*" Jim encouraged her, "*let's get going before they come back to unload the boats.*" He looked up into the mass of overgrown vines and trees that they were about to clamber into. "*I don't think there's a path big enough for your chair,*" he told Calamara. "*I'll have to carry you.*"

"Delightful," Calamara replied in a deadpan tone of voice. Jim moved across to her; she reached about his neck and linked her hands. He didn't even blink as he lifted her and hooked her legs into his arms.

"You can carry my chair," Calamara said to Graeme, like he was her slave or something. Wordlessly, he folded the chair and lifted it.

“I hope it’s not too heavy for you,” Calamara laughed over her shoulder as Jim tramped into the trees. If Graeme had laser vision he would have burnt a hole in the back of her head, and that was the mildest of the evil things he was thinking of doing to her. He did his best to calm himself and stomped after them.

Nobody could have been in the woods they were moving through for ages. There was no sign of human life. The plants had taken over. The floor was carpeted with stinging nettles and holly bushes grew everywhere, so much so that before long they were being pricked and stung with almost every step they took. Creepers were creeping and curling, reaching out and grabbing a stranglehold on anything and everything in an effort to get to fresh air. Graeme could understand why: it was incredibly musty in that semi–gloom; he felt like he couldn’t breathe properly.

And it didn’t take long to realise that humanity might have abandoned this place, but they certainly weren’t alone; there were birds and insects in there with them. As the trio came crashing in on their homes, the birds flew off. Midges and moths were more of a pest, flitting crazily hither and thither.

As they got further into the trees, Graeme raised his head up to the tangled canopy of skeletal branches they were marching under and walked right into a thick spider’s web that was strung across his path. He called out in surprise and did his best to pick the sticky mess from his face. As he pulled his hand away he realised he was holding a meaty, silk-encrusted slug, yellow and orange and black and pulsating, like a living bruise. He reeled back and threw it away, wiping his now slimy hands on his legs. He felt really stupid; it was only a slug. He glanced at Jim and Calamara, who were walking slightly ahead and off on his right. Jim was making so much noise as he clumped along that Calamara hadn’t noticed what had happened. Graeme was kind of grateful about that.

The plan to look for an entrance wasn’t really a great one. They could barely make out the castle wall for the trees and bushes and vines. Graeme didn’t say anything, but if there was a door or whatever somewhere, the chances of them spotting it were slim. They didn’t speak much, either, beyond Calamara telling Jim which way she thought they should be heading and where they should look to see if there were any hidden doorways or loose stones. She was always sending Graeme off to stick his hand into the largest pile of stinging nettles she could see. They found nothing, of course, and Graeme’s mind began to wander as the search progressed. His pace slowed a bit and he fell behind the others. Jim never slowed down, probably because he had Calamara clinging to his back like an evil genie, whipping him on. In fact, it was Calamara who eventually commanded that they stop because she was "exhausted".

They paused in a small glade. There wasn't much greenery in the winter; dead leaves crunched underfoot, but at least it was dry and free of anything that might sting them if they sat on it. There was a slight breeze, which must have been coming from the sea. Jim set Calamara down and Graeme put her chair beside her, then the boys sat on the ground as well.

Graeme leaned back against the castle wall and closed his eyes, letting the sun warm him. He was playing back what Lord Raversham had been saying and, after a while, realised there was something he needed to ask Jim. "What was all that about the Gunpowder Boy?"

"Um," Jim said. "*I kind of foiled an attempt to blow up the Houses of Parliament.*"

"You were involved with that?" Graeme asked him. "That hit the news and everything!"

*

In February 1998, there had been a big scandal in London. It had turned out that the Prime Minister of the day, who had learnt of a brewing back bench rebellion aimed at deposing him, was planning to blow up the Houses of Parliament, with the Queen and just about every minister inside. He'd used every pound he could lay his hands on – what he couldn't get by increasing taxes he had simply robbed directly from people's bank accounts – to raise a private army. Immediately following the explosion, he was going to take control of the country by force. Luckily, someone had stumbled upon his plans and alerted the authorities. The identity of the so–called "Gunpowder Boy" had been kept a closely guarded secret, until now.

*

Jim smiled and shrugged. "*I – accidentally – found some stuff while I was on line one day,*" he started to say. Then he stopped, scratched his head, and added, "*I shouldn't say any more. I've been told not to talk about it. The Prime Minister was very specific.*"

(By that, he meant the new Prime Minister, Thomas Penny. Penny, prior to the Gunpowder Plot, had been resigned to being leader of the opposition for ever and a day and was therefore only too delighted when, following the subsequent and speedily arranged general election, the Queen asked him to form a government.)

"It would never have worked anyway," said Calamara. She was looking down at the ground, raking through the leaves. "Nobody's ever going to remember, remember the 17th of February. Doesn't trip off the tongue, does it? I'll never forget the look on your Dad's face. He went loopy."

Jim made a face. "*Yeah,*" he said. "*One minute, the new Prime Minister's congratulating me and saying how we need more enterprising youngsters, the next Mum and Dad are banning me from the computer and I've got a fish tank to 'keep me occupied'.*"

"A fish tank? That doesn't make sense," said Graeme, although actually he was thinking it was funny that it should have happened to Jim, since his parents had done a similar thing to him.

"*They're parents,*" Jim said, shrugging again. "*And they decided to send me to Peashingle Academy because it doesn't have a computer department! It's like studying in the dark ages!*"

"There's no difference between that place and Peashingle Comp," said Calamara, "apart from the fact they can afford to clean the toilets so things smell nicer when they flush your head down the loo."

Graeme was dead eager to find out more, but didn't really feel that he could press Jim about it any further. After all, Jim wasn't pushing him about anything. *Everyone's entitled to a bit of privacy*, he thought; but that did lead him to think of something he needed to ask.

"Is that why you didn't answer my emails?"

"What emails?"

"If you couldn't use your computer, then you wouldn't have got my messages. There wasn't a Minicom, so I sent you some emails while… over the summer," Graeme finished lamely. He was all too aware that Calamara was watching him as he spoke.

"*Mum and Dad would have passed them on,*" said Jim. "*Oh, hang on; they had a virus over the summer. Or rather, I should say, viruses. Our computer was completely trashed about four times. That's what they get for not letting me keep an eye on it. Mum and Dad click on anything that moves.*"

"I thought you didn't want to talk…"

Jim picked up on what Graeme meant immediately. "'Course not." He smiled. "Don't be an idiot."

Calamara cleared her throat. "When you two lovebirds have quite finished," she said, "can we move on? I'm rested now."

"*Hang on, what about you and the Queen?*" Jim asked her. "*You never said anything about the Queen. And you twisted my arm all those times to make me tell you about the Gunpowder Plot.*"

Calamara scowled. "It was all so long ago. There's nothing to tell. It was before we moved here. I met the Queen; I may have bitten her – ever so slightly. The end. Can we go now? Or we'll be here for ever."

Jim and Graeme looked at each other and smirked. Graeme felt a bit ashamed to admit it, but it was fun to see Calamara feeling awkward.

"Shut up!" she shouted. "Or," she rounded on Graeme, "perhaps you'd like to tell us why Lord Raversham looked like he was going to pee in his pants when he saw you."

"I don't know why," said Graeme. He wasn't exactly lying. It was kind of true. It was a fair bet it had something to do with that newspaper, but he didn't have a clue why Lord Raversham was so spooked by it.

Now Calamara and Jim looked at each other. Graeme hoped Jim hadn't told Calamara all about him; he sort of thought that Jim hadn't, at least not all of it, otherwise she would have been really laying into him.

"So, let's go, shall we?" Calamara asked again. "The wind is getting stronger."

Jim got up and dusted himself down. Calamara wasn't wrong about the wind. Leaves were beginning to whip up and swirl around; but the sky was clear.

"It is a bit brisk, isn't it?" said Jim, walking across to Calamara. "Never mind. It can't get much worse. We're pretty sheltered here."

It was as if the wind were listening to him and had taken that as a challenge; in a split second, it went from blustery to full blown hurricane–force.

"What's going on?" Jim shouted.

Now sods of earth were being ripped up, flying into the air, leaving a hole in the ground right in front of them, at the centre of the clearing, a hole large enough to swallow them one by one if they got close enough to it. The wind buffeted them; it was howling, moaning even, as if they'd disturbed a gravesite and the dead were clambering from their coffins. Graeme grabbed hold of a vine that was clinging to the wall of the castle, just as Jim and Calamara were hanging on to whatever they could.

There was a flash of what looked like metal in the centre of the hole but with so many leaves spiralling around it was difficult to be sure. Graeme couldn't see clearly. It definitely seemed to be silver, whatever it was, and it was rising up.

Graeme tried to brush the leaves away from his face to get a better view. The wailing continued all around them and it seemed that there were more and more leaves and twigs being caught in the whirlwind, until it was impossible to see anything. Something with barbs on it scratched Graeme's face as it whipped past. He hunched up, wrapping one arm around his legs as the other gripped that vine; he screwed up his eyes and kept his head down.

And the wind stopped.

Even more suddenly than it had appeared, it just stopped. Everything that had been caught in it, all the foliage, all the brushwood, dropped to the ground and all over them. Graeme's face stung as he looked up. He touched his cheek; he was bleeding.

"What's that?" asked Calamara. "Help me up, you two."

Standing in the middle of the clearing was an oblong, silver box, about the size of a tea trolley. It was humming. Graeme and Jim held Calamara between them and walked over to it. They could feel the ground vibrating underneath their feet in time with the hum of the box.

"*What's going on?*" Jim asked.

The hum got louder until it was a deep, monotonous buzz. The box got warm, too; Graeme could feel the heat coming off it in great waves. A section from the top, at the end nearest to them, popped open. A short pole extended straight up out of it and at the top, a small piece of white cloth, like a pocket–handkerchief, unfurled until it was taut. It might actually have been a pocket–handkerchief; it had the initials FP embroidered in one corner.

Another panel opened towards the back of the box. Graeme stuck his head behind the hanky to see what was happening and was nearly blinded by a shaft of bright light that shot out from the depths. He blinked, spots momentarily clouding his vision. The light was shining on the cloth and a blurred image was forming. It was like they were watching a tiny cinema screen.

The picture leapt into focus. Numbers flashed in front of their eyes:

5 … bleep … 4 … bleep … 3 … bleep … 2 … bleep …

"PICTURE START" was displayed and then:

"Hello."

They were watching a black and white film of a young man with a patchy beard. He was wearing a collarless shirt, trousers, and no shoes. The picture zoomed in on his face.

"Hello," he said again. He sounded posh. "Welcome! Welcome to Raversham Isle! I am Fitzpatrick Parkes. Or rather, I am a recording of Fitzpatrick Parkes. The real me is, well, I could be anywhere, who knows? But welcome! Welcome!"

The picture vanished. There was a grinding sound from inside the box and the hum changed pitch. It was now more of a whine. The screen lit up once more. The smiling face of Fitzpatrick Parkes re–appeared. This time it was in colour. He had ginger hair.

"This is rather awkward," he said. The picture clicked off and back on again, this time in black and white. "It appears that you are trespassing on private property."

The pole the screen was on telescoped out so Fitzpatrick was more–or–less eye to eye with Graeme, Jim and Calamara. "Judging by your size," he said, "you do not appear to be – " – the picture went off and on again – " – Carreg Arswyd – " – it flickered once more – " – and you are far too tall and in possession of too many limbs to be members of the Mawrtywysen. Therefore I conclude that you are – merely children – but I do not see Master – Uriah – amongst you, so I am wondering – why you have – a key?"

The three of them looked at one another. Again, the picture went off and after a short pause, it came back on. "Any answers?" Fitzpatrick asked. Whatever this was they were watching, it seemed very disjointed. It was as if something were taking lots of different, separately recorded, pieces of film and splicing them together on the spot.

Jim was excited. "*What did it say?*" he asked.

There was a clunk inside the box and subtitles started appearing as Fitzpatrick spoke. He – it – he – could obviously understand sign language.

“I do not care for being referred to as ‘it’,” he said. The picture froze and the box whirred. “Would you prefer subtitles or signing?” a colour Fitzpatrick asked.

Jim looked at Graeme, wonderment filling his eyes, then back at the screen. “Signing, please,” he replied.

The picture pulled back until the whole of Fitzpatrick could be seen. He rolled the sleeves of his shirt up one by one and continued, now signing everything he spoke.

“As I was saying, I do – not – recognise you and – you appear to be in possession of what I must presume to be – an illegally obtained – key. As such, I am afraid I have no choice other than to eject you from this isle. Please stand by.”

The earth began to shake. They all fell, rolling apart. Fitzpatrick’s screen craned over so he was still looking at them. “Thank you for visiting.” He smiled. “Do – not – come again!”

The ground opened up under Jim and he fell in with a panicked scream that quickly faded. Calamara looked at where he had been and then back to Fitzpatrick. “You can’t do that to me,” she cried. “I’m disabled.”

“You should have thought of that before you decided to take up trespassing as a hobby,” Fitzpatrick told her; and Calamara dropped down a hole of her own, screaming all the way.

“I’ll send her chair down later,” Fitzpatrick told Graeme. “Are you ready?”

“No,” said Graeme.

Fitzpatrick beamed. “Excellent! That’s the best way to go!”

And then Graeme was falling and the light was fading further and further away as the darkness claimed him.

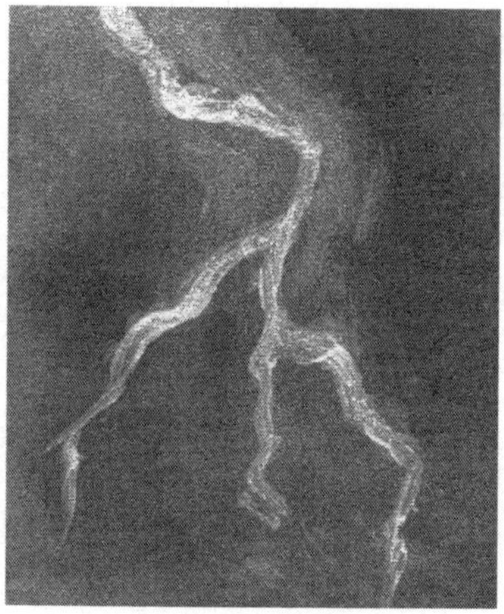

CHAPTER FIVE

Raversham Relations and Fevered Dreams

Graeme was plummeting into nothing. He skidded down and round in the dark, twisting in a corkscrew, out of control, air rushing past his face, eyes stinging. He hurtled around hairpin bends, went up and down, was shoved left and right, pushed and pulled by he didn't know what until he had no idea what direction he was going in.

And then he slammed into a wall and stopped. He sneezed as a cloud of dust engulfed his head. He waved his hand around his face to clear the air, coughing and spitting out the dust he had breathed in. Cobwebs tangled in his fingers.

It wasn't so dark here – wherever 'here' was. There was a little light creeping in from off on the right. Graeme got on his hands and knees and crawled towards it. He went carefully; other than that speckled patch of yellow light, it was still almost pitch black.

As he got closer, he realised that the light was filtering through a small bush of some kind. He grabbed hold of the branches and tugged. It wouldn't budge. Shuffling into a better position, he tried again. Still nothing. He got a firmer grip at the root. This time, as he pulled, the whole thing erupted from the earth. He was covered in a shower of dirt and fell backwards, ending up on his back with his feet in the air and the bush still in his grasp. He sat up and chucked it away.

He'd uncovered a small, metal grille. It must have been an air vent of some kind. Tiny squares of light shone on his face as he got his nose up against it to see what was on the other side.

What he saw was a deserted cavern. The light was coming from grand, red–hot braziers that were positioned along the walls at regular intervals. Rough stone columns supported the ceiling. At the far end of the room was a raised platform, with a staircase that led up to a darkened doorway.

Graeme heard a familiar humming from somewhere nearby. He'd hardly had time to think about that when he was blasted by a surge of hot air and white light flickered on the side of his face. A screen had extended on a pole from the wall. Fitzpatrick Parkes was smiling at him.

"Terribly sorry," said Fitzpatrick. "There appears to be a slight hitch. If you will bear with me, I shall see what I can do to fix the problem. Thank you for your patience."

Fitzpatrick's face vanished and was replaced by the word "INTERLUDE", behind which played a black and white film of an old woman with hair drawn back into a tight bun. She was sitting outside, on a patio overlooking a sunny garden, making industrious use of a spinning wheel. Tinny music burbled all around Graeme for a moment and then the woman was gone and Fitzpatrick was back.

"Righty–ho," he said. "I've had to re–route you. Once again, do accept my apologies. A dinghy has been launched. I'd hate for you to drown while you wait for the authorities to pick you up. Please – don't – come again! Out you go, Eskimo!"

The ground shuddered and then fell away under Graeme at an angle, forming a slide. He tumbled down it and found himself falling again, the light shrinking as he sped away.

If he'd thought he was going fast before, it was nothing compared to this. There were no twists and turns now. He wasn't even touching the sides until the chute levelled off, but by that point he'd picked up so much momentum that he wasn't slowing at all. He could smell salty air and see a circle of light that started out the size of a dot, but it grew and grew, faster than it had any right to grow, until it filled his vision and he was hurtling out of it, up and out into cold, fresh air.

He was tearing through the sky, turning over, twisting round, the clouds above him and the sea below, startling the seagulls as he flew past them. There was an orange dot bobbing on the sea; and he tumbled towards it.

He gasped as he plunged feet first into the ice cold water. Gasping was a stupid thing to do, not that he could help it, but it meant that he swallowed a huge amount of salt water and choked on what he didn't swallow. He couldn't breathe. The water soaked his clothes, all those clothes that Adrian had made him wear, making him ten times heavier than he should have been. Everything sounded so distant. He couldn't see because bubbles were rushing all around him, racing for the surface. He dimly realised that's what he should be doing as well, so he kicked hard, straining every muscle, forcing himself up and up and up.

His head broke the surface and he gulped air. Hands grabbed at him and he found himself being pulled head first onto an orange rubber dinghy, upside down with his legs pedalling at nothing, looking at a soaking wet, sullen Calamara.

"For goodness' sake, pull yourself together," she said. She had gathered herself up into as tight a bundle as she could at the far end of the dinghy.

"Are you okay?" Jim asked out loud as he helped Graeme to right himself. He was drenched as well.

Graeme nodded. In fact, he was freezing. He wrapped his arms around his knees and shivered.

"*Your lips are turning blue*," Jim told him. Jim's hands were shaking with the cold, so it was hard to tell what he was saying.

"I'll be f–fine," Graeme stammered.

Jim didn't look convinced.

"What are we going to do now?" Calamara was whining.

Graeme's teeth chattered. He could feel the cold seeping in through his clothes, chilling him to the core.

"I need to get dry or I'll catch something," Calamara continued.

What a surprise, thought Graeme: she was only thinking about herself.

"Whoever's boat this is, they obviously don't clean it very often," Calamara said, disgusted. "It's all sticky." She pressed her hand to the dinghy floor; it seemed reluctant to let her go, clinging on as she pulled away.

"Maybe someone left – " said Jim.

"Maybe someone left what?" Calamara interrupted him, but he didn't answer: the floor was stretching down, like someone below had pinched a hold at the centre and was tugging at it, only it was stretching far further than it should without ripping. It was extending to infinity. Slowly – they couldn't get loose because the surface was so gummy – they slid over the lips of the orifice that had formed and into what felt like a very tight surgical stocking.

Anacondas can eat a pig, whole; as they were kneaded at, Graeme thought: *now I know how the pig feels*. This wasn't any surgical stocking: it was an intestine; and they were being digested!

Jim tried to grab onto the inflated rim of the dinghy, but the way back sealed shut as they were sucked in. The tract pulsed as they were squashed, squeezed, suffocated. They were contorted into all kinds of shapes as they progressed, the fleshy canal undulating, hugging them so tightly that Calamara's muffled shouts were senseless. She must have known she wasn't doing any good, but still she shouted. Graeme was too weak to fight. He just let it take him, let the gross digestive juices slime all over him.

A cacophony of gurgles and burps accompanied them as they were pulverised and drawn in deeper still. Graeme wondered exactly how deep you had to get before the pressure made your skull implode. Judging by how his head was feeling they weren't far off that point; and then, just as they were being crushed so hard he thought his bones were about to shatter, his body turn to pulp, the whole thing relaxed and they plopped out onto a damp white floor.

Graeme's eyes fell on a pair of black shoes, highly polished. They belonged to a smartly dressed man who was the spitting image of…

"You look just like the butler," said Jim. "I mean, Lord Raversham's butler."

"Indeed, young sir," said the man, proffering a towel. "I am his son, Lightston Kendall. You'll find there are a few of us about."

"Where are we?" asked Calamara.

"Questions can be answered later," Kendall replied. "For now, I would consider it more of a priority for you to get dry. No?"

"Stop treating us like children!" Calamara exploded.

Kendall acted as if she weren't there. "I think," he said to Jim, eyeing Graeme, "your friend may need help."

"I'm fine," Graeme lied. His teeth chattered. He tried to stand up. "I'm fine," he said again. He lurched and fell back down. Calamara tutted at him.

Kendall raised one eyebrow. "Yes, you're in tip top shape."

Graeme opened his mouth to reply but no sound came out. His head felt heavy. Fog seemed to be settling all around him. He gagged once.

"Are you going to be…?" Jim asked him.

“No,” Graeme said; but then he was, all down his front. He passed out.

*

“He probably just needs food,” a woman’s voice was saying. “How long has it been since you last ate?”

Graeme heard Calamara reply. “Breakfast.”

“There you go, see? Malnutrition. Have we got any Pavlova left?”

There was a pause.

“I didn’t catch that?” the woman asked.

“The boy was just letting us know that he had two slices of toast and a multivitamin tablet for breakfast, Summer,” a male voice said, “and I don’t think Pavlova is what they need right now. I think I read somewhere that chocolate is good in situations like this, or orange juice. You know, maybe it was bananas. Definitely not Pavlova, though.”

“Oh, what do you know, Harvest? Child Nutritionist Extraordinaire!”

“I think Master Harvest is correct about the Pavlova,” Graeme heard Kendall say.

“For once,” giggled Summer.

“But his other suggestions are… ill informed choices, if I may be so bold.”

“Of course you may, Kendall,” Summer gloated.

“They require something more substantial, miss,” Kendall finished.

Graeme wondered if he dare open his eyes. He didn’t want to throw up again. He was warm, wherever he was, and wrapped – mummified, more like – in a blanket.

“Well, what do they feed children these days?” Summer asked.

“We’ll make the boy on the couch a hot whisky and lemon when he wakes up. That should sort him out,” Harvest said. “Get a fire going in his belly, as Dad always says. Kendall, do you think you could cobble some food together for these two?”

“I’ve never known Chef to ‘cobble’,” Kendall replied, “but I will ask, sir.”

There were footsteps and a door opened and closed.

"Well," Summer said after an age, "isn't this nice?" Graeme felt her breath on his face. It smelt sweet. "What's up with your sleeping friend?" she asked. She must have been inches from him.

"He's been in hospital," Jim said. "He was ill."

"No! In hospital because he was ill? What a revelation!"

"What was up with him, then?" Harvest asked. Nobody said anything.

"Anyone?" Harvest persisted.

"There's something they don't want us to know," Summer breathed. "What could it be?"

"I don't know that I can be bothered," Harvest sighed.

Summer's voice took on a very theatrical air. "Well, I can. We need to know, Harvest. These three children are in our care. They're in a lot of trouble. Goodness knows what the police will say. All we want to do is help, but how can we unless we know what we're dealing with? Now, wouldn't – wasn't your name Jim? Wouldn't Jim like to help us help his friend?"

"I don't think it would help him if I told you," Jim said. He sounded a bit defensive.

"It might be very important," Summer cajoled.

"No."

"You can tell us. We're grown ups. You can trust us."

"No," Jim said again. "I'm thir– fourteen, not seven."

Graeme could have sworn that he heard Summer hiss.

"Oh for goodness' sake," said Calamara, sounding exasperated. "Not everything you know is top secret, Jim. I'll tell them."

"What?" Jim cried.

"You will?" Summer was thrilled. She had moved away from Graeme now. He had an image in his mind of her hovering over Calamara like some sort of vampire. He wished he could open his eyes.

"How wonderful!" Summer was saying. "Spill the beans, then."

Graeme tried to keep still but he could feel a rage burning inside him. Part of him wanted to leap up and stop this before it went any further. How dare Calamara tell them anything! He couldn't help but wonder, though, how much she knew.

"He had pneumonia," Calamara began. "That's why he was in hospital. He was in a house and it caught on fire and he was trapped inside. The fire brigade only just got to him in time. He was nearly burnt to a crisp."

"And that's it?" Summer asked.

"Yes," Calamara said.

"This is what… Jim," she seemed to have trouble remembering names, "didn't want to tell us? I would have thought there would be more, given his reaction."

"He's funny like that," Calamara replied.

"Oh," said Summer. She sounded disappointed. "How dull the truth can be. Oh well. Harvest, shall we get back to the game?"

"All right," Harvest agreed. They both walked away.

There was silence for a moment and then Graeme heard Calamara whisper, "What do you mean? She wasn't giving up easily. The best thing I could do was to give her the facts, because they're quite boring. Not what she was hoping for at all. And who *doesn't* know he was in a fire, anyway?"

There was another pause as Jim signed something to her. Then he chuckled.

"No, I do not. It doesn't mean anything," Calamara snapped. "I don't want his thanks. I didn't do it for *him*. He's a fool, but whatever happened, it's none of *their* business."

Graeme heard her shifting position. "Idiots," she scoffed. She shuffled back round. "I want to know what really happened," she whispered to Jim. "I heard all the rumours about him being in a gang, and being in trouble with the police – didn't you know? It's all over the port. I might have believed the stories if I hadn't met him, but I've met him. Still, there's got to be more to it than him just being in a fire, or, like the woman said, why would you be so cagey? Why don't you tell me?"

Graeme thought now was the time for him to wake up. He stretched and yawned.

"Look!" Jim exclaimed.

"Well, would you believe," Calamara sighed. "What timing."

Graeme forced another yawn and gingerly opened his eyes. He didn't throw up.

He was lying on a couch in a large, white room. There were portholes all around, through which he could see the dark sea and bubbles skittering upwards. They were underwater. A table was right beside him, with a posh lamp on it. The lampshade was like stained glass. Jim and Calamara were nearby, sitting in high backed chairs, blankets wrapped around them. Jim was kind of grinning. Calamara was frowning at Graeme. Graeme frowned right back at her.

"Hello," said Harvest, getting up and walking across to where the three of them were sitting. He was a thin man with short black hair and a ski–slope of a nose. "I'm Harvest Acre Raversham. This is my sister," he stuck his thumb over his shoulder, "Summer Rain."

"Hi," Summer said. She hadn't moved. She only glanced at Graeme for an instant before returning her attention to the game of chess that was in progress on the table in front of her. She wore a simple white dress and had exactly the same nose as her brother. "Come on, let's get back to the game." She inclined her head towards the chessboard and looked pointedly at Harvest. Her brother seemed more interested in Graeme – at least for the moment.

"Pleased to see you're looking more alive," he said. "We've thrown out your clothes, at least the top layer. The other stuff is drying… somewhere. Kendall took it. Afraid my sister and I aren't very domestic, but hey, it creates a job for someone, doesn't it? You're in one of my shirts. A good one, too; but you can keep it. Especially if you puke again."

Graeme couldn't see that much of the shirt due to the blankets, but he could see that it was white, with embroidered flowers. No doubt Calamara would have something to say about that in due course. "Where am I?" he asked.

"You're aboard the *Fathomless Wonder*," Harvest told him. "My sub."

"Our sub," Summer Rain corrected him.

"I'm going to get you a drink," Harvest said to Graeme, walking across to a bar and starting to rummage around, boiling a kettle. He walked back after a minute, a steaming glass in his hand.

"What's that?" Graeme asked. He had a pretty good idea, but as he'd supposedly been asleep he thought he shouldn't give the game away.

"It'll warm your cockles," Harvest assured him. "Now, drink up."

"You're sounding more like Father every day," Summer accused her brother as Graeme took a sip. He screwed up his eyes and coughed.

Harvest and Summer both laughed. They both had the same musical, mocking laugh.

"Come on then, sister mine, let's see if I can't beat you," Harvest said, still chortling. He sauntered back to join his sister. They completely forgot about anyone else as soon as they continued their game.

"How are you?" Jim asked Graeme.

"Okay," Graeme said, making a face as he took another sip of the whisky. It felt like he was swallowing fire. He reached out and put the glass down on the table. "What's going on?"

"*Summer Rain and Harvest Acre are Lord Raversham's children. Summer Rain said the whole family..."*

"Or what's left of the family," Calamara smirked.

Jim carried on, "*They're visiting for Christmas. We ought to ask them to let Lord Raversham know where we are. Mort will worry if he finds we're gone."*

A door opened and Kendall the butler strode through with a tray of sandwiches, crumpets, and a pot of tea. He cast a glance towards the Ravershams before walking across and setting the platter down in front of the trio.

"It's good to see you're awake, young man," he nodded at Graeme, starting to pour the tea. "As we're not sure who likes what, Chef has made a range of sandwiches for you. If in doubt I'd stick to the crumpets."

He looked at the glass of whisky on the table, then back at Graeme. "Have you had any of that?" he asked.

"A little," Graeme said.

Kendall sighed deeply. "No more, I think," he said and whisked the glass away, vanishing back through the door by which he had entered.

They tucked into the food. The sandwiches seemed to be full of lettuce and some weird pastes, so Graeme stuck to the crumpets as Kendall had suggested. He was kind of wary at first in case he was sick, but his stomach seemed fine and he found that he was absolutely ravenous after his first bite, so he wolfed down loads. He was really thirsty, too, and drank two cups of tea really quickly, which burnt the roof of his mouth.

"*They wanted to know all about you,*" Jim told Graeme as he ate, indicating Harvest Acre and Summer Rain. That's one of the advantages of being deaf: you can talk with your mouth full.

"Really?" Graeme asked, spraying a few crumbs. He didn't want to let them know he'd been listening.

"Yes, really," said Calamara, squinting at him. "But I'm sure you..."

A claxon blared, seven times. Summer broke away from the game. "What is it?" she asked, up and heading for the door mid–sentence. Harvest wasn't far behind. Jim helped Graeme to untangle himself from the blanket.

Graeme swung his legs onto the floor and found that he still felt pretty unsteady. With Jim supporting him, they left Calamara and followed Harvest into the next room, finding themselves on the circular bridge of the submarine. Screens of all shapes and sizes filled every wall; there was a large table, lit from underneath, with a map laid out on it; and a persistent *beep, beep, beep* was being broadcast from wall–mounted speakers.

Kendall was studying one of the screens, his face bathed in blue light. "You two shouldn't be in here," he said, but Summer told him to be quiet.

"What on Earth can it be?" she asked nobody in particular.

"Whatever it is," Harvest said, "it's heading directly for us."

"You haven't been annoying anybody recently, have you?" Summer asked her brother. He gave her a laid back shrug.

"We're turning into its path," Kendall informed them.

"Didn't they say in the manual that's a bad thing to do?" Harvest suggested.

"It wasn't a course of action I would have chosen myself, sir, but it appears the boat has other ideas."

"You mean…"

"It has taken matters into its own hands, yes."

Summer was poring over an oval screen. "The bay doors are opening."

"Can we see it?" Harvest asked, his voice full of curiosity. At his command, the largest display in the room cleared of all the jargon that had been scrolling across it and instead brought up the image of a torpedo, headed directly for them.

"Let's hope the *Wonder* knows what she's doing, or you're going to wish we hadn't rescued you," Harvest said to Graeme and Jim.

The *bleeps* was getting more frantic; there were hardly any pauses between them now; it was more like a single tone, the kind you hear when heart monitors don't have a beating heart to monitor any more.

"I think perhaps we should hold onto something," said Kendall.

"Too late!" Summer shouted with glee.

The torpedo burst apart, inches from the hull, releasing a cloud of bubbles and a box. The box continued to travel towards the sub and vanished from view.

"We appear to have received a package," Kendall said, not flustered in the slightest.

"Bring it up here," said Summer.

"It's already on its way."

The illuminated table rotated and a square hole appeared at the centre, out of which rose a sopping wet box. Two grey metal arms, ending in delicate pliers, descended from the ceiling and pried it open.

"Calamara," Jim called over his shoulder, "your wheelchair's here!"

Graeme recalled how Fitzpatrick Parkes had said that he would send it along. He'd kept his word.

A pair of doors on the opposite side of the bridge parted, and a woman wearing a smart black and white trouser suit came rushing out. She had a silk scarf tied over her head which was streaked with red and orange and yellow; the scarf trailed down her back to well below her waist. Topping it all off was a black top hat with a red feather tucked into the brim, which she wore at a jaunty angle. "What was that? What was that?" she cried. "Summer? Harvest?"

"It was a delivery, Sigourney," Summer replied.

Sigourney smiled. "Is that all? Thank goodness! I was just having a nap and then I heard that awful racket and I thought for a moment… no, I shouldn't say. I don't want to tempt fate. But you're both here. Thank goodness, thank goodness." She stopped as she noticed Graeme and Jim. "Who are these?"

Harvest introduced the boys and explained where the sub was now headed.

"This," he told Graeme and Jim, "is our big sister, Sigourney."

"Sigourney Raversham–Quick," Sigourney said, tipping her hat. "You must have heard of me," she boasted, and wasn't very impressed when the boys just looked straight back at her.

"Well this has well and truly frazzled my nerves! I'm going back to my rooms," she announced with a huff. She fixed the boys with a stare. "You've *never* heard of me?"

Both of them shook their heads. "Sorry."

"No wonder the world is going to rack and ruin," Sigourney despaired, before turning on her heel and walking out.

“She’s a milliner,” Harvest explained as he caught the boys’ bewildered looks. “Raversham–Quick Hats.”

*

Graeme and Jim may never have heard of Raversham–Quick Hats, and it was probably a fair bet that Calamara hadn’t, either. However, the rest of the world was more than well aware of them. Sigourney had started out as a costume designer in amateur theatre while she was at university in Wales, and, after graduation (a first, as was expected of any Raversham worth their salt) she took off to America where she met and married Gethin Quick, a man who owned a thousand and one stores around the globe and his own fashion label to–boot. Gethin had a keen eye for up–and–coming talent: the marriage was seen more as a business than a love match; the pair spent less than a week of each year together.

Gethin’s hunch proved to be correct. Sigourney quickly became the rising star within the company, much to her father’s surprise: Lord Raversham had always thought his daughter’s designs were an affront to the eye, liable to cause permanent brain damage.

After thirteen years of designing couture, Sigourney was at the top of her game. No expense was spared at the launch of her “Extremo Fantastico” collection. She wowed the world at the El Chile Fashion Parade in Cancun with this new range, modelled by a troupe from the Ballet Sauter. Once the presentation was done she retired to her suite at the Hotel Concepto–Grande for the obligatory after–show party. Centre of attention at the exclusive gathering was the male lead of the ballet, Claude Roget, famous for championing the rights of amputees in dance. Claude had lost his right leg below the knee in his early days with a contemporary ballet company who employed chainsaws in their act. The loss had not stopped or even slowed his career; on the contrary, he was now a much sought after performer. He was holding court in the lounge of Sigourney’s suite, astonishing everyone with how naturally his state–of–the–art false leg moved, flinging it back and forth with gay abandon. During one particularly enthusiastic kick, the leg detached itself entirely from his body and cart–wheeled in a sweeping arc across the room to where Sigourney was enjoying a private chat with some of her more eminent clients. It hit her squarely on the back of the head.

She woke one morning, two days later, in a hospital bed, to find that her hair had started to fall out. The leg's impact, the doctors said, had caused some sort of trauma and there was nothing anyone could do to halt the hair loss. Within a month, she was piebald; only a few wispy clumps of her once lustrous hair remained. Another month later, after discovering that no hair restorer would work and that she had a nasty, potentially fatal, skin allergy to any form of wig, she founded Raversham–Quick Hats and its subsidiary, Purely Scarves of Silk, and became her own biggest customer.

*

The claxon sounded again.

"Something else that's being couriered to you today?" Harvest asked Graeme and Jim.

The main screen switched on. This time there was no torpedo to worry about.

"Roberta?" Summer asked. "Roberta Plastic?"

"Hello," said Roberta, her face filling the screen. The picture made her look all odd; she appeared to have a huge nose and tiny eyes and mouth.

Summer didn't bother saying hello back. "You're still here?" she asked instead. "I thought you would've been promoted ages ago. Why aren't you policing the mean streets of London, then?"

"I'm irreplaceable," Roberta replied. Her face was a little sour.

"I must say you're the last person I'd expect to see piloting a launch!" said Summer. "When we were in school you were petrified of water."

"I got over that," Roberta replied. "I did a course. Anyway," she said, clearly wanting to change the subject, "I'm responding to a distress call. I diverted this way as soon as I picked it up."

It was then that she noticed the boys. "What in heaven's name are you two doing there? Don't tell me you were the distress call… Why am I asking? I know, just *know* you were."

"We pulled them out of the sea about half an hour ago," said Summer. "There's a disabled girl with them, too. They'd been exploring the isle and got expelled, it seems."

"Calamara's with them? Things just go from bad to worse." Roberta glowered at Graeme. "What's your uncle going to say about this? And James, I thought after our little chat we agreed you were going to stay out of trouble."

Jim looked anywhere rather than back at her.

"How infuriating is this?" Roberta raged. "It's all I needed today! Bloody kids! They'll need to get home," she said to Harvest and Summer, "and I have other things to do. This is a dreadful imposition, but can you take them?"

"Of course," said Summer. "We wouldn't want to interrupt you messing about on the water!"

"Ha!" Roberta's laugh was mirthless. "No such luck. I'm playing the ferryman." She stepped aside to reveal a man, snoozing alongside a much smaller figure whose features were hidden by an overlarge bright yellow raincoat and hat. "I'm taking them back to the isle and I don't think your father's going to let me get away any time soon. I suspect he's annoyed that the news leaked out; and my money says he's going to blame me. Mind you, given the choice between facing him and having to be the first to tell Jim's dad what his son's been up to, I think maybe I haven't drawn the shortest straw for once."

"Summer," said Harvest, hearing that, "we should let Kendall reunite them with their families when we reach land. I'm not good with irate parents."

"Nor me. We're not parent people," Summer agreed.

Roberta didn't look surprised. "Well, I'll probably see you later then. I'll let Lord Raversham know what's going on." She redirected her gaze at Graeme and Jim. "I can see your little gang are going to be nothing but trouble. I don't know what I'm going to say to your uncle, and your parents, about this. You'd just better hope I'm in a good mood when I come back, and let's face it, that's hardly likely."

With that, she powered up the motor of the launch and sailed away. The view–screen went blank.

"Are you done now? Can I get my chair?" Calamara snapped from the other room, thumping her fist on the table.

*

By the time Kendall knocked on Adrian's front door, Graeme was lagging behind as far as he could, expecting the worst. Adrian didn't react like Graeme's mum and dad would have, though. They would have shouted at him non–stop for seven hours and then that would have been it. Adrian didn't say a word. He just *looked* at

Graeme, which was far, far worse. He thanked Kendall for bringing his nephew home and then he ushered Graeme inside.

Adrian went back to work for a while. Graeme was left alone, by the fire. When Adrian re–appeared and started preparing dinner, he still didn't say anything. They didn't look at each other, but Graeme could feel his uncle watching and it made his ears burn; it made him want to curl up and die.

It wasn't until they were half way through dinner that Adrian finally spoke.

"You feeling bad?" he asked.

Graeme nodded but didn't look up.

"Yes, well," Adrian said. "I thought you probably were. The fact you're managing to eat these eggs without any comment says a lot."

Graeme risked an upward glance. Adrian was smiling. "The best thing about people with a conscience of their own is that you don't have to scold them or anything. They do a far better job of it all by themselves."

Graeme kept quiet.

Adrian chewed on some rubbery egg for a moment. "I am disappointed in you, Graeme. I'm dreading speaking to your mum and dad. They're going to have such a go at me about this. It's just as well I'm not a parent. I'm not doing a very good job."

"I'm sorry," Graeme mumbled.

"I know," Adrian said.

Graeme didn't stay up long that evening and went to bed early. The wind and rain were picking up outside, making his window rattle, like someone was trying to get in. Strangely, he'd always found bad weather, storms especially, really comforting. Tucked up in bed late at night, hearing the wintertime cracks and creaks of an otherwise still house made him feel safe. Curling up under his duvet, within a few minutes he was fast asleep.

He woke in the middle of the night. The rain had got worse. It was hammering on the window now. The wind was howling, whistling through gaps in the window frame. But even above that he heard someone on the steps up to his room. At first he thought it was Adrian, coming to check he was okay, but the footsteps were too infrequent, too hesitant. His heart started to pound and he pulled the duvet tighter about himself. With his head right under cover he couldn't hear anything any more. He waited for ages, feeling the bed tremble in time with his heartbeat, before he lifted the edge of the duvet and peeked out.

A cloaked man was standing just by the trap door. He was facing Graeme. The light from the landing below reflected off his silver mask. Graeme wanted to yell but couldn't. They were both motionless, save for the rising and falling of their chests.

Graeme didn't know if the man had realised he was watching him or not. Letting the duvet drop down again so his head was covered, Graeme waited, and then lifted it again. The man had gone.

Graeme got up and drifted to the window. The man was standing in the street, his cloak being whipped around him in the wind. Again, it seemed like he was looking directly at Graeme.

Graeme didn't remember getting dressed or putting his shoes on, but he did, must have, because the next thing he knew he was out the door. The rain soaked his clothes immediately. The street was empty, but there was only one place he could think a cloaked man would be heading, so he went to the beach. Sure enough, there was a gathering there. Boats all ready to sail out. At first he couldn't tell which of these people had been in his room, but then one of them turned and Graeme saw his silver mask. The others might have been wearing masks as well, but they had deep hoods so their faces were completely hidden. The masked man was facing Graeme while the others all worked around him. They stared at each other, Graeme and the man. He turned and walked into the surf, climbed into a boat. Graeme followed. Nobody else took any notice of him.

The boats rowed out on the choppy water. There were only three in Graeme's boat: him, the man who had been in his house and one other man, who was rowing. The rower was muttering under his breath and cursing as they went up and down on the waves and as water splashed into the boat.

They were heading for the isle. The masked man didn't seem to take any more notice of Graeme. He just sat at the opposite end of the boat and stared out to sea. When they were a fair way out, he reached under his seat and brought out a rusted lantern. He lit it and held it aloft. Far off in the dark night, an answering light signalled twice.

This was the closest Graeme had ever been to the masked man. Looking deep into the cowl of the man's cloak, Graeme examined the silver mask. It was remarkably plain, with no etched patterns of any kind to mar the highly polished surface. There were no holes for the nose, nor one for the mouth; only two almond–shaped, angled holes for the eyes, utter blackness behind them.

They reached the rocks at the base of the cliff and started to weave their way into them. Rowing became increasingly difficult, and the rower was reduced to just pushing against the rocks with his oars in order to keep moving. With one final heave he forced the boat into a clear stretch of water. He pulled the oars in and the whole thing shuddered. To Graeme, it felt like something had gripped the hull from below.

A yellow light blinked on and off, right in front of them. It was an electric light that was fixed to the rock, with metal bars protecting the frosted glass.

The boat shook again. Graeme grabbed the board he was sitting on with both of his hands. The masked man folded his arms and looked left and right. He seemed to pause for a moment as his gaze fell upon Graeme. At least, that's what Graeme thought.

They began to sink. Whatever had a hold of them was pulling the boat under the water. Graeme now wanted to dive overboard but something stopped him; maybe it was terror: sometimes you can be so scared that you can't move.

The water was nearly spilling over into the boat when there was a small noise, like air escaping from a balloon, and extra wooden panels started to rise up on either side of Graeme, clattering as they curved over his head. They clicked together at the top, sealing everyone in, and then eight square sections of wood, four above and four at their feet, rattled back to reveal windows. The water rose up and up around them, lapping at the glass. Graeme thought it felt weird as they gradually submerged, the dark sky finally vanishing as the sea closed in above their heads.

The water gently rocked the boat as they continued to descend. Narrow beams of light shone from the hull, letting Graeme see a little of what was out there, not that there was much to see, other than a few curious fish swimming towards the boat out of the gloom. There were sparks as the fish nudged the windows and Graeme could see them jump and their scales curl as they were instantly fried. Their lifeless bodies floated away into the murk.

The boat came to a halt after a few minutes. It shuddered twice more and then they were pulled forward. A blinding array of lights lit up a gigantic tunnel. They were pulled inside. Graeme glanced behind; the other boats were following. All the hulls had turned bright yellow.

They were a string of mammoth lemons, lost overboard from a giant's ship.

The tunnel was long, with offshoots on either side. Their boat sailed past the first three of those and took the fourth on the left, which lit up as they entered. This was much smaller than the main tunnel. Only some lights were working and even those that were flickered on and off, on and off. They sailed past line upon line of rusty pipes, upturned barrels and old, unreadable signs until the boat finally gave another now–familiar shudder and they started to move up.

Surfacing in a large cavern, Graeme could see the orange glow of fiery braziers as he looked intently out of the boat's upper windows. He jumped once as shutters closed over the glass, nearly chopping off his nose; and then the wood panels enclosing the boat fell away as it came to rest at the edge of the pool. The masked man and the rower got out as the others surfaced behind. The two of them waited until everyone had arrived and then they all walked off through an archway which had a red curtain drawn across it, leaving Graeme all alone.

He got out, then. The boats were now lined up in single file, nose to tail, jostling one another like a queue of first sale day shoppers. A hatch opened in front of them and they glided through it. The hatch closed.

Wherever he was, it looked like Graeme was stuck there for the time being. He followed the same path the others had taken, pulling the curtain aside and walking through the archway.

He found himself at the back of a cavern. With a jolt of surprise he realised that this was the place he'd seen earlier, through the grate, when Fitzpatrick had thrown him off the isle. There were the pillars supporting the roof; and there were the braziers, full of crackling flames. Of course, this time it was chock full of cloaked people. They were all in front of him, facing forward towards a raised platform, cross–legged on the floor with their heads held down. They seemed to be meditating or something. They were all chanting. Graeme could see over their heads to the steps at the back of the platform. Standing in the doorway at the top of those steps was the man in the silver mask. Graeme moved to one side and began slowly walking up towards the front, not creeping exactly, but trying to stay out of sight.

The masked man held his arms wide.

"Brothers!" his voice echoed all around. "Sisters! Children of the Night! The time is almost at hand!"

Everyone looked up and began to sway from side to side.

Gathering his robes, the masked man made his way down the steps. He didn't have anything on his feet. He'd nearly reached the bottom when he let out a loud yelp.

"Ow!" he cried, stumbling the rest of the way down. He lifted his left foot and put it in his hand, twisting to examine it. He was hopping on one leg. People in the crowd looked at each other. They seemed bewildered.

The masked man looked to one side, off into the wings. "I thought I told you to sweep these steps?" he fumed, still hopping around. "Get up here."

A short, cloaked man scurried out to join his master. "I'm sorry," he apologised. "I did sweep, honest. Perhaps, perhaps, you should have worn, um," he lifted his robe and held out a foot, which he waggled about. He was wearing bright blue flip–flops.

The masked man gingerly put his own foot back on the floor. His head moved from the face of his servant to the flip–flop and back again.

"I did my best, sir," the short man whimpered.

"Of course you did," the masked man replied, "just like you did when you lost the key; just like you did on your trip to Las Vegas the other night." He reached into his robe, pulled out a curved sword and ran his servant through with all the efficiency and precision of a highly skilled surgeon. He then pulled his blade free, letting it clatter to the floor. The short man sighed and collapsed alongside it. A pool of blood formed around the body.

"But your best is never good enough," the masked man said. It looked as if he were about to turn away, but he paused, turned and kicked the corpse. "And you cut the telephones off two days early you imbecile."

He beckoned another member of the congregation to come forward. As the figure rushed to join him, the masked man raised his voice. "So perish all who disappoint me," he declared.

The person who had joined him on stage bowed so low that their hood dipped into the congealing blood on the floor.

"You are now my number one," the masked man announced.

If it was possible, the person bowed lower still. "Yes, Lord." It was a woman's voice, but disguised: it sounded like she was trying to speak through a mouth of gravel. She looked at the massed followers grovelling in front of her as she stood up and Graeme could see right into her hood. She wore a blood red mask. It had huge yellow eyes, a long, hooked nose and a demoniacal grimace with white fangs painted on it.

"Now get rid of that and bring on our guests," the masked man instructed her.

The cloaked woman stood up and grabbed the body, dragging it away. She returned almost immediately with two people who were very much alive. There was a woman and a man. They both had short, wavy blond hair; the woman had a pointed nose. They wore white smocks and had masking tape stuck across their mouths. Their hands were tied in front of them.

The cloaked woman prodded them in the back and marched them across until they were standing in the middle of the dais, facing the crowd. She untied their hands and backed away, again bowing so low that her head was almost touching the floor.

The masked man walked around the prisoners, his hands clasped behind his back.

"So," he said, "thank you for joining us."

The captive pair stared wordlessly back at him.

"What?" the cloaked man asked, "nothing to say? How unusual. I would have thought you…" and here he rushed up until he was nose to nose with the captive woman, "of all people would have had something to say about this."

The woman frowned.

"Or perhaps age has brought with it wisdom," the cloaked man continued. "But somehow I doubt it, I doubt it very much."

He walked behind them and put his head between theirs, looking from one to the other. "I'm sure you're wondering why you're here," he said. "Why I require your presence. Well, it's more that I *don't* require you any more." He walked back around so he was in front of them again. "I never did," he said. It sounded like his voice was shaking.

"Perhaps I can help make things a little more clear," he said. He raised a hand to his face for a moment and then stretched out his arm. In his hand he held the silver mask. Only the two people in front of him could see his face. They both stumbled back. The woman tried to scream.

"Yes," the cloaked man boomed, replacing his mask, "now you understand. Who's laughing now? Look at me!"

As he commanded them to look at him, the captives both stopped and stared straight at him. Graeme couldn't make out if he was talking to them or what. After a few minutes, he untied their hands and stepped to one side.

"They have agreed to dance for us, my friends," he said. "Their last dance."

A panel in the floor slid back at the very front of the dais. Smoke billowed out of it and a bed of burning hot coals rose up. The captive man held out his hand and the woman took it. With a stately grace they stepped onto the coals and started to dance back and forth, whirling round and round like they were dancers from the golden age of Hollywood, gliding across the silver screen in glorious black and white. There was no sound, other than the strange, soft chanting of the crowd. The dancing couple didn't make a noise as their clothes caught alight, as the flames licked up around them, as their skin burnt and cracked.

Graeme felt sick. He tried to turn his head away, but couldn't. The masked man was ignoring everything going on in front of him. He was looking right at Graeme again as the couple continued their gruesome dance, their movements becoming more and more awkward. They tripped and stumbled, staggered and lurched, but they didn't stop, they never stopped. Smoke filled the air, great billowing clouds that swept through the room.

The devil–masked woman marched to the front of the dais. "Rejoice!" she cried.

"Graeme?"

Graeme's heart was beating faster and faster. He couldn't breathe. He couldn't see for smoke. There had been so much smoke, he thought, so much smoke.

"He's alive," they'd said. Graeme could see, see the faces staring at him, hands pulling at him. Everyone had been so panicked, then. He hadn't worried, then. But this was now. He screamed.

"Graeme!"

Graeme's eyes snapped open. He was cold, so cold, breathing heavily and sweating, standing at the window in his bedroom. The curtains were pulled back. Rain was battering the glass.

Adrian was standing in front of him, grabbed hold and hugged him tight. Graeme's arms just hung at his sides.

"It's all right," said Adrian.

Graeme didn't dare close his eyes. He didn't know what to say.

There was a burst of lightning and an ear splitting *crack*. The air was alive. The whole room shook; outside, the beach lit up for a second and in that brief moment Graeme saw someone standing at the water's edge, braving the storm.

Graeme could still smell the smoke; he could still feel the heat making his skin prickle; and he knew that the eyes of the masked man were still on him. He wanted to shut out the world, but words, the words of that cloaked woman were searing across his brain:

"Rejoice! For the Pyn King has returned to claim the world!"

CHAPTER SIX

An Unexpected Invitation

"All right, everybody! 'I Saw Three Ships'! And you gentlemen at the back, let's sing the proper lyrics, shall we? We don't want a repeat of the Withelwain Shopping Centre last week, now, do we?" The short, fat choirmaster looked over his shoulder and treated everyone to a sheepish grin.

Graeme and Adrian had arrived at the Cymylog Gardens ten minutes earlier, at about half past one, and it was packed. Lots of people wrapped in their winter clothes had been tempted out by the clear blue sky and had gathered at the entrance to watch the Peashingle Academy Youth Choir.

Graeme had been up been up at the crack of dawn; not surprisingly, he hadn't slept that well after the dream. Thankfully, Adrian hadn't mentioned it, even though they'd spent a really boring morning doing nothing in particular during which the subject could have cropped up at any moment. Still, Adrian had been really happy. Graeme realised, with a little shock, that his uncle was simply pleased that they were finally spending some time together.

The choir, all dressed in the black and burgundy uniform of the Peashingle Academy, burst into song. Three tall boys in the back row, who must have been about fifteen or sixteen, were obviously ignoring the choirmaster's plea for decency. Seven girls in the next row down were glancing back at them and giggling; and right in the front row were Adam, Archibald and Margaret Raversham. They weren't singing. They were just opening and closing their mouths like puppets while their heads swivelled back and forth, watching everything going on around them.

The choirmaster gave an exaggerated sigh. "Stop! No! No! No! Didn't you hear anything I said? You three!" he shouted, though his voice didn't sound that forceful, "you three boys!"

He pointed at the boys in the back row with his baton. "Gabriel!" he called out, indicating the one with wide blue eyes and untidy brown hair. "Gabriel Wellington! Yes, I'm talking to you! Please nudge Mr Finder for me, would you? See if he has finished excavating his nose and then maybe we can continue!"

Gabriel nudged the pallid boy standing to his right, who looked like a thick stick of lard with grease oozing from every pore.

"Found anything good, Reeves?" Gabriel asked him.

Reeves Finder pulled his finger out, showing off a giant, spongy yellowish–green lump that anyone could have made out, even at the back where Graeme and Adrian were standing.

"Delightful," said the choirmaster, a slightly ill look on his face. "No need to show everybody, not in public. Put it away, eh?"

Reeves stuck his hands in his pockets.

The choirmaster rubbed at his temple. "All right, then! From the top! And Aled," he said, directing his remark at the boy with deeply tanned skin who was standing to the left of Gabriel, "if there is anything resembling a brain between those ears of yours, remember what I said about the using the traditional lyrics, please, or I shall have to inform the vicar of your behaviour… and you know what she's like. Are we ready?" he asked, lifting his baton. "And a one, two, three…"

The choir started singing again. The results weren't any better second time round.

"Have you had enough of this?" Adrian asked. A man with a camcorder turned around and shushed at him. Adrian and Graeme exchanged a weary glance and shuffled through the crowd towards the main building, a massive place built of wood and glass, all sharp angles framed by the tallest of eucalyptus trees.

Adrian pushed the door open and the two of them passed through a curtain of warm air into the garden centre. The ticket desk was immediately in front of them and a restaurant with panoramic windows that looked out over the sweeping landscape was on their right. With the sky outside so bright, inside, in the warm, looking out, you could almost have believed it was a summer's day, were it not for the multitude of stoic, bare–limbed trees.

Sitting at a table in the restaurant, nursing a cup of coffee, was Josephine; by her, with his nose in a book, was Lord Raversham. The book's title was printed in bold lettering. It read, "I THOUGHT HE WAS GONE, BY DOCTOR TANIA HERNANKOWITZ". A plate with a single doughnut on it was positioned between them.

Josephine waved at the newcomers.

"We'd better say hello," said Adrian. Graeme gave Lord Raversham a wary glance, which his uncle noticed. "You can apologise for yesterday as well, can't you?" he said. Graeme had kind of hoped to just avoid Lord Raversham rather than have to say he was sorry for anything. It wasn't that he minded apologising, but he thought they never sounded like he meant them when he did. Still, there wasn't a lot he could do to escape it now. They walked over to the table.

Lord Raversham didn't even seem to notice Graeme approaching at first. When he did, he got that same look in his eyes that he'd had before, like he thought the boy was going to attack him. Josephine was as cheery as she had been the first time Graeme had seen her. She had sugar round her mouth and was still bundled up in the fur coat she'd worn on the beach, despite the fact the heaters in the restaurant were going full pelt.

"Had enough of the singing, then?" she asked.

Adrian said, "It's very crowded out there."

"It is, isn't it?" Josephine agreed. "And it's cold," she added as an afterthought, pulling her coat lapels together for effect.

"It's bloody boiling in here," Lord Raversham snapped.

Josephine slapped him lightly on the arm, her amused expression unaltered. "Maybe you have better circulation than me. Mind you, even if it were baking hot I'd be as far away from Pip as I could get at times like this. He gets so tetchy when there's a crowd; I find it's best to stay out of his way." She pointed through the window at the choirmaster, who was looking very serious as he worked. "I wish he'd just relax," she sighed. "Do you want a doughnut?" she asked Graeme.

Graeme looked at the fat ring doughnut. You couldn't see the doughnut itself for sugar.

"It's the last one," Lord Raversham complained under his breath.

Josephine smacked him on the leg. "Don't be a baby." She winked at Graeme. "Go on, have a bite!"

Graeme had to admit that it did look tasty. He picked it up and started to eat. Adrian hadn't been wrong when he said the doughnuts were fabulous.

"Good, eh?" said Josephine, as if she could read Graeme's mind.

He nodded.

Josephine licked her lips. "Where's your friend?" she asked.

"This is an uncle and nephew day out," Adrian told her.

"Oh," she said, her eyes still sparkling in Graeme's direction. "What fun for you. I wouldn't worry; he'll in all likelihood show up before long. It seems like everybody I've spoken to and more besides are coming to see the choir. For some reason people seem to think standing about catching their death is Christmassy."

"More fool them," grumbled Lord Raversham.

Adrian elbowed Graeme, who was in the midst of licking his fingers.

"Yeah, um, sorry about yesterday," said Graeme.

Lord Raversham didn't acknowledge that Graeme had said anything at all.

Outside, the carol was finishing. Josephine sighed. "I suppose they'll expect me to say something now." She hugged herself. "Maybe in a few minutes." She didn't have a few minutes though, because the choirmaster, Pip, turned and beckoned her out. Josephine just hunkered down further in her chair. Pip then scurried in to stand next to the table. He folded his fat arms and stared at her.

"Are you coming, vicar?" he asked.

Graeme looked at Josephine and then at his uncle. She was a vicar? She didn't behave in a very vicar–ish way. Josephine saw his face, wrinkled her nose and giggled. Reaching out, she patted him on the cheek. "He looks so confused," she said to Adrian. "How sweet. There, there," she comforted Graeme, pouting with mock sympathy. "You're perplexed, aren't you, dear? How wonderful!"

"Well?" an irritable Pip asked her. "Are you coming?"

"Of course, of course, of course, of course. Will you excuse me?" she asked. "I have to tend my frozen flock. Come on, old man," she said to Lord Raversham, pulling at a loose fold in his coat. "You can come out as well, pillar of the community that you are."

Lord Raversham said something virtually inaudible that probably wasn't very complimentary; but he closed his book, tucked it under his arm and followed Pip and Josephine outside.

"Next year we're doing this somewhere with central heating," Graeme heard Josephine say. "Or if I win the lottery, Bermuda."

"Come on, let's go and find a tree," Adrian said.

He and Graeme went out to the deserted yard, where there was every sign that there had been Christmas trees galore in the weeks gone by. Pine needles were scattered all over the gravel. There were a few trees left, but they looked pretty pathetic. A lone man sloped out of the shop. He was pulling on a body warmer and scowling, muttering under his breath. He stood off to one side, hugging himself and stamping his feet.

Adrian grimaced as they looked at the meagre pickings. "I suppose this is what comes of leaving things too long," he said. "Come on, let's choose one."

Graeme nodded.

Adrian worried over the trees for ages. There really wasn't that much choice, but Graeme got the impression that his uncle was trying to make a bit of an event of it. Eventually, just as Graeme's fingertips were starting to get numb, the stroppy guy stepped over to them.

"Why don't you try a fake tree?" he suggested, rubbing his hands together. "We've got loads in the shop."

Adrian wasn't sure about that. "I was really after a real one."

"We've got some really good fake ones," the guy said. "Honest."

"What do you think?" Adrian asked Graeme.

"We can have a look," Graeme replied.

"Well, can you hold…" Adrian looked at the two threadbare trees he was currently holding, "… what do you think? This one?" he asked Graeme, holding out the one in his right hand.

"Yes," Graeme agreed. Of the two, it looked the least dead.

"Right, can you hold this one for us?"

The guy took the tree off Adrian.

"We'll go and have a look at the artificial ones, but we may be back!" said Adrian.

The guy smirked. "I'm not expecting a rush."

"Everyone's a comedian," Adrian said as he and Graeme walked across the courtyard into the shop.

It was certainly all decked out for Christmas: everywhere was covered in tinsel; garlands were strewn about; lanterns were hanging from support struts; a happy plastic snowman was sitting outside a pile of flat–pack garden sheds; and festive panpipe music was being played over the speaker system. It seemed a bit odd to Graeme, that anyone would bother putting ribbons on bags of compost, but then he supposed somebody might have wanted one for a (boring) present.

The fake trees were stacked in boxes against one wall. They came in all colours and sizes and just as the assistant had said, there were loads of them. In fact, judging by the quantities left out on show, as well as the stickers reading "MONSTER REDUCTION!!!" and, "50% OFF!!! TODAY!!!" they obviously hadn't sold that well this year. A few had been taken out of their boxes and set up. A few of those few were even almost life–like.

Adrian started looking through them, asking Graeme's opinion at every stage.

"Do you think this one would be too tall?" he asked, pointing at a massive tree, its topmost branches bent over as they hit the polystyrene–tiled ceiling. "You'd think I'd remember the height of the room, wouldn't you?" he said, laughing. The laugh stopped as something over Graeme's shoulder caught his eye. His face froze for a moment and then he turned back to look at the trees and frowned.

"Um… yes, I think that one is too, too, too, um…"

"Tall?" Graeme prompted him.

"Yes, exactly. Too tall."

Graeme looked for what might have disturbed Adrian. Behind him, the shop had filled up. The carollers must have finished singing, because he saw Adam, Archibald and Margaret, who were inspecting a spade and giggling. Other shoppers, their faces showing nothing like goodwill to any man, were knocking against each other like bowling pins in an alley as they made their way through the store, cursing under their breath as they were forced to push past people who had decided to stop for a chat in the middle of the aisle.

Graeme spotted Captain Murgatroyd and Mortimer. They were standing in front of a counter laden with holly wreaths, talking to each other as people moved around them. The Captain caught sight of Graeme and pointed at him, then started barging past everyone. Even the persistent aisle–chatters moved out of his way.

"You!" he said as he neared Graeme, "so you made it back then."

"Yes," said Graeme.

"You got me into a lot of trouble!" the Captain told him, wagging his finger. "Llewellyn was not impressed."

"I'm sorry."

"As you should be!"

"Now, Pop," Mort tried to calm his dad. "Hi, Graeme."

"Hello," said Graeme.

Captain Murgatroyd elbowed Mort in the ribs.

"Hi, Adrian," Mortimer said.

Adrian turned around. He blinked and frowned again, then sort of half–smiled. "Hello," he said, still frowning.

"How are you?" Mort continued.

"Um… fine."

Captain Murgatroyd rolled his eyes and said, "So, I see you are choosing trees?"

"Yes," said Adrian. He scratched his head. "We're choosing a tree."

Mort chuckled, stuffing his hands in his pockets. "You've left that a bit late!"

"So I gather," Adrian said, giving Mort another wry smile in return.

"Which ones are you considering?" Mort asked.

Adrian pointed awkwardly at a couple of the trees. "These I, um, think."

"Right. They look good."

There was a moment's silence while all four of them stood there and Adrian and Mort shuffled their feet.

"They're certainly better than what Pop's got in his sitting room," Mort joked.

Adrian chuckled, but he sounded very nervous to Graeme. His ears were purple.

"Hey! Graeme!"

It was Jim. He ran over, dodging through the smallest gaps in the crowd. He was wearing a beige jumper with a white tee shirt underneath and dark khaki combat trousers that had zippered pockets on the legs. "*I didn't think you'd be out, not after yesterday*," he signed.

"I didn't know you were going to come along, either."

"*Well, it's the choir, you know. We come every year. It's kind of a ritual. Mum says, 'Let's get in the Christmas spirit', Dad says, 'We could just pop to the off licence', she hits him, and then we come here. They're outside, thanking the vicar for finding us, you know, yesterday. She's trying to persuade them to get me to join the choir! Can you believe it?* Hello, Captain. Hello, Mort."

"Here is the other troublemaker," the Captain growled. "You bad boys."

Jim looked a bit guilty, but then his face lit up and he pulled at Graeme's arm. "*Come on,*" he said. "*You won't have seen the maze yet. I'll show it to you.*"

Graeme looked at Adrian. "Do you mind if I …?"

Adrian didn't seem to hear him at first; it was as if he'd been in another world, forgotten who his nephew was.

"Um… sure," he said. "That is, no, no, I don't um, no, go ahead."

Captain Murgatroyd looked all around. "Yes, I suppose I should go and… check my birds are not annoying people… or… something…" he murmured. "I'll leave Mort here to help you pick your tree," he told Adrian. He elbowed Mort again and tramped off.

Adrian and Mort looked at each other, at the trees, at each other very briefly and then back at the trees again. Graeme and Jim left them and made their way out into the gardens.

"What's this maze, then?" Graeme asked Jim once they were outside.

"*It's massive,*" he replied. "*You'll love it!*"

They ran down the hill, past the winter garden; through the bog garden with its pond full of frogs and flies; and past an old, white–painted Victorian house that served as tearooms where a mother was wiping jam from her toddler's mouth while her husband jiggled a baby in his arms.

It was necessary to go down a path lined with marble statues to get to the maze. The statues, of supposedly famous men and women pointing or peering grandly into the middle–distance, were well weather–worn, cracked and discoloured. This part of the gardens was deserted.

The maze was constructed from towering stalks of yellow and black and green bamboo. The stalks had been bent over to form an archway of sorts at the entrance, where a sign read, "For Jocelyn".

Jim didn't pause. He ran straight in.

The bamboo was thick and massive, planted in tight clumps and forming virtually solid walls that were about ten feet high. They ran along the passageways, darting left and right. Jim seemed to get more excited each time they ran into a dead end. Graeme couldn't understand why they were getting so lost. He tugged at the back of Jim's coat to get him to stop.

"Haven't you been in here before?"

"*Yes*," replied Jim, "*but Calamara's normally with me. She's much better at finding her way than I am!*"

Graeme wished Jim had told him that earlier. They ran on, with Graeme taking the lead, but it turned out that his sense of direction wasn't any better than Jim's. Having been thwarted for the fifth time, Graeme finally decided that he couldn't run any more and they slowed to a walk. Graeme thought he'd take the opportunity to ask Jim whether they were going to try and get back on the isle.

"*Fat chance of that now*," Jim said, looking rueful. "*I thought we could try going down to the beach today, see if Calamara's key opens the boat cave, but as we were all under house arrest... Well, we can do that later on, as long as Calamara's been let out, too!*"

They rounded a corner and came face to face with a small girl with shoulder length blonde hair, wearing a red cardigan over a simple white dress. She was standing in the middle of the path, hands in her pockets.

"Hello," she said. "What are you doing?"

Graeme and Jim looked at each other.

"We're trying to get to the centre of the maze," Jim said.

"You've got a funny voice," she told him.

"I'm deaf," Jim said, signing it at the same time.

"Oh," she said. She laughed. "You're the bad boys."

The bad boys didn't know what to make of that.

The girl's eyes narrowed. "I heard what your friend said about wanting to get on the isle. Are you spies?"

"We want to get to the centre of the maze," Jim said, ignoring her question, "because that's what you're meant to do."

She sniffed. "My family are worried about spies," she said. She leaned closer. "There are people about," she whispered, "people who are after me."

"Like who?"

"I don't know!" she shouted, stamping her foot on the ground. "If I knew, the police would arrest them and they wouldn't be about. I want to know if you're them. Are you the spies?"

"We're not," Jim told her.

"Spies would say that," she said. "I'm very important, you know. My name's Fanny Lennox. I won a prize for judo," she boasted, "back in Delhi. My teacher, Mr Seth, says I am as deadly as an angry scorpion! And that was before I started the lessons! So watch it! I'm here to stay with my grandfather. He does anything I ask."

"I'm Jim," said Jim, "And this is Graeme. Hello."

"Well, it's lucky you bumped into me. I know the way to the centre of the maze. My grandfather built it. Do you want to follow me?"

"Okay," Jim said.

"I hope you can keep up," she told them. "I'm the fastest runner in my class."

She whirled around and sped off. Graeme and Jim ran after her. It took about fifteen minutes of running back and forth before they finally realised that she didn't, in fact, have a clue where she was going, either.

"Don't be silly," she said when they confronted her. "Of course I know the way. It's just a *very* big maze," she explained. "It takes a while to get anywhere."

"All right," Jim said. "Lay on, Macduff."

Fanny frowned. "What?" she asked.

"I mean get going!" Jim said.

"All right, Mister Fancy Pants," said Fanny, and ran off again.

Seeing as neither Graeme nor Jim had any better ideas, they continued to follow her. As it turned out Graeme was quite grateful that Fanny was in front, as she was the one who tumbled over Calamara as they ran out of yet another dead–end.

"Clever," Calamara sneered as Graeme helped Fanny get up off the ground.

"*Hi Calamara*!" Jim signed. "*What are you doing here?*"

"Mum and Dad, you know…" she said. "They just had to see the choir. They didn't even like singing before they moved here." She fixed Graeme with a stare. "I saw your uncle and Mortimer talking, or not talking, actually. They mostly seemed to be looking at their feet. When I could get a word out of them they said you'd come down here, and I know what you're like in this thing," she said to Jim, "so I thought I'd be *nice* and come and see that you got out okay."

"*I did once have to spend a night here*," Jim confessed, grinning sheepishly.

"That's very good of you, but *I* was just taking them to the centre of the maze," Fanny announced.

Calamara screwed up her face. "Who's this?" she asked.

"I'm Fanny Lennox," Fanny told her. "I'm staying with my grandfather, Lord Raversham. And I'm investigating *strange people*."

"Oh." Calamara was unimpressed. "You've come to the right place. You won't find any shortage of strange people around here." She looked pointedly at Graeme. What a wonderful girl she was.

Fanny missed that entirely.

"Never mind," Calamara said. "So you think you're heading to the centre of the maze?"

"Yes!" said Fanny.

"Well, you're doing a splendid job," Calamara congratulated her, "because if you turn that corner you'll find you're right by the entrance. *Where you came in*," she stressed.

Jim and Fanny looked at each other and both of them went a bit red in the face.

"Come along," said Calamara. "You want to get to the centre?"

Fanny nodded furiously. "My grandfather will probably think I have been kidnapped!"

"Yes, I'll bet he's started the party already," Calamara said, under her breath. "Come with me, then."

They were only another minute or so before they reached the centre of the maze now that they had Calamara to guide them. At every turn, Fanny kept on saying, "Oh, yes," and, "Oh, you're going *this* way."

"If you look to the left you should be able to see the top of the gazebo," Calamara informed them, sounding so confident Graeme could have strangled her; but she was right: a domed roof was clearly visible above the wavering tops of the bamboo. "The gazebo marks the centre of the maze. The way in is just around here," she said.

"That's right, well done," Fanny agreed.

Calamara growled.

"*Do you think we should get between them?*" Jim asked.

"*No*!" Graeme signed back.

They all froze as they heard a voice.

"Can we start now?"

"Not until we're all here, Summer," Graeme heard Mathilda say.

Fanny clapped her hands together. "That's my aunty!" she whispered, "and my other aunty! Let's see what they're talking about!"

She crouched down and parted the stalks to peer through. The rest of them did the same.

They were looking into the central courtyard of the maze. There was the gazebo on one side. Its doors were wide open; it was empty.

Opposite the gazebo and separated from it by a long, shallow pool was a gleaming white statue of a woman playing the flute. White benches were placed all around the pool. Every adult member of the Raversham family that Graeme had met so far was there, apart from Lord Raversham. Michael was sitting on a bench by himself, surrounded by a collection of shopping bags. He was staring at the statue. His wife was pacing back and forth in front of him. Harvest Acre was on the next bench along, lying flat on his back with his feet up. Summer Rain was on the other side, sitting on the statue's plinth, leaning back with her eyes closed; and Sigourney was sitting nearby, wrapped up in woolly scarves. She was wearing a white coat and a furry white hat.

"Why did we have to come here, of all places?" she asked.

"Because we need to talk about Father," Mathilda said, "and this is the one place I'm sure he won't come."

Everyone looked at the statue.

"That's my Grandma," hissed Fanny. "She's dead."

"And how is our Father, who art not in heaven?" a new voice asked.

A young man with a black goatee, dressed in dark trousers and a black turtleneck sweater was standing in the doorway of the gazebo. Exactly how he'd arrived there was unclear.

"Is there another way to get into the courtyard?" Graeme asked Jim.

Jim shrugged. *"There must be."*

"Intentional," Mathilda greeted the stranger. "You finally made it, then."

"Intentional!" cried Sigourney, rushing over to hug her brother, entangling him in scarves. "How are you? Are you all right?"

"I'm fine, Sigourney," Intentional assured her. He had to put a fair bit of effort into pushing her away from him. Sigourney rested one hand momentarily on his cheek before returning to her seat.

"Of course he's fine," Mathilda snapped. "Monsters, indeed! He was just drunk."

Intentional glowered at her. "I'm sorry I'm late," he apologised, though it didn't sound like he meant it. He ambled his way to the statue and sat next to Summer Rain. "I haven't missed anything, have I?"

"We were waiting for you," said Mathilda.

"And now you can suffer along with the rest of us, brother dear," Summer remarked without opening her eyes. "Look upon it as a penance for being such a show off."

"Me? A show off?"

"For using that thing," said Summer, pointing at the gazebo. She still had her eyes closed. "You always have to rub it in, don't you?"

"Oh. I can't help it if I was one of the trusted few."

"The trusted two, you mean. I always understood about Uriah. He was always freakishly tidy, but you..."

Intentional grinned at his sister. "The youngest always gets the easiest ride; and never forget: you got the boat."

"There is that, yes," Summer Rain admitted, "but I have to share." Her eyes swept towards Harvest Acre, who yawned, stretched and then gave her a lazy smile. He closed his eyes. "So good," he said, "having all the Wastrels together again…"

*

Lord Raversham had christened his three youngest children "The Wastrels" at the onset of their adolescence. Harvest Acre, Summer Rain and Intentional had initially riled against it. To single them out was, to their mind, spectacularly unfair. Even if you discounted Michael, Sigourney and Penelope (all of whom Lord Raversham declared were as close to having "proper jobs" as they were ever likely to get), Finlay and Uriah were still there to consider.

Finlay loved his life of performance poetry but there was little doubt that he would have starved in his garret above the Café du Plume in Paris if it weren't for the family fortune. By comparison, travelling to the back of beyond, seeking out lost species and putting one's life in danger in order to befriend and document savage, sometimes cannibalistic tribes might have been seen as quite a worthy cause, but Uriah had a tendency to wait until after dark, purloin sacred tribal statues and other artefacts and then scarper before the affronted tribes and their poison darts (not to mention knives and forks) could catch him. The authorities considered this to be theft; Lord Raversham considered that it was not a respectable line of work. If you were rich and wanted to be a thief then you made your living stealing diamonds and other precious gems from the well–to–do who frequented the high class beach resorts on the continent, his reasoning went.

The thing Harvest, Summer and Intentional missed was that everyone else in the family was *busy* with something. They, on the other hand, had a skill for idleness that could almost be idolised. They had themselves chauffeured over (or, where applicable, under) land, sea or air to wherever they pleased and once there they sat back and let life drift by. If they had put as much effort into something productive as they did into doing absolutely nothing they could have conquered the world.

The name, therefore, couldn't be shaken, no matter how hard they tried (which was never that hard: too much effort, you see). Much as they hated it, like any name used over time, "The Wastrels" eventually stuck and even they came to use it when referring to themselves.

*

"How long has it been?" Harvest Acre asked. "It must be a year…"

"Or more," said Intentional.

"I do wish you wouldn't run yourselves down by using that derogatory name," said Mathilda. Running people down, destroying their self–confidence (and being oblivious to her own nature, Lord Raversham would add), that was her job. "And I think," she continued, "given the circumstances in which we have come together, a little less frivolity would be appropriate! Father – "

"He's not your father, actually," said Harvest Acre.

"Ooh, don't upset her!" said Intentional, pretending to cower as Mathilda shot him a look that could kill.

"He's better than my father ever was!" Mathilda announced, her voice quavering. "You lot don't realise how lucky you all are! You'll miss him when he's gone! We need to talk about this!"

"What is there to talk about?" Harvest Acre asked her.

"You always want to talk about everything," Summer Rain complained. "Father's been declared nearly dead so many times that everything's planned to the *n*th degree. Kendall will take care of everything, he always does. There really isn't anything to talk about. You just have a morbid fascination with Father's health."

Intentional lifted his foot and started to pick at the sole of his shoe. "He's not really dying is he?"

"He'll probably outlive us all," said Harvest Acre. He didn't sound at all concerned.

"Exactly!" cried Sigourney, her voice sounding a bit desperate. "Exactly!"

Michael sighed, still staring at the statue. "You know, I could have been a flautist, but my teacher said I had the wrong lips."

Everyone stopped talking and looked at him. Sigourney put her hand to her bosom and gazed pityingly at her brother.

Harvest Acre opened one eye. "It was about the only instrument you didn't play, Michael," he said.

"That is," said Summer Rain, "play in the loosest sense of the word. Every now and then you'd give it another go, wouldn't you, Mickey? I always thought you were hilarious with that oboe. The triangle was your one great success, wasn't it?"

Michael was blushing. He was focusing on the ground, not looking anyone in the eye.

"What about the opera?" asked Harvest Acre, scratching his chest. "Or was it a concerto? Weren't you composing a concerto?"

"I was so happy when you found music, Michael," said Sigourney. "I remember hoping that it may prove to be your calling. I'd forgotten the concerto! You were always hiding your light under a bushel! Have you kept it? It could be a legacy for you to pass on to future generations!"

Michael's shoulders had slumped. "It was only a song..."

"So modest! You used to run away, didn't you? I remember now! You'd run away as soon as we mentioned it! You were always so quiet!"

"Staying quiet was the sensible option if you ask me," said Intentional. "Father never went on at Michael like he did the rest of us, did he?"

The Ravershams all nodded, lost in a common memory.

"Michael knew when to abandon shilly–shallying with aimless pursuits, unlike the rest of you," said Mathilda. "He always had both feet on the ground. Fath – Llewellyn, um, Lord Raversham – he was just pulling you all into line."

"I'll kind of miss Dad's lectures when he does pop off," said Intentional.

Sigourney blazed back to life, picking up where she'd left off before Michael's interruption. "There's more danger of us popping off before him! You of all people should know that! We're marked for death!"

"That's a bit strong, Sigourney," said Harvest Acre.

"We've seen neither hide nor hair of Uriah or Finlay in weeks!" Sigourney shrieked. "Nobody has! In this day and age that can mean only one thing! And what about Intentional? He knows! Tell us, Intentional! Tell us everything that happened!"

"It's all a bit of a blur, now," said Intentional. "But I can't forget that thing, that creature. Every time I close my eyes I see it staring back at me, that gaping, drooling mouth."

He shivered.

Nobody said anything in reply to that. They all looked at each other, avoiding Intentional's gaze. Well, everyone apart from Sigourney was avoiding his gaze. She was nodding furiously.

"I know it sounds far fetched," said Intentional, reading their thoughts.

"Far fetched or not," Sigourney wailed, "something is going on! It's undeniable! And the police won't do anything! You can't have heard! They think it's one of us! They think we're after Father's inheritance!"

"That's a bit off. We're all richer than rich, after all," Intentional pointed out.

Harvest Acre squinted at his younger brother. "Yes, well, they think one of us wants to be richer than rich… than rich."

"And they're going to wait for the last one of us to be left standing and they think then they'll have their man!" Sigourney exclaimed. "Imagine! This is what twentieth century policing has come to!"

"It's just lazy," yawned Summer Rain. "Typical Roberta. She hasn't changed since school."

"If we look at this calmly, no offence, Sigourney, but you are a bit excitable, it isn't even guaranteed that anybody's after anybody," Harvest said. "Uriah's probably just lost in the rainforest again. You know what he's like when he thinks he's found a new species of tree frog."

"I hate to speak ill of a fellow family member," announced Mathilda, "but I have to say that Finlay isn't one to keep in touch at the best of times, either. And we all know about his, his *enthusiasm* for good wine."

"Don't you criticise my family! Finlay is a tortured soul and a prescient poet!" Sigourney shouted. She pointed a finger at Mathilda. "I'm keeping my eye on you! You're at the isle every opportunity you get, fawning over our Father, poisoning him against us! You hover over him like the Angel of Death!"

Mathilda looked shocked. "Michael and I are just more local than the rest of you! We don't go gallivanting off around the world!"

"*Galivanting?*" shrieked Sigourney.

"Mathilda's right about Fin, though, Sigourney," said Intentional, holding his arms above his head and stretching, "and she may well be right about me."

"I can't believe you're all sitting there dismissing what's happened!" Sigourney continued. "What about Penelope, then? What about Penelope and Harrison? Why would they leave poor little Stephanie?"

"That's me," said Fanny.

"Why *wouldn't* they leave poor little Stephanie, is what I'd ask," said Summer Rain. She and Intentional leaned against each other and laughed.

Graeme looked down at Fanny. She was humming a little tune to herself; she didn't seem bothered that she was being insulted; either that or she simply wasn't paying attention to what they were saying about her.

Sigourney put a hand to her forehead. "How cruel! When I think of that poor little girl… how she may never see her parents again… I worry how it will affect her, I really do worry…"

"That sad little wretch!" snorted Mathilda. "She couldn't pick that Victorian throwback of a father, or Penelope for that matter, out of a line–up, they spend so little time with her. It's no wonder she's as odd as she is, being passed from one inadequate nanny to another. And when they can't find a nanny, she's packed up and sent here! I'd imagine she knows Raversham Isle better than her own home! I wonder why they ever bothered having a child at all!"

There was an ear–splitting scream and before anyone could stop her, Fanny ran around the corner to her family. Graeme watched with eyes bulging as Fanny launched herself at Mathilda, flying through the air with her arms stretched out in front of her, her hands forming claws. Landing on Mathilda's shoulders like a little devil, she proceeded to scratch and bite whatever she could. Everyone, with the exception of Michael (who moved the bags out of the way of the scuffle) raced to help. There was a lot of shouting and even some pleading before they managed to prise Fanny's fingers from Mathilda, whose coat was fast becoming little more than a tattered ruin. It took four adults to separate the two of them.

"You see?" Mathilda clutched at her heart. "They've managed to raise a delinquent! A savage!"

Fanny growled at her, eyes blazing. Intentional and Summer Rain were holding her arms. Fanny still seemed mad but she wasn't straining to get away from them or anything.

"Michael," said Mathilda, "hand me one of my new coats."

Michael silently reached into a bag and passed a heavy, dark brown suede coat to his wife.

"It's just as well I went shopping, isn't it?" Mathilda said to him in a conversational manner as she shrugged herself into the coat. Michael didn't reply.

"Fanny," said Intentional, "are you going to behave if we let you go?"

"Of course she will," a familiar voice called out from directly behind where Graeme, Jim and Calamara were hidden. The three of them span round and found themselves face to face with Roberta. A man in a long, green coat was standing beside her.

"James, Calamara and Graeme," said Roberta, a stern look on her face. Her arms were folded. "I see you have a new recruit."

"Who's out there?" Sigourney called.

"Come along all of you," Roberta continued, herding the trio round and into the courtyard. The man in the green coat walked to Fanny. "What are you up to, little lady?"

Fanny looked down and twisted from side to side. "Nothing, Benjamin," she said meekly.

"Those horrible children!" Mathilda shouted, pointing at Graeme, Jim and Calamara. "Again! They're back again! What were they doing, officer?"

"They appeared to be watching whatever you were up to," said Roberta.

"Look, Michael! You're always on about them being children, having innocent fun! Try defending them now! They've been spying on our private conversation!"

Michael didn't say anything.

"Stephanie!" Sigourney shrieked. "Were you with these children?"

Fanny nodded.

Sigourney bore down on Mathilda. "You take back what you said about my sister! It's clear now, these ruffians are seducing precious little Stephanie with their evil ways! Poor mite! Benjamin! What are you paid for, if not to look after my niece? Penelope told me that you came highly recommended!"

"I've…" Benjamin started to say.

"Highly recommended?" Mathilda asked, interrupting him. "And he can't even manage to keep an eleven year old girl under control? Disgraceful!"

Benjamin wasn't listening. He didn't appear interested in anything they had to say, which stopped them in their tracks.

"That's a good trick," Roberta said to him out of the corner of her mouth. Benjamin rubbed his eyes.

"What's a good trick?" he asked her.

Summer held up a welcoming hand. "You're looking healthier," she said to Graeme.

"Well, isn't this nice, all of us together?" said Intentional.

"I'm sorry for the intrusion," Roberta apologised, when it became clear that nobody else appeared about to say anything. "I'll get these three out of your hair. Come along," she said to them, "let's go and see what Lord Raversham has to say about this."

"Father's here?" Sigourney asked.

"He shouldn't be out in this weather!" Mathilda exclaimed.

"I… agree, Mathilda," said Sigourney, astonished to find that she and Mathilda were, for once, of one mind.

"He arrived a while ago," said Roberta. "When I left him he was trying to kill Johan Murgatroyd's corncrake. I warned that I might have to arrest him. The corncrake is an endangered species, after all. I did the course, you know."

*

All interested parties had gathered in the yard where the last few Christmas trees were spending their final days. The Ravershams, along with Benjamin, Roberta and Josephine, were standing behind Graeme, Jim, Calamara and Fanny. Captain Murgatroyd, Mort, Adrian, Jim's parents, and a smart looking man and woman who Graeme assumed were Calamara's mum and dad, were to one side. There was a small boy by Calamara's mum. He was clinging to her leg.

Adrian didn't look happy.

Graeme felt like he was on trial.

"Why me?" asked Lord Raversham, pacing up and down between the two groups. "What," he asked, "is so fascinating about my island and my family that you can't leave me alone?"

"You can't really blame them, Father," said Michael.

"I don't know why you stick up for them."

Josephine coughed, weaving her way forward until she was standing directly behind Graeme. "Michael does have a point, Llewellyn," she said. "Sometimes you're your own worst enemy, keeping everything so secret. They are children, after all, and your reclusive nature does make you and your blessed island something of a mystery."

"Reclusive nature?" Lord Raversham was apoplectic. "Where do people get this from? I'm not a recluse! I get out! What am I doing here if I don't get out?"

"Perhaps you should look upon this as an opportunity," said Josephine.

"An opportunity? What kind of opportunity?"

"Take them to the island."

"You're mad!"

"Take them home, Llewellyn," Josephine said again. "Take them home and let them see where you live. Give them a sneak preview of the preparations for the party. Once they've seen that your castle is nothing more than a mouldy old pile of stone – "

"Well thank you very much," said Lord Raversham.

" – once they've seen it's nothing special, that should be the end of your problem. Dispel the myth," Josephine finished with a flourish of her hand.

"That's a terrible idea," said Mathilda.

"Actually, I think it's quite sensible," said Roberta.

"Quite the best idea anybody's had in an age!" agreed Michael, winking at Graeme. Mathilda looked at her husband as if he were a traitor to the cause.

"They can stay the night!" said Fanny. She jumped up and down.

"What?" Lord Raversham was aghast at the thought of that.

"Oh, please, Grandpa," Fanny pleaded, running up and pulling on Lord Raversham's sleeve. "Pleasepleaseplease! I don't have anybody to play with!"

"I don't think so."

Fanny stamped her foot. "Grandpa! I do things for *you*!"

Lord Raversham chewed his tongue and then cursed. "What about the gardener's son? I thought I'd arranged for him to spend some time with you."

"Dickie's boring," said Fanny.

"Oh," said Lord Raversham. He shook his head. "How did we get on to the topic of them sleeping over? I haven't even agreed that they should visit yet, anyway."

"Do any of you have objections?" Roberta asked, turning to Adrian and Jim and Calamara's parents.

"No objections here!" said Jim's mum, rather too quickly.

Calamara's parents didn't appear to care one way or the other. Graeme didn't suppose they could have stopped their daughter doing whatever she wanted in any case.

"I don't know," said Adrian. "Since Graeme's been here, we've spent so little time together… and I don't want him to get into any more trouble."

"This is to keep him *out* of trouble," said Josephine.

"Like we're going to pay any attention to you," Roberta, highly amused, said to Graeme's uncle. "You're behaving like a new parent! Talk about taking your responsibilities seriously!"

Jim's mum linked her arm with Adrian's. "If you had any experience in the parenting game," she said, "you'd have his bags packed already!"

"Well, I suppose…" said Adrian, though he still sounded unsure.

"I'll be fine," Graeme said.

"We'll look after him," said Jim, laying a hand on Graeme's back.

"The boy doesn't want to be spending a dull evening with you when he could be gallivanting around with his friends," said Josephine.

"And it'll give you some time for other things," said Roberta. Her face was alive with mischief as she looked meaningfully at Mort.

Captain Murgatroyd caught on to what she meant. "Excellent idea! You can both stop moping at opposite ends of the bay and actually talk to each other for once!"

Adrian and Mort exchanged a quick, shy glance.

"Excuse me," said Lord Raversham, "have we forgotten that I haven't agreed to any of this yet?"

"You will, Llewellyn," said Josephine. She put her hands on Graeme's shoulders, gently so he wouldn't be alarmed.

"No, I won't!"

"Quite right, too!" said Mathilda. "We don't want them hanging around with poor Stephanie! They're a bad influence! She attacked me, you know!" She pointed at Fanny, as if Lord Raversham wouldn't have recognised his own granddaughter.

Lord Raversham considered first Mathilda, and then Fanny. "Did she really?" he asked. He winced as he crouched to look her in the eyes. He held her chin in his hand. "It is very wrong to attack people without warning," he said.

"She did scream beforehand," Jim pointed out.

Lord Raversham's face brightened. "Really?" he asked, his attention never leaving Fanny. "A battle cry, eh? Well, then, I think that's all fair and above board," he decided, straightening up. "You can't complain if you were given fair warning, Mathilda."

Mathilda looked so angry that Graeme thought her head was about to launch itself into orbit. "Of course, Fath… I mean, Llewellyn," she eventually managed to say, her voice quiet but a bit unsteady, like she was trying to keep a check on her emotions.

Lord Raversham beamed at her.

"So they can come?" Fanny asked, worming her way under Lord Raversham's arm. Lord Raversham's expression was almost tender as he looked down at her. He then looked at Graeme, then Jim, then Calamara, then back to Graeme. "No," he said.

Fanny took a breath, preparing for round two; but just before she could speak, Lord Raversham coughed. "I mean yes," he said. He cleared his throat again. "For the night? I suppose so. Yes, yes of course."

CHAPTER SEVEN
Raversham Castle

Lord Raversham pointed to the left. "Those," he intoned, "are the forbidden towers. You are not to go there under any circumstances."

Everybody swung their gaze towards the thin towers that he was indicating. They were the ones you could see from anywhere in Port Stilton, linked by a curving flight of stairs. Scaffolding supported them both. If he'd been any closer, Graeme thought, looking up at their spires would have made him feel at best dizzy, at worst he would have fallen over; and wouldn't Calamara have just loved that?

"Or go there," Lord Raversham said, apparently changing his mind, "I don't care. Just take a duster and broom if you do. They haven't been cleaned in an age."

Jim, whose eyes had lit up at the word "forbidden", looked disappointed.

Graeme, Jim and Calamara were finally inside the castle grounds and crunching up the gravel drive towards the front door of the castle itself, lugging their suitcases along with them. Graeme, dressed in jeans with a blue jumper pulled over a black, yellow and brown striped collarless shirt, was beside Lord Raversham, with Jim, Calamara, Fanny and Roberta. Benjamin and all Lord Raversham's children were trailing behind. Michael and Mathilda's kids were even further back, walking in a row like robots. To either side of the path were splendid lawns with fountains dotted at irregular intervals. Anywhere there was a clear patch of land people were busy erecting tents and tables.

Banners reading "Merry Christmas" and "Season's Greetings" were being strung between the trunks of massive, gnarled trees; any that were deciduous also had people up in the denuded branches, busily weaving multicoloured bunting.

Sigourney caught her breath as they passed an ornate fountain which emptied into a round pool. Mottled orangey–white fish were swimming in there, weaving in and out of the weeds. She wasn't gasping at the pool, though. She pointed repeatedly with one finger at an imposing stone stage that was standing to their left. It was taller than a two–storey house, with a grey stone, flat–fronted roof that had the Raversham crest as its centrepiece. The crest stood out, not least because rather than being painted, it held a real, really big, gleaming sword (hopefully well clipped in place), and the wolves chasing round the outside actually moved, making a *tick–tock* sound. Graeme half–expected a cuckoo to pop out at any moment.

"It's still here!" Sigourney cried out. She looked ecstatic. "Daddy! I thought you were going to demolish it!"

Lord Raversham grunted. "I should have," he said. "It's unstable, and a bloody eyesore."

"Oh, no! I have so many happy memories of that stage," said Sigourney. "I created all the costumes, discovered my talent for design, on that very spot!"

"Many would say that'd be reason enough to raze it to the ground. All I remember," Lord Raversham said, "is Jocelyn forcing me to sit out here in all weathers watching you lot prance about. At least Michael had the sense to stay out of it, apart from when you dragged him in to play the violin during the performance of … 'All Fair's Foul', wasn't it?" He paused. "I never did get Murgatroyd to refund me the money for those so–called music lessons. I wonder what he spent the money on? It certainly wasn't on his boat."

Sigourney didn't pay any attention to her father. Instead, she sagged on one hip slightly, put a hand on her heart and let out a sigh. "Such happy days!"

The front door of the castle made an imposing entrance, constructed of heavy–looking dark wood, fortified with equally sturdy iron bars and bolts. It was set into a recess in the castle walls. The walls were knobbly, made of ancient grey–white stone. Though not as tall as the not–so–forbidden towers, they still soared skyward. Looking left to right from the entrance, a keep marked one corner, a fat turret the other.

Roberta turned to Lord Raversham. "Well, you've made it home," she said. "Unless there's anything else you need, I ought to be getting back. Pip Thornton wants to talk to me; he wants to complain about something."

"That choirmaster complains about everything and anything," said Lord Raversham. "What is it this time?"

"Oh, he was awake in the night with his 'troubles' and saw some people moving on the beach."

Jim elbowed Graeme in the ribs.

Roberta continued: "They were looking suspicious, he says. I told him to come to the station and I'd take a statement." She screwed up her face. "I'm in for a fun afternoon."

Lord Raversham pulled her to one side. "Not that I'm worried, but see if you can't find at least some news of where my children are," he quietly reminded her.

"I haven't forgotten about them."

"Good."

"I'll be off, then," Roberta said. She turned and walked back the way they'd come. She glanced at Graeme. "See you. And behave!"

As she departed, the front door opened and Lord Raversham's butler came striding out.

"My Lord," he said, inclining his head to Lord Raversham.

"Kendall," said Lord Raversham, a sly smile on his lips. "You're slipping. I escaped."

"If it pleases you to imagine so, sir."

"Hello, Bertrand!" Fanny squealed. "Look! I've got some friends!"

"So I… see," said the butler. He looked questioningly at Lord Raversham.

"Don't ask," Lord Raversham replied. "These three will be staying the night. Put them on the tenth floor."

"Of course," Kendall agreed. He turned to Fanny. "Miss, Richard asked me to let you know that he would be in the kitchen for the afternoon, helping with the baking, should you wish to visit him."

Fanny made a face. "He's so boring."

"Why don't you run along there?" Lord Raversham suggested. "Go and see if you can't get under Tatum's feet. She'll love having four more helpers. I have things to see to here."

"I'm sure we'll manage without you getting involved, sir," Kendall told him. "You need your rest before tomorrow night."

"Why?" asked Lord Raversham. "I always spend the whole evening in my rooms. I never actually make an appearance. Do you think I'm going to break with tradition and go disco dancing?"

Kendall didn't answer that.

Lord Raversham was cheering up. "You'd never think we've been doing this for – how many years it is now? It must be forty–odd," he told anyone who cared to listen. It still seemed the old man was avoiding looking Graeme's way. "Something always goes wrong at the last minute," he continued. "It's almost a tradition. Somehow it just doesn't feel right unless we have at least one person running around like a headless chicken."

"Well, this time there's really nothing to worry you, my Lord," said Kendall. "There are a few issues with the Ferris wheel, but that's all."

Lord Raversham didn't look very enthusiastic. "Doesn't sound like the sort of thing I'd be any good with," he said.

"Indeed not. As I suggested, maybe you should consider retiring for the afternoon."

"I was thinking more of visiting the wine tent."

"You really should do as you're told, Father!" Sigourney called out.

Lord Raversham looked at Kendall and rolled his eyes. "Tell you what, take this lot." He waved his hand vaguely at his family. "They could do with the exercise and it means they can keep an eye on one another, in case one of them *is* trying to bump the others off."

There were moans of protest from the Ravershams.

"But Father, I was going to take afternoon tea!" complained Sigourney.

Lord Raversham rounded on his daughter. "You were going to watch that soap opera, more like."

Sigourney cast her eyes downward for a second before replying. "*The Wind Blows Warm* could never be described as a mere soap opera."

"And it's just getting good," Intentional added.

Lord Raversham shook his head. "Not you too," he moaned. "That thing was on the radio when I was a lad and it was a right dose of tripe back then. How it ever got on television, how it keeps going, is beyond me."

"Twenty million people can't be wrong, Dad," said Summer Rain. "And in any case, *you* might not need to, but I need to relax."

"All you do is relax," snapped Lord Raversham, "you *and* your brother."

"Do you mean me? Why am *I* getting pulled into this?" whined Harvest Acre.

"If you all think you've come home to lounge all day in front of the goggle box then you've got another think coming," Lord Raversham said to his children. "Helping out will do you good."

Intentional grinned and pulled at Summer Rain's hair. She punched him right back. Graeme noticed that Adam, Archibald and Margaret had already escaped.

Fanny laughed. "Can we go now, Grandpa?"

"Of course," said Lord Raversham.

"Are you sure that's a good idea, Father?" pleaded Mathilda.

Lord Raversham's eyes went dead. "Shut. Up."

"Please take heed of my advice just this once," Mathilda persisted. "They're troublemakers, all three! They're insolent and they flout every rule! I don't know what possessed you to bring them here! I suppose you have your reasons and you don't have to explain them to us, but now they are here don't let them go unsupervised!"

"Michael!" Lord Raversham shouted. "If you don't keep your wife quiet I shall have her gagged."

"Of course, Father," agreed Michael, all the while shifting the bags and bags of shopping he was carrying from one hand to the other. He didn't make it clear which option he would go for: keeping her quiet or allowing her to be gagged.

"Don't worry, Mathilda," said Benjamin. He put a hand to his mouth and yawned. "I'll make sure they behave."

"That's so reassuring," replied Mathilda, a sarcastic smile on her face.

"Leave your cases here," Kendall told Graeme, Jim and Calamara. "I'll see that they get taken to your rooms."

"Don't think I won't know what you're up to, Fanny," said Benjamin. "I have eyes everywhere."

"Yes, Benjamin," Fanny sang, before grabbing Graeme's hand and pulling him along with her. Her touch shocked him a little.

They ran through the front door and into the cavernous hallway of the castle. A huge staircase that led to the upper floors was directly in front of them. Towering, bushy Christmas trees stood to either side of it, festooned with lights, figurines, baubles and tinsel; and a shield bearing the Raversham crest was suspended high above their heads.

Stained glass windows were set into every wall, depicting all kinds of scenes: there were knights fighting in front of crowds; kings and queens on thrones with people celebrating; kings and queens being beheaded with people celebrating more. Light spilled through the windows, casting kaleidoscopic patterns on the floor. There were gleaming suits of armour; bright tapestries hanging from the ceiling; thick white candles on stately iron holders with long knobbly wax stalactites trailing to the stone floor. It was exactly like a castle should be; and completely unlike all those cold, draughty ruins that Graeme had been dragged round by his parents. You could believe a king would live in Raversham Castle.

The front door burst open and Mathilda strode past them and up the grand staircase. The light streaming through the windows created a halo around her. Michael hobbled along behind, straining under the weight of the packages.

"I need to bathe my feet," Mathilda was saying. "Did you hear how your father spoke to me? He's clearly deteriorating. You should try and talk to him again; we ought to be in a room that's closer to his. It's not right, that we should be tucked away in that tower. What if he needs us? I love your brothers and sisters, I really do, but sometimes I doubt they have his best interests at heart. Michael, once you've seen me to our room you should go back outside and help. Don't leave them alone to talk about us behind our backs." She paused, turned and looked down her nose at the children.

"I don't know what you urchins are up to," she said, "but remember this: I know the kind of miscreants you are; I know the kind of wicked deeds you contemplate. Despite my warnings, Lord Raversham has allowed you into his home. I hope you will not abuse his trust. Considering your assorted dysfunctional backgrounds, I realise it will be nigh on impossible for you to ignore your natural instincts… If you were children of mine you would have been brought up properly but as it is…" She left the sentence hanging, regarding them from on high like she was a heavenly angel and they weren't worthy to be in her presence. They didn't say anything.

She breathed in, her nostrils twitching. "Lord Raversham is a great and brave man, but he is not a well man. He is frail; he is old; he is dying."

Fanny squeaked.

Mathilda was demented. "If his condition worsens, or, God forbid, he dies as a result of any bad behaviour on your part, I promise you will regret it for the rest of your days."

She stood on the spot and stared, waiting for some kind of response. Jim just seemed confused. Calamara and Graeme stared right back at her. Only Fanny, her hand held over her mouth, seemed affected by what had been said.

"Insolent brats," Mathilda spat. Then she clucked her tongue at her husband and resumed her march up the stairs. Unusually, Michael didn't look at Graeme even once as he passed by, but then he did have all the bags to manage. He was staring straight ahead, right at his wife's back.

"Are you going to go and see your friend now?" Calamara asked Fanny.

Fanny looked at her as if she were mad. "No! I've got you! I'm the hostess. I'm going to show you to your rooms."

"You know," said Calamara in honeyed tones, "I don't think it's very polite to ignore a friend just because you've met some new ones."

Graeme and Jim looked at each other. This didn't sound much like the Calamara they knew.

"*What are you up to*?" Jim asked her.

"*Shut up*," Calamara's fingers flickered.

Fanny was looking up at the ceiling, far above. She swung back and forth on one heel. "I suppose you're right," she said, grudgingly accepting Calamara's advice. "But you'll have to come with me," she added. "I can't leave you alone."

Calamara's face hardened in annoyance; it was only for a second, though, as she then went all glassy–eyed. "Well, let's go then!"

So Fanny ran to the left, followed by the others, and down a short but steep flight of spiral stairs (which pleased Calamara no end) that were lit by flaming torches. From there they went along a narrow corridor towards a heavy oak door. A cloud of steam billowed out into the corridor as Fanny and Jim heaved the door open.

"Shut the bloody door!" someone shouted from inside. "I don't want the castle smelling of cabbage!"

They hurried through and shut the door behind them.

They found themselves in the largest kitchen Graeme had ever seen. A long table stretched from one end of the room to the other with a rack of pots and pans suspended above it. Some staff rushed back and forth whilst others threw pizza dough above their heads, or boned turkeys, or rolled pastry, or chopped vegetables. A shout from someone for salt was met with a sharp cry of, "yes, chef!", and a cellar of salt tumbled through the air to one of the four chefs who were hovering over the stoves on the opposite side of the kitchen. The one who caught the salt tapped it once over his bubbling saucepan before taking another pinch to throw over his shoulder. He then tasted his creation using the tiniest of teaspoons.

One of the chefs who had been running around watching the others came up to the new arrivals. "What are you doing here?" he asked. "We're busy. No time for tours." His face was so red he could have hidden in a strawberry patch.

"Grandpa told us to come and visit. Kendall said Dickie was here," Fanny said. She seemed completely unruffled by the chef's attitude.

"He's peeling potatoes outside," called a woman who was standing by the sink with a sieve full of rice in one hand. Even in the heat of the kitchen, she had skin that was as white as her uniform. "Let them through, Hans," she told the chef who was blocking the way. He walked off in a huff, immediately starting to shout at one of his colleagues.

Graeme, Jim and Calamara followed Fanny across to the woman, who put down her sieve and took out a large wooden spoon and mashed something in the sink. She started to sing:

"Who needs a waste dis–po–sal?
Who needs a waste dis–po–sal?
Who needs a waste dis–po–sal when you've got a wooden spoon?"

When they reached her she stopped and turned to smile at them, revealing a mouth of perfect, white teeth. Her eyes were sapphire blue.

"Hello," she greeted them.

"This is the head chef," Fanny said.

"My name's Tatum, Tatum Lyle," said the head chef.

Fanny winked. "She's a spy."

"Used to be, used to be!" Tatum gabbled.

"Like in the films!" exclaimed Fanny.

Tatum raised an eyebrow. "Not really," she said. "It just becomes like any other job, in the end. I much prefer this. It has far more intrigue."

The angry chef was passing as she said that. He leaned close. "If she kept her nose more in cookery books and less in other people's business we'd all eat a lot better, I tell you."

"Thank you, Hans." Tatum smiled. "Why don't you go and empty the bin?"

Hans grunted and stomped off.

Tatum sniffed. "We are a little busy. It probably would be best if you weren't underfoot. Go outside and see little Richard. Make sure he hasn't lost another finger to the potato peeler."

Fanny nodded. "Follow me!" she said, and led them across the black and white tiled floor to the back door.

Calamara cursed under her breath. "Is she a cheerleader in the making or what?"

Fanny twirled around. "Ooh! You think so?" she giggled. "How splendid!"

Outside, they found a boy about Graeme's age. He was sitting on the back steps beside a bucket and a heap of peeled potatoes that was taller than any of them. Graeme thought, *Everyone's so bothered about me piling on pounds, I reckon he could give me over half his body weight and not miss it.*

The boy was wearing brown trousers with a bunch of keys fixed to his belt loop and an untucked shirt that was a bit too tight for him. His face lit up as he saw Fanny and he looked away from what he was doing for a moment. The potato he was peeling dropped to the ground and the peeler dug into his finger.

"Ow!" he yelped, dropping the peeler and sticking the bleeding finger in his mouth. He stood up.

"Hello, Dickie!" Fanny said, running up and hugging him.

"'Ello, 'iss," he said.

"You are funny," Fanny told him. She seemed very happy to see him, which Graeme thought was odd, considering how she'd been saying how boring he was not quarter of an hour earlier.

Dickie blushed.

"These are my new friends," Fanny said, reeling off names and indicating Graeme, Jim and Calamara in turn.

"'ello. 'ello. 'ello."

Calamara made a meal of stretching; she took off her glasses and rubbed her eyes. "I'm so tired all of a sudden!" she announced. "I think we'd better go to our rooms."

"I'll show you the way!" Fanny said.

Dickie's face fell. "But you've only just got here."

"He's quite right," said Calamara. "It would be very rude for you to leave him, Fanny, having only just got here."

"Wouldn't it be just as rude for us to leave, then?" Jim asked.

Calamara's head snapped round to look at Jim. There were daggers in her eyes.

"Yes!" Fanny said. "It would, wouldn't it?"

"Yes, but we're not as well bred as you," countered Calamara, sounding slightly desperate. "Besides, there are probably lots of potatoes left to peel."

Everyone looked at the mountain of peeled potatoes. Then they looked at the bucket beside Dickie. There was one potato rattling around in it. Calamara continued, nonetheless. "Dickie only has a few uncut fingers left. Are you going to leave him to cope on his own? Surely not."

"That's nice of you to consider me, but I don't really have that much more to do," Dickie said, speaking very slowly. "I was going to look for my friend cock robin, if you wanted to come along?"

"What an excellent idea!" Calamara smiled. "Fanny, you should do that while we – "

"No," said Fanny. "Benjamin said he was going to keep an eye on me, and I think I should keep an eye on you. Dickie, why don't you come with us? That way, nobody's being rude."

"Thank you, miss," Dickie said, pushing himself to his feet. He tucked his keys into a pocket.

Calamara's eyes bulged and she gritted her teeth. "Fine," she said. There was steam coming from her ears. "That's just fine."

*

"What's the 'llawr o nefoedd'?" Calamara asked, squinting at a panel of buttons on the lift wall.

"It's the top floor," Dickie mumbled.

"Why not just call it the top floor, then? How pretentious."

Dickie shuffled from side to side, staring at his feet. "My Dad says that the floors were originally numbered top–down," he said. "The llawr o nefoedd was floor one, and the ground floor was floor twenty four. The Ravershams didn't like that, though, so after the architect left they switched it all about; but the llawr o nefoedd is still at the top."

(One might ask, where else would the *floor of heaven* be? Fitzpatrick Parkes had a number of whimsical ideas when he was constructing the castle, amongst them the llawr o nefoedd and the unpopular concept of numbering the floors top–down. There were others.)

Calamara saw the sense of Dickie's explanation and nodded her approval. "Sounds about right."

Jim hadn't been able to see what Dickie was saying, so Graeme had been signing it for him.

"*Sounds boring*," he said. "*It would have been more fun the other way round*!"

The brass indicator above the lift doors moved right, a bell ringing every time a floor was passed. Dickie continued to stare at his muddy boots and Calamara drummed her fingers on the arm of her chair.

The lift pinged. "Floor ten," said a familiar voice. It was Fitzpatrick Parkes. "Nursery, children's rooms, nurse's station, armoury."

The outer doors parted, leaving them looking out into the hallway through the lattice–like inner door. Dickie unlatched it and pulled it to one side. Fanny skipped out and down the corridor. "Come along!" she called to the others, as if she were speaking to pets.

"Coming," Dickie answered and dutifully trotted after her.

Calamara shook her head. "Hopeless," she said, wheeling out with Graeme and Jim in tow. "Absolutely hopeless."

Fanny was waiting for them, a finger held to her lips. They crept up to her. She was looking into a small room; its door was ajar. Fixed to the wall by the door was a brass plaque, which read "NURSE". Through the door, Graeme could see Benjamin, his feet up on a table. He was sound asleep and snoring. Fanny looked first at him and then at her new friends, holding her hand over her mouth to stop herself laughing out loud.

If Benjamin did, as he had said, have eyes everywhere it did him little good as they were almost always shut.

Fanny beckoned everyone further along the corridor. "They've delivered your luggage," she said. She pointed to her left. "This is my room," she told them.

The suitcases had been placed outside three rooms on the opposite side of the corridor to Fanny's.

"You overlook the inner courtyard," Fanny said. "Bad luck. It's so dull. My room is the best. It looks out over the gardens," she boasted. "Come and see!"

Fanny's room was enormous. Hundreds of square glass panels formed a gigantic bay window through which they could see a panoramic view of the grounds. There was the gravel pathway that led up from the front gate; all the tents being prepared for the party; and the fair, complete with the Ferris wheel that Kendall had been talking about. It looked like they'd got it up now, but there were still ropes hanging from it. Beyond all that were the walls that they'd been exploring the day before and beyond that, the ocean.

"What do you think?" asked Fanny. She was sitting on the edge of her bed. The bed was so big she looked like a doll, sitting there swinging her legs to and fro.

"Very nice," said Calamara, eyeing the frilly eiderdown with disgust. She had moved across to a dressing table, which had a doily, a small vase of posies and a photo frame on it. She picked up the frame and brandished it at Fanny. "Who are these?"

Fanny twisted her legs back and forth. "It's my Mum and Dad," she said.

"Really?" Calamara passed the frame to Graeme as she continued to gaze around the room for something to criticize. She said something else, but Graeme didn't really hear it. He was looking down at the photo. The couple in it were hand in hand, smiling under a palm tree on a wide stretch of beach. He recognised them immediately. As he stared at it, the photo seemed to come alive. The man took the lady's other hand and they started to dance, spinning round and round. They danced out into the water, but the water wasn't water any more. It was fire. They were twirling and whirling through the inferno, their clothes catching alight; and just like the last time, they didn't stop dancing and he couldn't tear his eyes away as they died all over again.

"Ignore him, it's just for attention," he heard someone say. "Selfish."

He was feeling really weird.

"Is he all right?"

"He probably needs to lie down. He was at the back of the queue when they were handing out stamina." Only Calamara could have said that.

"Mind he doesn't drop the…"

*

Penelope Raversham was not one of the Wastrels, but she probably should have been and would have been, if she had never met Harrison Lennox.

Harrison belonged to the Lennox clan, another famous family. Lennox Ices were renowned the world over; but the family were almost more famed for obstinacy: they refused to change the company motto, "Lick a Lennox", even though it had caused more than a few expensive court cases over the years. There had been a small flurry of them when Fanny's classmates had teased her on the first day of school. Fanny's retribution was decisive, swift and bloody. Though the family and the courts disagreed about the amount of damages that should be awarded to the children with bruised and swollen tongues, broken noses, arms, legs and missing teeth, they couldn't help but agree that the girl had the makings of a great judge.

Lennox Ices had the best ice cream in all the best flavours and Lord Raversham only provided the best for his guests at his annual Christmas party. (Actually, Lord Raversham always wanted to order cheap vanilla ice cream for the hoi–polloi, the kind that's a violent shade of yellow, comes in a giant white tub and definitely doesn't have "no artificial preservatives" all over it, but Kendall was in charge of the ordering and therefore his employer's reputation for providing quality foodstuffs was blemish free.)

Now it happened that, in Penelope's fourteenth year, Harrison Lennox was on his apprenticeship with the company, delivering and serving the ice–cream with his father. Penelope, who always had a sweet tooth and a particular weakness for Lennox's Chewy Caramapple Chocolate Chunk Fix (known as "The Destroyer" by dentists worldwide), was caught by the boy with her hand in the freezer and, in the best tradition of love at first sight, their hands might as well have been frozen together for the remainder of the party, if not the rest of their lives.

Penelope was carefree, free–wheeling, thought she knew everything by the time she was seven and was more than a bit of a pest. Summer Rain, Harvest Acre and Intentional worshipped the ground she walked on. None of her other siblings were so devoted to her: she could wind up Sigourney and Michael just by walking in a room, but Finlay was too spaced out to notice her and Uriah was never at home anyway, always off at some scout camp.

By comparison, Harrison was a serious lad with a strong work ethic, a family trait that was whipped down the line from generation to generation.

A professional matchmaker would never have put these two in the same country, let alone the same room, but their opposite natures complimented each other. He, the uptight, straight–laced boy had his laces loosened; and Penelope the potential Wastrel was given direction in her life. After a five year courtship they moved to Delhi, home of the Lennoxes, where they worked hard and played harder. Children were certainly not on their agenda. Harrison had two older brothers, both of whom had provided heirs to continue the family line. When Penelope found herself pregnant it was a big surprise to the pair of them, but it was hardly a problem. The Lennox family had been brought up almost exclusively by nannies since 1783 and Fanny would be no different. Harrison and Penelope's lifestyle would not be disrupted by the arrival of their daughter. One might wonder how Fanny would have coped with such remote parenting, had she been made of less stern stuff. Following family tradition is all well and good in some respects but, when it comes to people (of any age), what works for one rarely works for all. What terrible doom might lie in store when a child possessed of a more fragile nature and subject to such an upbringing is loosed upon the world?

*

"Hello!" Jim grinned at Graeme.

They weren't in Fanny's room any more. This white room was stark by comparison. Other than the large four poster bed Graeme was sitting on, there was only a thin wardrobe against the far wall. Jim was kneeling by the bed, a glass of water in his hand, with Calamara, who was sporting a mustard yellow hooded top and slim black trousers, alongside him.

"What happened?" Graeme asked.

"You lost it a bit," Jim told him. "We're in your room. We've all got connecting doors. How cool is that?"

"Not very," said Calamara.

"Did I faint?" Graeme asked Jim.

"No, well, not at first. It just looked like you were listening to a voice that nobody else could hear. You went a bit white. "

"Whiter," Calamara corrected him.

"… then you shouted out, 'The King!' and collapsed," Jim finished. He handed the glass of water to Graeme. "Have a drink."

Graeme took a gulp of the water.

"For once you did us a favour," Calamara said to him.

"*What do you mean*?" Jim asked her, getting up off his knees.

"That girl was a thorn in my side. Didn't you notice me trying to get rid of her? I thought you might have caught on a bit sooner. She's like a limpet." Calamara gestured at Graeme "Your turn did the trick. Never thought I'd hear myself say I was grateful to you. When you had your fit she didn't want to see you, so we brought you to your room and now we're finally free of her – and her simple friend. He said something about them going off to see 'mister fox'. Pathetic!"

She treated the boys to a very self–satisfied smile. "So! What's the plan?"

"*We should find Lord Raversham,*" said Jim. "*We need to follow him and see where he goes.*"

"I don't think so," Calamara disagreed. "I don't suppose he's going to be up to anything in broad daylight. Right now, though, we can be pretty sure that he's not in his rooms and I think we ought to try there first. I bet whatever this," she brought out the key and waved it at Jim, "opens, it'll be there."

"*You think that'll be the – key – to the whole thing?*" Jim suggested, grinning.

"You're so funny!" Calamara squealed, doing a very good impersonation of Fanny. Then she made a face.

"I had a dream," Graeme said then. He didn't know what made him say it and even as he said it he started to regret it. He knew he shouldn't have said anything. Both Calamara and Jim looked at him in odd ways. Calamara looked quite happy; it was as if Graeme were confirming her suspicions of his madness. Jim was just concerned.

"You had a dream," Calamara said back to Graeme. She sighed.

"Yeah," he said. He really wasn't sure about this now, but he was so aware of them expecting him to say something more. "I had a dream. Last night. At least, I think it was a dream, or I thought it was, until…"

"He's off again," said Calamara. "Well, don't stop there. Tell us all about it."

So he started to tell them. The stupid thing was, as he went on, the whole thing seemed more and more unreal. He'd had this kind of feeling before, trying to talk to his parents. He remembered them sitting, waiting for him to talk; him hearing his own voice and even as he started to try and say what he wanted to say he realised how daft it would sound and how, really, it wasn't anything to bother with, nothing important, he was probably mistaken. He remembered how he'd ended up mumbling about nothing in particular, and them giving each other *that look*, the "what are we going to do about him?" look before they got up and left. *That look* haunted him.

And now it was happening all over again. It had seemed so real: the stranger, the boats, the cave; but now, with Calamara's eyebrows getting higher and higher as he went on, he found himself thinking that he must have been mistaken, it was all so far–fetched, it couldn't really have happened, not to him. He was a babbling idiot.

He started off telling them about seeing the cave when Fitzpatrick flushed them into the sea – that, he was pretty sure about. Then he mentioned the man in his room, the boats, seeing the cave again in the night, and the Pyn King, but his voice trailed off before he got to the fire. He just couldn't face telling them about that. They'd really think he made the whole thing up if he did. He wasn't feeling sure of himself at all.

True to form, though, Jim was really excited by it all. "*You saw the man?*" he asked. "*The bloke we saw on the beach?*"

"Yeah."

"*Did you recognise his voice? Was it Lord Raversham?*"

Graeme thought about that. He hadn't considered it at the time. He tried to remember the voice. It had been distorted because of the mask, but now Jim had made him think about it, there was something that had sounded familiar. Was it Lord Raversham, though? It probably had been; it all fitted, didn't it? He wasn't sure, but Jim was looking so expectantly at him and Calamara was getting more and more sceptical, so he didn't want to start saying that he didn't know.

"Yeah," he said.

"Wow!" said Jim.

"I guess."

"That means he must be the leader!"

Calamara only repeated what Graeme had said, "You guess." Her voice was flat.

Graeme hated the way she seemed to see everything; it was like his every thought was appearing on a flashing neon sign above his head, just for her. He said, "Yes," far more firmly.

Her eyes narrowed and his darted to his feet.

"Is that so?" she said, clearly not believing him.

"Yes," he said again, through gritted teeth.

"*This is great*," Jim was saying. "*This has confirmed so much!*"

Calamara still didn't look convinced. "Yeah, right. You're so gullible," she said to Jim. "How can you even start to think he really knows what he's talking about? Isn't it a little bit too convenient, that he should come out with all this now – and it's exactly what you wanted to hear?"

"Well," Jim said out loud, "I believe him."

Graeme felt like he could fly, then.

"Bully for you," said Calamara.

"*You think Graeme's lying?*"

Calamara wailed, "He's desperate to please you! I don't know if he believes what he's saying or not, but…"

"If you doubt him then you can stay here," Jim said, interrupting her. "We're going to do some investigating."

"Investigating?" Calamara scoffed. "What exactly are you going to investigate?"

"*We're going to find that cave*," said Jim. He turned and went to walk out the door. Graeme felt like sticking his tongue out at Calamara; he ignored that impulse and followed Jim.

"Hey!" said Calamara. She slammed her fist down on the arm of her chair.

Graeme tugged at Jim's pullover to stop him. Jim glanced back over his shoulder.

"Caves, caves, caves. Why does everything revolve around caves for you?" Calamara asked.

Jim stood there in the doorway but he didn't turn round. "Well, you don't need to worry about that, do you?"

Graeme watched Calamara. Her eyes were darting from the floor, to the back of Jim's head, to Graeme, and back to the floor as she tried to think.

"You stay here," Jim said to her again. Then he walked out the door, leaving her spluttering on the spot.

Graeme followed him.

As they walked along the corridor Graeme was thinking about what Calamara had said. How could he be sure any of what he'd told them was real? Seeing the cavern when Fitzpatrick had caught them – that, he was pretty clear on, but the rest of it really was like a dream.

Only, some of it had seemed so familiar. Like memories, all jumbled up; but then, isn't that all dreams are?

Jim could tell Graeme was worried. He stopped and smiled. "*Don't let her get to you. I believe you really saw it all*," he said.

Graeme nodded, still feeling pretty bad. He wondered if he should say something, but he kept quiet.

"*Don't worry*," said Jim. He put his hand on Graeme's arm.

Graeme heard Calamara let out a small cry of despair and looked back. She was making her way towards them. "All right, all right!" she said. "I'll come along."

"*You've changed your mind? You believe Graeme?*" Jim asked her.

Graeme could see that she didn't.

"I will… reserve judgement," she said. "But we don't need to find any cave, not yet."

"*Why not? You want to look for Lord Raversham's rooms instead?*" Jim asked her.

Calamara's mouth formed a wide, reptilian smile. "We can do that later. I think perhaps we should follow up on some of Graeme's information first." She pulled herself forward so she was in the lead. "That man, the one in the mask: what was he called?"

"The Pyn King," Graeme said, spelling it out.

"That's a funny way to spell it. How do you know it's spelt like that?" she asked.

Graeme shrugged. "Dunno. I just do."

"Wonderful," Calamara sighed, flicking her hair out of her eyes. "This just gets better and better."

"*Sounds kind of oldey worldy, don't you think*?" Jim suggested.

"I've heard it before," Graeme said.

"Yes, yes," said Calamara, "in another life, no doubt. My point is: you said that they said he had returned. If he's returned then he's got to have been around before; and that means we can look him up. There must be stuff somewhere about him if he tried to take over the world. We need to find a computer and get on the Internet."

"*I'm not allowed to use a computer*," Jim reminded them.

"I know," Calamara told him with a withering look on her face. "What I'd love to know is what makes you keep that promise. Your Dad's not here now."

"A promise is a promise," said Jim.

Calamara didn't look convinced. "Yes," she drawled. "Well, be that as it may, you're not the only one who knows how to use a computer."

Graeme wondered if she was referring to him. Somehow he doubted it.

"*Fanny would know where to find one*," Jim pointed out. "*We could tell her and Dickie about everything, let them help.*"

"You want to tell her that we think her grandfather is out to conquer the world?"

"*Well, maybe not yet...*" He glanced at Graeme and in that instant, Graeme realised that Jim didn't really believe him, not a hundred percent, anyway. Calamara caught that as well. She smiled in satisfaction.

"*... but we could tell her about the Pyn King,*" Jim continued. "*We don't have to say who we think he is. Besides, right about now Mr Thornton's telling Roberta about the boats. How long do you think it'll all remain a secret then*?"

Calamara was quiet for a moment. "You always have an answer, don't you? I don't want the girl knowing. Imagine having her tagging along, squealing and screeching all the way. Now, did either of you see a computer while we were wandering the hallways earlier?"

"No," Jim and Graeme said together.

"*We could try the library*," Jim suggested. "*There's got to be a library. If they're going to have web access anywhere, it'll be there!*"

"Right," said Calamara, happy to be back in control, "follow me."

They went to the lift and got in, closing the doors behind them.

"Which floor would the library be on?" Calamara asked, not that she was asking Graeme, or even Jim for that matter. She was asking herself. She was the only one she ever really listened to, anyway.

None of them were expecting the reply they got. "The library," said the voice of Fitzpatrick Parkes, "is on floor eighteen."

"Where did that come from?" Calamara asked, looking all around her.

"From down here," Graeme said, pointing to a small speaker just below the lift buttons.

"*What was that*?" Jim asked.

"I think it was Fitzpatrick Parkes," Graeme told him. "You know, from yesterday. He says the library is on floor eighteen."

"*Fair enough,*" Jim said, leaning over and punching the number in on the keypad. The lift burst into life and started going up. It came to a halt a minute later and the outer doors swept open.

"Floor eighteen," Fitzpatrick said. "Library, wood store, matches. Don't mix and… match."

Jim pulled the inner door aside and they got out. There was a small wooden gate alongside the lift that led to a flight of spiral stairs. Those stairs coiled away to other floors, both up and down. In front of them was the library itself. It had row upon row of bookcases jam packed with dull coloured volumes. Each bookcase had a ladder on wheels, so you could reach the upper shelves. Dusty shafts of honey–coloured afternoon sun shone through lofty windows on the far side of the room. High above them, flimsy lights dangled on wires from beams that ran across the ceiling.

As they moved further in, Graeme heard the sound of people scrabbling to their feet. The three Raversham kids appeared from an aisle off to their right, hiding something behind their backs.

"What are you doing here?" demanded Adam. "You're not allowed." Even as he spoke they were edging around Graeme, Jim and Calamara, towards the lift.

"Looking for a computer," Calamara told them.

"We're telling Mummy," Margaret said. "You shouldn't be here."

"I'm scared," Calamara snarled. The two groups were circling each other now, like they were cats preparing for a night–time spat. From Graeme's point of view, the thought of having Adam, Archibald and Margaret behind him with nobody else in the way was not a good one.

"We mean it," Margaret said. "We're telling." The Ravershams were right in front of the lift now.

"You're going to be in so much trouble," Adam gloated.

"See you later, James," said Archibald, leering at Jim. They all giggled, stepped backwards into the lift and pulled the doors shut with great difficulty, as they were unwilling to drop whatever it was they were hiding. The lift started up.

Calamara looked at Jim. "You should just kick them," she told him.

Jim just smiled at her. "*It's not my thing.*"

"It's probably the *only* thing they'd understand," Calamara replied.

“I recognise those dulcet tones,” someone said. It was Fitzpatrick Parkes. His voice had come from under the floor. Some of the flagstones slid aside and a very old television set rose up through the hole. It was made of dark wood and had the smallest of screens. You could imagine a 1950s family huddled around it to watch the coronation, inviting the neighbours over to show off the fuzzy picture.

The tiny screen lit up and a black and white image of Fitzpatrick Parkes appeared. “I thought I recognised your voices in the lift,” he said, “but I couldn't see, so I couldn't be sure. It's you three again. How on Earth you ever got in here I do not know.” He was still signing everything he was saying, and the picture and sound were still pausing every now and again, just like before.

“*We've been given permission by Lord Raversham*,” Jim told him.

“Yes, of course you have,” Fitzpatrick said, in a tone not so much dripping as full–on pouring with sarcasm. “Few have ever challenged my defences with such effectiveness. I am quite, quite impressed. Or maybe I'm just in need of a service. I really must make time for that. But, I digress. I'm afraid that I will have to ask you all to leave...”

“Hang on,” Calamara shouted, “we're not lying! We *have* been given permission!”

“I feel I should point out that by continuing to lie you are only serving to compound the severity of the case against you,” Fitzpatrick said. “As I believe I mentioned the last time we met, please – don't – come again. Goodbye.”

CHAPTER EIGHT

A Legend of the Pyn King

"Aieeeeee!"

A tiny blue whirlwind twisted out of one of the aisles and bore down on Graeme, Jim and Calamara.

Calamara was resigned to her fate. "Here we go again."

Dust and papers and books flew into the air as the cyclone curved around the room with sparks of static electricity coursing over its blurred surface. They braced themselves; it got so close Graeme could feel its edges pulling at him, ruffling his clothes; but instead of swallowing him it span right past and slammed into the television. A long crack appeared in the wooden casing and the whole thing quaked. The screen went blank.

The whirlwind stopped spinning, revealing a wild, dishevelled Fanny hopping from one foot to the other. She was wearing a sky blue dress. "Hello!" she said as she smoothed her hair. "I went to your room to see how you were," she told Graeme, "but you'd gone." She looked at all three of them. "You'd all gone," she added, sticking out her bottom lip, a cross expression on her face for a split second before she went back to being her old merry self. "So, I thought I'd come and find you!"

She span around, making the skirt of her dress flare. "Dickie!"

Graeme followed Fanny's gaze to the top of one of the colossal bookcases. Dickie was up there, wobbling on a ladder. He stepped down, the rungs bending somewhat alarmingly at each foot–fall, and plodded to stand by Fanny.

“How did you find us?” Calamara asked. She had sunk into her chair and her arms were folded.

Fanny giggled. “I asked my cousins.” She took a step closer. “They don’t like you very much,” she tried to whisper, but Fanny’s idea of a whisper was more of a shout.

“Really?” asked Calamara, sounding not a bit surprised.

“How did you get here?” Jim asked Fanny.

“That’s a point,” Calamara agreed. “How did you get here? You didn’t use the lift or the stairs. We would have seen you.”

“You big silly! This is a castle, you know!” Fanny laughed. “There are loads of secret passages! I know my way around here!”

“Yeah? Like you knew your way around that maze?” Calamara asked her.

“Ooh, better than that!” Fanny exclaimed. No doubt it annoyed Calamara greatly, but Fanny was immune to her sarcastic comments. Whether Fanny was too innocent to realise Calamara was trying to wind her up or she was simply happy in her own little world was unclear to Graeme, but as long as it thwarted Calamara’s attempts to be clever it was good enough for him.

“I’ll give you a tour,” Fanny was saying. “I’ll show them to you if you like!”

Jim was thrilled. “Yes, please!”

Calamara cursed under her breath. “Not right now,” she said. “We’re busy.” She paused, looking at Fanny in a peculiar way. “We’re hunting for a computer,” she announced. “We need to look up something on the Internet. Do you know where we can find one? A computer, I mean.”

“My Grandpa only has this one computer,” Fanny told her, patting the television to indicate that’s what she was talking about, “and it keeps going wrong. It was built *years* ago, back in the olden days. Grandpa doesn’t like computers much.”

“Well, even if we could get this one working it wouldn’t be much use to us, the state it’s in,” said Jim.

“It’s okay sometimes,” Fanny said, leaping to Fitzpatrick’s defence. “It’s just very old,” she added, walking around to the front of the set. “All you have to do,” she told them, flexing her fingers as she crouched, searching for something, “is to push… here!” She jabbed at a ribbed section of wood. It fell open with a soft click, revealing a white panel with one big, black knob. Fanny let out a triumphant cry and clapped her hands together, really fast. She twisted the knob, first one way and then the other. All the lights in the library dimmed, flickered and blazed back to life. Moths up in the rafters swirled crazily in the brightness.

On the television screen, a load of letters and numbers scrolled past; nothing that made any sense to Graeme, although Jim was taking a keen interest up until the screen went blank again.

"It'll take a while to warm up. It's the valves," Fanny told them, closing the panel.

"You could always – " Dickie started to say, but Fanny cut him off.

"What do you want to look up, anyway?"

"We're investigating," Calamara told her. She gave Graeme and Jim a long, hard look. Before Graeme could think what that meant, she started to tell Fanny about the people on the beach and how Graeme and Jim had seen them sailing out to the isle. At various points, Fanny gasped and put a hand to her mouth, but that must have been more for effect than because she was actually scared by what she was hearing. In fact, she seemed to be enjoying it all; her face was lit up with an impish glee and her cheeks had deep dimples.

"Graeme there," Calamara stuck her arm out at him, "reckons he had a dream, or maybe it wasn't a dream, and says their leader calls himself the Pyn King. We want to find out about that man."

Graeme thought he must be dreaming. He couldn't just have heard Calamara telling someone what they were up to, could he? Not after everything she'd said earlier. His mouth fell open in shock.

"Why is he being a goldfish?" Fanny asked, looking sideways at Graeme.

Calamara shrugged. "He's a boy," she said, as if that explained everything. Apparently it did explain everything to Fanny, who nodded very seriously. Then a really strange thing happened. Calamara and Fanny smiled at each other. Calamara even giggled a bit.

Graeme looked questioningly at Jim, who just said, "*Don't ever say Calamara can't surprise you.*"

"Ooh!" squealed Fanny, watching Jim as he signed to Graeme. "Wriggly fingers! You'll have to show me how to do it one day!"

"Sure," said Jim. "And you can show me those secret passages."

Calamara looked at the television screen and then at her watch. "Is this going to take much longer?" she asked.

"Well," Dickie said, "we are …"

The floor began to vibrate. There was a grinding sound. The television started to descend into its hole, stopped, then rose back up and settled in position. The words “London to Peashingle in Thirty Seconds” appeared on screen, slowly fading away to be replaced by an obviously speeded–up film of a puffing steam train. They watched as it hurtled along the tracks under a perfect, cotton–wool cloud sky with smudged banks of earth and trees to either side of it. It went under bridges, past windmills, past rows of houses, past forests and up and down hills; it sped by fields filled with waving grass, cows and sheep and through train stations so fast that their names couldn’t be made out.

The driver was leaning out of the cab, pulling on a chain to sound the whistle as the train went under another bridge. He turned to the camera. Even though his face was black with coal dust, you couldn’t mistake that it was Fitzpatrick Parkes. He opened his mouth, as if he were about to speak, and the film stopped. It literally froze in place. Graeme thought the whole thing might have broken down again, but then the picture went completely white, with just Fitzpatrick standing there. He put his hands behind his back.

“Hello!” he said. “Hello and welcome to Raversham Isle Management Controller – Version Zero Eight Point Zero Six. I am now loading previous run time settings: enhanced communications for the deaf and hard–of–hearing are – on. The system is now ready.”

Fanny moved to stand right in front of the screen. “Hello!” she said, patting the top of the television.

“Miss Stephanie,” Fitzpatrick greeted her. “And Master… Richard, isn’t it?” he asked Dickie, who didn’t say anything. Fitzpatrick tried to get a look over Fanny’s shoulder at the others. “And these are…?”

“These are my friends,” Fanny told him, moving to one side. “Don’t attack them!”

“As if I would!” Fitzpatrick smiled back. The television juddered forward slightly so it was closer to them.

“I’ve seen you before,” Fitzpatrick murmured. He looked perplexed and turned to Fanny. “They appear to match earlier records that I have of some… intruders.” His eyes narrowed as he studied Graeme, Jim and Calamara intently. “It’s like… déjà vu… how strange, how very strange.”

Graeme started to brace himself, ready for the floor to open up at any moment; but Fitzpatrick didn’t seem that interested this time;

instead he gave a flamboyant shrug, said, “C’est la vie!” and stood there, happy and patiently awaiting instructions. Every now and then he’d look down to examine his shoes and do a little tap dance.

“You can ask him now,” Fanny told Calamara.

Calamara pushed herself up so she was nose to screen. She glanced back over her shoulder. “I just ask about whatever I want to know?”

Fanny nodded furiously.

“All right, then.” Calamara turned back to face Fitzpatrick, who was patiently waiting for them. “Tell me about the Pyn King,” she commanded him. “P – Y – N – K – I – N – G.”

The picture of Fitzpatrick wavered and became a very grainy black and white. He splayed out his hands. “There are no records that meet your search criteria.”

“I told you! No such person!” Calamara shouted at Jim, wheeling around and throwing her arms in the air. She thrust an accusatory finger in Graeme’s direction. “He’s a prize moron! I knew it!”

“I normally get ‘syntax error’ when I ask for things,” said Fanny.

“Don’t despair,” said Fitzpatrick. He was now clutching a thick book under one arm. “I could perform a more thorough search for any likely partial matches. Would you like me to do that now?”

“*Yes, please*,” said Jim.

“As if that’ll produce anything!” snorted Calamara. “Why not just admit your friend’s an idiot?”

“You know,” said Dickie, “just because that thing doesn’t know about it, it doesn’t mean nobody knows.”

“What is it with everybody that you’re all sticking up for this attention seeker? What’s so special about him?” spat Calamara, glowering at Graeme.

“I’m sorry,” Dickie apologised. Graeme thought, *I wouldn’t have apologised to her, no matter what.*

“I was just saying,” said Dickie, “we could always just…”

There was a cough from behind them and they turned around. Lord Raversham was standing at the gate to the stairs, leaning on the balustrade. He was wheezing. This was the third time in two days that someone had crept up on Graeme; it was the second time it had been Lord Raversham.

"Young… Richard? Yes, Richard has a point," he said between breaths. "Computers, especially this computer…"

"I heard that!" said Fitzpatrick. As his hands were full, the words were also displayed as subtitles on screen. He paused in the process of leafing through the pages of his book to gaze out at everybody.

"Shut up," said Lord Raversham, "or I'll unplug you. These things," he continued, slowly getting his breath back, "these things are not the be all and end all. Have you noticed what room you are in? If you want to look something up, why not try it the old fashioned way? I have the odd tome in my collection, you know," he said, waving his arm to indicate the shelves and shelves of books.

"That's what I was trying to say," said Dickie.

"Well, you're a rare boy," replied Lord Raversham. "Now, what are you lot up to? There was I, just wandering back to my room, albeit in a somewhat roundabout route so as to avoid my tenacious butler, after a pleasant half hour sampling the delights to be had in the wine tent while my children toiled in the fields, when the power goes out and I'm plunged into darkness in one of the lower corridors. When the lights come back on I've got my grandchildren standing in front of me – which, by the way, would be enough to scare anybody in their right mind half to death – telling me that you were in the library and 'being bad', I think were their exact words."

"We're not being bad," said Fanny, fluttering her eyelids.

"I'm sure. What are you wanting to look up?"

Graeme, Jim and Calamara looked back and forth at each other.

"Come along, out with it!" barked Lord Raversham.

Fanny opened her mouth but Calamara rolled onto her foot.

"What's so secret that you can't tell me?" asked Lord Raversham. His eyes widened and his face filled with dread. "Unless… unless it's a teenage thing."

"They're looking for information about the Pyn King," said Fitzpatrick. This was followed by one of those time–stood–still moments of ominous quiet that probably only lasted a second but, to Graeme, seemed to take an eternity to pass.

"The Pyn King, eh?" Lord Raversham asked, his voice sharp, his eyes lighting up. "The Pyn King," he said again, this time sounding more reflective. He started to pick idly at a fingernail. Graeme, Jim and Calamara still hadn't dared breathe once. Calamara looked scared to death. (A bit of Graeme was pleased about that.) What was Lord Raversham going to do?

"I can tell you about the Pyn King," he said.

Graeme and Jim exchanged worried looks. Was this going to be it?

"You don't even need to consult a book," Lord Raversham continued, "unless you want to see the family tree, though I think that's on the upper shelves, so one of you lot would need to clamber up there."

This certainly wasn't what Graeme was expecting. He glanced at Calamara. She wasn't looking frightened any more. She was watching Lord Raversham with her eyes narrowed to slits. Her eyes flicked briefly towards Graeme as she caught him looking at her, her expression unchanged.

Lord Raversham didn't seem to notice any of this. He shifted position slightly, wincing as he did so. "There are only a few stories about the Pyn King, and fewer people know them. Most are twaddle. I know the truth: the Pyn King was never a king at all, but he did come perilously close. No, he was never a king, unless you count how he perceived himself in his own, sick mind. He was a man called Aefford Avers.

"Old Aefford stormed out from the marshlands of what used to be known as West Wales years and years ago. In a very short space of time he managed to rally an army dedicated, so he said, to uniting the peoples of England, Scotland and Wales; or rather, what would become England, Scotland and Wales. The boundaries weren't as

rigidly defined as they are today. He claimed to have been gifted with a divine prophetic vision; in fact, he was more akin to a psychotic madman who swept across the country, press–ganging men, women and children to his cause as he went from town to town. Some, of course, joined him willingly, mostly those who delighted in causing agony to others and recognised that their basest desires would be permitted under his rule. Those few became his inner circle, his trusted honour guard."

"But what *was* his cause?" breathed Jim, already totally caught up in the tale.

"I was getting to that," snapped Lord Raversham. He was enjoying telling the story and didn't like being interrupted. "His sole ambition was to be crowned King of Britain, and no doubt, in due course, the world. He oversaw sacrificial rites in these very parts. Blood, it is said, flowed like water in those dark days."

Fanny whimpered and held Dickie's shirttail. Lord Raversham didn't pay any attention to that, though. He really was having fun.

"The kings and queens of Britain, of which there were many, looked at the growing unrest and were astonished at how a single man had managed to unite a country against them, albeit by brute force. They, after all, had been trying to depose one another for centuries without much luck. They took stock and realised that they in turn would need to unite for what was probably the very first time in history if they were to overcome their new foe.

"They launched a massive strike against his forces. The battle blazed and the Pyn King found the combined armies of Britain a force to be reckoned with, for sure. He drove his people on, though, whipping them to the edge of death until they ran willingly to their doom, but he saw the undeniable truth: that it was not enough; and he fled, leaving everybody, the flogged and the faithful, behind.

"When they saw their leader abandon them, the Pyn King's honour guard were furious at the betrayal. They left the battle and gave chase. The remnants of the downtrodden forces of the Pyn King, now rudderless, collapsed. They were put to death in any number of imaginative ways. Mercy wasn't a concept at the forefront of many people's minds back then. Hot pokers, however, were, or so I am led to believe."

Lord Raversham gave a grim chuckle.

Jim asked, "Did the Pyn King's honour guard catch him?"

"Will you *wait*?" Lord Raversham asked him, frustrated at another interruption.

"Sorry."

"Hmpf. The guards did find him, but not until it was too late. You see, the kings and queens of Britain had despatched a lone assassin to seek out the Pyn King. This assassin came upon him not far from the battlefield. The Pyn King, having deserted anybody who might have defended him, had no choice but to stand and fight. An epic struggle between the two ensued but the assassin's mettle proved to be more than a match for that of his beleaguered opponent and the Pyn King died that day.

"The kings and queens of the land celebrated: they had beheaded the snake that would have eaten them. The short–lived rebellion of the Pyn King was over."

Calamara was signing something at Graeme. "*So the Pyn King is real.*"

She seemed really put out about that. Graeme wanted to burst out laughing.

"*But,*" she added, "*are you sure it was Lord Raversham's voice that you heard?*"

He ignored that. He hated the way she doubted him. He hated the way she wound him up. He hated everything about her. But what he really hated was that he was thinking the same thing, asking himself the same question. He didn't really need to ask; he knew that it hadn't been Lord Raversham's voice that he'd heard. Why had he lied before? Now when the truth came out Jim would hate him.

"How come we've never heard of the Pyn King before now?" Calamara asked then, eyeing both Lord Raversham and Graeme with a suspicious expression. "You make him sound quite important, so you'd think we'd have learnt about him in history. He'd at least have a footnote in some book or other."

"Records were sketchy in those days," said Lord Raversham, "but yes – you would have thought there would have been something, wouldn't you? Maybe there would have been, but as it turned out while the battle was raging, a horde of Vikings were landing much further north. The British army might have been mighty, but it wasn't mighty enough to fight two wars on consecutive days. They were confronted by the Vikings and duly crushed; and then not long after, the Vikings were overthrown by the French, and so on and so on. So there weren't that many people left to tell the tale."

He stood there, looking quite pleased with the speech he'd given. Graeme half thought Lord Raversham might be expecting a round of applause. Well, Fanny, now over her short–lived bout of fear, certainly clapped her hands together, even if everyone else remained silent.

"You know *so* much about him, Grandpa. You're *so* clever!" she said.

Lord Raversham looked at his granddaughter with despair in his eyes. "He was *family*," he said as if he were talking to a bunch of idiots. "We have the only documents in existence that make any mention of the man! I know more about him than most. And given that my children, even the one who considers himself a teacher, pay scant attention to family history, no doubt his story will die with me…"

He looked directly at Graeme for the first time since he'd set foot in the library, like he was about to ask him something, but then he said, "Hang on… Where exactly did you hear about the Pyn King?"

None of them could face him. Graeme hoped Jim or Calamara would come up with something soon or else Fanny would no doubt blurt out the truth.

"And where," Lord Raversham bellowed, sounding far more like his normal self, "is Benjamin? I thought he was keeping an eye on you. I don't want you running wild again!"

"He's sleeping," Fanny told her grandfather.

"Sleeping? On what he gets paid? The lazy – I don't know why Penelope ever employed him. I want you all to go to your – " Lord

Raversham had to finish that sentence later because he was cut off by a blood–curdling scream.

"That's Sigourney!" He whipped around, ran back through the gate and up the stairs. The gang went to follow him, but hadn't even reached the first step when he stopped, turned and said, "You lot go to your rooms! And stay there!"

They looked at each other as he rushed off.

"Yeah, right," said Calamara. "Jim, carry me. You," she ordered Graeme in that haughty manner of hers, "pick up my chair."

"Where are you going?" Fitzpatrick called as they started to pursue Lord Raversham. His voice faded as they climbed the stairs. It was a shame they didn't bother to go back and hear what he had to say.

"You ask me to do a job and then you tootle off! You don't want to hear about the mine, then? The accident? Llewellyn's only told you one version of events, but fine, if you're not interested… The bad manners of modern youth! Talk about a five second attention span! This wouldn't have happened in my day! Hello? Hello? Honestly! It's only good manners to say good–bye…"

*

Graeme had noted how strong Lord Raversham was the first time they'd met. Now, once again, he considered that for someone reportedly at Death's door, the old man was in more than good shape. If anyone were ever on their last legs, they'd want a pair just like Lord Raversham's: he couldn't half move fast. The room he ran to was two floors up and looked out over the gardens. It looked like half the gardens had been transplanted to the room. It was like an indoor jungle. Amongst the overgrown, dusty foliage were giant palms, a near–to–death yucca plant which sat forlornly by the window and, huddled in a shady corner, a motley collection of ferns. There was a single, canopied and unmade bed with feathered spears resting against one of the bedposts and loads of trunks against the walls, poking out between the greenery. The walls themselves (at least, the parts that could be seen) were covered in tribal and ceremonial masks. Several dozen of the masks were lying broken on the floor. Sigourney was standing by the window, clutching her bosom. Intentional and Michael were with her.

"Oh, Father!" she cried as she saw Lord Raversham.

"What happened?" Lord Raversham asked her. "I haven't heard you scream like that since I let you stay up late to listen to the "Dial Dread" night when you were eleven."

"I… I… I…" she stammered, sinking onto one of the chests.

"She was helping me hang a banner," said Intentional. "I was in my room next door and she'd come in here; we were tying the thing in place when she dropped her end and started screaming."

Graeme wandered over to the window, fought past a rambling, wide–leaved plant that he didn't recognise, and leaned out. A crumpled banner that read "Happy Christmas" was resting on the gravel, twitching in the breeze.

"I thought I told all of you to go to your rooms?" Lord Raversham said, noticing Graeme.

"Oh, don't worry about them, Dad," Michael told his father. "Tell Papa what you saw, Sigourney."

Sigourney took a deep breath. "It was awful!" she cried. "So huge! A ghost, I swear to you, a ghost as big as a bear! It came right for me! It was white, white with awful, pale eyes!"

Fanny screamed.

"Were the eyes purple?" Intentional asked his sister. Sigourney's face drained of any colour as she nodded.

"Yes," she said.

"That's exactly like the thing I saw!" Intentional shouted. "Exactly it! Why couldn't your wife have been here, eh, Michael?"

"Hmm? She's resting," said Michael.

"You're sure about this?" Lord Raversham asked his daughter.

"Attacked! Attacked in Uriah's room! What was it doing here?" Sigourney was whimpering.

"Where's Kendall?" Lord Raversham asked.

"I am here sir," Kendall said, walking into the room. "I believe congratulations are in order. You managed to lose me for half an hour." His face took on a concerned expression. "What if something had happened to you?"

"Forget that for the moment, Kendall. My daughter needs a lie down and something to soothe her nerves."

Kendall took one swift look around the room, assessing the situation for himself. "Of course, sir."

"Escort her to her room, please."

"Yes, my Lord." Kendall proffered his hand to Sigourney but she seemed too far out of it to do anything, so he put his arm around her shoulders and led her away.

"And get in touch with that police woman! I don't care if the phones are working or not! Swim to the mainland and bring her here if necessary!" Lord Raversham shouted. For the first time since Graeme had met him, he sounded genuinely worried.

"I'm already here," said Roberta, walking through the door. Her face was dead serious.

Lord Raversham nearly jumped a mile.

"The comms are down," Roberta explained, "surprise, surprise; so I thought I should make the trip across. I have news from Belém."

*

"News? What news?" Lord Raversham asked Roberta.

"The expeditionary force reached Uriah's encampment yesterday," she said. She looked around her. "Isn't this Uriah's room?" she asked.

"Yes," said Lord Raversham.

"Oh," said Roberta. "Perhaps you'd prefer to go somewhere else for this?"

Lord Raversham sank onto one of the chests. "Just get on with it."

Roberta nodded. "So, they reached the encampment yesterday," she said. "I would've had word earlier, but with all the problems, you know… well, here's the thing: they found nothing, apart from remnants of the camp itself."

"Nothing?"

"Absolutely nothing."

"You said, 'remnants'. What had happened to the camp?"

"There was a fire. Seven square miles of forest have been decimated."

Graeme's stomach started to churn.

"A fire in a rainforest?" Intentional asked her. "Sounds impossible."

"Rainforest doesn't mean it just rains, idiot boy," Lord Raversham admonished his son.

"I assure you it is possible," said Roberta. "I know that much, even though I'm no ecological expert. I'm booked to do the course next year but for now, strictly amateur, I'm afraid."

Lord Raversham stared into the middle–distance. "And Uriah?"

"There was no sign of anybody, but the fire was intense. It may be that any remains would have been..."

"Cremated," Lord Raversham finished for her.

Roberta gave the old man a sympathetic look. "We can't be sure if he was there or not," she said, trying not to sound overly hopeful.

Graeme couldn't read Lord Raversham's face at all. "Well, that's good," he said after a while, taking a deep breath. "There's still hope."

Roberta gave him a steady look. "Yes," she said.

"What about Finlay?"

"Absolutely nothing there, I'm afraid. Stations round the country – and on the continent – are following up on leads, but there's nothing positive as yet."

Lord Raversham bowed his head. He didn't say anything for a long time. "Well, what do you make of all of this?" he eventually asked her, sweeping his arm in a wide arc.

Roberta scrutinised the room. "Hmm," she said, "it looks like somebody's gone a bit mad in here."

"Sigourney was attacked!" said Intentional. "She was attacked by the same creature that tried to kill me!"

"There's no proof that anything tried to kill you," Roberta said. She said it so fast it was like an automatic response.

Lord Raversham glared at her. "When are you going to take any of this seriously?"

"I have always taken this seriously," said Roberta. "It was my impression that until quite recently, *you* were the one treating this with frivolity."

Lord Raversham stood up. Then he sat down. "Yes," he said.

Roberta walked across to him and put a hand on his shoulder. "It's my job and I'm bloody good at it," she said, "even if I get scant recognition. These things, they just take time."

"That might be something we're running out of," said Intentional. "If they can get here…"

Roberta was sizing up Intentional, trying to work out whether or not she should believe his story. "I suppose I ought to talk to Sigourney," she said.

"Leave her for now," said Lord Raversham. "You can talk to her later, once she's rested. I want you to stay, anyway."

Roberta shook her head. "I'm not your personal security guard, you know. I'm the local bobby. If you wanted round the clock protection why didn't you get private guards?"

"I don't want private guards turning my home into a prison, snooping around with me paying for the privilege," said Lord Raversham. "I pay my taxes: ergo I pay for you, so you can earn your pay by staying here. I'm sure the good folk on the mainland will survive without you for one night."

For a moment it looked like Roberta was going to put up a fight, but then she just shrugged. "Okay," she said. "I think all I'd be doing in any case would be cooling my heels waiting for Pip Thornton to finally make an appearance. He sounded so anxious when he spoke to me before but I've seen hide nor hair of him all afternoon. Mind you, if I hadn't been waiting for him I wouldn't have heard about the campsite."

Michael coughed. "We'll leave you to get on," he said. He and Intentional left the room.

Roberta bent down and picked up half of a broken mask. "Do you know if there are any of these missing?" she asked, turning it over in her hands.

"No idea," said Lord Raversham. "Uriah must have an inventory somewhere. He loved… loves lists."

"Oh," said Roberta, still staring at the mask in her hands. "I was just wondering, whoever or whatever it was, maybe it wasn't after Sigourney at all. Do you think someone might have wanted to take some of these? Are they valuable?"

"I'm not bothered about the masks!" said Lord Raversham. "I'm bothered that somebody, or something, was in here."

"All right," said Roberta, putting the mask down, "I'll do things by the book and question everybody present at the time. I'll need to speak to your sons. Shouldn't really have let them go. I don't know what I was thinking. Can you get them back?"

Lord Raversham yelled, "Michael!"

"Roberta," said Jim.

Roberta looked at him and then took in Graeme, Calamara, Dickie and Fanny as well. "And you lot didn't actually witness anything, is that right? I see you've got yet another new member of the gang," she said, one corner of her mouth turned up as she acknowledged Dickie, who blushed. "You're building quite the little army, aren't you? How come if there's anything going on recently, you lot are always nearby?"

This is it, Graeme thought. Roberta was correct. Every time there had been a problem in the last few days, he and the others had been there and Roberta had worked out they were the common denominator. She was going to take them home, he was sure; but Roberta didn't pursue the matter any further.

"*I think, maybe, we need to –* " said Jim, but he was cut off by Lord Raversham.

"I told you to go to – " he started to say, but then Calamara cut *him* off.

"Come on," she said, pulling at Jim. "Let's go back to our rooms."

Michael and Intentional re–appeared.

"You called, Father?" Michael asked as the gang squeezed around the two of them and out the door. Michael smiled at Graeme and ruffled the boy's hair. "Little scamp!" he said.

Lord Raversham grunted. "I'll send some food up for you later. I don't want to hear from you for the rest of the evening! I have enough to worry about!"

His voice echoed out into the hall. "Where were you sloping off to, anyway?" Graeme heard him ask his sons.

"To see Mathilda," said Michael.

"What hold does she have over you, son?" asked Lord Raversham. "You rescue her from a life of drudgery and take on her children, all for what?"

"Hmm?" Michael sounded as out of it as usual.

"I said… oh, never mind. Roberta wants to ask you some questions about what you saw, if anything."

"Of course, Father," said Michael. The voices were growing faint, as by this point Graeme and the others were right by the lift. The doors were already open. They got in and Dickie pulled the doors shut.

"I should really be getting back home," he said.

"Dickie lives in the gatekeeper's cottage," Fanny informed them.

"I'll escort you to your room, miss," Dickie told Fanny, "and then I'll be on my way."

"All right, Dickie," said Fanny, patting him on the cheek.

Calamara rounded on Jim. "What were you going to do back there?"

"We need to tell Roberta," said Jim. "Mr Thornton knew about the boats and he didn't show up to talk to her! What if he's vanished, just like the Ravershams? We have to say something!"

"And what were you planning on saying?"

"I was going to tell them about the boats, about Lord Raversham!"

Fanny yelped.

Calamara ignored her and shot a look Graeme's way. "You see?" she said. "This is what happens when you lie."

Turning back to Jim, she continued, "If you say anything, all you'll do is cause unnecessary pain."

"What do you mean?"

"Did you not see how Lord Raversham reacted – or didn't react – when we mentioned the Pyn King? Are you blind as well as deaf?"

"Maybe he's just good at masking his feelings."

"Are there two Lord Ravershams? Because I know you can't be talking about the one I've met."

"Who else could the Pyn King be? What makes you think it's not him?"

"We know he was on the beach that night because of the piskie; so he's not just some senile old fool who misplaced a keepsake. But is he the Pyn King? We'd know one way or the other, *if* we'd followed *my* plan; but as it is, the only 'proof' we have comes from Graeme."

Everyone looked at him.

"I," Graeme started to say. He couldn't face any of them. He concentrated on the lift walls. He hadn't noticed before, how they were covered in coarse fabric, embroidered with roses. "I could be wrong about it being Lord Raversham's voice that I heard," he said in a small voice, "and Calamara's right. The way he reacted in the library, he isn't the Pyn King."

Calamara blinked. She seemed surprised. "Thank you," she said. It was the first time Graeme had heard her say anything to him that didn't reek of sarcasm.

"Of course it's not Grandpa!" laughed Fanny. "How silly of you to think that!"

"Are you sure?" Jim asked Graeme. He didn't sound angry.

"Yes," said Graeme.

"And what about the rest of it?" Calamara asked. "What about your, 'underground encounter', and all the other stuff from your, 'dream'?"

“I saw the cave,” Graeme said. The awful thing was he wasn’t even sure about that now. What if he’d imagined the entire thing?

“Oh, the cave,” Calamara was saying, “of course, the cave. It always comes back to caves.”

Jim gave Fanny a speculative glance. “Maybe this would be a good time to explore those passages Fanny knows about.”

“Oh yes!” Fanny agreed.

“Do you know of any that lead to caves underground?”

“I don’t know. I don’t go down that far. I’m too scared. But if you’re with me…”

Calamara wasn’t happy. “Fine,” she snapped. “Go crawling through dusty tunnels all you want. When you don’t find any caves, I hope you shut up about them. For now, let’s just get back to our rooms and play along with the grown–ups’ plans. You can go off on your wild goose chase later.

“Now is anybody going to start this elevator?”

Jim punched the buttons to take them to floor ten.

Fanny jumped up and down. “Ooh, Dickie,” she exclaimed, “you’ve got to come along, too! You can get a ladder and climb up to my window at midnight!”

“I don’t know that my ladder’s long enough, miss,” said Dickie.

Graeme listened to them plotting what they were going to do, wondering if Jim really still had any faith in him. He lost track of what they were saying as he let his attention drift off. Something was bugging him, something other than Calamara for a change; something wasn’t quite right. He bit his lip, making it bleed, as he thought; and his eyes slowly widened as he realised what was wrong.

“We’ve gone past floor ten,” he said. “We’re still going down!”

Sure enough, the indicator above the doors hadn’t stopped at floor ten and was slowly clicking down floor by floor.

Calamara pursed her lips and scowled. “You’re right,” she said. Admitting Graeme was right was like swallowing thorns for her, he guessed. He smiled back at her.

She saw him smirking. “For once,” she added in clipped tones.

The indicator reached the ground floor and didn’t move any further; the lift kept going.

“Where is it taking us?” asked Fanny, suddenly afraid. She clung to Dickie.

“I don’t know,” he said.

“I’m scared,” said Fanny.

"Don't worry," said Jim.

The lift hit bottom.

Fitzpatrick's voice came over the speaker. "The llawr o annwn. Certain death and damnation await. No consumable items beyond this point."

The doors opened.

Fanny screamed.

CHAPTER NINE
Caves Galore

Skeletons! Skeletons hanging upside–down, suspended from the ceiling by chains tied round their ankles, grinning to welcome the newcomers to the llawr o annwn. Some had rats in their eye sockets, long–whiskered, quivering noses poking out to smell the new arrivals; all were dripping with blood that formed rivulets on the floor, pooling in places.

Calamara wrenched the latticework door open and wheeled part–way out of the lift. She hoisted herself up, running a fingertip along a length of matted hair that was dangling from one of the skulls, catching a droplet of blood.

She tasted it.

Fanny screamed again.

"It's just rust," Calamara told her, "rusty water. There's no need to get excited."

"We're probably under the foundations of the castle," said Graeme. Having an architect for an uncle could be useful, sometimes.

"Hark at you. I don't recall asking your opinion," Calamara said, sniffing.

Jim said, "I think Graeme's right."

Calamara sniffed again and then said, "Are you all going to sit there and rot or join me?"

It was more an order than a question, but that didn't stop Fanny trying to get the lift to go again by running her hands up and down over all the buttons. It went nowhere, though, so they stepped out into the tunnel, crouching to avoid the skeletons.

The room they were in had rough stone walls and smelt damp. The air was clammy too, neither hot nor cold, somewhere between the two that was simply uncomfortable. At the far end, past the decayed corpses, there was a wooden door covered in moss and cobwebs. They wove their way along and somehow, by the time they reached it (and Graeme didn't know exactly how this happened) he and Jim were in the lead.

"Someone have a listen," said Calamara. She swivelled in her chair so it hit Graeme. "Go on, you do it."

If Graeme could have thought of a good reason to refuse, he would have. As it was, he cleared the muck off the wood as best he could and put his ear to the door.

"Nothing," he said, probably too quickly, but he could feel gooey stuff – gooey *alive* stuff – crawling into his hair and down his neck.

"There's no keyhole. It can't be locked. See if you can open it and have a look."

Graeme wondered why he hadn't noticed that a few seconds earlier. He brushed off the doorknob with the cuff of his jumper and inched the door open so he could peek through.

"I can't see anything," he whispered. "It's very dark."

He stuck his head through the door a bit more and squinted into the darkness. He blinked a few times to get his eyes to adjust.

"I still can't see anything," he hissed, "but there's a strange smell…"

And something grabbed him by his hair and yanked him into the gloom.

*

"Look what I found!"

Another door opened and Graeme was dragged into a dimly lit cave. Water was trickling down the walls, dribbling into green pools lined with lichen. Held in an awkward position, looking at everything sideways on, Graeme was facing a row of desks with computers, behind which sat girls wearing microphone headsets. The girls wore white shirts with half–undone burgundy ties. They seemed a little familiar but Graeme couldn't quite place them. One of the girls looked at him and then up at whomever it was who had a hold of him.

“Do you mind? I’m on the phone!” she said, indicating a telephone with a flashing light on it. “I thought we were expecting our Lord?” she asked, frowning down at Graeme.

“We got this instead.”

“Have you got time to play, then? I thought you were getting everything ready.”

“Oh, that won’t take long.”

The girl shrugged. “On your head be it,” she said. “I would have checked and checked again. If there’s not enough you know he’ll be mad.”

“Don’t worry, *mother*,” Graeme’s captor drawled sarcastically. “There’s tons left over from when the Parliament gig went up the swanny.”

“I hope so for you sake,” said the girl. She punched a few buttons on her phone and then said in a perky voice, “Thank you for holding! Good Evening! You’re through to Con Support, Stella speaking. Oh, hello! How are you? I almost didn’t recognise you, it’s been that long! What can I do for you? Right… right… and you want to kill him? Okay. Not a good day, eh? Well I can talk you through that. Have you got any idea what he was doing? You’ll have to tidy up after we’re done.”

Graeme was dumped on the floor and looked up into the face of a tall, skinny boy with huge blue eyes and messed up hair. He knew then where he’d seen him – and those girls – before. The boy was Gabriel, and the girls had been in the choir with him, back at the garden centre. What was going on?

“Hang on,” Gabriel said in a surly voice. “I’ve got to go and help get your friends. I’ll be back. Don’t try going anywhere or they’ll kill you,” he advised, indicating the girls. They all smiled and waved.

The girl who was on the phone, Stella, appeared to be getting a bit flustered. “No,” she said, sounding weary, “you’re not getting it right. It’s quite simple. Pull to the left, then to the right, then left and left again. No, he should be choking by now.”

She looked at the other girls, went cross–eyed and tapped the side of her head, then returned attention to her caller. “No, yes, I’m sure you’re doing your best. Well, would you like us to arrange for someone to visit and do it for you? Sure, we can do that, not a problem. We can’t do it this week, though, what with it being Christmas and all. We have another thing on, I’m afraid. Yes. I’ll book you in for the first slot after New Year, how about that? Could I have the intended's name, please? Thank you, that's great. No, I've never known it not to work before! Oh, that's okay! It's what we're here for, isn't it? No, it probably won't be me who comes out. I'm chained to this desk, I tell you! Okay then. We'll let you know how things go. Have a happy holiday! Righty–ho! Bye then! Toodle–oo! Bye!"

She stabbed at a button to disconnect the call and pulled off her headset. "Moron!" she spat at the phone.

Gabriel re–appeared and hauled Graeme to his feet. Twisting around, Graeme saw that Jim, Calamara, Fanny and Dickie were all being manhandled as well. Without her chair, Calamara looked like a rag doll, albeit a fuming, dagger–eyed rag doll.

"Not a good day for you, eh?" Gabriel asked upon hearing Stella's outburst.

"You're not wrong," Stella replied. "Where are you taking them?"

"To the cells, I s'pose. Our Lord can decide what he wants done with them when he arrives."

Stella took a deep breath and put her headset back on. Graeme could hear her voice as she answered another call, sounding all happy again, fading away as they were forced through a narrow gap in the rock and out into a cavern. It was the one he'd seen before, the one he'd told Jim and Calamara about. So he hadn't imagined it. He smiled to himself even as he was dragged along.

Their captors took them across the floor and through an archway on the other side of the room that led to a row of dingy cells. Gabriel dropped Graeme again and fumbled with a set of keys. He had great difficulty getting the cell door unlocked. When it finally clicked, he pushed the door open and all five of them were tossed inside. Calamara heaved herself into a corner beside a pile of chalky rubble, gathering her legs up and hugging them to her chest. It was odd how pathetic she looked.

The metal bar door slammed shut and the boys swore as they went through the rigmarole of locking it again. They laughed and walked off.

"Well, that didn't go too well," said Jim. "Sounds like we might get to meet the Pyn King, though, eh?"

Graeme nodded.

"I don't know that I want to be around when he comes," said Dickie.

"Nor do I," said Fanny, cowering by his side.

"Well we could always try to escape," said Jim. He got up and examined the door.

Dickie joined him. "I helped my dad with some of the locks on the garden gates," he said, squinting in the semi–light, "but all we did was bash the rusted ones out with a hammer."

"Could you use a hair–pin?" asked Fanny, now positively bubbling with happiness. "They used a hairpin in 'Georgina Ace' last week. I watched it on satellite TV while Benjamin was out. Georgina Ace said 'bum' three times!"

Graeme was amazed all over again at how Fanny managed to sound so frightened one minute and then be okay the next.

"Thank you miss, but I don't think hairpins actually work," said Dickie, "where locks are concerned."

"Could any of us squeeze through the bars?" Jim asked. He looked at Graeme and Calamara.

"Like I'd be of any use if I got out while I'm in this state," said Calamara.

Graeme got up and gave it a shot, but the bars were fused too close together. Even Fanny couldn't manage it.

They collapsed on the floor.

"Nothing to do but wait, then," said Jim.

There was noise building up outside the cell, back in the cavern. It was too distant for Graeme to make out exactly what was going on; there was just the general hubbub that you get when a large number of people are meeting.

They'd sat there for a few minutes when Fanny got up. "Right," she said. "All right, then."

Walking to the door, she grabbed hold of the bars, took a deep breath and screamed, "Let us out! Help! Help! I can't take it any more! I'll tell you everything, everything! I can't be locked up! I need air! Don't fence me in! Help!"

She kept going for ages. For such a small person, her lung capacity was incredible. Eventually, Gabriel appeared. He didn't look impressed. He folded his arms as Fanny reached out through the bars and tried to grab hold of him.

"Please! Help me!" Fanny pleaded. She was loud, but she wasn't the greatest actress in the world.

Gabriel's face broke into a lopsided grin. "Yeah, I'll bet," he said. "This is a bit of an old ploy, don't you think?" He reached into his pocket and pulled out a bunch of keys. "These what you're after?"

he laughed. "Fat chance. Now why don't you," he said, pushing Fanny roughly to the floor, "sit down and be a good little girl?"

Dickie's eyes blazed and he shot up off his feet and took hold of the boy, pulling him right up to the bars so their faces touched. "Don't you ever push her again," he said. His voice was trembling.

"Too right," said Fanny, now at Dickie's side. She kicked Gabriel's shins a couple of times.

Dickie pushed with all his might, sending Gabriel spinning across the corridor where he collided with the wall. Bending down to rub his legs, Gabriel said, "You'll regret that later," and limped away.

"That went well," Calamara said. She seemed to be getting her usual foul temper back again.

"*Oh ye of little faith*," said Jim. He'd obviously seen something that Graeme and Calamara had missed.

Fanny turned around, grinning from ear to ear. Dickie reached into his pocket and pulled out his keys, only they weren't his keys. They were the keys –

"They're the keys to the cells!" squealed Fanny, clapping.

Jim got up. "Well done," he congratulated both of them.

Dickie blushed. Fanny looked dead pleased with herself.

"Now let's get out of here," said Jim.

"It's not going to be as simple as that," snapped Calamara. "Listen to all the noise out there. We're never going to be able to sneak past."

"Let me go and have a look first, then."

"Oh, that's such a good idea," said Calamara. "You're really going to be able to hear if someone comes up behind you."

"Graeme will come along as well."

"Yeah," said Graeme. "Of course I will."

Calamara sighed. "Oh, good."

Dickie unlocked the door. Graeme winced as it squeaked open. He and Jim craned their necks out to make sure nobody had heard anything.

"*Come on*," said Jim, taking the keys from Dickie.

"Take this thing, too," said Calamara, throwing the key with the Raversham crest on it to Jim. "You might need it. I want it back, mind."

Graeme and Jim walked out of the cell and shut the door behind them. Looking right, they saw the archway that led back to the cave. Just as Graeme had thought, all the noise seemed to be coming from that direction. To the left was a hefty wooden door; and there was yet another passage next to that.

They approached the wooden door first. There was a tiny window set into the top half of it which Graeme could see through if he stood on tiptoe. There were steps leading up to he didn't know where on the other side. The door was locked. Jim tried each of the keys in turn, but none worked, so he and Graeme made their way into the passage instead.

This tunnel twisted and turned. It wasn't lit. They stumbled along, and when they did eventually see some light they both almost broke into a run. It was only the sound of something up ahead clattering on the floor that made Graeme stop. He pulled Jim to a halt as well. Now edging along, they flattened themselves against the wall and peeked around the corner.

It was a kitchen: a rather basic one; it had a large, single oven, four tables and that was about it. A girl in a white tunic, chequered trousers and a floppy chef's hat was chopping up some meat and yelling at a boy who was cleaning up where he'd spilt a pot of what looked like cauliflower on the floor.

An older boy marched across from the other end of the room. "What's going on?" he asked. "What's all the noise?" He stepped over the boy and the pot to reach the girl. "Can't you keep your skivvies under control?" he asked her.

"Bog off, Ashley," said the girl.

The older boy wasn't impressed. "What have you got in the oven?"

She gave him a contemptuous look. "Take a look yourself and see."

Ashley opened the oven door.

"Hello?" someone said from deep inside. "Hello? Can I get out now? It's getting very hot in here."

Ashley shut the oven door. "Who's that?"

"It's call 42357," the girl said, continuing to chop up the joint of meat, "a disappearance. He's got to mysteriously vanish." She stopped her chopping long enough to wave a hand in what was no doubt meant to be a mystical manner. "What better way for that to happen," she explained, tossing her meat cleaver in the air so it tumbled over and over, then catching it again as it fell back down, "than for us to have bacon and chops and prime rib and whatever for the week? Evan," she indicated the boy and his pot, "likes the brains best. And what we don't eat, we give to the Carregs. Nothing goes to waste!"

Graeme and Jim pulled themselves back completely out of sight.

"*Interesting, eh? Let's see what's going on in the cave*," said Jim.

Calamara seemed less than impressed as the boys ran past the cells again and into the archway that led to the cavern. This was it all right; this was the place where the Pyn King had held that ceremony. Graeme was even more convinced now because it was full of people, just like it had been in his dream. *Which wasn't a dream*, he thought to himself; but the brief thrill of proving himself right, or rather, proving Calamara wrong, started to fade as memories of what he'd seen began to come flooding back.

The braziers cast elongated, quivering shadows onto the reddish–brown rock walls. There were loads of children in there now, about a choir's worth, most dressed in black cloaks. A few, about six or so that Graeme could see, wore white jumpsuits with gold braiding down the arms. There were also a number of cloaked adults. All of them, children and adults alike, seemed to be waiting for something.

"*This really doesn't look good*," said Jim.

They made their way back to the others and told them what they'd seen.

"You must be in heaven," Calamara drawled at Jim. "So many caves!"

Jim smiled in a good–natured way. "We can't get through the kitchen. They're... cooking. The other door's locked and there's nowhere to hide in the meantime."

"And the cavern is crowded," Graeme said. "We could creep round the back of the room, maybe, but..." he looked at Calamara.

"You couldn't make it if you had to lug me along with you," she finished for him, knowing exactly what he was going to say.

Graeme nodded.

"Well, you'll just have to go without me then," she said. "All of you can get out, raise the alarm, then come back for me."

"But what will they do to you when they realise we're gone?" asked Fanny.

"We can't..." said Jim.

Calamara held up a hand. "Don't be stupid," she said. "You should all go."

"Okay," said Graeme.

Fanny was stunned. "How could you?"

"I wouldn't expect anything else from him," said Calamara, picking at a lump of chalky rock.

Everyone was looking at Graeme as if he'd said something terrible. He supposed he could have said that he just realised that it was the sensible thing to do and that Calamara had suggested it herself, after all. He could have said that, but it would have been a lie. He hadn't thought anything of the sort. He just wanted to get out of there as quickly as possible.

Calamara grinned, her face triumphant. She was really annoyed that the cave had turned out to be real; but her spirits had improved because Graeme had just gone and dropped himself in it again. He really did need to try and think before opening his mouth, especially around her.

She savoured the moment; but then she said, "He is right, though. You need to go now."

Fanny plonked herself down. "Well, I'm not leaving you," she said.

Dickie looked at them. "If you're not leaving, miss, then I'm not going, either," he declared. He sat down as well.

Calamara gave them both a disparaging stare. "More fool you."

"Are you sure you're both going to stay?" Jim asked them. They nodded. "Then it's just us," he said to Graeme.

"Let's go," Graeme said.

The two of them turned to leave and stopped short. Gabriel and another one of the boys who had captured them earlier were standing in their way. They were both wearing those white outfits.

"I see you got the door open," Gabriel said. He pulled out Dickie's keys and chucked them on the floor. "Yours, I believe. Clever, but did you really think we wouldn't notice?"

He and his friend pushed Graeme and Jim back into the cell. "You're not going anywhere."

Without warning, Fanny flipped up and kicked Gabriel in the chest, then pirouetted and karate–chopped him. The other boy went to help, but Jim stuck out his foot and tripped him up. The two boys landed heavily on the floor and before anyone knew it, Fanny was on top of them, banging their heads on the floor.

"You… should… brush… your… hair!" she chanted to Gabriel.

Jim gently pulled her away. "I think they're unconscious now," he told her.

"Good," she said. She wasn't out of breath or anything.

Jim grinned at Calamara. "*Looks like you'll be okay, anyway.*"

Calamara didn't look convinced. "*I think she's as crazy as him,*" she signed, pointing at Graeme.

"*Let's wear their uniforms,*" Jim said. "*It might help us get through.*"

They struggled into the suits. A disguise was a good plan but Gabriel and his friend were that much bigger than Graeme and Jim, especially Graeme; once the suits were on, even over the top of their winter clothes, the sleeves still fell way beyond their fingertips and they were forced to roll their trouser legs up so they didn't fall over as they walked. Fanny did her best to try and get Graeme's hair to spike up, "so you look more like one of them," she explained. He wished she hadn't used so much spit. He pulled his collar right up to try and obscure his face.

They said goodbye to the others and cautiously made their way into the cavern. Everyone's attention was on the dais at the front, where the Pyn King was standing. Graeme froze on the spot. He was unable to budge, even when Jim prodded him.

"The time is nearly at hand," the Pyn King was saying. "Tonight, the final stages of my great plan will set in motion a chain of events that will ultimately lead us to our glorious destiny!"

The cloaked woman in the red mask that Graeme had seen before stepped forward. "We have long planned for this time," she said. "You all know the part you must play. We are gathered here now to send the beloved chosen ones on their way. They are honoured to be responsible for this, the first task. They are emissaries. For the first time in an age, the name of the Pyn King shall be spoken outside of these confines. The world shall tremble as his Word is spread."

She held out an arm. "Bring forth the creatures!"

Four huge white beasts lumbered out to the centre of the stage. They were the size of rhinos but walked on two legs, shambling along, feet scraping on the ground, arms with massive five fingered hands hanging at their sides. Their tiny, light purple eyes were expressionless.

The Pyn King raised his face to the heavens. "Here to serve the Purpose are the Carreg Golau! Come forward, my emissaries, most blessed of the Children of the Night! Come forward and ready yourselves to start your journey!"

The crowd began to part in places and various kids, the ones in white, made their way up to join the King. Everyone around Graeme and Jim also moved aside. There was nothing the two of them could do to escape. They had to walk forward; and Graeme was surprised to find that he actually could walk.

They did their best not to look anyone in the face as they stepped up onto the dais. The others were lining up behind the creatures, their heads down, two to a beast. Graeme and Jim followed their lead.

Graeme glanced to the side and spotted Aled and Reeves, Gabriel's friends, standing behind the Carreg next to theirs.

The Pyn King clicked his fingers and one of his cloaked followers stepped up, carrying a stack of masks. The King took them and moved along the line, handing them out. They were tribal masks; each had a different design. Just as Roberta had suspected, someone *had* wanted to take those masks from Uriah's room.

Graeme kept his head right down as the King neared him. When they were level, the King passed a plain white mask to Jim and Jim took it. It was wooden, painted white with slight, curved indentations for eyebrows. Then the King held out a polished silver mask for Graeme. Actually, it wasn't silver: it was made of tin; but it gleamed in the torchlight, nonetheless and was almost identical to the King's own: featureless, save for the almond eyes.

Graeme reached for it, but the King didn't let go. Not daring to look up, Graeme started to panic as they stood there, his heart racing as he and the King both gripped the mask. He felt sure that the King must have known who he was. Surely if these people were the Pyn King's emissaries then they'd be well–known, recognisable. It would be easy to spot an impostor, wouldn't it, especially this close?

And the moment passed. The King let the mask go and Graeme quickly put it on, feeling safer now his features were concealed.

The King strode back to face the throng and the Children of the Night clambered up onto the Carregs' backs, sitting in place behind the hunched shoulders. Graeme glanced at Jim and they did the same. Then they sat in place and waited. When Graeme's hands touched the creature, he was surprised to find its skin felt solid and cold, like rock. He scratched at it and bits came away, the residue lodging under his fingernail. The Carreg shifted where it stood, its colossal shoulder muscles undulating, as if it enjoyed the sensation. Graeme hoped it was tame. If he or Jim were expected to try and control it then they'd really be in trouble.

The King raised his arms above his head. “Fly!” he commanded.

As one, the Carregs crouched to the ground and then with a massive burst of energy they leapt straight into the air, hurtling towards the ceiling.

Graeme looked up, expecting the rock above him to part, or for the monsters to change direction. Neither of those things happened. Instead he felt a sharp jolt, like you get when you dream you’ve tripped and fallen and wake up all of a sudden; and then they weren’t about to hit the ceiling any more. They were soaring into the night sky, past snowy mountain–tops and on up, up until the air was so thin Graeme found it hard to breathe, up so far he could see the curve of the Earth.

CHAPTER TEN
Always Another Way

The Carreg Golau stepped from cloud to cloud, travelling miles with each bound. They had appeared so clumsy; yet now, in free air, they were nothing of the sort. Now, they were graceful, moving in precise time with each other; and they made no noise. The only sound Graeme could hear was the wind whistling about him.

They were racing through the night to Graeme knew not where. Jim was looking around and down at the patchwork land; every now and then he'd let out a whoop of delight.

Graeme took a sharp intake of breath as the creatures did whatever it was they did and he and Jim were wrenched out of place, only to find moments later that they'd landed on the wing of a plane. The other monsters and their riders were perched nearby, some on the wings, some on the body of the plane, one right on the nose, looking like an oversized hood ornament. The plane didn't seem affected; it didn't shake or drop out of the sky, instead continuing on course. Graeme looked sideways into a window and saw a family, all asleep, apart from one little boy with jam smeared round his mouth, his face pressed to the glass. The boy waved, not at all disturbed by the sight of the Carreg Golau. Graeme looked left and right before waving back.

And they were gone. The stars became streaks for a second and again Graeme felt like he had started in his sleep. Now they were atop Tower Bridge, the beasts hanging onto the stonework with one arm, their purple eyes scanning the skyline, the lights below glaring into Graeme's eyes. The traffic didn't grind to a halt; nobody walking over the bridge stopped. London was unaware of what was going on.

The Carreg Golau looked around once more, like they were getting their bearings, and then lifted into the air again, lightly touching the tip of Big Ben and bounding on across the rooftops, staying lower this time, stepping on chimneys and trees, even touching the ground on occasion, until they reached the Mall and one giant jump later came to rest on the rooftop of Buckingham Palace, next to a fluttering flag.

With one more jolt they found themselves in a deserted corridor in the palace, lined with portraits and paintings. The Children of the Night dismounted, so Graeme and Jim got off as well.

"*Wow!*" said Jim.

The two of them trailed after the others, creeping along the corridor towards a large pair of double doors and sidling into a stiflingly hot grand ballroom, which was packed to the gunnels with equally grand men and women in evening dress. The walls were white, panelled with gilt edging and were lined with groaning tables of food and drink. At regular intervals there were towers of glasses over which cascaded waterfalls of bubbling champagne. Everything was covered in a swirling mass of diamond light, reflected from crystal chandeliers hung far above. An orchestra, led by a sedate conductor, was playing soft music that was almost drowned out by chatter. Waiters and waitresses hovered in the midst of it all, balancing trays heaving with little pastries and more glasses of champagne.

One of the Children of the Night pulled off his gruesome green mask. It was Aled. "Let's go," he said, and they melted into the crowd, leaving Graeme and Jim standing there, sticking out like sore thumbs.

Graeme felt Jim pulling at his sleeve. Jim pointed across the room. "It's the Prime Minister!"

He hauled Graeme around before he could look. Now they were facing one of the tables. An old woman was inspecting the impressive spread, her two walking sticks propped up against the table. Behind the table was an alcove, all but covered by a hanging tapestry.

"*Quick*," said Jim, "*be you and I behind an arras then!*"

Trying not to be conspicuous and therefore, Graeme thought, probably looking really dodgy, they edged backwards until they were able to duck out of sight.

Now safely concealed, they let their masks fall to the floor and peeped around the edge of the tapestry. The Children of the Night were nowhere to be seen.

"*What do you think they're up to?*" asked Jim.

Graeme shrugged. "*No idea. I hope they don't notice that we're missing!*"

"Mother! What are you doing?"

Jim nudged Graeme in the ribs so hard that it hurt. It was the Queen. She was wearing a violet dress and a tiara. In one hand she had half a glass of champagne. The old woman, who was hovering over a bowl of fruit salad, paused.

"You startled me, dear," said the Queen Mother, her voice quite weak. "I was just getting another helping…"

"Another one?" The Queen looked disapprovingly at her mother.

The Queen Mother blinked. "Yes?"

"You've had fifteen now."

"It's very good."

"It's very alcoholic," the Queen corrected her. "You can see the fumes rising from the bowl even way across the room. I think they emptied an entire bottle of kirsch in there!"

"Really?" The Queen Mother's eyes were slightly unfocused.

"And you haven't moved from this spot for an hour. Nobody else can get close enough to have the merest smidgeon of a taste."

The Queen Mother licked her lips and leaned closer to her daughter. "I'll make this my last then," she promised, tapping the side of her nose with one finger.

"See that you do. People are starting to talk."

"Oh, don't be cross with your poor old mum," said the Queen Mother, her voice quavering.

The Queen raised an eyebrow. "My poor old mum? My poor old mum? I wasn't aware I had a poor old mum. If she comes in you'll be sure to point her out, won't you?"

That struck Graeme as a very Calamara–ish thing to say. Of course, they'd met before. Maybe some of Calamara's DNA had transferred from tooth to nose.

The Queen Mother popped a sausage roll in her mouth, grasped her walking sticks and shuffled around to watch the room. "Anyone arrived yet?" she asked, though it was hard to make out what she said because her mouth was so full.

"Well, the Prime Minister's here. He's over by the orchestra, having his ear chewed off by Lord Harries." The Queen waved across the room at a bald man in a dark suit who towered over everyone else. He inclined his head and waved back.

Jim elbowed Graeme again. *"It is the Prime Minister!"* he said. (Graeme knew that, of course.) *"He'd have a fit if he knew I was here!"*

"We're still waiting for the First Minister of Scotland," the Queen continued. "He'll no doubt be trying to leave it as late as possible so he can make an entrance."

The Queen Mother said something but Graeme missed it.

"Quite," said the Queen. "Oh, look out. The PM's escaped. He's coming over."

"Oh, 'uggr," said the Queen Mother.

"Ma'am," said the Prime Minister in his barrow–boy cockney accent as he neared them, inclining his head towards the Queen, "and Ma'am," he winked at the Queen Mother. "Delightful, as ever, to see you both." He had a large glass of yellowy–reddish something in his hand. It had a chunk of pineapple trying to float in it… and a few cherries… and a tiny umbrella… and a bendy straw. There was probably more paraphernalia than drink.

"Hello, Thomas," the Queen greeted him. "Are you having a good time?"

"I'm hoping it will improve now I've managed to shake off Harries."

"But you looked like you were having such a nice chat," the Queen lied.

The Prime Minister rolled his eyes. "If that man asks me once more about setting a definitive timescale for the inauguration of the Welsh Parliament I think I'll scream."

"This is hardly the time or place for such questions, after all," said the Queen, apparently sympathising with him.

"It's good to know someone understands," said the Prime Minister, closing his eyes and pinching the bridge of his nose. "And I'm feeling somewhat… delicate tonight," he added.

"One too many late nights?" the Queen asked.

"Yeah, it was the office Christmas party yesterday," said the Prime Minister.

The Queen Mother swallowed the remainder of her sausage roll and treated him to a winsome smile. "I would have thought you'd be hardened to all that sort of thing by now, the number of shindigs you throw," she said, using a fingernail to pick at bits of sausage meat and pastry that had got caught between her teeth.

The Prime Minister looked slightly guilty. "Well, we do like to have the odd bash or two," he admitted. He joggled his head from side to side. "Work hard, play hard, you know."

The Queen and her mother exchanged a very quick glance.

"Yes…" they both said at exactly the same time.

"Anyway," said the Prime Minister, "last night's was the last until New Year. Apart from the one on Boxing Day, but that's more of a damage limitation thing, technically speaking. I had to invite the opposition, you know, keep 'em sweet, so I don't think it counts, at least not in my book."

The ladies were watching him and simply smiling. It seemed to be throwing the Prime Minister off balance somewhat. He sloshed his glass around and sucked air through his teeth, gazing around the room for something to talk about. His eyes narrowed as they fell upon the tapestry the boys were hiding behind. Jim pulled his head back, tugging at Graeme as well.

"*Did he see us? What are they saying?*"

Graeme started to sign everything he could hear for Jim.

"Thomas, are you all right?" the Queen asked the Prime Minister.

"I thought I saw – " he started to say, and then he laughed.

"Saw what?"

"Don't worry. It's just me, the paranoid politician!"

Jim breathed a quiet sigh of relief. They peeked out from their hiding place again.

"It really annoys me when people don't finish their sentences," said the Queen, irritated.

The Prime Minister shook his head. "Sorry, sorry. I just thought… for a moment… I thought I saw that boy, the Gunpowder Lad, you know…"

"Oh," said the Queen. "I would have thought you'd have been happy to see him. I seem to recall reading a report about you professing eternal gratitude."

"That was almost a year ago," said the Prime Minister, "and I'd only just taken up office. Back then, he was an asset. Now though," he licked his lips, "now's a different matter."

"Such a short time in power and already so much to hide?"

The Prime Minister didn't answer her. His eyes twinkled as he sucked hard on his straw.

The doors at the other end of the room opened and a grossly fat man in a green tweed suit strode in, stopped and struck a pose. He was already sweating; it would only get worse once he entered the room proper. Nobody paid him any attention, but he seemed oblivious of that, continuing to preen as he looked around the room. When he spotted the Queen and the Prime Minister standing together he waved.

"Halloo!" he shouted, skipping towards them and bowing as he neared the Queen.

"First Minister, how good of you to join us," the Queen greeted him. The man stood up straight, his sharp eyes, as pea green as his clothes, searching her face for any sign of sarcasm.

"My pleasure, your Majesty."

"How are things north of the border, Lord Gelding?" asked the Prime Minister, handing him a glass of champagne from the table.

"Ticking along, thank you, Thomas," said the First Minister. "Things are going very smoothly, now we don't have to put up with the interference from you damn southerners!"

Everyone laughed. It sounded a bit forced on the part of the Prime Minister. Once again, there was an awkward lull in the conversation.

All of them let their eyes wander around the room as they furiously racked their brains for small talk.

"Oh no," groaned the First Minister, "here comes Harries."

Everybody turned as one to look in the same direction.

"Well, well," said Harries, a stocky man with a square jaw who looked as if he'd be more comfortable in rugby kit than the grey suit he was currently wearing, "all the leaders gathered together. I hope you ladies and gentlemen weren't having a powwow without me, now."

"Would we, Harries?" the Prime Minister pretended that he was shocked at the suggestion. "Never!"

Lord Harries didn't seem to be convinced. His eyes moved to the table. "Mmm! Fruit Salad!" he said, a broad smile spreading across his face. He reached out to get a bowl.

There was a clatter as the Queen Mother dropped her walking sticks. Lord Harries' face became a picture of pain as she gripped him by the wrist of his outstretched arm.

"Now Lord Harries," she simpered, "are you sure you wouldn't prefer to have a piece of pecan pie?"

"I'm allergic," he said. He gave a small yelp as the Queen Mother tightened her grip.

"How about a fig roll, then?"

"They give me the, the runs! Ow! Ow! Ow! Although, one can never be too regular, I suppose," he said. "Yes! A fig roll! Sounds delicious!"

The Queen Mother let go of him. Lord Harries cradled his hand and started to massage it.

"You have a strong grip, your Majesty," he said.

"Me? What nonsense," the Queen Mother told him. "Don't forget your fig roll," she said, grabbing one and passing it to him.

The Prime Minister bent down and picked up the Queen Mother's walking sticks for her while the Queen just frowned at her mother.

"*Look,*" said Jim. He pointed to the doors around the room. The Children of the Night were positioned at each entrance, blocking the way.

"*We should warn somebody,*" he said. "*They could be in danger!*"

Graeme didn't think there was any "could" about it, but if he or Jim stepped out and did anything they'd be exposed and then *they'd* be in danger. He was about to say as much to Jim, but Jim was already gone, having leapt into clear view.

The Prime Minister sprayed champagne all over the Queen as he let out a terrified cry of horror. His arm flailed wildly in Jim's direction. "It's the – it's the – boy!"

The Queen took a wad of napkins and patted the front of her dress, trying to dry herself. She looked at Jim. "It's a boy, yes," she said. "I don't know how you're going to react when your wife gives birth if this is your normal reaction to children. Is he with the caterers? That's a very smart uniform."

"No, you don't understand," said the Prime Minister. "That's *the* boy! The computer kid!"

"Really?" asked the Queen. "So you did see him. Maybe you're not as paranoid as you think."

"How did he get here?" asked the Prime Minister, enraged.

"It would take too long to explain," said Jim. "You're all in danger. You have to call security now!"

As he said, "now", the room fell silent, so that last word seemed to echo from wall to wall. The conductor of the orchestra turned around, clutching at his throat. Blood was seeping between his fingers. He collapsed. People screamed; they dashed for the exits, but the unfortunates who reached the doors were cut down.

Aled, now masked again, climbed on top of the conductor's body.

"We come on behalf of the Pyn King!" he declared, taking the thin blade he had used to cut the conductor's throat and wiping it on his sleeve. It left a streak of red on his arm. His masked face looked down at it, and at the gurgling man beneath his feet.

The Carregs appeared in the room. There wasn't a puff of smoke; there was no flash of lightning, nor a thunderclap of noise. One second they hadn't been there, the next they were, silent as the grave. The only accompanying sound was the cracking and crunching of bones as they crushed the unlucky people who were standing where they had now settled.

The Children of the Night had left their posts and managed to surround the Queen, Queen Mother and the ministers. With the doors now unguarded, the brave party guests were leaving fast.

"Do not be afraid," a girl who was holding the First Minister said, "for my Lord wishes to discuss a most glorious future with you all."

Aled pushed his way through to join the others. He grabbed Jim.

"Seen enough, have you?" he asked. Jim, of course, couldn't tell that he'd said anything behind the mask.

"He's with you?" asked the Prime Minister.

"No," Aled replied. "He is not. And neither," he added, reaching behind the tapestry and pulling Graeme out, "is this one."

The Prime Minister seemed really unnerved. "Who's that?" he screeched.

"My Lord will explain all," said Aled. He pulled Graeme close and whispered lovingly in his ear, "and then you shall die."

*

Flying through the sky on the back of one of those creatures had been a thrill; being tied up in a net, suspended by a rope from around one of their ankles while travelling was much less fun. It was pretty difficult for Graeme to move, but he could see, by twisting and squirming, that the other creatures were carrying similar nets, all containing sacks with red circles on them. Graeme supposed they hadn't expected that he and Jim would be along for the ride, so they didn't have sacks for the pair of them. The mesh of the net dug into Graeme's face. For some reason the creatures were travelling a lot lower, skimming across land and sky. They were either unaware or didn't care that the interlopers were being dragged along on the ground and bumping over rooftops, sending tiles tumbling to the earth, or getting soaked as they were dipped into lakes and seas.

The journey, being more uncomfortable, of course seemed to take much longer. When Graeme finally caught a glimpse of Raversham Isle out of the corner of one eye, he breathed a mental sigh of relief. Yellow light spilled from every window of the castle and the festive lights installed for the party twinkled in the trees, making the place look peaceful, serene even, and welcoming; Graeme doubted they'd get a hearty welcome, no matter who was there to greet them when they landed.

One more gut–wrenching leap and they came to rest in the cavern, surrounded by the cloaked followers of the Pyn King. The riders dismounted and their great lumbering beasts were marched away. The nets were loosened and the captives tumbled onto the floor. Graeme and Jim sat up immediately. The sacks were tipped upside down and the others fell out, looking overcome. They were given no time to orient themselves; instead they were pushed and kicked until they were facing the dais. The door at the top of the staircase opened and the Pyn King strode out, a large map of some kind in his hand. He virtually ran down the stairs and was joined by his second in command as he approached the cavern floor.

Together they came to a halt by Graeme, who could see right into the woman's hood. He caught a glimpse of her green eyes, her real eyes, staring out at him from the pupils of the terrible painted eyes of her mask. She averted her gaze as soon as she realised they had made eye–to–eye contact.

"What have we here?" the Pyn King asked, starting to roll up the map. Graeme noticed it wasn't a map; they were blueprints, the layout of a building marked with crosses at various points.

The King patted his cheek with the rolled up document. "We weren't expecting you," he said to Graeme. The woman's fingers danced as he spoke, signing everything he said.

Aled stepped forward, removed his mask and bowed. "We discovered them, my Lord. They took the places of Gabriel and Tristan."

“We found your brothers unconscious in the cell with the boys’ friends,” said the woman. “They will live, Aled, though they will pay for their error.”

“At least let me deal with these two myself, my Lord,” said Aled.

“No,” said the Pyn King. Aled nodded, but shot Graeme an evil look.

“Take the prisoners to the cells,” said the woman.

Aled nodded again, stepped back, and started barking instructions. The crowd parted as the still befuddled ministers, and the Queen and Queen Mother, were taken away.

“Use the upper cells,” the Pyn King called after them. “Let our esteemed guests have a view!”

“What do we do with these two, my Lord?” asked the woman. She leaned so close to the King that the gross nose of her mask nudged his hood. “Is it time?”

The Pyn King turned his head until the gleaming silver mask was facing Graeme, so Graeme could see his own reflection, all crooked, a disfigured copy of his face staring back at him.

“I think – ” the King started to say, but there was a sudden burst of noise from beyond the door that led to the cells. There were yells, followed a thunderous crash and the walls shook, cracked, and fell in. Light, bright orange light flooded into the room, forcing Graeme to cover his eyes; and amidst the sounds of settling rubble and the screams of frightened people he heard – he *felt* – a roar. The room shook again, and again. It sounded like the cavern was in chaos. People were fighting to get out of the way of whatever was coming. The floor quaked and something very heavy thumped down in front of Graeme and Jim.

The light dimmed. Graeme took his hand away from his eyes. He and Jim were the only ones left. All the followers of the Pyn King, and the Pyn King himself, had vanished. The bowed head of one of the Carreg Golau was looming over Graeme’s head. Calamara was sitting astride its neck.

“Hello,” she said. “How did I know that you’d be in trouble by now? I thought I’d come and see if you needed some help... I’m sorry, I meant to say, some *more* help. *Again*.”

*

"This is amazing!" shouted Jim. He whooped. They were flying again, travelling through the night on the backs of the Carregs. Graeme and Jim were together on one; Fanny and Dickie were on another; and Calamara had one all to herself.

Jim turned around so he faced Graeme. "Have you noticed," he asked, "how we're being rescued by girls a lot lately?"

Graeme nodded as they passed through a wispy layer of cloud. He was looking at the skin of the Carreg he and Jim were riding. It was brown.

"You did a good job of getting out and raising the alarm," said Calamara as her Carreg neared theirs, "I *don't* think. Did you manage to do anything useful at all?"

"We saw them kidnap the Queen, and Queen Mother, and the Prime Minister, and the First Minister of Scotland, and some Lord from Wales!" said Jim.

"Lord Harries," said Calamara, "and I could have told you that. They brought them past our cell right before we escaped."

"How did you escape then?" asked Jim.

"I had some help from Hek–Hek here," said Calamara, patting the creature she was riding on.

"They have names?" Jim asked.

"Of course they do," piped up Fanny. "Mine's called Justyn!"

"We rode some things like these," said Jim, "but they were white. Are these like them?"

"These *are* them!" shouted Calamara. "Hek–Hek here was sleeping at the back of our cell. I was leaning against him. I just thought he was a pile of rock, but as I picked at it I realised that it was paper, coming away. They've been covered in papier–mâché, or something like it. It keeps them subdued, apparently. While you were off gallivanting, we uncovered the rest of him and when he woke up he agreed to help us escape."

"You talked to it?" asked Jim.

"Of course."

"They can talk?"

There was the sound of stone moving on stone as the Carreg that Graeme and Jim were riding on twisted its neck and looked at them. Its face was a soft, glowing blue; its eyes were two jet–black beads and its mouth a jagged crack.

"I can talk," it said in a very slow, deliberate voice. "My name is Reality."

"Hello Reality," said Jim.

Graeme didn't say anything.

Reality turned to look where he was going again.

"Where are we heading?" asked Jim.

"Somewhere safe," replied Calamara. "I hope."

They flew on into the night, eventually landing on a grassy hill in a park lit by old–fashioned streetlights. The creatures shrugged the kids off onto the ground and started to stretch. Their backs were all different colours: one grey, one brown and one black. As they turned around Graeme saw their fronts clearly for the first time. If they curled up they would have looked like nothing more remarkable than giant boulders, but standing in front of him now they revealed an inner core of coloured quartz, each one a unique shade. As they stretched they glowed brighter and brighter until they outshone the lights and blotted out the stars.

The grey one Calamara had been on, Hek–Hek, thumped onto the ground and yawned as the other two continued to stretch their legs.

"Where are we?" asked Jim, starting to pull off his white uniform now it was no longer required. Graeme followed his lead.

"My favourite place," said Hek–Hek, shuffling forward on his bottom. He snuffled, though it was anyone's guess where his nose was. "I need food," he said.

"Hek–Hek!" said Reality, putting one massive hand on his fellow's shoulder. "No."

"You don't know what I was going to say," said Hek–Hek.

"Oh yes I do, and the answer's no. We don't eat them."

Hek–Hek looked slightly disappointed. "Well, what else are we going to do with them?" he asked, ready to sulk.

"I don't really know," said Justyn.

"We could take them back with us," said Hek–Hek.

"Take them with us?" Justyn looked unsure. "No human has seen our home in an age."

Reality was smiling. "It's a great idea," he said.

"What?" Justyn asked him.

"Well, the Great Leader's always pontificating about how he knows best. Let's take them to him; let's give him the opportunity to demonstrate his profound wisdom."

Hek–Hek rubbed his hands together. "Good, good," he said. "I've got crackers at home. They're lovely with crackers."

"You're not going to eat them!" Reality exclaimed.

Fanny stuck her hand in the air. "I need to eat something. I'm hungry!"

"Me too." Hek–Hek began to mope.

"Let's go. Climb on up," Reality instructed Graeme.

So Graeme and Jim climbed back onto Reality, Fanny and Dickie clambered up to sit on Justyn's massive shoulders and Hek–Hek got to his feet, reached out and picked Calamara up. Fanny screamed.

"I won't eat her," Hek–Hek promised, gently placing Calamara behind his head.

"Let's go home," said Reality.

*

It felt like they dropped a thousand feet all at once. When Graeme's eyes stopped watering he found that they were making their way along a rough–walled tunnel. Criss–crossing amber veins ran through the rock on all sides, helping to light the way. They weren't really needed, as the three creatures generated more than enough natural illumination.

The tunnel went on for another few minutes before it opened out onto a grotto. There were more crystals making up the walls here than rocks, and they were all gold, so the entire cave felt warm and inviting. There was a shallow pool in the centre, with a path of blue slate slabs curving around the edge. A large egg shaped rock was at the far side.

The creatures set the passengers down and approached the pool.

"Ho, Great Leader!" Reality called, his voice echoing all around.

Cracks appeared in the egg–like rock and bright green light shot out through them, getting brighter and brighter as the Great Leader unfolded himself. He settled in position at the water's edge, one foot dangling in the pool. He had exactly the same black eyes as the others.

"We're back!" said Justyn.

The Great Leader frowned. "Had… had you gone somewhere?" he asked. His voice was slower than Reality's. It was as if he were concentrating very hard in order to talk.

"We've been gone for eight weeks or more," said Reality. "Some human had kidnapped us."

"Oh," said the Great Leader. He didn't seem very interested. "And in eight weeks you have regressed so far that you are talking in the human tongue?"

"We have company," said Reality. The creatures moved to one side so the Great Leader could see Graeme and the others. "They helped us three to escape," Reality told him. "There are more of us still held, back there."

"Oh," said the Great Leader. "And why did you bring these people here?"

"They'd seen us," said Reality. "No human has seen us in a long while..."

"Ah."

"We thought if anyone would know what to do, it would be you."

"I see."

"Can I eat one?" asked Hek–Hek.

"No you can't," said the Great Leader. "Leave us. I will talk to these humans myself and determine what their fate shall be."

Hek–Hek was crestfallen but didn't argue; he patted Calamara on the head and then he, Reality and Justyn walked out the way they had come, leaving the gang alone with the Great Leader, who leaned back against the wall of the grotto.

"What am I going to do with you?" he asked himself.

"You're not going to eat us, are you?" Fanny whimpered.

For a moment, it looked like the Great Leader was considering it. "No," he said eventually. "We're the Golau, not the Arswyd. Unlike our depraved cousins, we stopped eating humans when you started showing signs of a rudimentary intelligence."

"Thanks," snorted Calamara.

"Oh, it wasn't any great hardship," said the Great Leader, missing the sarcastic tone in Calamara's voice. "I never really cared for the taste, anyway."

"What did we taste – " Jim started to say, but stopped when he caught the exasperated look Calamara was directing at him. "We really ought to get back," he said instead.

"Back? So soon? How un–inquisitive you are."

"There's stuff going on, really bad stuff, and I think that maybe we ought to be warning someone. It might even be on a global level!"

"Oh." The Great Leader didn't seem very concerned. "Is the end nigh again? Some of us thought you wouldn't survive much longer. Mind you, some said you wouldn't make it out of the dark ages. I knew better, of course. What's the problem?"

“There’s a man calling himself the Pyn King. He wants to take over the world.”

“Indeed? What other goal could there be, I wonder,” said the Great Leader. “The Pyn King, you say?”

“Yes,” said Calamara.

“Well, well. I find that hard to believe.”

“How come? We know all about him,” Calamara assured the Great Leader.

“Do you really? Do you, really? What version of events did you hear? Let me guess. A tragic accident befell the man. He was buried alive in a collapsed mine, supposedly driven mad from being alone for so many years. When he escaped his mind was bent on an illogical revenge and he came rampaging out of the heathen lands and conquered the world. Something like that?”

“Something like that, yes,” said Calamara.

“We never heard about an accident,” said Jim.

“It’s all wrong, so very wrong,” said the Great Leader. “The Pyn King was merely a figurehead; a symbol for a bunch of do–gooders to rally round as they traversed the globe in an ill–fated attempt to fix the world. If somebody is claiming that the Pyn King has returned, they are mistaken, I assure you, for he was never there in the first place.”

“You sound like know that for sure,” Calamara accused him. She was less than convinced.

“I do,” replied the Great Leader.

“But if it was a thousand years ago…”

“We’re not like you, you know,” said the Great Leader. “We don’t lead such pitifully short lives. The Carreg Golau were born from the bubbling magma that formed the Earth. We watched as life other than our own fought for a foothold, we watched the dinosaurs hatch and lumber to extinction, we watched you take your first steps on dry land, as you floundered – and continue to flounder – to grasp the nature of your surroundings. We watched as you soared into the skies, we shall watch as the last human dies, we shall always be, for we are eternal, enduring until the very end of days, until the universe itself takes its final, shuddering breath.”

As he had spoken he had glowed brighter and brighter. Now, that glow faded. “I envy you, sometimes,” he said. “I don’t think those final days will be pleasant.”

“I’m still not convinced,” said Calamara.

"You surprise me," said the Great Leader, meaning the exact opposite. "It seems that you haven't really changed that much since I last spoke to one of your kind. I keep on hoping that one day you'll surprise me, but as time marches on it looks less and less likely. I'm afraid you'll always be lagging behind."

Calamara bristled at that. "We're not the ones living in dank caves. We're not the ones who drop into a dead faint when someone waves a sheet of paper at us!"

"Well, we're not the ones who die if we're held under water for any length of time, or break every bone if we fall," retorted the Great Leader. "That would be you done and dusted wouldn't it?"

He gritted his teeth and closed his eyes. Apparently Calamara could wind up not just anybody, she could wind up any*thing*.

"We could trade weaknesses all day," he said. "Let's go outside."

"I think we really should..." Jim started to say, but then the ground dropped away and they were standing under a starry night sky.

"... be... getting..." Jim never finished his sentence. He was marvelling at the sky. He faced the Great Leader and said, "This isn't Earth!"

"Indeed not," said the Great Leader, casting a superior glance at Calamara, who was sprawled on the ground.

Jim, on this whole other world, was lost in a world of his own. He wandered off, his mouth gaping wide open as he took it all in.

"Dank caves, indeed!" said the Great Leader, smiling in a very condescending manner at Calamara. "You need a wheelchair," he said, and one appeared alongside her. Graeme had seen one like it in a museum once. It was the wheelchair equivalent of a Penny Farthing.

"Thanks," said Calamara, though she didn't look too happy. Dickie moved to help her but she slapped him away and lifted herself into the chair.

"It's an antique," said the Great Leader.

"You don't say?" said Calamara. "I think I'll call it *'The Boneshaker'*."

The Great Leader smiled. "A splendid name," he said. "I'll give you some time to acclimatise yourselves." He walked away and Graeme, shivering due to the cold, took a proper look around.

They were in the middle of a desert, with gentle rolling sand dunes as far as the eye could see. The sand seemed almost blue; it was giving off a soft glow. A paddle steamer was chugging its way along a wide river that snaked through the landscape; and there was a chain of upside–down pyramids hovering in the sky, slowly rotating with their tips pointing to the ground. There wasn't any sign of a moon.

Fanny was whimpering. She looked petrified and had clamped herself to Dickie.

The Great Leader pointed towards the riverbank, where a white ironwork table and five chairs had been set out. "Come on," he said, "you must need to eat something."

Fanny brightened up a bit at that; she and Dickie started to make their way across the sand, followed by Graeme and Calamara.

As she passed Jim, Calamara clipped him round the ear. "Help me, then," she said, not that she needed any help. It was the strangest sensation, walking on that sand. Feet (and wheels) didn't sink into it at all. Instead, Graeme found that he and the others glided, like they were skating; but it clearly wasn't ice, because he could scoop it up in his hand and watch the grains trickle through his fingers.

"How far?" Jim asked as they reached the table and sat down. "How fast?"

The Great Leader shook his head. "How far and how fast really don't come into it," he said. "Dear, oh dear. Don't you ever consider the terrible distances that seemingly separate you from the rest of the universe and think that maybe you're looking at things in entirely the wrong way?"

"Well, no," said Jim.

"Well, maybe you should," said the Great Leader. "Now, who's hungry?"

A huge, steaming plate of mashed potato appeared in front of them, along with five glasses of pink lemonade.

"I'm not very good with human food," the Great Leader admitted, "but I think there's something very comforting about mashed potato."

Fanny stamped her foot. "I hate mashed potato," she complained.

"Oh. There's cheese in it," said the Great Leader, as if that would make all the difference.

"We haven't really got time," said Jim, although he appeared quite torn.

" 'eak 'or 'rself," Calamara mumbled as she stuffed her face. She swallowed before continuing. "If I'm going to foil an insidious attempt to take over the world then I need to eat first."

She grabbed a glass of lemonade and took a long swig.

"The survival instinct," said the Great Leader, for some reason fascinated by Calamara. "You know, a lot of us think that humanity is too far down a dead end of evolution to ever be saved; but every now and then one or two of you show that there's a little hope left."

"You seem very interested in us: humans, I mean," said Jim.

"What a very… human observation," said the Great Leader. "We take an interest in all Earthly delights. Maybe you caught the news report about the turkey being the next dominant form of life on Earth, taking the reins, as it were, from yourselves?"

"'hy 'ould we be int'rested in 'at?" asked Calamara. " 'at scientisht wa' 'onkers."

The Great Leader chuckled. "Why indeed. I thought it was quite amusing," he said. "My point is: it's not as if we – the Carreg Golau – have left the Earth. We might not poke our noses in and interfere, but we still like to keep an eye on the old country. Some of us still live there, even."

"You're gigantic though," said Fanny, who didn't seem very happy with the idea that these creatures were strolling around England. "We'd have seen you."

"We might be gigantic but you have very big feet," said the Great Leader. "You're sidetracking me," he said. "I'm meant to be deciding what to do with you."

"We just need to get home," said Jim.

The Great Leader twisted his head from side to side, looking at the five of them. His eyes narrowed, so much so they almost vanished. "Yes, I think that might be the best course of action," he decided. "I hardly have to worry that anyone's going to believe anything you'd tell them about all this."

"Are you going to come back and get the other Carregs that weren't freed?" Jim asked.

"No. As I said, we don't interfere. They can't come to any harm and will return in due course, I'm sure. Now, if the rest of you are certain you don't wish to partake of the refreshments, where would you like to go? I can take you anywhere you want," he said, "anywhere at all."

Calamara licked her fingers. "Can we have a moment?" she asked.

"Certainly," said the Great Leader. "I have all the time in the world."

"Thanks." Calamara jerked her head, indicating that they should move away. They followed her across the sands and formed a huddle. Graeme felt Fanny worm her arm around him. He could feel her shivering.

"For a so–called superior species they aren't half boastful," said Calamara, looking back over her shoulder at the Great Leader. "Where to then?" she asked. Graeme was surprised she was even bothering to consult anyone.

"Well, now we know that the Pyn King's real," said Jim.

"Yes," agreed Calamara.

"And what Graeme said is right."

"*Some* of what he said is right," Calamara corrected him. "I haven't seen any boats that turn into mini yellow submarines yet."

"How much more incredible is that than anything else that's happened?"

"I'll believe it when I see it."

"Stop being so contrary," Jim snapped at her. Graeme had never heard him sound so stern. "You know that we're caught up in something serious here and we need to tell someone what's going on before it's too late!"

Calamara was clearly taken aback. Her voice was much quieter when she spoke next. "Do you really think that only we and Mr Thornton saw the boats? How come nobody else has mentioned them? We don't know who to trust."

"We could tell Grandpa," suggested Fanny.

"Don't be daft. We really don't have any reason to trust him, of all people. He attacked Jim and Graeme on the beach the other night."

Fanny let out a little scream and covered her mouth.

"I've said it before and I'll say it again: if we'd have followed my original plan and gone to his rooms to have a look around, we might very well have discovered what this," Calamara brandished the key, "is for, and maybe we'd know one way or the other about him. But no, we had to go chasing after Graeme's 'vision', didn't we?"

Graeme thought how wonderful it would be if she could walk, because then he could boot her up the behind.

"But the Great Leader said he could take us anywhere," Jim reminded her. "I mean, the authorities must be hunting for the Queen and the others by now. So we could tell someone outside of Port Stilton."

"The 'Great Leader' said some other stuff as well and much as I hate to admit it, he was right: even if we did find someone who would listen, nobody who's remotely sane is going to believe us about this, or any of it. And even if we did find one person who did believe, they're going to crucify us for not having said anything earlier. No, there's only one thing we can do: we've got to sort this out ourselves. We've got to go back to the lair of the Pyn King…"

Fanny screamed again.

"…we've got to go rescue the prisoners; and we've got to stop that madman from doing whatever he's got planned."

"Stop him? How do we do that?" Jim asked her.

"You're the brains. I'll leave you to figure that one out."

"Oh," said Jim.

"Then, once we've saved the world, if they still want to kill us for not having spoken up any sooner, well, in that case, we'll die heroes."

*

The Great Leader was watching the pyramids when they made their way back to him.

"That was quick," he said, not taking his eyes off the sky. "Where to, then?"

"How exact can you be?" Calamara asked him. "We need to be very careful about where we end up."

The Great Leader chortled. "I could position you to within a fraction of a micro–millimetre of a hair's breadth. You wouldn't understand, of course. How quaint you are."

"*He's really getting on my wick,*" Calamara signed. Her jaw was set.

"We are the Golau," the Great Leader was saying, once again literally glowing with pride. "Are you ready? Tell me your destination."

"I want to see my Grandpa!" wailed Fanny.

"Your wish is my command," said the Great Leader.

Calamara put her head in her hands. "Oh, good God."

But it was too late.

CHAPTER ELEVEN

The Truth Will Out

Graeme put his hands out as he felt himself falling, stumbling forward. Spots of light danced in front of his eyes. The Great Leader had vanished and now he couldn't see a thing.

"Shh! Did you hear that?"

He was outside. The man's voice had cut through the still, freezing air. It sounded like Lord Raversham.

"How did they…" the voice continued, but stopped abruptly. "Come on."

There were hurried footsteps; a door banged once; and then there were more footsteps fading to nothing.

Graeme blinked hard, trying to get his eyes to adjust. He wasn't alone. Jim, Calamara, Dickie and Fanny were with him and looked just as confused.

"What are we doing here?" Calamara asked. Her voice sounded very loud in the otherwise quiet night.

They were in the centre of the bamboo maze at the garden centre, stood close together, right by the statue of Lady Raversham. High above them, clouds parted to reveal the crescent moon. Everything was covered in a layer of frost. The door to the gazebo was open and swinging back and forth.

"Why, why, why?" Calamara was moaning at Fanny. "Why did you ask to see Lord Raversham? I thought we'd agreed!"

"I was scared," said Fanny.

Calamara snorted. "Well, no harm done, it seems. Looks like the 'Great Leader' isn't so all knowing after all. No sign of LR here."

"I heard him!" said Fanny.

"Me too," said Graeme.

"Sure about that, are you?" Calamara drawled at him.

"I heard him," Fanny said again, "and then I saw two people run into the gazebo!"

Jim walked over, pushed the door open and went inside. "There's another door in here! In the back!"

They followed him in. He was right: there was another door, though you could only tell because it was open. It would have blended in with the back wall if it had been closed.

"What's down there?" Calamara asked Jim.

"I can't see much," he replied.

"Let me see, then," she said, moving alongside him. Jim pushed the door completely open so everyone could see.

Something was glowing at the bottom of a steep flight of narrow stairs.

"Well, let's have a look down there," said Calamara.

"I don't think we should all go," said Jim. "A few of us should investigate first."

"Don't be stupid," Calamara replied. "There's no need for a few of us. We only need one guinea pig."

She gave Graeme a push and he was sent tumbling down the stairs. He somehow regained his balance all of three steps from the bottom and stood there for a moment, feeling his ribs, which were aching like mad. He ignored the impulse to rush back up and whack her.

He heard Fanny say, "How awful!"

That was followed by a mad clatter of feet as she started down the stairs to join him with, he guessed, Dickie not far behind.

He was in a tiny store room which had been carved out of the earth. There were old mining lamps hanging from the ceiling; a skew–whiff wooden table with one leg that was shorter than the other three by at least an inch; and in one corner sat a sack of rocks. The candles in the lamps were lit; their light formed guttering, sickly orange halos. A plaque was screwed to the wall on the right, one of those name plates that some people put on their houses. "*Porthgosod*" was written on it in fancy letters, with flowers all the way round. To the right of the plaque there was a small section of rock that appeared smooth, polished even. It was no larger than the size of a hand.

"What can you see?" Calamara shouted.

"Ooh!" Fanny breathed, dashing up to Graeme, taking his hand and then running the fingers of her other hand over the sign.

"Miss, don't touch…" said Dickie.

Fanny ignored him. She looked at Graeme and bit her lip. "This isn't very nice," she said. Then she reached out and touched the smooth patch of rock.

Graeme heard Dickie cry out, "NO!" and then it felt like someone was driving white–hot nails up his arm and into his brain. Fanny was gone and Graeme's hand was being sucked into the wall as someone or something tried to twist his arm off and someone else reached down his throat and did their best to pull his stomach up through his mouth. He heard a loud clicking sound, a damp squib of a bang, like a failed firework, and then he was lying face down on the ground and somebody was pulling him by his hair.

Fanny was giggling with delight. "Grandpa!"

"What are you doing here? I'm going to kill that Benjamin."

"See to the portal," said a woman's voice. Graeme thought it was kind of familiar.

"Damn, I forgot to switch it off."

There was a low–pitched buzz.

"What is it about me that's so irresistible to children? Do I give off kiddie–friendly pheromones or something?"

"Be quiet and give me a hand," said the woman. "What happened to chivalry, eh?"

"Typical!" said Lord Raversham. "You lot are all for women's rights, want to be treated as equals, but when it comes to a spot of not–so–heavy lifting it's back to 1952 values we all merrily trot!"

"A less tactful lady than me might ask exactly what values were being applied when she was called at an ungodly hour and commanded to get up, throw on a coat and hightail it to a beach to search for a lost trinket."

Silence.

"I'm sorry," the woman apologised, "I know it's more than a trinket. That was a poor choice of words on my part. I'm sure you get my drift, though."

Graeme, again, didn't hear a reply, but he did feel Lord Raversham's hands grab hold of him.

"You're not sulking now, are you, Llewellyn?" the woman asked as she and Lord Raversham dragged Graeme along.

"Ow!"

"What is it, Grandpa?"

"I've twisted my ankle! Ow! Ow! Ow!"

The woman sighed.

"I'll have to sit down," said Lord Raversham.

Graeme was released; he thudded to the ground. Rubbing his backside, he turned over so he could see properly. They were on the beach, right by the boulders he and Jim had hidden behind the other night. Lord Raversham was resting against one of them, nursing his ankle, with Fanny by his side. The woman Graeme had heard was Josephine. She didn't seem the least concerned about Lord Raversham; she was not far off, raking at the sand with her feet.

Fanny reached for Lord Raversham's foot, her tongue sticking out the corner of her mouth. "Shall I massage it for you, Grandpa?" she asked.

Lord Raversham flinched. "No!"

Fanny looked very disappointed.

"What you can do, young miss," Lord Raversham continued, "is tell me what you're doing here. Another sleepless night?"

Fanny's eyes went wide as her face took on an expression of innocence. "No, Grandpa," she said. "We were captured by the Pyn King and we escaped and we met rock people!"

"I can't have a moment's peace," Lord Raversham complained. He hadn't listened to a word his granddaughter had said. "If it's not Kendall trying to imprison me, it's you trailing behind me. And why did you bring this one with you?" he asked her. "I suppose you told him all about this? I should have known not to trust…"

Graeme was so confused and Lord Raversham noticed; his eyebrows rose slightly. "You didn't tell him," he murmured.

"You said not to," Fanny replied.

"Well, yes, but… well, well. Wonders will never cease."

They were both staring at Graeme now.

"Don't gawp, boy," Lord Raversham told him. "You look gormless enough as it is without sitting there with your mouth gaping wide open."

Graeme closed his mouth.

Josephine didn't stop her aimless wandering as she said, "You might as well tell the boy what you've been up to, Llewellyn, or he'll only go and come to all the wrong conclusions."

Lord Raversham grunted. "You tell him," he said to Fanny.

Fanny smiled and sat cross legged on the sand, facing Graeme. "It was the first night I was here," she said. "I came from the airport by helicopter. Have you ever been in a helicopter? I've been in loads. This one wasn't brilliant, but they flew very fast *just for me*!"

"Stop showing off and get on with it," said Lord Raversham.

"Yes, Grandpa. I'd been looking forward to visiting for ages! Christmas takes for*ever* to arrive! I was so excited, wasn't I, Grandpa? I was so excited I couldn't sleep!"

Lord Raversham said nothing.

"It got really late," Fanny continued, "and I was so tired but I still couldn't sleep. I couldn't wake Benjamin up and I was bored, so I went to see Grandpa. *I've* got a key to his room."

"Not any more, you don't," said Lord Raversham.

Fanny giggled. "When I got there, I saw him vanish as he touched a shiny stone on his wall, so I touched it too. It's not very nice, is it?"

"No," Graeme agreed. He was grateful that he hadn't eaten anything. His stomach was only just beginning to settle.

Fanny held out her hands, fingers spread wide. "Look what it does!"

On one hand, there was a pinprick of blood on each of her fingertips; and on the other, the hand that had been holding Graeme's, there was a single dried spot in the centre of her palm. Graeme looked at his hand; he had a dried spot of blood dead in the centre of his palm, too.

"It magicked me to the cave on the beach."

"It didn't magic you. It's not magic," said Lord Raversham.

"I followed Grandpa to the church and he saw me peeking in the window…"

"Twenty twenty vision, I've got," said Lord Raversham.

"He told me to go back to the beach and wait for him there; but when I got to the beach I saw all those people in the boats, and Jim, so I went back and hid on the porch of the guest house. That's when I saw you run past."

"People in boats?" Lord Raversham asked her. "You never said anything about people in boats."

"I tried to tell you when you came to find me, but you said to be quiet and if I ever breathed a word to anyone you'd skin me alive with your own bare hands."

"That does sound like me," admitted Lord Raversham.

"You were on the beach?" Graeme asked Fanny.

"Yes! Grandpa was getting very worried because you were by the cave, and we needed to get there…"

"So I thought I'd try and scare you off," said Lord Raversham, "you know, open and close the door a few times. You just got more intrigued, though. In the end, I thought it would be best to let the cave deal with you."

"You gassed me and Jim!" Graeme said.

"And?" said Lord Raversham, as if gassing people were a perfectly acceptable, everyday occurrence. "Maybe," he said, "maybe if I'd had time to think; maybe if this little harpy hadn't been on my back; maybe if boys stayed in their beds at night instead of rampaging all over the local habitat! Besides," he added, "I made sure you were safe, didn't I? I put you up in the rocks…"

"I helped!" said Fanny.

"… out of the way of the crocodiles."

"There aren't any crocodiles round here," said Graeme.

"No?"

Graeme couldn't think what to say back. It appeared the explanation was over and Lord Raversham didn't seem in any hurry to start talking, either; but then Josephine chose that moment to meander back towards them.

"So Llewellyn," she said, "it would appear to be the perfect time."

Lord Raversham, so boisterous until then, wilted where he sat. He literally seemed to shrivel into his massive brown coat.

"Just ask him," said Josephine, so softly Graeme barely heard her; and then she gestured to Fanny. "Come on my little one, let's leave the boys to talk."

"All right," said Fanny. She tried to take Josephine's hand but the vicar shook her off. The two of them walked into the night.

Lord Raversham had his eyes fixed on the sky for the longest time. "It's amazing," he eventually said, though he wasn't looking Graeme's way, "how as you get older, people treat you more and more like a child. Kendall has rarely let me out of his sight since my last health check. He'd have a conniption fit if he knew I was getting out at night. Seems odd to you, doesn't it, a man of my stature being dictated to? Stature has nothing to do with it. When you reach my age, not that you'll ever reach the giddy heights that I have scaled to, don't say I didn't warn you."

Scraps of dark blue cloud were scudding by overhead. Again, Lord Raversham paused; and though Graeme didn't know if the old man was going to say any more, he knew he shouldn't speak.

"Visiting Josephine – getting out – helps me feel, well, normal. And she listens. Everyone else around here treats me as if I'm liable to drop dead at any minute."

"Are you going to?" Graeme asked him.

Lord Raversham licked his thin lips. "My doctors have been saying that I'm going to die on a semi–regular basis since I was five."

There was another long silence.

"I've lived here all my life, you know," he breathed. "Not on the isle, of course – I commissioned that – but the family have always lived hereabouts. Visitors think Port Stilton's a pretty funny name for a place, and that always surprises me a little. Living here so long, the name's just become, well, it just is. You don't really think about the literal meaning of the words any more as you say them."

He angled his head so he could look at Graeme, briefly, out of the corner of one eye. "It's the same with death," he said. "'You're going to die'… The words just lose all meaning if you hear them often enough. But now, at this late stage of life, I find myself having to face the fact that my physicians may be fools, but they're fools that know their prognosis is going to be proved correct sooner rather than later. Suddenly, I'm seeing the words and thinking about what it all means. One day, I'm going to die. One day, it's going to happen to me.

"I sound daft, I know. After all, none of us can avoid it, as Josephine has reminded me time and again. She has a wonderful, down–to–earth manner. Ultimately, though, she also has an unshakable faith that I can't fathom. Much as I'd love to be like her, even though we have talked at length, long into the night, I keep coming back to what Murgatroyd says: what's so special about being human that means we're going to be singled out for life everlasting? Maybe we are just 'long pig', after all.

"The thought of that, though… the thought that one day I will just stop… when I wake up at three in the morning with those kinds of thoughts on my mind, I can feel my heart beating so hard it's like it wants to break out of my chest and go running for the hills. Sometimes I lay awake all night, afraid to go to sleep, afraid to stay awake, thinking and thinking until the first birds start cheeping outside my window.

"Seeing you at my front gates the other day, it startled me," he said. "I didn't recognise you the other night, in the dark; but there, in broad daylight… there you were. It was like Death himself was standing in front of me."

"Thanks," said Graeme. His tone was such that Calamara would have been proud.

"I didn't mean it like that. You'd have thought I'd have been eager to talk to you, wouldn't you? After all, I'd read all about you, and so much more besides. But no, I was scared, scared of a teenage boy. I was scared that you might confirm my worst fear, that there really is nothing once we're gone, that this life really is all that there is. I might not believe in an afterlife; but I want to, so very, very badly. And I was afraid – I still am afraid – that you will rob me of the last vestiges of hope."

He let out a long, laboured breath. "But now here we are," he said, "and I can't escape it any longer. So…"

"So?" Graeme asked. Now Lord Raversham was staring right at him and Graeme was the one doing anything to avoid making eye contact. He felt sick; he knew what was coming.

"What's it like to die?" whispered Lord Raversham.

*

Graeme never died. He didn't know where that story came from. They said he said he wanted to die, but he never died.

His parents said he'd been very quiet. He'd always been quiet; it wasn't something that had occurred to him before: he'd always heard his own voice in his head. Sometimes he never seemed to shut up. His parents said they noticed he was, "withdrawn" they called it, especially after the move. They said he didn't have friends round any more, which shows how well they knew him. He hadn't had any friends round in ages, even before the move.

Graeme didn't consider himself to be one of those people who can easily tell how they're feeling. He tended not to realise how happy or sad he was in the moment. It was only later, when he looked back, that he could really see what was going on.

He couldn't say exactly when it all started. Over time, he was just getting quieter and quieter; more and more depressed. He didn't realise it at the time; and even as he sat on the beach with Lord Raversham he couldn't think of a reason for it. It kind of scared him, looking back, how he got on with everything, went through the motions of life. He'd get up, go to school, come home, eat dinner, watch TV and go to bed. But if anybody had asked he couldn't tell them what he'd done that day. Nobody did ask, though.

He could never describe exactly how it was. Once, he said that it was as if, if someone had decided to cut off his hand, he wouldn't have noticed. It was like he was dead but his body hadn't realised yet. It was like he was a ghost that everybody could still see.

He'd watched enough TV, seen enough programmes where they said that you should talk to someone. He did try, eventually. Three times, he tried.

He tried talking to one of his friends. Darwin was quiet, like Graeme, and spent most of his breaks and lunchtimes holed up in the library to avoid the school bullies who zeroed in on him as soon as he was in the open. It didn't help that Graeme couldn't find the words. He never found out what Darwin thought he was going to tell him, but he'd just started when this so-called friend laughed a really awkward laugh and changed the subject. Graeme didn't bother pushing it any further. He felt stupid for even trying. After that, Darwin avoided him, or maybe Graeme avoided Darwin, he was never sure. Graeme felt guilty, like he'd let something slip out that he should have kept to himself. Eventually, he just avoided everybody. He was the weird kid in the playground who stood all alone, staring into space.

He was standing in the playground the second time he thought of saying something. He'd been watching some leaves being blown around when Miss Parry, his form tutor, came up to him. He liked Miss Parry. Do it, he was saying to himself. All he had to do was open his mouth; but anything he thought of saying was so lame, like something out of a soap opera. And all he could hear was his parents saying, "Depressed? Don't be so stupid! What have you got to be depressed about? Pull yourself together!"

So he kept quiet.

Then there was the third time. He'd tried his friend, he'd tried a teacher. And one night, even though he knew what they'd say, he almost told his parents.

They'd sat him down. They were worried, they said. They wanted him to get out, go on courses, like the sign language one he'd been on. They said they were going to take away his Con–*Sol*8. They thought the games machine was making him anti–social. Actually, he hadn't used it in ages. They were all at the table; and somewhere inside his head Graeme was screaming that he should be telling them how he was feeling, but that part of him was so far off and only getting further away, or being buried, more like.

They went out, then. Graeme had a sudden urge to run after them; but the words weren't there, still. So instead, he sat in the lounge as the sun went down; and then he sat there in the dark. He went to bed before they got back. He sometimes thought it would have been better if he'd stayed there. They'd have known something was up if he'd still been there when they got in. They couldn't have avoided it.

It was about a month later when his parents went out again and he was left alone. He was sitting in the lounge. The TV was on. He could never recall what programme it was. He sat in front of the fire, staring into the flames. He was ripping up pages of a magazine, folding them into thin tapers and lighting them in the fire, watching them burn.

His stomach always knotted up when he tried to remember the rest of it. He would break out in a sweat. At some point he went to his bedroom. He didn't remember switching the TV off. He did remember sitting on the floor, at the foot of his bed, the bed frame sticking into the small of his back. He was staring at the radiator. He remembered the shadows in the grooves. He remembered the smell of the smoke. He couldn't remember the rest of it. He had dreams sometimes, but he didn't remember them, either.

He went more than a bit loopy when he woke up in hospital. The doctors told him that, much later. They said he went mad for a few days. He hit people, bit people, even. They had to restrain him.

He could remember his Mum and Dad visiting during those first few days. The doctors said he was too heavily sedated, but he heard the two of them. They said he'd only done it for attention. He never forgot that.

He stayed in hospital for ages. His lungs were weak and he got pneumonia. He had a hard time shaking it off. They said it was a miracle he'd survived at all, a miracle that he wasn't badly burnt.

Doctor Willis was the one who told him about how he'd said he wanted to die. He spoke to her a lot; or rather, he spent a lot of time with her. Sometimes she talked non–stop. Sometimes she didn't say anything, but that was rare. About the only thing Graeme would say was that he didn't want to see his parents. He knew they'd visited before, when he couldn't stop them; and he was pretty sure they came in to see Doctor Willis, but he never saw them. He went crazy if anyone suggested that he talk to them.

It was about two weeks before Christmas when they said Graeme could go home. He said some bad stuff, then. Not so bad that they kept him there, there were "limited resources", but bad enough that they called Adrian and he agreed that Graeme could stay with him. Doctor Willis had driven Graeme to the coach station and seen him off.

*

"So I never died," said Graeme. He felt so tired.

Lord Raversham was solemn when he said, "Josephine was right. I am a fool. She told me that I was grasping at straws, straws stuck in a milkshake of mist, as she put it. She'll have a field day when she hears this.

"Did you know you made the papers? They didn't tell the story exactly the way you did. There were several versions, not bad considering you only have two local rags, lots of tales about gangs and suchlike."

"That's…" said Graeme.

"Bollocks?"

"Yeah."

"*The I.I.I. Bi–Annual Psychic News* interviewed one of the hospital's orderlies. He said how your heart had stopped when they brought you in, that you were dead, how he'd overheard you, later, talking about seeing a tunnel of light, and your great grandparents waiting for you, with your dog, beckoning you to join them."

"That's…"

"More bollocks?" suggested Lord Raversham.

"Yeah."

"Yes. So it would seem, so it would seem."

"Mum and Dad never let me have a dog, anyway."

Lord Raversham rubbed the back of his neck. "You paint your parents as quite the ogres, don't you?"

Where did *that* come from? Why did he have to bring *them* up? All the time Graeme had been having problems, in all that time, all they'd done was sit him down once for a chat and confiscated his games console. They should have seen what was going on inside him. Instead, they'd been quite happy to send him away. They didn't fight to get him to stay for the holidays. Yet everyone wanted to talk about them. Back at the hospital, everything had seemed to end up being about them. Doctor Willis had said how interesting that was. It just made Graeme mad. Everywhere he went, even if they weren't there, it always came back to them. Why did it always have to be about them?

Graeme shot to his feet and yelled, "WHAT ABOUT ME?"

Lord Raversham leaned back, as if he'd been buffeted by the words; then he just seemed amused. "And there it is," he said.

Graeme's eyes were wild. He was breathing heavily.

"Sit down," Lord Raversham told him. Graeme didn't sit down, though. He started pacing back and forth on the beach.

"'What about me', indeed," said Lord Raversham. He chuckled. That just made Graeme madder.

"I haven't heard 'what about me' in ages!" Lord Raversham continued. "Almost all my children bawled 'what about me' at me at least once during their formative years. You're about the right age for shouting, 'what about me'. There can't be too much wrong with you."

"It's just," Graeme said, "it's just…"

"Yes?"

"Now you're on about them, just like everybody else."

"I only asked," he said. "Don't talk about them if you don't want to. I don't care about your parents, boy; but you obviously do."

All the anger drained out of Graeme as quickly as it had appeared. He sank onto the sand. His head was hot; he felt like he wanted to cry.

"I don't care," he said. "I don't care."

Lord Raversham watched him. They didn't speak.

For so long there was just the rush of the waves; they seemed to get louder and louder as time went on, constantly pounding the shore.

Lord Raversham cocked his head to one side. "Can you hear that?" he asked.

There was something hammering from behind the door of the boat cave.

"It might be the others," said Graeme.

Lord Raversham reached into his pocket, pulled a bleeper out and pointed at the door, which swung open. Jim and Dickie ran out. Calamara followed them, stopping occasionally to lean over the side of her chair and throw up.

"I switched it off," said Lord Raversham, "I know I switched it off…"

Calamara paused in throwing up long enough to shake a small coin–like object at Graeme. It was the key.

"We found a use for it," she said and promptly threw up again.

Lord Raversham pushed himself into a standing position and stalked across to her. "It's a bad idea to eat before you use a Porthgosod," he said. He sounded quite distracted. His eyes were fixed on the key.

Calamara shot him a look of pure hate. "No! Really?" she said; and then she threw up again.

"Serves you right for taking other people's property," said Lord Raversham, still more focused on the key. One bony hand darted out and snatched it from her. His voice became harsh. "Where did you get this?"

"It was on the beach," said Jim, "a few weeks ago."

"This is Uriah's key," said Lord Raversham. "It was on the beach?"

Jim nodded.

Lord Raversham pulled at his nose and strolled back to sit beside Graeme. Jim followed. "*Are you all right*?" he asked Graeme, who was still looking dog tired. He touched Graeme's leg.

"Yeah."

"Where's Fanny?" asked Dickie.

A new voice came floating out of the darkness. It was a hollow voice, a little muffled. "She's safe, she's safe."

The Pyn King strolled up from the shoreline. Graeme wondered how long he had been stood there.

"Who the bloody hell are you?" asked Lord Raversham.

The Pyn King put his head to one side, like a bird. "You'll find out soon enough! You can't see further than the end of your nose, can you? I am the instrument of your doom! Tonight, old man, or rather, today," he relished the word, "today is the beginning of a new age! If you wouldn't mind handing over your key…"

"That's hardly likely to happen," said Lord Raversham.

The Pyn King drew himself up to his full height, enraged and threatening. "You dare…" he started to say; and then he was looking at Graeme, again with that birdlike cocked head. He stepped back.

"Why not?" he said. "Why not? Yes, one last midnight boat ride."

CHAPTER TWELVE
The Good Girl

Lord Raversham didn't say a word as they sailed out to the isle; neither did Calamara. Graeme kept catching her throwing hateful looks in his direction, as each thing he'd told her and Jim about his dream came true. This time, he could be sure: he wasn't imagining anything.

They entered the main cavern, led by the Pyn King himself and guarded by a phalanx of the Children of the Night. The place was like a ghost town now, but must have been a hive of activity earlier; the rubble created by the Carreg Golau during the escape from the cells was gone, the floor completely swept clean. You could still see where the wall had been broken down, but the hole was plugged, albeit in a makeshift manner. Gathered at the foot of the dais were a few Children of the Night, poring over what Graeme assumed to be the blueprints he'd seen in the hand of the Pyn King.

Gabriel was lounging against the dais, watching the others. His hands were bandaged in bloodstained rags. As soon as he caught sight of the Pyn King – and more importantly, who was with the Pyn King – he jumped up and scurried along just behind his master, frequently glancing back over his shoulder at Graeme and Jim, like he was afraid they'd vanish again if he took his eyes off them.

"My Lord," he pleaded, "let me have those two."

"No. I have other plans for them," said the Pyn King, "and besides, you should be far too busy. Have you finished the preparations?"

"Mostly."

"Mostly?"

"We're doing the last bits now, Lord."

"I see," said the Pyn King. He took hold of Gabriel's head and forced the boy to look at the other Children of the Night. They were still staring at the blueprints, twisting them one way, then the other, quite clearly not making a lot of sense of them.

"Some might think it appears otherwise," the Pyn King said, then. "I would suggest," and his tone made it clear this was anything other than a suggestion, "that you return to your fellows and ensure they are clear in their purpose. If anything goes wrong tonight you will look back on the punishment you have already endured – I hear you sobbed throughout, how mature – with the fondest of memories."

"Yes, Lord."

The Pyn King added, "And once you're done, round up the remainder of your brothers and sisters and join the choirmaster. You need to practice for later. Stay out of my way."

Gabriel stopped walking and let his arms fall to his sides. Graeme and the others were marched past him and into the corridor that held the cells they had been imprisoned in earlier. They, like the cavern itself, showed signs of having been repaired in a hurry. Graeme could see vague shapes of people, slouched behind the bars.

"No room there, my Lord," said one of the Children of the Night. "We have them all."

"I wasn't planning on putting them *there*," said the Pyn King. He took out a large iron key from the depths of his robes and unlocked the wooden door next to the cells. Everyone was forced through.

"I've reserved accommodations for you on the upper level," he explained, sounding like a hotel concierge. "I urge you not to try to escape. Though I could resort to… certain measures to ensure your co–operation, I'd rather not for now. Neither do I want you dead yet and if you try to get out, there is a danger my associates will let their natural instincts come to the fore."

*

The Children of the Night were famous throughout the underworld for their dogged enthusiasm in all bloody tasks undertaken, their lack of morality, and for their competitive rates. The rumour went that they needed to kill in order to stave off ageing; the so–called parents of the Children of the Night were truly parents in some cases, but equally they were still Children of the Night; they were merely less successful Children of the Night.

Given this particular need to murder, the fact they got paid to kill was an added bonus for them. Jobs, such as their current assignment, that initially required little killing of people, were either refused or endured as a means to an end. The odds for success were admittedly long but if everything went well, the world – specifically the human race – was their oyster. A police force would no doubt be required; population control was their speciality. Even failure had an upside: thwarted would–be tyrants had the best tasting intestines.

*

The prisoners were pushed up a flight of stairs and entered another corridor. The stark cells there were nearly identical to the ones they'd seen below, apart from the fact that the fronts were made of criss–crossing bars that formed a mesh; and there were small barred windows set into the back walls that let strips of pale blue night–time light filter through onto the straw–strewn floor. Graffiti covered the stone walls.

Graeme could hear a familiar voice, barely more than a whisper.

"To be honest," his uncle was saying, "it was a bit of a blessing in disguise. I didn't even have a chance to carve the soup."

They came to a halt outside Adrian's cell. He was sitting with Roberta. One of the Children of the Night unlocked the door and then Lord Raversham and Graeme were shoved inside. Calamara, Jim and Dickie were forced into the next cell along. The doors were slammed behind them and locked.

Dickie let out a small cry and ran to the vertical bars that separated the cells. "Miss!"

"Dickie!"

It was Fanny. She'd been sitting alongside Roberta.

"Where's Josephine?" asked Lord Raversham, peering into the gloom to see who else was in there. It was the first time he'd spoken since the beach.

"I don't know," said Fanny. "They took her away."

The Pyn King stood in the corridor with his arms folded. He looked into the cells for a few seconds and then strode away without saying a word, the children running after him.

Adrian stood up and grabbed Graeme. "Thank God!" he said. "Are you all right?"

"Yeah," said Graeme. "Yes, I am."

Someone swore. The Prime Minister moved into the light from wherever he'd been skulking and swore again. He pointed into the next cell, at Jim. "The boy!" he cried through a mouthful of food, spraying crumbs everywhere.

Another person joined him from the darkness. "The hideous girl!" shouted the Queen, her arm outstretched towards Calamara. Almost instinctively, her other hand shot to cover her nose.

"What's wrong, dear?" Graeme heard the Queen Mother say. She was in there with them as well. She'd taken her shoes off, stretched out her legs and was wriggling her toes. "Oh, my poor feet," she moaned. "Oh, my legs. How rude these people are. In my day, if someone was going to kidnap you, you'd get at least a week's notice. You could get packed; you could pick out suitable clothes. This lot just don't know how things are done. Look at my shoes! They're just not suited to the purpose, are they?"

The Queen was too distracted to start bantering with her mother. "I've got a restraining order against her!" she announced, her attention still fixed on Calamara. "She can't be in here with me!"

Calamara gave the Queen a disdainful glance and then turned her head the other way. "There's not a lot you can do about it, is there?" she said. Graeme couldn't see her face but he thought it was a fair bet she was smiling.

She, Jim and Dickie had been put into a cell with the First Minister, Lord Harries and Captain Murgatroyd. Captain Murgatroyd was asleep. Lord Harries and the First Minister were having an argument about who should have done what and when to avert their current predicament.

"All I'm saying," said the First Minister, "is that, had you not been so bothered with trying to find out what we were talking about –"

"You were talking about me behind my back!" yelled Lord Harries.

"Ah, the paranoia!" said the Prime Minister, chewing merrily.

"We were not!" insisted the First Minister. "What on Earth makes you think we'd be interested in talking about you?"

"Oh! So you think I'm inconsequential? A provincial bore? Don't think I haven't heard those names bandied about the House! Now I know where they started, don't I?"

"Your own imagination, Harries, that's where."

"I don't think so! I was talking to Thomas over lunch only the other day and he agreed that you – "

The First Minister was shocked. "You've been speaking to the PM about me?"

"Oh, no," said the Prime Minister.

"Ha!" Lord Harries was triumphant. "Not so great when the boot's on the other foot, is it?"

"You've been speaking to him about me?" the First Minister asked the PM.

"Leave me out of this. That's what you were both after, wasn't it, getting your own parliaments? That means I don't have to get involved."

"That's not what you were saying the other day!" said Lord Harries. "You were agreeing – "

"I was trying to eat," said the Prime Minister. He waved his plate in the air. "Like I am now? I would have said anything to be left in peace with my food!"

The First Minister put his hands on his hips, thrusting out his sizable stomach. "Are you trying to play us off against each other?"

The Prime Minister saw that he was in a no–win situation, one that could go on and on. "Please, somebody," he begged, "change the subject!"

The Queen Mother had finished rubbing her feet and was fed up with the raised voices, so she obliged. "Have you finished your letter, dear?" she asked her daughter, sounding quite sleepy. The Queen stopped casting evil looks Calamara's way, muttered something and sat back down. She had a piece of paper and was scribbling a message on it using the stub of a pencil.

"Where did you get that paper and pencil?" the First Minister asked the Queen.

"A lady never reveals her secrets," the Queen replied.

"Or what she keeps in her knickers," the Queen Mother added, smiling at nobody in particular.

"*Thank* you, Mother," snapped the Queen. "Obviously the pain in your legs isn't *too* distracting."

"This is all my fault," said Adrian, hugging Graeme so hard the boy could hardly breathe.

"Don't be daft," Roberta told him from where she was sitting. "How were you to know any of this would happen? You don't even know what's going on… unlike your nephew."

Adrian pushed Graeme out at arms length and held him fast, staring at him. "Do you know what's going on?"

"I wouldn't be too hard on him," said Roberta. "I mean, it's all so far–fetched, who'd have believed a bunch of kids? Especially these kids."

Adrian looked quizzically at her. "What do you mean?"

Before Roberta could answer, two women arrived outside the cell door, accompanied by two girls, Children of the Night, one of whom was carrying a dark cloak and blood red mask. One of the women was Tatum Lyle, the cook, still in her whites; the other was Josephine.

The girl not holding anything unlocked the cell door and thrust an elbow into the small of Tatum's back; Tatum fell forward into the cell, landing on the floor right by Graeme.

The violent child, her eyes murderous, turned to Josephine.

"I wouldn't, if I were you, Miss Albright," said Josephine, holding a hand up. "I can walk in, thank you." And walk in she did, calm and composed, until, that is, she noticed her royal cellmates. Her face took on her trademark expression of suppressed amusement, deep dimples appearing in her cheeks. She batted her eyelids coquettishly. "My! Such esteemed company. I don't know that I'm worthy."

"Hello, Josephine," said Roberta.

"Hello, you," Josephine replied. "We're all bunched in here, aren't we? Does anyone want to scoot up so I can have a sit?"

Roberta ran a hand through her lank hair and stood up. "Take my place," she said. "Looks like it's time for me to go, in any case."

"What?" Adrian said. He let go of Graeme; his arms just fell away.

The girl holding the robes bowed and held them out. Roberta walked across and ran her hand over the dark material.

"What's going on?" asked the First Minister, standing up.

"You are all here at the behest of my Master," said Roberta, still fondling the cloak. "Your lives are in his hands, now."

"What gibberish is that?" the First Minister shouted. "You can't do this to us! We're important people! What do you think will happen when we're missed? You'll be sorry, then! Just you wait!"

Roberta whirled around and smacked him through the bars. "Wait? Wait? Just *you* wait, my friend, just *you* wait! I'm not going to be the one who waits any more, not for anybody. In my youth, I was always the good girl who waited to be asked. How proud my parents were of me; what a model pupil I was at school! Destined for great things, they said. She'll go far, they said. And where am I? Five miles from where I grew up, in this miserable, run–down backwater. And why, do you think, that is? I'll tell you why," she said, her voice venomous, her eyes narrow as she whipped about to face Graeme. "They always say, 'Wait until you're asked', don't they? I bet you're told that all the time, aren't you? I certainly was. What they haven't told you is this: at some undefined point, just *you* wait, it'll happen, it becomes, 'Ask or you don't get.' Nobody says it. You're just meant to know. And suddenly you, the good child who always waited to be asked, you'll be stepped on, pushed aside, left behind and forgotten while everyone else, all your friends whose parents looked upon you as an example of the perfect child, all those who were told off for speaking back to their elders, who ran around doing exactly what they pleased, flouting the rules, they end up on the top of the heap. I've learnt from my mistake; you can learn from it, too. I'm done with playing the waiting game. Now I'm just going to take what I want, like the rest of them."

She stepped across to Adrian, put her hand under his chin, lifted his face and kissed him hard on the lips.

"Don't be worried," Roberta smiled as she let him go, resting a hand briefly on his cheek. "Soon you'll understand."

She put her cloak and mask on and banged the cell door shut; and then she and the children walked down the stairs.

"Rejoice!" Graeme heard her shout. "Rejoice! For the Pyn King has returned!"

Adrian was staring after her. So was Jim. There were tears in their eyes.

"Well," said Josephine, sitting down in the spot vacated by Roberta and crossing her legs, "that wasn't rehearsed at all, was it? Should we applaud, do you think?"

Lord Raversham was looking intently at Graeme. "The Pyn King…" he muttered. "You were looking up about the Pyn King," he said.

Graeme licked his lips.

"And you," Lord Raversham shot a look at Fanny, "you… boats in the dark, sailing to the isle…"

"Yes," said Fanny.

Lord Raversham's face was wild as he finally connected all the dots. There was a moment's absolute silence, like all the sound was being sucked from the room, and then…

"WHY DIDN'T YOU TELL ME?" Lord Raversham exploded. "YOU KNEW! YOU LITTLE HORRORS KNEW ABOUT IT ALL!"

"They did?" asked Lord Harries, leaping to his feet. "Why didn't they say anything? Why didn't you say anything?"

"You could have trusted me," Adrian said.

"Really?" said Calamara. "If we had told you, who would've been the first person you'd have told?"

"Well, Roberta, of course…" Adrian was quiet for a moment. "Point taken," he said.

"What are we going to do now?" Lord Harries asked everyone.

"We can't let them get away with this!" bellowed the First Minister.

The Queen looked up from her writing. "Isn't it nice to see such zeal?" she said to the Prime Minister. "You can tell he's not been in office long."

The Prime Minister was wistful as he replied, "Was I ever like him, all those many months ago?" He spilt crumbs down his front as he spoke.

The First Minister turned to the Queen. "Your Majesty," he wailed. "Surely you are concerned?"

"I suppose so," said the Queen. "The royal family are usually available at a moment's notice should a radical despot try to take over the globe."

"What was that, dear?" the Queen Mother asked.

"Stop playing the fool, Mother."

Jim's eyes had lit up. "You save the world?"

"I don't just sit on the throne every day," said the Queen. "That wouldn't pay very well now, would it?"

"*Wow! So you're like superheroes, guarding the planet?*"

"Don't be stupid," said Calamara.

Jim ignored her; his eyes were like saucers now. "*Do you have a costume?*" he asked the Queen.

"I find a crown works well enough for me."

"And very lovely you look in it too," said Captain Murgatroyd, yawning and stretching as he woke up. It was debatable, Graeme thought, as to whether the Captain had actually been asleep at all. Graeme was a past master of that sort of thing and considered that Murgatroyd's performance of someone waking up wasn't very convincing.

"We have to get out!" the First Minister was screaming now. "I'll be lying dead before I let scum like this take over my country! Thomas, surely you have something to say about all this?"

"Me?" asked the Prime Minister. He wiped the corner of his mouth with one finger. "Not really. If this guy, whoever he is, wants to be King of the World let him try. We were going to have to present the New Year budget review in a few days, which I certainly wasn't looking forward to. Let him do it if he's so keen. The digs here could be better, but the bacon sarnies are up to snuff." He waved a half eaten sandwich in the air before taking another giant bite out of it.

The First Minister and Lord Harries started gabbling.

"Do be quiet," said the Queen. "I'm sure Thomas is just joking."

"I'm not sure of that," said the Prime Minister, happily munching away.

"Well, we have a way out, now," said Lord Raversham.

"What do you mean?" asked the First Minister.

"My cook may not be a good cook," said Lord Raversham, gesturing to Tatum Lyle, "but she's one hell of a spy! She'll have us out of here in no time!"

Tatum looked worried. "Um," she said.

"Um?" Lord Raversham asked her. "Um? Come on, girl! I put up with your lousy cooking because I knew you'd come in handy in this kind of situation."

"I thought you liked my cooking," said Tatum.

"Well, your omelettes are okay," conceded Lord Raversham. "Don't get all prima donna–ish on me. Do the spy thing. Get us out of here!"

"I don't know that I can," said Tatum, looking very uncomfortable as now everyone's attention was fixed on her. Her pale skin was turning a deep shade of red.

"It's only a simple lock, I'm sure it'll be nothing to you!" laughed Lord Raversham. "Don't be shy! You're the spy!"

"Yes, but not that kind of spy."

"What?" Lord Raversham's voice was flat.

"Well, yes, I'm a spy," she said.

"Good!" Lord Raversham grinned.

"But really more of an industrial spy."

"What?"

"An industrial spy," Tatum repeated. "More soufflé than sabotage; more torte than torture; more aniseed than assassination."

"But on your curriculum vitae…"

"Everybody stretches the truth on their C.V. don't they?" said Tatum, a sheepish smile on her face.

"Oh, good God!" Lord Raversham and Calamara said it together.

"We're never going to get out of here!" wailed the First Minister. "Oh, my beloved brethren!"

"Mother," said the Queen, holding up the letter she had just written, "how does this sound as a sign–off?

"'Enjoy holding the fort for me, son. Don't get too comfortable. I will be back. Soon. Lots of Love, Mum.'"

The Queen Mother looked sad. "You're always so hard on the boy."

"Have you forgotten what happened that time we went to Kenya and left him at home?"

"What time was that, dear?"

"You know."

"Oh, yes." The Queen Mother got misty–eyed. "Wasn't he an imp back then? But that was years ago, decades ago. He was only five."

"Exactly. Imagine what he could get up to these days! Every time I sit on that throne I dread the day they want to move it."

"Bless him. He's my little mudgrumble," said the Queen Mother.

The Queen's face took on a curious but kind–hearted expression as she gazed at her mother. "You'd forgive him anything, wouldn't you?" she sighed. "It's lucky one of us lives in the real world. Oh, now, don't try that look on me, I'm not changing it," she added, folding the letter. "All done, then. Now, has anyone got a pigeon?"

Captain Murgatroyd stuck his hand in the air. "I have a seagull, your Majesty," he said.

"Would that work?" asked the Queen. "My troublemaking eldest is the nature lover, but I have to say I don't ever remember anything about seagulls being good for carrying messages."

"Seagulls," said Captain Murgatroyd, "they have a great instinct."

"Well, I trust in your expertise, Captain," said the Queen. "Do you have it on your person? Perhaps like a magician, in your coat?"

"You really don't know much about nature, do you?" the Captain said. "Wait. I will call her."

"Oh, it's a her. Splendid!"

Captain Murgatroyd let out a three tone whistle. There was the fluttering of wings and Canary, Joan the seagull and Corncrake all appeared at his window. "If you'd care to give me the note," he said, holding out his hand. The Queen rolled up her message and passed it through the bars. Captain Murgatroyd then gave it to Joan. The other two birds started making an awful racket.

"Oh, shut up!" said the Captain. "You know she's the best at this."

"Tell her to take it to my son at the palace," the Queen instructed him.

"I'm sure she got that, your Majesty," said Captain Murgatroyd. He patted Joan. "You heard the lady," he said. "Off with you, now."

All three birds launched themselves from the window and disappeared into the darkness outside.

"We'll be dead before that bird gets anywhere!" sobbed Lord Harries.

Jim reached through the bars and tapped Graeme on the shoulder. "*We may be able to get out of here sooner than that*," he said.

"What?" asked the First Minister. "What did you say, boy? Stop talking in code."

Fanny stood up. "He's deaf!" she shouted.

"Oops!" The Prime Minister laughed. "Watch it, Gelding! No reporters here, are there? That's a gaffe they'd have on the front page if ever there was one."

"He said we may be able to get out of here," said Calamara.

The Prime Minister stopped laughing. He didn't stop eating. "Really?"

"Yes," said Jim. He walked across the cell to the far wall and pointed at some graffiti. "*Porthgosod*," he said, grinning.

Lord Raversham smiled. "Well, well," he said.

"Well, what?" asked the First Minister.

Everyone in the same cell as Graeme crowded to the bars that divided them from the others. There was a patch of smooth stone just under where Jim was pointing. Flecks of crystal shimmered within it, like it was a tiny window to the universe.

"Use my key," said Lord Raversham, tossing his Porthgosod key through the bars to Jim. "Click it to get the blade to pop out – there's a bit of a knack to that – and then insert it into the rock. Let it guide you. It'll home in on the keyway."

"He knows how to use it," said Calamara.

"Fine," said Lord Raversham, "clever girl. Then I needn't tell you how to control your destination."

"Actually," said Jim, "that might be…"

"Oh, just get on with it," snapped Calamara.

Jim tried, but nothing happened. "Do all the keys work in the same way?"

"Yes," said Lord Raversham.

"Are we supposed to be impressed?" said the First Minister.

"Maybe it's broken," suggested Jim.

Lord Raversham fished in his pocket and brought out Uriah's key. "Try this one."

That didn't work, either. Lord Raversham began to swear. Fanny screwed her eyes shut and put her hands over her ears.

"What is that thing?" the First Minister asked again.

"I wouldn't mind knowing, myself," the Queen added. "Lord Raversham?"

"It's a transport," said Lord Raversham.

"Of sorts," Calamara added. She was looking quite queasy.

"There are several of them dotted around the place. A few are still working. I never thought Parkes would have put one here," Lord Raversham was saying in a distant voice.

"Why ever not?" said Josephine. "He had a romantic streak a mile wide, that one."

Jim tried the Porthgosod again. There was a grinding noise from the ceiling. A hatch popped open and a thin white screen lowered itself into his cell. A box was positioned behind it. Graeme heard a familiar *hummmm*; and a scratchy black and white image of Fitzpatrick Parkes appeared.

"Hello, prisoners of Raversham Isle," he said in a cheery tone, though his sentences were still punctuated with moments of frozen silence. "I see you have tried to – activate the portal. I'm afraid that you'll find there are quite a few safeguards in place to stop that."

"Switch them off then, you bloody fool," said Lord Raversham.

The screen tracked across the room until it nudged up against the bars. "Is that… Llewellyn Raversham?"

"Well done," Lord Raversham congratulated Fitzpatrick, "ten out of ten for observation to that man. Now prove yourself useful for once and let us use that thing to get out of here, unless of course you can unlock the doors."

"You want me to unlock the doors?"

"Yes."

"All right."

"Now we're getting somewhere!" said the First Minister, rubbing his hands together. Graeme wondered for a moment what everyone else was making of this. It must have looked pretty odd.

They waited for the doors to open. Fitzpatrick walked from side to side on the screen. He paced back and forth several times before saying, "I can't unlock the doors. I'm sending the signal. The circuitry must be damaged."

"What a surprise," said Calamara, resting her head in her hands.

"I'll have to add it to the 'Bug Fix' list," Fitzpatrick continued. "My goodness! This is item number two thousand, two hundred and forty five since my last service! Would you believe it?"

"Well, if that won't work, get the Porthgosod up and running," Lord Raversham commanded him.

"Ah, well, that I can't do. I have no reason to believe that it isn't functioning. These being dungeons, however, I did take a few precautions. Only a member of the Raversham family can activate it. It isn't something that can be overridden."

"Bloody useless computer! I can't reach it from here! And no, before any of you ask, I'm not hacking off any limbs so we can get out!" Lord Raversham started to cough, batting away Adrian, who had moved to help him. His eyes happened to fall on Fanny, who had been standing quietly, holding hands with Dickie through the bars.

"Raversham!" Lord Raversham wheezed. "Computer said… Raversham!"

He took a deep breath and then in one swift move grabbed Fanny and flung her against the bars between the cells. "Through you go, my girl," he said, trying to force her through, first one way, then another. Fanny screamed, but Lord Raversham seemed possessed. He poked her and pushed her, grimacing with effort. "Why – do I – have – to have – a – chubby – granddaughter?"

Fanny was getting red marks on her where she had been repeatedly thrust against the metal, but she was starting to ease to the other side. Dickie got a hold of her hand and started to pull. Fanny screamed even more.

"Shut up, girl," snapped Lord Raversham. "Do you want to alert those fools out there?"

With one final shove, he managed to push her through to the other cell. She collapsed on top of Dickie.

"Now try the wotsit," said Lord Raversham, pointing at the Porthgosod.

Fanny struggled up and rubbed at a welt that had appeared on her forehead. She didn't look very happy with her grandfather, but she did go and stick the key in the activator.

Nothing happened.

"Oh, joy," said Lord Raversham, sinking to the floor.

The picture of Fitzpatrick changed to colour. He was standing in the middle of a field of bluebells, all apologetic. "I'm sorry. That makes it two thousand, two hundred and forty six items to fix."

The screen started to retract, but then stopped. Jim was under the hatch, dangling from the rods that were extended out of it. He was gazing past them, into the ceiling cavity. "I think there might be another way out," he said.

Captain Murgatroyd went to help him.

"Excellent!" the First Minister agreed. "What a clever lad!"

"You have no idea," said the Prime Minister, a wry look on his face.

"Indeed," said Lord Raversham, sounding brighter and struggling to stand up. Josephine stood over him, holding out her arms.

"Old men with old bones should be more careful where they plonk themselves," she said. "Come along, old fool, heave ho!"

"Shut up, shut up, shut up," Lord Raversham replied; but he did hold her hands and allowed her to help him right himself. He cuffed his nose and pointed at the square hole in the ceiling. "Someone can get out and find their way to the computer room. That's your area, boy," he said to Jim. "You can re–jiggery it, or whatever you do, and get us out of here."

Jim blushed. "I shouldn't really. My Dad said I mustn't use computers…"

The Prime Minister stopped chomping long enough to say, "Well, I'm the Prime Minister and I override your Dad. You go for it!"

"Okay," Jim agreed, though he still didn't look very happy.

"Right," said Lord Raversham. "The computer room is on the…"

"Actually," Jim said, "I'm not very good with directions."

"That's an understatement," Calamara announced to the room at large.

"I know the way!" Fanny squealed, jumping up and down. "I know the way! I do! I do! I know *lots* of secret passages!"

"That's settled then," said Lord Raversham. "The two of you can go."

"If Miss Fanny is going, then I'm going too," said Dickie, his fists clenched, ready for a fight.

Nobody said anything, but everyone looked at the small hole in the ceiling. Then they all looked at Dickie, standing in a defiant pose with his shirt buttons almost popping off. Then they looked back at the hole.

"I'm not letting Fanny go off facing who knows what danger," said Dickie. "Not without me."

"We don't have time to argue," said Lord Raversham, waving his arm in the air. "Feel free to try getting up there. Just let the other two go first."

"Please release me," said Fitzpatrick. "Let me go!"

The screen was shuddering as Jim, Captain Murgatroyd and the First Minister held onto the rods and projection box.

"I shall be forced to raise the alarm if you do not let me go," said Fitzpatrick.

Lord Raversham laughed. "What makes you think that's still working?"

Jim clambered up onto Captain Murgatroyd's shoulders and from there hoisted himself up into the small opening. His clothes ripped as they caught on something up there in the dark.

"I'm in," he called down.

Fanny went up next. She screamed once as Jim seized her hands to help her.

Captain Murgatroyd was left to hold onto Fitzpatrick's workings by himself while the First Minister and Lord Harries attempted to lift Dickie. As they'd all expected, it was a difficult job and he was a very tight fit, but with a bit of wiggling and after being told to suck in his stomach, up he went.

"You can let Fitzpatrick go now," Jim called down.

Captain Murgatroyd released his grip and Fitzpatrick vanished into the ceiling. The hatch shut behind him.

There were hurried footsteps on the stairs. The Pyn King strode in with Roberta at his heel. He came to a halt in front of them all.

"What is going on?" he asked.

"Nothing!" sang the Queen Mother, looking about as innocent as a child with brown teeth sitting next to a pile of empty chocolate wrappers.

"Back for an encore?" Josephine asked Roberta. Roberta ignored her and leaned close to the Pyn King, whispering something in his ear.

"I see," said the King. "Those boys and the girl are nothing to worry about. They are not in any danger; they are amongst the first disciples."

Graeme wondered, *what did he mean by that?*

Roberta bowed and stepped back. The Pyn King's gaze was still concentrated on the prisoners. Graeme wished he could see something of the man's face, or anything other than just the reflection of them all in that mask.

"I have a proposition for the leaders amongst you," said the Pyn King.

The First Minister sat up at that news.

"Dawn is about to break on a new age," the Pyn King announced. "The world is about to be united. I extend my hand to you at the cusp of this momentous day. Join with me and we shall put the world to rights!"

"Mate," said the Prime Minister, "we can't even agree with people who are supposedly on our side. What makes you think you and your lot are going to fare any better?"

"Our triumph is inevitable. I have seen the folly of the world as it is now, and I have foreseen the perfection of the world that is to come. People will rally to join our great cause! Embrace this opportunity now!"

"The Scottish people will never bow to you!" The First Minister's voice rang out.

"See?" said the Prime Minister. "I told you. Can I ask: what happens if we don't, um, embrace your kind offer?"

"You will die, as will all who oppose us."

"Ah."

"I'd rather die a free man than live under your rule!" cried Lord Harries.

"Hear, hear!" said the First Minister. He linked arms with Harries. "You've bitten off more than you can chew, my friend. Attack one and you attack us all. We shall stand with our brothers, shoulder to shoulder, united against you! You may kill us, but you'll never kill our national pride! We may be Welsh and Scottish and English, but we are also British and we do not stand for this sort of thing!"

Lord Harries and the First Minister began a boisterous rendition of "Rule Britannia", swaying from side to side.

"You've got them going now," said the Prime Minister, ignoring the frantic gestures coming from the other side of the bars. (The First Minister was trying to get the PM to join in, so all three leaders could stand together.)

"I'll take that as a 'no', then," said the Pyn King. "Such as shame you cannot join me. Oh, and gentlemen," he said, raising his voice so he could be heard over the din of the ministers, "we will bring *real* national pride, and *inter*national pride, as our new order unites the world!"

"What about me?" Lord Raversham asked. "Why am I here? Are you planning on asking me to join in with your little coup?"

The Pyn King laughed then. It was a rich, warm laugh. "You, old man? No, the offer is not extended to you. You will not be able to participate; your fate, and that of the rest of your family, is already sealed. *Not long to wait now!*" he crowed. "I had hoped not to do this, but I don't want any more of you wandering off… I think you need some rest."

He gestured to Roberta, who peeled off her mask as she stepped forward, her eyes alive, red and burning.

"Don't resist," she said. "The choirmaster resisted and you wouldn't like what happened to him to happen to you..."

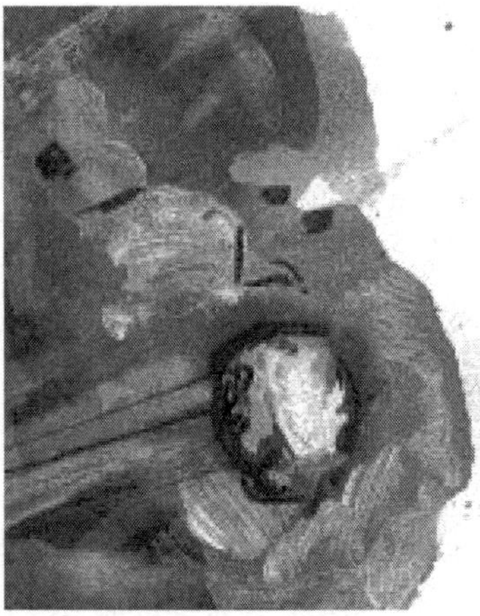

CHAPTER THIRTEEN
Unmasking

Graeme dreamt that he was skating across a frozen sea of blood, under a rusted iron sky. He was racing towards the horizon, had to reach the horizon; he couldn't see what was chasing him but something was there, snapping at his heels, messing with his hair. Other, invisible things circled him, their voices changing from whispers to muddied chanting to a scream which made the ice crack and shatter. He fell into the freezing water.

The babbling voices continued, even in the dark, under the ice. This is what he heard:

"What was he thinking?"

"Why don't you think?"

"... if I'd had time to think..."

Then... silence.

Then:

"Is he all right?"

"Yes."

"What will he hear?"

"Everything."

"What will he see?"

"Everything."

Then... silence.

Then:

"It's this way! Hurry!"

This is what he saw:

Jim, Fanny and Dickie crawled out of the hatch onto a flagstone floor. They were in a cavernous hangar. A clunky computer with chunky keys and an integral, tiny green screen sat on a dusty desk, beside a red pillar postbox with multiple slots in it. Lengths of film rattled into the box and out of it, strung across the room like spaghetti, rising up in a zig–zag fashion, through a complex series of suspended steel poles to vanish through slots in the ceiling.

The computer had a rats' nest of cables plugged into the back of it, snaking away on the floor to a bank of dull, old, beaten–up grey metal cabinets that housed large, spinning spools of magnetic tape. Behind those were aisles of racks reaching from floor to ceiling, with spools of tape and film stored on them. Mechanical arms were browsing the racks, picking out spools and dropping them into wooden carts that waited below. The carts then trundled along railway tracks to either the cabinets or the pillar box, where another set of arms loaded the media ready for use.

"Wow!" said Jim.

As he, Fanny and Dickie walked towards the computer, one of the arms that had been loading tapes shot out and held up its six–fingered hand to stop them. One of the flagstones directly in front of them slid to one side and the ancient television set that they had seen in the library (or one just like it) rose into view.

The television screen lit up.

"Hello," said Fitzpatrick Parkes.

Jim rubbed his hands together. "Right," he said. "Let's get to work."

*

It was dusk and Graeme was sitting in the wings of the stone stage, outside Raversham Castle. He could hear the *tick–tock* of the wolves on the crest, somewhere above him, still engrossed in their endless pursuit of each other.

He was all alone, with a thin white robe over his normal clothes. He couldn't move his hands or feet and was tucked in the shadows behind one of the great stone columns that supported the roof, well out of sight; but from his vantage point he could see all the goings–on.

The babbling from the dream he'd been having turned out to be nothing more than people milling in and out of the tents that had been set up for the Raversham Christmas Eve party. Amongst the crowd –

and the place was packed to the gunnels – he picked out a young boy and girl who were walking under the twinkling fairy lights eating candy floss; some kids playing tag, running between the legs of their parents, waving sparklers; an old man hopping up and down, happy he'd won a giant pot of gherkins in the raffle; and a chatty line of people waiting for cups of hot chocolate, their breath steaming in the air.

It seemed so weird to see the happy scene laid out before him. Such terrible things were going on and yet nobody here was aware.

The choir were standing in front of the main door to Raversham Castle. Gabriel, Aled and Reeves were larking about in the back row; the girls were in the next row down and, yes, Adam, Archibald and Margaret were in the front row again, as creepy as ever. Mr Thornton was standing on a small podium, baton in hand as he addressed them.

"Are we all ready?" he asked in his permanently panicked voice. He cast a quick glance over his shoulder. Graeme shuddered as he did so. His voice may not have been any different, but his face was a ruin: he had no nose to speak of, his lips were caked in blood and his one remaining eye was clouded over with a milky film. "'Ding Dong Merrily on High', then," he said, "and I have a tube of Frooty Booty that I'm willing to share if we all stick to the correct words…"

It seemed almost like a replay of their performance at the garden centre, even down to the small detail of all their parents vying for position with their camcorders held aloft.

They certainly know what's going on, Graeme thought. But why hadn't anybody else reacted when Mr Thornton had turned round?

There was an ear–piercing scream. Finally, someone had noticed! They hadn't, though. The scream had come from a girl at the top of the Ferris wheel and the next moment she was laughing with embarrassment, throwing her arms around her boyfriend's neck and burying her head on his shoulder.

Roberta breezed onto the stage, standing at the centre. She took a sidelong glance at Graeme. "What a night!"

"Where is – " Graeme started to say.

"Everybody?" Roberta finished for him. "Some of them will be joining you later," she said.

Graeme wondered what would happen to the others, those who weren't included in the "some" Roberta was referring to.

Roberta folded her arms and stared out at the sea of bobbing heads. "You have lots of questions," she said. "The people, for instance. Some, of course, are with us. More than you might think. Those who are not have been dealt with. You must have wondered why you and your friends seemed to be the only ones to have seen the boats sail out to Raversham Isle. You weren't, of course. We took care of those who did. Some came more quietly than others; you wouldn't have thought the choirmaster would put up such a fight, would you? Best not to judge a book by its cover."

Graeme was still confused.

"Hypnosis," said Roberta. "Hypnosis, you see? Not any bog standard hypnosis, though. This takes a fair amount of effort to keep everyone… happy. They came to me, you see. Well, you would, wouldn't you? Who better to tell than your local policewoman, who you trust implicitly, such a good soul who'd never do any harm, who's been here for ever and ever and ever? 'Strange people on the beach', they said. 'Up to no good, Roberta.' And so I took their worries away." Her face was etched with grim amusement as she added, "I did the course, you know. Last year."

Graeme thought, *So had they known about me, Jim and Calamara all along? Why had they left us alone?*

"Who says we left you alone?" Roberta asked him. She wandered over and kissed him on the cheek. "Had any odd dreams recently?"

The Pyn King arrived before Graeme could think too much about that. Roberta joined her master and the pair of them surveyed the party.

"Is all well?" the Pyn King asked.

"Yes," Roberta said, bowing.

"Good." The Pyn King beckoned to someone in the wings on the opposite side of the stage to Graeme. "Bring them on."

Lord Raversham, bound by his wrists, was led up to stand before the King. Trailing behind him was the rest of his family, all bar the dead, the presumed dead… and one other. It didn't look like they'd been hypnotised. Mathilda, especially, was struggling with her bonds.

"What are you doing? Where's my husband?" she warbled.

The Pyn King slowly turned to face her, bending as he did so, so he was whispering in her ear. "I have every hope," he said, "that he will grace us with his presence shortly."

"With any luck he'll be off raising the alarm!" shouted Sigourney. She didn't sound hopeful; from the looks that she shared with the other members of her family it definitely seemed that they didn't have much faith in Michael. They weren't expecting to be rescued by him any time soon.

"Well, we might as well get the show on the road," said the Pyn King. He gestured with one hand and four white Carreg Golau popped out of nowhere. They sat on their haunches before the footlights at the edge of the stage.

Roberta stepped forward. "Behold the Carreg Golau, who will carry the message of the Pyn King to the furthest reaches of the Earth! Gather, faithful friends, and watch the beginnings of the new era!"

The Pyn King held his arms out and the crowd immediately stopped what they were doing, emptying from the tents, forsaking the attractions, dropping their food, instead congregating at the foot of the stage. The parents of the Children of the Night kept filming. They filmed everything, it seemed.

The Pyn King watched them all from behind his silver mask. "Let's get the personal business out of the way before we rally the army and set forth!" he shouted. The crowd cheered.

"Hello, old man," said the Pyn King, standing by Lord Raversham. Then he stepped back one pace and bowed his head. With one hand he reached up and gripped his mask. There was a soft sound as it detached itself from his face. Then he held the mask out at arm's length and raised his head. His hood was so large that Graeme couldn't see anything from where he was sitting, but he did hear Mathilda gasp. The mask fell to the ground where it span around like a coin, making a hollow, tinny sound, and finally settled right side up. And then the Pyn King turned so his family could all see him. The light spilled onto his face.

It was Michael Raversham.

"Michael?" Mathilda was aghast. Her husband didn't answer her; instead, he simply waited as his family gawped at him. He smiled as their faces turned from shock to anger to confusion.

"So, at last you know. And look – no laughter. How strange. For once I'm the centre of attention and yet nobody's laughing."

"What are you on about?" Summer Rain asked him.

"You all laughed at me," he accused them. "You've always laughed at me, not even just behind my back, laughed at everything I've ever done, thinking you're so much better."

"Don't be stupid, Mickey," said Summer Rain.

Michael gripped his sister by the throat. "You see?" he screamed. "You see? Even now, you think I'm being stupid! And don't call me that," he added in a far quieter, sinister voice. "That's not my name."

"Let her go," said Lord Raversham. His face was ashen, but his voice remained calm. "They're your brothers and sisters, Michael. Would you rather have grown up alone? Being an only child's no great shakes, I can tell you."

Michael let go of Summer Rain. His face was red; he was opening and closing his mouth; he couldn't find the words.

"Where did this rage come from, son?" Lord Raversham asked him. "If you were so upset, why did you never talk to me? Why did you never say anything? The others were never shy about letting us know when they were even mildly aggrieved. Don't say you were scared to talk to me. You must know I certainly never laughed at you."

Michael found his voice. "No, you were worse," he said, turning on his father. "You ignored me. You ignored me and even when I tried to be like them you still ignored me. I listened to all your tales, I tried to be the best son you could have, I followed you, watched your every move, modelled myself after you; but I was never good enough, was I? All the others had to do was squeak and you'd go running to them. Don't think I didn't see you revel when you learnt of their latest wild escapades; how you delighted as they drifted after their gossamer dreams."

He was incensed now, literally shaking. "But what about me?"

And Lord Raversham could finally say that *all* his children had asked him that question at one point in their lives. That was unlikely to be a thought he would have precisely at that moment, however. Right then, he was just shocked. "You used to closet yourself away in your room, doing goodness knows what," he said, then. "Well, now I suppose we know."

"Yes," said Michael, spreading his arms wide. "How ironic is it, that I am the one who had the greatest dream of all?"

A Child of the Night scampered up to Roberta and handed her a long mahogany box, which had golden patterns painted on it. The child ran off stage and Roberta moved alongside Michael.

"I thought you might be worried about the others, Father," Michael said, regaining some composure. "I thought that you would want to learn what happened to them before you die."

Lord Raversham's expression became stern, but he didn't say a word.

Michael opened the box and reached inside, taking out a glass casket. Inside that was a bloody lump of something with pink and white veins running over its surface.

"Here is what's left of my dear brother Finlay," said Michael, as if he were making casual small talk. He tossed the casket to Lord Raversham.

Michael reached into the box again, this time bringing out a casket that contained a tongue. "Uriah was kind enough to let me make use of his extensive collection of masks, and his key. At least, I presume he had no objection. It was very difficult to tell as by that point I'd already taken this little souvenir."

He passed that one to Sigourney, whose face was blotched with tears.

"And finally," he said, reaching in and taking out two more of those same glass caskets, "here's my beloved sister, Penelope, and her husband." The caskets each contained a charred skull. "Maybe if they'd put their heads together earlier their daughter wouldn't have turned out quite so simple…

"I was going to do away with you each in turn," Michael continued. "I did worry that I wasn't going to be able to manage to see to you all before tonight, but of course I was forgetting about your overblown egos. You saved no end of time by deciding to return home. How thoughtful."

"Michael, you idiot!" cried Mathilda. "Stop this nonsense! What on earth do you think you're doing? We're your family!"

Michael slapped his wife hard on the cheek. "Yes," he said, "yes, of course."

"Daddy! Daddy!"

Adam, Archibald and Margaret had broken ranks from the choir and came rushing up to join their father. "Merry Christmas! Merry Christmas! See, Daddy! See what we've made you!"

They handed him a flimsy paper castle, made from what looked like pages of an old book. Michael didn't give them so much as a glance as he took the gift and turned it over in his hands.

"It's of here," Margaret told her father, "Grandpa's home. Do you like it?"

When Michael spoke next, his voice was shaking. "Where did you get the paper for this?" he asked.

"From the library, Dad," said Archibald, beaming with pride.

Michael crushed the model, let it fall to the floor, stamped on it and lashed out, belting all three of his children. "You destroyed a book for this pathetic thing?" he shouted. "You mutilated a book?"

Adam, Archibald and Margaret fell to the floor, bawling as they huddled together for protection, shuffling back as one to get away from their father.

"The best decision I ever made was to keep you out of my preparations," Michael told them. "You *freaks*."

"Michael!" Mathilda's face was a picture of incredulous disbelief.

"Shut up, woman. You have served your purpose."

"My purpose?"

"The nature of my vision meant that we had to make preparations in secret, my love," Michael explained to her. "You think I cared for you? You really think I wanted to see to your every whim and tend to your mutant offspring? No, my dear, oh no. I needed someone to shield me, to draw attention away from my business. Who would spare me even a fleeting look when I had such a hideous, self–centred monster of a wife to distract them?"

Michael turned to Lord Raversham. "What's wrong Father?" he asked. "I thought finding that out would make your day."

It was true. Under any other circumstances, it was a sure thing that Lord Raversham would have been beaming ear–to–ear upon hearing that. Now, though, he just looked sick to the stomach and so, so disappointed.

"So, even at the end, I cannot do a single thing right," said Michael. He turned to the crowd. "What's a loving son to do?" he asked them. An answering wave of laughter washed across the audience.

A movement in the throng caught Graeme's eye. Somewhere near the front, he'd seen something. He scanned the sea of faces but no–one now leapt out at him.

"What is a loving son to do?" Michael repeated as he looked up to the coat of arms, positioned at the apex of the stage. He kicked one of the Carreg Golau; the creature shimmered for a moment and the sword on the Raversham crest was dislodged from its position, falling into Michael's waiting hand. In one smooth movement, he swung around with the sword extended, aiming at Lord Raversham's neck.

"No!" With a scream, Mathilda pushed Lord Raversham back, sending him tumbling, and the blade meant for him instead sliced clean through her neck. Her head went soaring into the sky as her twitching body ran in a tight circle and then collapsed, blood spurting everywhere.

"No!" cried Michael, echoing his wife's final words.

Lord Raversham watched Mathilda's heroic end without uttering a word. If he lived long enough, he knew he would be spending many a long winter's night pondering how he could have, as it now appeared, misjudged the woman to such an extent.

Michael roared and threw the sword away with such force that it smashed through one of the stained–glass windows of the castle. Silence descended; the only noise was that of falling glass. "Fine," he said, breathing heavily. "Fine." He summoned Aled. "Take him, take *them* back inside. Tie them up on the main stairs."

Aled crooked a finger and a motley collection of his fellows, all cloaked, surrounded the Raversham family and led them away with Aled blazing a trail through the crowd towards the castle. Mathilda's body was dragged off–stage, leaving Michael, Roberta and the brooding Carreg Golau.

"It is nearly time," Michael said, addressing his followers, "time for our great mission to start. And my family, as their final act on this good Earth, are going to give us the greatest, most heartfelt, most spectacular of fare–thee–wells!" Then he held out his hand to Graeme and Graeme, pulled by an invisible will, stood up, walking out to join him.

Everyone cheered. Again, Graeme thought he saw something. He couldn't move his head but his eyes swept back and forth, scrutinising every face, searching for anyone, anything that looked familiar.

And then, in the midst of everyone watching, he saw the grin, a single, bright grin shining from within a hood, a grin that faded as its owner saw him. Now hands were flicking, forming words; but people were moving, blocking Graeme's view. He kept missing the message.

"*Get –* "

" – stage!"

"Bring me the control!" Michael commanded. Aled, who had now returned, climbed back up onto the stage and handed over a black remote control which had a single, green button on it.

" *– off –* "

" – powder – "

" *– going to –* "

"They are in there?" Michael asked.

"Yes, Lord."

"And everything is in place?"

"Yes, Lord."

Graeme could clearly see Jim now, fighting his way through to the front row.

"Good." said Michael, turning to face the castle. "Adieu, family," he said and pushed the button.

"Getoffthestagegunpowerundreneathit'sgoingtoexplode!"

Finally, Graeme got the message but he still couldn't move. He could see Fanny and Dickie now, frantically trying to pull Jim back; he could see Roberta, who had also noticed Jim and taken in what had been said; he could feel the panic rising in her gut as she gripped Michael; he could see Michael look back at him as the two of them fled from the stage; he could see the crowd and their confusion; he could feel the stone stage start to break up underneath him; he saw cracks appear, running up the columns that supported the roof, every block preparing to shatter; he could move.

He could move! He was running now, throwing off the robe, running past the Carreg Golau who had not budged, running to the very edge of the stage and leaping, his arms flung out in front of him, into the crowd as they too started to run. He saw Jim and the others caught in the rush, being carried away from him.

Behind, the stage exploded, belching smoke and flame, heat billowing, hitting him square on the back and pushing him further than he could ever have jumped un–aided.

Below, the ground cracked wide open, creating a bottomless orchestra pit in front of the stage, splitting the earth in a jagged line from the keep at the leftmost corner of the castle to the outer wall of the grounds. Those who had been too slow fell in and Graeme fell after them, but thanks to the forewarning and therefore being a little more prepared he reached out and sank his fingers into the soil at the edge of the crevasse. If he'd flown that bit further he would have landed on firm earth, but at least he wasn't falling into the void yet. He didn't know how long he'd be able to hold on; people were tumbling past him, trying to save themselves by whatever means. If any of them tried to snatch at him, he'd lose his grip.

Swinging himself up to safety was never going to work. Every time he moved he could feel the ground he had his fingers dug into giving way a little more. Boulders – actually lumps of the stage – rushed past him, bouncing on the slate walls of this newly formed chasm. His breath quickened. If he managed to find some support and tried to haul himself up, there was a fair chance the rock wouldn't bear even his weight and if he slipped he could lose his grip then, too; but it was either that or just dangle and wait to be hit by falling debris or until he couldn't hold on any longer.

He tried to get a foothold and surprised himself by actually finding one. He could feel his leg shaking as he pushed himself up. He'd nearly got his head above ground level when the slate ledge he'd been relying on gave way. He fell heavily against the wall; the air blasted out of his lungs and he was showered with dirt as he lost one of his hand–holds.

He swung in place, with only one hand now delaying his fall. He risked a look down; there was no bottom to be seen, just walls of slate fading to emptiness. It was inevitable now that all too soon he'd be finding out how deep it went.

And something above gripped his arm. It was such a shock that the fingers of Graeme's hand, the one he was hanging by, sprang free; he was now at the mercy of whatever was holding him. He was pulled up a bit but sank back.

"Your other hand," said an indistinct voice. Graeme raised his free arm and that too was grasped. He was dragged over the lip of the crevasse and onto the grass.

Roberta let go of him. "We couldn't lose you," she said; but then another explosion rocked the remains of the stage. An uneven chunk of stone went sailing over their heads; Roberta turned away from Graeme to watch it crash into one of the seats at the top of the Ferris wheel; the wheel span around, unbalanced by the weight, causing the ropes holding it to snap. It started to fall to one side, still spinning. As the crushed seat containing the rock came half–circle, the rock was spewed out and hurtled back the way it had come. But now it was angled much lower. It hit Roberta square in the chest. She tripped over Graeme where he sat and fell into the abyss, screaming.

It had happened so fast, Graeme couldn't be sure that it had happened at all. He crawled to the edge and looked in; he watched as Roberta got smaller and smaller, until he couldn't see her any more.

The grounds of Raversham Castle were in chaos. Explosion upon explosion was ripping through the stage – or where the stage had been – and by the look of it the castle itself had been hit by a block or twenty. Windows were broken, there were gaping holes, and one or two parts of the wall were beginning to collapse, sending more rubble flying to injure those who hadn't managed to get a safe distance away.

In fact, there were still loads of people about, most running through the smoke laden atmosphere with little to no idea of where they were going. Some others were looking at their surroundings, dazed and clearly wondering what was going on. The trance that Michael and Roberta had them in was evaporating.

There was no sign of the Carreg Golau. No doubt the fire had burnt their papier–mâché coverings and, free of restraints, they had gone home.

"Hello, boy," said a familiar voice. It was the Prime Minister. He had a fresh cut on his forehead. "I wouldn't stay that close to the edge if I were you."

"Graeme!" And now Jim was there. He came running up and hugged Graeme. Calamara was behind him, with Dickie and Fanny.

"What's going on?" Graeme asked.

"They were going to blow up the castle," said the Prime Minister. "Jim here – "

"And us!" squeaked Fanny.

"And those two," said the Prime Minister, "located where they'd placed all the gunpowder. They freed those of us who were left in the cells and we shifted the explosives under the stage. We'd rather hoped it would have blown the Pyn King to bits."

"*Seeing you was a bit of a shock!*" said Jim. "*I had to warn you, but of course that meant we warned him. What were you doing up there, anyway?*"

Graeme didn't have a chance to answer that, not that he'd have known how to answer if he had.

"But the Pyn King is still on the loose," said the Queen, joining them. She noticed the Prime Minister had been hurt. "Hello, Thomas. Not been scrapping, have you?"

"Hit by a brick," said the PM, "and I was well back from the big bang. The Pyn King was right on top of it. He's probably been crushed by masonry."

The Queen Mother peered around from behind her daughter. "Why are you lot just standing here?" she asked. "There are bad people to sort out, and who's going to do it, if not us?"

"Yes, Mother," said the Queen. She extended a hand. "Shall we?"

"You're not going anywhere," said Gabriel. He'd appeared without a sound from Graeme didn't–know–where, with Reeves at his side. Each had a hold of one of the Queen Mother's arms.

"Get your bloody hands off me," the Queen Mother said to Gabriel.

"Not a chance, Grandma."

"Silly boys," said the Queen Mother. She twisted around, slipping free of them with ease and then stuck two fingers of one hand up Gabriel's nose, and did the same to Reeves with her other hand. She made a face as runny yellow mucus came oozing out of Reeves' nostrils, dribbling onto her arm.

"Did your mother never tell you to use a handkerchief?" she asked.

Both of the boys squealed like pigs. She ignored their cries; she walked them to the very edge of the abyss and then chucked them into it. They fell, wailing, into the pit.

The Queen Mother looked back over her shoulder at Graeme and the others, all standing there with their jaws on the floor. "I think it's time to go and kick some goolies," she said.

"Absolutely," said the Queen, rolling up her sleeves.

The Queen Mother started to walk purposefully away, followed by her daughter and the Prime Minister. "And if you find any wine," she said, "keep it safe. This is going to be thirsty work."

"STOP!"

It was Michael. The crowds parted. He stood before them with the Children of the Night behind him.

"This will stop now," he said. "Get them!"

The Children of the Night, slavering like rabid dogs, charged. Aled led the way. They pushed past the royals and the PM and were within a few metres of Graeme when Calamara let an awful war cry escape her lips.

She launched herself at Aled. Maybe she thought she was going to knock him over, but he dodged her charge and grabbed her, locked his hands about her throat and started to squeeze. Jim went to help, but the others swarmed over and around him, and around Graeme, Fanny and Dickie, holding them all back.

The Children of the Night formed a semi–circle, fencing Calamara and Aled in between them and the crevasse, and an unintelligible chant started up from their massed ranks. Their parents, standing just outside the circle, were still jockeying for the best view so they could continue videoing the whole thing.

Calamara was being strangled. Her tongue was flopping out of her mouth as she fought for air. She was using her free hand to whack Aled, trying to force him away, but she was getting weaker, it was clear to see. Her life was ebbing away; her arm just started waving at her side, not able to even reach him now. He was going to kill her. She gasped for air. Her eyes bulged. Aled held onto her neck, grinning all the while. Calamara's arm fell to the side of her chair and hung there, limp as anything; but still Aled held on, shaking her and crowing with glee.

Calamara was leaning forward now. The fingers of the hand at the side of her chair were twitching. She gave a sudden, really guttural cry; and the chair collapsed. It literally fell to pieces. Calamara keeled over, falling sideways to the ground, taking Aled with her. A single spoke from the wheel of her chair was sticking straight up in the air. Calamara dove to one side. Aled tried to twist away but failed, instead falling right on it. He screamed as the spoke went into his ear; and the scream stopped as the spoke continued its passage, skewering his brain.

Calamara sat up, rubbing her throat. "In one ear and out the other," she croaked. "These old chairs are death traps."

"My baby!" screamed a woman from somewhere back in the crowd. The stunned Children of the Night let go of their prisoners as she and a man, who still had a camcorder clamped to his eye, rushed into the makeshift arena. They fell at Aled's side and the woman cradled him in her arms.

Michael pushed his way to join them. With him were other Children of the Night, who had re–captured the ministers and the royals. “Kill them all,” he instructed the Children of the Night.

The man with the camcorder stood up. “Hang on a minute now,” he said.

“What?” said Michael, the skin under his eyes tightening as he glowered at the man.

The woman, who was weeping over her son’s dead body, gritted her teeth. “There was never any mention of our children being put in danger when we signed our son up for this army! No mention of death, was there? No! No! Only talk of all the excitement, the places he’d see, the food he’d eat! Oh, my baby! Oh, my beloved!”

“That’s true!” said someone from the other side of the crowd.

“She’s right! Nothing said about death!” someone else called out.

“They’re only children!”

There were several shouts of “Hear, hear!” and those were soon joined by more and more until there was a full blown chorus. Michael began to look like a cornered animal. He snarled and then charged into the crowd with his cloak flapping about him.

“Get him!” someone shrieked; and the Children of the Night and their parents seemed to forget that anyone else was there and instead pursued the Pyn King. The ministers, always quick to take advantage when they spotted a change in the tide of opinion, gave chase themselves.

Jim went straight to Calamara and helped her to right herself. Graeme was about to help too, until…

“Graeme!” Adrian appeared from the smoke, running up to him, nearly bowling him over and giving him a fierce hug. “You’re all right,” Adrian said, over and over again. “You’re all right.”

From somewhere not too far off, Graeme could hear the sound of politicians fighting, but not each other, for a change. There was Fanny, holding onto Dickie; and then he saw the Ravershams. He watched them as they filed out of the castle, as they took in the war zone their home had become and as they sat on the ground, shell–shocked and mute, as the stars came out.

CHAPTER FOURTEEN
I Thought He Was Gone

Graeme was listening to the ministers.

"No, we didn't catch them," Lord Harries was saying to the Queen.

"They move fast!" said the First Minister, panting. He had yet to regain his breath even though the politicians had arrived back outside the front door of Raversham Castle over half an hour previously.

The well–lit gravel entranceway and nearby lawns had become an unofficial congregation point for anyone who had not fled the scene. The grounds were now divided by the great crack in the earth. On the far side of the abyss, the big muddy bunker where the stage had once been was now silent; the fire had died, leaving only swirling grey smoke trails climbing to heaven. Kendall, Lord Raversham's butler, was handing out blankets (stripped from the many beds of the castle) in an effort to keep everyone warm. Graeme was sitting with Jim and Calamara. The detached feeling he'd had while on the stage was starting to return, no doubt due to tiredness.

"I don't think we'll be seeing the Pyn King again any time soon, in any case," the First Minister continued. "At least, not alive. He was one of Raversham's sons, was he?"

The Queen coughed and indicated that the Raversham family, Fanny and Dickie amongst them, were well within earshot. Graeme had watched as Lord Raversham had told Fanny about her mum and dad. Unsurprisingly, Fanny had not taken the news well and the entire family were gathered in a tight group, shutting out the world. They still hadn't said anything to anyone outside the family; everyone had rightly left them alone. What would be the correct thing to say in this kind of circumstance? Graeme certainly didn't know.

"You think he's dead, then?" the Queen Mother asked the First Minister.

"Definitely. If I couldn't catch up to those evil kids and their parents then he won't have been able to outrun them!"

"Oh?" said Lord Harries. "And you're so speedy? I was ahead of you for the majority of the chase!"

"In your dreams!" scoffed the First Minister. "I was on the athletics team at uni."

Lord Harries patted the First Minister's somewhat expansive midriff. "Well, that was a fair few years ago."

"I was never really into sports," said the Prime Minister, attempting to defuse another row before it began.

Nobody looked surprised to hear that.

The Queen asked, "So you didn't catch them, but did you see where they went?"

"They went into the underbrush," said the First Minister, "by the walls."

"*Some* of us tried to follow them," said Lord Harries, "didn't we, Gelding?" Both he and the First Minister eyed the PM accusingly.

The PM tried to plead his case by rolling up his trouser leg, revealing a shin covered in red blotches. "I had to stop! I got stung!"

"We thought we had them cornered," said the First Minister, "but we came up against the outer wall. They'd just disappeared, back to the sewers they came from, with any luck."

Graeme felt like something was poking at his mind. It was kind of like a lost memory, dancing right behind his eyes. If he tried too hard to pin it down it would skitter away, so he did his best to ignore it, hoping it would come back.

"It's just one massive room, with racks and racks of film, and more film strung across the ceiling feeding into projectors! You should see all the tape drives! And inside the computer itself, inside its got loads of burnt out valves! Being in that room, it's like going back in time, I couldn't believe it! I found a toy chest, stuffed with boxes and boxes of punched cards and reels of paper tape!"

Jim was really getting excited. In turn, Graeme was making all the right noises, but he wasn't really listening as his friend continued to ramble on about Fitzpatrick and the possibilities if the systems were upgraded. Calamara, on the other hand, was paying attention and groaned before asking if it wasn't too late to revive Aled so he could continue strangling her, as that would be preferable to listening to Jim talking computers.

The tallest towers of Raversham Castle were twin black pillars in the midst of a spangled dark blue midnight sky. They were swallowing the night.

Graeme said that he needed to go for a walk. Nobody seemed to hear him. Maybe they just didn't care. He got up and left.

He didn't know he was going to the towers until he got there. Rickety scaffolding surrounded them, but the door to the shorter tower would be unlocked. It was around the other side. He had to duck under a low bar to get to it. There was a flight of steps inside. He went up. The steps were worn; they went around and around. It took him ages to climb them and find the room. Moonlight streamed through a crumbling arch that led to the external stairway linking the tower to its twin.

There was a cloaked man standing outside, half way between the two towers.

"Don't be afraid," said Michael Raversham.

Graeme was frozen for a second. A part of him wanted to run but a calm inner voice said that he shouldn't. There was no need to flee. He wasn't in any danger.

"Join me, please," said Michael. He had obviously eluded the Children of the Night, but the chase had left him dishevelled. The wind was hard and cold; the tatters of his cloak fluttered out behind him, twisting like snapping black eels.

Graeme walked across the dusty floor to the arch. The stairway, which had a short, decaying rail of stone along one side, was ancient; Graeme doubted that it would support two people.

"Join me," Michael said again. Graeme stepped out.

The stairs, at their mid–point, were just taller than the flat roof of the main castle. Graeme looked down upon the scarred ground, picking out the doll–like people dotted across the lawns. He could see the Ravershams, the royals, the ministers, Adrian and Josephine, Captain Murgatroyd and Mort; and there were Jim and Calamara. They hadn't moved since he left.

"It's quiet up here, isn't it?" Michael said. "I used to come up here when I was young, to think. I could never think down there. There

were too many voices. I was always surrounded by them, my family; they never shut up, too many arguments, too many people to compete against. Here I could always make sense of it all. Why didn't I think of coming back here until now, when it's too late? I can see it all now.

What did I do? I've killed my brothers and my sister. And more. What did I do?"

This Michael was an entirely new person; neither the quietly odd man Graeme had first encountered nor the madman who had just attempted to blow up Raversham Isle. Maybe this was the real him, honestly full of remorse for what he had let himself do. Or maybe the craziness was still lurking under the surface. Graeme stood quite still.

Michael went on, "I never planned to kill anyone. Not in the beginning. But they were always so smug, I could see them, looking down at me, if I got rid of them all –" He closed his eyes, breathed deeply. "But they were not part of the plan. They were never meant to be part of the plan. I made them a part of it. It's still there, that rage. I can feel it. I must stay calm… Been there, done that, after all! I'm so tired."

He took another breath. "I only wanted to continue my mother's legacy when I first read about the Pyn King. There's a book all about him in the library. That's how it started. I wanted to help the world, help everybody, everything." He barely suppressed a laugh as he corrected himself, "Well, everything apart from those bloody snails."

But the tortured man returned. "That's not wrong, is it, to want to help?" he asked, doubting himself. "What's so bad about wanting to save the world?"

"Nothing," Graeme said, "in theory; but you wanted to kill anyone who didn't agree with you."

Michael's jaw set hard.

Stupid, stupid, stupid, thought Graeme. *Big mouth strikes again.*

Then Michael chuckled. "*Bob amser arall ffordd*, eh? Is that how you think the world should work? That's where all the trouble starts. You've seen a small part of the chaos out there over these last few days. Look at the leaders you've met. I have no doubt they started off with the best of intentions but see how they have been reduced to squabbling amongst themselves, fighting for their little plans. No one person can ever win, can ever lead effectively, when life is one big compromise. *Unig un ffordd*, that's the ticket. Only one way."

"Your way or the highway, you mean?" Graeme asked him.

Michael was puzzled by that question; then the puzzlement changed to amusement. He reached out as if he were about to ruffle Graeme's hair but stopped himself. "Legend," he said, "speaks of a man who survived an accident so horrendous that anyone else would have died. By rights, so should he, but he was spared and emerged to face the rest of his life with a renewed vigour, a sense of purpose, a *vision!* And people flocked to him, were inspired by him. He became more than a man. He became a figurehead, the embodiment of an ideal that transcended even death, and his disciples worked tirelessly in his name to put the world to rights. They worked wonders, his way, the only way. That's what the world has been needing, waiting for again: that one man to return and lead us proudly, bravely into the future. And now he has come. You have come."

It took a moment for Graeme to realise what Michael had just said. "*I* have come?"

"Yes, you. The Pyn King has returned, and not before time."

"But the Pyn King, that's you…"

"It's not me. That destiny is all yours."

"No."

"Yes it is; and it's just as well. Look at the mess I've made. I used this whole situation for personal gain. Personal *gain*! That's laughable. I was… I let myself get… carried away. What was I thinking? If only I could bring them back."

Graeme didn't know what to do. Guilt seemed to be keeping Michael subdued; but who knew what little thing might send him spiralling back into the violent madness that had possessed him only hours earlier? Suddenly, Graeme felt very alone. Jim would have known what to do. Calamara, much as he hated to admit it, would have known what to do. But he, Graeme, didn't. Michael's words were clogging up his head, making it impossible to think. The one thing he knew, the one thing he was sure about, was that the idea he was meant to lead the Earth into a new age really *was* laughable, proof that Michael's head still wasn't screwed on tightly enough.

Michael put a hand on Graeme's shoulder. Graeme jumped.

"I'm sorry," Michael apologised. He let Graeme go. "I wish I could stay," he whispered, "and see what you become."

"You're going? Where?" Asking the question made Graeme realise that if anyone should be going, it should be him. He tried moving back down the steps a little way. Michael appeared to be too caught up in his own predicament to notice.

"It doesn't matter. Wherever I go, I go to die. I deserve it, I truly do. And it doesn't matter. I don't matter. I've done, ultimately, what I was meant to do. I have prepared the way for your arrival. I await the coming of the Children of the Night with my arms open wide."

"They're coming back?" Graeme stopped moving.

"For me. I doubt they ever left. They're probably watching now. I'm on their death list. No doubt I have been assigned a job number. I wonder what it is? I won't be attempting to evade them. It wouldn't do me any good if I did; once you've made the death list, you're done for. Nobody has ever outrun them. That's the risk you take, employing them, I suppose."

Graeme started to wonder exactly how close the Children of the Night were. Was he in danger if he stayed?

"Yes, yes, what have I done?" Michael bemoaned. "What was I thinking, bringing you here when they are after me? You're not safe." It wasn't clear whether he was reading Graeme's mind or just continuing with his own train of thought. "You have to go," he announced.

Graeme nodded and started towards the lower tower again.

"Don't forget," Michael called after him, "it's your world now."

Once in the comforting twilight of the tower, not to mention out of Michael's line of sight, Graeme pelted down the stairs, tripping over himself in an effort to get away. When he got to the bottom he bolted out of the door, past the scaffold and fell onto the grass.

"Hello."

Graeme sprang to his feet. Ten Children of the Night, dressed in their uniforms, were bearing down upon him. They stopped short and their leader, a girl, took one pace forward. Graeme tensed.

"Hello," the girl said again. "Remember me?" She mimed being on the phone. "Good evening, Con Support!"

It was Stella. She saw that Graeme recognised her. "Nice to see you again. Oh, don't worry, we're not here for you. And even if we were, I might let you off. I've finally been unshackled from that call centre and given some fieldwork. It's all thanks to you! You have no idea how long it takes to get a promotion when you live as long as us. People just stay in their jobs forever! You and your pals have created a few openings tonight."

Two shots rang out. One of the Children of the Night slammed to the ground, dead. All the others immediately closed ranks, growling, ready to meet their attacker.

Michael was leaning in the tower's doorway, out of breath. Crooked in one arm was an open, smoking, double–barrelled shotgun. He was hurriedly reloading it. "Leave him alone," he said, readying the gun and twitching it to indicate Graeme.

“We’re –”, Stella started to say but then Jim came running into view, carrying Calamara on his back.

“What’s going on?” he asked Graeme. “You sneaked off quietly! It was a while before we noticed you were gone. Was that gunfire we heard? Oh.”

Michael, startled, swung the gun wildly towards Jim. Taking advantage of the distraction, Stella and the other Children of the Night surged forward to attack, forward towards Graeme, who was between them and their quarry. Michael yelled, heaved the gun back to aim at them and let off two more rounds.

Pain exploded in Graeme’s stomach and in his chest. He felt himself physically lift up into the air, driven backwards by the force of the impact. In front of his eyes, fireflies of silver and jade swirled out of and around him. The Children of the Night swarmed past, leaving him to collapse.

Jim ran to Graeme’s side and set Calamara down. “No!” he cried.

Calamara took charge. “Give me your jumper,” she demanded. Jim tore his jumper off and handed it to her. She pressed it against Graeme. “Go and get help.”

Jim raced away.

Graeme’s face was screwed up in agony. Calamara put as much pressure as she could on his wounds. The jumper went dark, soaking up blood.

Behind them, Michael was struggling to get away from the Children of the Night, who had him held fast. “What have I done?” he sobbed.

“Oh, do be quiet,” said Stella. “Let’s go,” she said to her fellows. “It’s dinnertime.”

And then Graeme and Calamara were alone together.

“You really are an attention seeker, aren’t you?” Calamara asked him. She obviously wasn’t expecting a response.

Graeme thought his body must be going into shock. He was shaking but the pain was fading, slowly.

“This jumper’s not going to hold much more blood,” said Calamara. “I should have made Jim take off his tee shirt as well.” She lifted the sodden jumper off Graeme and did her best to wring it out. She was about to put it back over him when she stopped and dropped it alongside him instead. “You know, I always thought, with wounds like this, there’d be more blood,” she said. “Surely it should be pumping out of you still?" She tugged the sleeve of her own top over her hand and wiped at the congealed blood through the gaping holes in Graeme's jumper; she breathed in sharply; and then she just ripped the jumper apart, revealing skin: perfect, pallid, skin.

She leaned back, away from Graeme, and then leaned in close. Their eyes met.

"What *are* you?" Calamara asked him.

And then Jim was back; and everyone else was with him; and there was panic and shouting and there were tears; and then there was confusion and relief and Jim was laughing; and Adrian was hugging a barely conscious Graeme; and there were explanations galore, how the blood couldn't have been Graeme's, obviously, they'd just been confused in the moment; and Jim was never so happy to have been wrong; and Calamara, her lips thin and pressed together, said nothing.

*

"You've just missed your parents," Adrian said from the kitchen.

Graeme, wrapped in his duvet, slouched, bleary–eyed, into the lounge. He blinked.

"They said they'd call," Adrian reminded him. "They just wanted to wish you a Merry Christmas but I told them you were sleeping and, given the time…" He indicated the clock; it was three in the afternoon. "Well, that led to a fun conversation, is all I can say."

"I'll call them back in a minute," Graeme promised.

Adrian clearly wasn't expecting that reply; happy astonishment was writ large across his face. "Okay," he said.

Graeme sat down in one of the chairs by the fire and yawned.

"Are you still tired?" Adrian asked him.

"Not really. Just a bit… spaced out."

"Well just sit there a while. I've got dinner under control." Adrian had the good grace to look a bit embarrassed about that little lie. "It'll be ready in half an hour," he added, pushing his luck. "Are you hungry?"

"Yes," said Graeme, and he meant it. How long had it been since he'd last eaten properly? The smells from the kitchen were driving his taste buds to distraction in anticipation of the feast to come. He could smell the roast turkey and hear the sizzle of roast potatoes cooking in the basting dish with it. He didn't doubt there would be sausages wrapped in bacon as well, and probably Brussels sprouts (a dubious pleasure) if his uncle was really intent on going the whole hog.

"Merry Christmas," Adrian said, risking everything by leaving the stove for a while. He handed Graeme a mug of tea. "Not seasonal, I know," he apologised, "but then, this is turning into a pretty unusual yuletide."

"Thanks," said Graeme, taking a sip. "Happy Christmas." He put both hands round the mug. Silently, he marvelled at his uncle. Adrian had coped in an insane situation with no warning; and he had lost someone he'd thought to be a good friend; yet here he was, trying to make everything all right again, trying to make it a good Christmas… all for Graeme.

"Don't be surprised if Jim pops over in about ten minutes. He's been visiting on the half hour, every hour since we got home."

"Okay. When *did* we come home?"

"Good question. About nine–thirty, quarter to ten this morning, I think."

Something was starting to bubble over on the hob. Adrian pulled a face and raced back to tend to it. "I thought it was going to take forever to get off the isle. It turned out that some people had run off with the boats when all the explosions started. The Ravershams set to work ensuring everybody got home quickly and safely. We got a lift back in the family submarine, if you can believe that! Talk about a surreal experience!"

There was a knock at the door. Adrian went to answer it. "I wonder who that is?" he called over his shoulder.

It was, of course, Jim, dressed in a white, collared shirt and cords. Calamara was with him, in jeans and an olive green long sleeve tee shirt. They both had heavy coats with them which they hung up inside the front door. Jim hugged Graeme while Calamara hovered in the background.

Adrian had already gone back to the kitchen and was investigating the contents of a saucepan like it was a strange and mysterious new life–form. "Oh," he said to Graeme, "so you know, Lord Raversham said he wanted to be kept up to date on how you were. I don't think he wanted to be as in the loop as Jim here, and they probably have other things on their mind at the moment, but you should call and leave a message with their butler. Tomorrow, though, eh? I think Lord Raversham was asking more for his granddaughter than anything. What's her name again? Fanny, is it? She was so worried about you! Think of what she's going through. What a little trouper she is."

"That's one way to describe her," muttered Calamara.

"Anyway, I'll let you guys chat. Don't mind me; I've got enough on here."

"*How are you?*" Jim asked Graeme, sitting down in the armchair on the other side of the fire. He picked up the poker and started jabbing at the logs.

"Kind of, I don't know, light–headed I suppose, but okay," said Graeme.

"We can't stay long," said Calamara.

"Speak for yourself!" Jim laughed. "I'm only next door, after all."

"All right then, *I* can't stay long."

"So," Jim asked, "where did you go when you left us? How did you end up with Michael Raversham shooting at you?"

Graeme told them everything that he could remember about what had happened, how he'd gone to the tower and what Michael had said. He didn't leave anything out, but he did stick to signing when he got to the part about him supposedly being the Pyn King. There was no need to alarm Adrian any more than he had done already.

"Do you think... " Jim wondered out loud.

"*Don't* think," Calamara stopped him in his tracks, "and don't be daft. Michael Raversham was potty. He didn't know what he was talking about." As she spoke, though, her eyes met Graeme's. There was doubt there, on both sides. "Besides, it's Christmas," she said. "Take your mind out of cloud cuckoo land for once and just enjoy the holiday. I'm sure you'll want to spend as much time as possible with this one before he goes back home." She politely turned to Graeme. "Are you staying for long?" she asked.

"Well," said Graeme, "I have to call my parents in a bit. I was going to ask if I could stay a while longer."

Calamara took that news on the chin. "So, until New Year, then?"

"That's only a week!" Jim complained.

"After that, school will start again and you'll be off to the Academy so you wouldn't see him anyway," said Calamara. She shuffled in her chair. "I hate this spare," she said, then oh–so–casually added, "Will you be back at weekends?"

Jim nodded. “I’ll be here all the time. Mum and Dad said they’re not sending me back there to be taught by nutters.”

“So you’re coming to Peashingle Comp?”

“No, I’m going to be home schooled.”

“What?”

“I’m having you on!” Jim laughed. “Yeah, I’ll be enrolling there. I think Dad’s trying to get the headmaster on the phone right now. Striking while the iron’s hot.”

Calamara was, for a second, in danger of having a genuine smile spread across her face.

“So,” Jim quietly asked Graeme, “when are you planning on leaving?”

“Well, I hadn’t asked Mum and Dad, or Adrian, yet,” Graeme said. “But I was going to ask if I could stay here, kind of, for the time being.”

A tray of something was dropped in the kitchen. Graeme thought, somewhat belatedly, that he should have signed that last remark.

“Seriously?” Jim and Calamara asked as one, although in two entirely different tones.

“If they agree,” Graeme said.

Jim was euphoric. “Of course they will! This is going to be so great! Don’t you think, Calamara?”

“Oh, good God,” said Calamara Jones.

THE END

* D I D 1 4 7 4 0 0 7 *

#0316 - 060616 - C0 - 229/152/17 - PB - DID1474007